THE McKANNAHS
~ *together again* ~

. . .

SEQUEL

Part II

of

The McKannahs

Western Adventure Novel

by

Rick Magers

GBP

Grizzly Bookz Publishing

www.grizzlybookz.net

DEDICATION

To Jack and Audrey, Larry and Beth,
Gary and Lynn, and all of my children.
They provided what I needed to be able
to write this book, and hopefully, others.

Cover art & illustrations by

Don Christy

~ OOO ~

*Please read western novels.
If you stop reading them
we stop writing them.*

*If that happens, a valuable piece of
Americana will be lost forever.*

Rick Magers
Member WWA
Western Writers of America

*An author without a loyal following
is just another unknown writer.*

White Buffalo Returns

The sun was going down as Jesse entered Fort Connah. Angus McDonald was no longer there, but his replacement, Everett Bullock, seemed happy to finally be meeting the man that Angus had spoken so highly of. Everett was born in Scotland but was raised in Dublin, Ireland and obviously loved his Irish liquor as much as Angus. Jesse smiled as the man poured himself a glass of the Irish whisky from one of two bottles Jesse had brought, hoping Angus might still be there.

"Mmmmm, lad, that's real whisky n' I bloody well thank you for it, life's blood for Scots n' Irish alike it is, by Jesus."

~

Jesse McKannah rode away disappointed after his visit to Fort Connah, partly because the new Indian Agent seemed inept and out of place compared to Angus McDonald. But mostly because Jesse had been thinking about his Flathead friends and wanted badly to sit around a fire outside with Angus and listen to his side of this tragic story. *Everett's okay I reckon and I doubt there's anybody that could fill ole Angus' shoes.*

He stopped to look out over the vastness of an area that at one time in the near past was filled with millions of buffalo. After a few minutes he shook his head slowly thinking, *not even a small herd left. It's as if they never existed.* He nudged his horse toward the area of the new reservation on the southwest end of Flathead Lake. "Sure don't sound like eighteen fifty-five was the best year for The People," he said aloud. As the horse walked slowly ahead, Jesse's mind replayed the same thoughts it had several times during the trip, *I don't know where to start,*

Rose, but I'm gonna do whatever I can to help your people. He sucked in a deep breath, *The People, our people, Rose. I don't feel as though I'm part of this new white man's world I've been seeing.*

Cresting the hill, he stopped the horse and scanned far left and then right. He could see their camp in the distance, but it did not appear to be large enough. Leaning forward, Jesse rested one forearm on the pommel as he patted Shadow's neck and tried to imagine the size of the camps they had made each time they stopped during the long trek to their ancestral buffalo hunting grounds.

Surely they didn't split up and half returned. No! Lame Wolverine wouldn't allow them to; there's nothing here, but even less back there. He would have helped the chief convince them that they must stay together. Another possible reason surfaced but he forced it back into the darkness of his mind.

He gently urged the horse ahead as he recalled one particular conversation he had with Everett Bullock two hours prior to his leaving. Now, as the sun peeked through the eastern trees, it ran through his mind again .....*and the Flatheads signed a treaty with the government giving them their many thousands of acres in exchange for a little piece of ground to whither away on while eating white man's food, and learning white man's ways, while drinking the white man's whiskey.*

Jesse caught movement in his peripheral vision as his horse moved cautiously down the hill toward the Flathead Indian camp next to Flathead Lake. He reached back to his right saddlebag and pulled out the folding telescope that his father, Sean, had given him many years earlier.

With it finally adjusted, his eyes then strained to identify the movement among the early morning shadows. He realized with a start that it was at least two dozen men, *might be twice that many,* he thought. Jesse patted the horse saying quietly, "Go slow boy, everything's okay."

A full minute later he was certain that each man carried a rifle and they were being very stealthy. *They're gonna hit the sleeping camp any minute and start shooting.* Once that thought registered, his pistol was out and his horse was responding to Jesse's spurs. He knew the pistol would never reach them, so he began firing in the air as his horse raced toward the sleeping village. *I sure hope Lame Wolverine ain't the first out and starts shootin at me, because he was gettin good with that rifle.*

Lame Wolverine was one of the first braves out, and his rifle was in his hands, but his cool ability to think on his feet, even from a sound sleep, had not deserted him. "Get down and wait," he screamed repeatedly to the braves who had rushed outside. A few moments later he heard someone yelling in the Flathead language, "Ambush, ambush," over and over. He watched with extreme apprehension as the shooting man on the horse rapidly approached waving his empty pistol in the air.

Lame Wolverine squinted into the early morning darkness, trying desperately to determine why the man on the horse was riding full-gallop into their camp. Moments later the men who had been sneaking around began firing at Jesse.

Within a split moment almost fifty Flathead braves, led by Lame Wolverine, began firing their rifles at the muzzle flashes in the distance.

The Indians stopped shooting when Jesse brought his mount to a slathering stop near his friend. When the Flathead Indian saw who it was climbing down from the horse he grinned wide. In his native language he said, "All of my people believe that the legend of White Buffalo is true, and now so do I, old friend."

"Who are those men that were trying to overrun the camp as you slept?" Jesse was observing the Flathead Braves as he spoke; noticing that they had stopped firing and were looking at his friend to issue a command. *Lame Wolverine must now be chief and they await his orders.*

"Come old friend, let us drink sassafras tea and I will tell you what has happened during the time you have been gone." He issued a command, and then turned to Jesse, "The braves will take up positions to keep the camp safe."

"Just a minute, Lame Wolverine, I have a better idea." The Indian watched as his friend walked around the horse to start digging in the left saddlebag. Returning, Jesse tossed him a small package. "I brought this for Rose's father, but it appears that you have taken his place, so let us share it."

As he smelled the package, Lame Wolverine spoke. "Yes, the old chief began weakening the day he realized that the buffalo were forever gone. He died in his sleep a few months after you left." His grin was wide when he said, "Let us not run, but go quickly to the fire so my woman can pound these beans." He shoved the package to his ample nose, "Ah, mmm, I have not smelled or tasted coffee since you left."

As the two men sipped the strong black coffee, Lame Wolverine explained all that had happened during his friend's absence.

An hour later Jesse shook his head slowly, "So your general counsel refused to listen to your pleas and voted to accept the government's offer of this fifty thousand acres, a large part of which is unusable lake, in exchange for nearly a million acres of prime fertile land that the Flathead Nation has held for a great many centuries?"

Lame Wolverine was silent for several moments after Jesse stopped talking, but finally turned to face him. "The old chief could have convinced them to keep the land, I think, but as their new chief I did not have a solid power base among my people." The Indian paused as his mind searched for words in the Flathead language that would convey his thoughts. After a very deep breath he said slowly, "Since arriving to these plains that no longer are home to our partners in life, the buffalo, I have watched as many of the people became like children." The look of sorrow on his friend's face saddened Jesse. "Losing the buffalo was to them like the fish," he swung his arm like a scythe, "losing the water. They cannot imagine a life with no buffalo meat, no warm buffalo robe when the wind is angry, and no warm buffalo pocket to slip their babies into as they go in search of bitterroot, onions, and cama. They feel as though the end of their life has arrived, and they are ready to accept the white man's offer of food and clothing, plus this small piece of land they call a reservation." He turned again toward Jesse, who could now see and feel the hopelessness of these proud people. "They now feel," Lame Wolverine continued, "as a child that has been punished does. They prefer to appease the evil white men so that their next punishment will be less severe. They sit as totems, gaunt and starving, while awaiting the wind that will blow their remains into the hereafter." His coal black eyes penetrated Jesse's soul as he said, "My people have lost their will to live."

A long silence filled the air as the two friends looked into the fire. Jesse stood and stretched before lifting the coffee pot from the smoldering coals with the short stick. Holding the pot in a hook at the end, he used his bandana to lift the bottom and fill their clay cups. After returning the pot to the coals, he said, "The wife who pounded the beans for our coffee is not familiar to me. Is Gentle Breeze okay?" Jesse silently thought, *she was a healthy two hundred plus pound woman when I left here. I hope she isn't ill or already gone.*

Lame Wolverine lowered his cup and looked hard at Jesse for a moment. He turned toward the front of their tepee that was covered in canvas with PROPERTY of the ARMY stamped on it in several places. He yelled in Salish,
"Woman, come to the fire."

Moments later a skeletal-thin old woman barely five feet tall shuffled around the corner of the bench the two men sat on. The first thought that entered Jesse's head was, *this must be Gentle Breeze's mother, here to look after Lame Wolverine. He always said that he would have but one wife, and never replace her if she died.*

"Do you know White Buffalo, woman?"

"Yes, I saw him many times when he was with Prairie Rose." She smiled and Jesse knew immediately who it was. He stood and embraced her for several long seconds, and then held her at arm's length. "Gentle Breeze, I am so sorry that I did not recognize you." He hugged her closely again, "Your sweet smile could never be hidden." Jesse held her away from him again, "Even though there were two of you waving at me when I left." He held her hand and moved to the log bench, "Please sit with us a moment and tell me what Rose has been doing since she left us."

Gentle Breeze was a medium who received messages from the departed members of her shrinking tribe. She looked lovingly at her husband's best friend when she spoke, "Rose has been very busy helping the wanderers find their resting place, and told me on the last round moon that you were coming back to us. Rose said that you were bringing the magic yellow to help The People live through the no buffalo times."

Jesse's mouth dropped open at her statement. His mind was spinning as he thought, *how could she have possibly known about the gold we found? She couldn't have. It must have been Rose who led us to the gold. Yes, the day I woke up and told Huff that we're gonna move a mile north where the river has the dogleg.*

He smiled at Gentle Breeze, "I am not surprised that Rose is still helping her people; it was always her way of thanking The Creator for giving her life. I now know she is happy. Thank you,

Gentle Breeze; you have lifted a weight from my heart. I shall always miss her, but to know that she is happy makes me feel good." He hugged her again, "And now, can I get you a cup of coffee?"

Gentle Breeze turned to her man. He knew that she enjoyed few things as much as a cup of steaming coffee, so he smiled and said, "White Buffalo, would you get the coffee pot while I get a cup so this lovely star gazer can enjoy a cup of the evil white man's potion." Lame Wolverine chuckled as he headed into their tepee for another clay cup.

After thoroughly enjoying her one and only occasional treat, Gentle Breeze returned to her morning chores inside their tepee. Jesse spoke in a soft voice, "She has lost half of herself since I was here among you, and when I saw your camp this morning it was less than half the size it was. Has there been no assistance from the white men at all to help your people?"

Lame Wolverine remained silent as he placed his empty cup on the flat rock beside the coals. He finally spoke, but in a soft subdued voice, "The soldiers brought barrels of salted meat that was good; not tasty like fresh buffalo, but edible. That was when they wanted us to give them our land in exchange for this," he paused to swing his arm in a wide arc, "and if we would agree then the food, blankets, robes, cooking pots, and all the other things that we would ever need, would be given to each family. They said you will no longer be cold in winter and your people will be fed better than ever before in their lives."

Lame Wolverine then stared into the morning fire as though searching for a way out of an ambush. Finally he continued, "My people were already starving, because it had been a year since we arrived to see empty prairies where the buffalo once moved like giant shadows across the land. In that first year we lost more that two hundred people, mostly the very young and the very old." He turned toward Jesse, who saw the hopeless plight etched across his brown face. "Jesse, we have already lost more than that this year, and some were much too young to die. Many women in this camp today are much worse than Gentle Breeze. Squaws do not eat much, because they know the braves must be ready to fight at all times. Since we traded our land for this reservation we have been given very little food, and none of the other things they promised. Our braves are getting thinner every day, and lately the white men from a village beyond that mountain," he pointed toward a high mountain in the distance, west from where they sat, "have been seen sneaking around out there watching us. This is the first time they actually attacked, and," he looked at Jesse, "had you not seen them and warned us, I fear that many of my people would be dead." He put his hand on Jesse's shoulder and said, "The Creator guided you to us."

Jesse turned to his friend, "Whatever or whoever it was, I am glad that I arrived here when I did." He couldn't stifle a wide yawn, and said, "Been a long time since I slept, old friend, do you mind if I rest in your tepee for a few hours?"

"Of course, Jesse, and you will always be welcomed into any Flathead lodging."

"Thank you. When I'm rested I'll go to the town where the men that tried to awaken you with bullets today, live. I will move among then as a ghost and listen. I'm puzzled why they are not satisfied with the land you gave them, and want this piece too."

Lame Wolverine himself was about half-convinced that his friend could actually change into the mythical White Buffalo and move among men unseen until he desired them to know that they were being watched. He said nothing as Jesse walked slowly, stiff and tired, into the tepee to rest.

Jesse slept very soundly knowing that he was among friends. He didn't move at all during the nine hours that Gentle Breeze kept an eye on him. After stretching to remove the stiffness, he smiled at her when she motioned with her thin fleshless arm while saying, "Come, you must eat now."

He followed her straight to the same log bench, where Lame Wolverine sat eating from a clay bowl. As Jesse scooted into position, his stomach growled loudly. He grinned shyly at Gentle Breeze who turned at the sound. She stopped filling his bowl to say, "See, dogs in your belly are fighting over your bones." She laughed and continued dipping into the pot, obviously selecting items that she knew he enjoyed. When she brought the bowl to him, Jesse realized how long it had been since his last meal. While chewing, Jesse watched as she scooped something from a flat stone protruding from the center of the hot coals. She sat the birchbark platter between the two men and said, "Acorn cakes."

Jesse balanced his bowl of food on his knees and plucked one of the hot acorn cakes from the tray. Passing it beneath his nose he crooned, "Mmmmm, my favorite treat."

Gentle Breeze said, "Yes, I know. Prairie Rose made them for you often." She reached into the pocket of the huge U.S. Army coat that had room for three like her, and pulled out a small canteen. "I have honey." Her smile broadened when both of her favorite men crooned.

With a mouthful, Lame Wolverine mumbled, "I had to leave while you slept, Jesse, so I didn't know she made these." He looked up at his beaming wife. "Come, lovely one, and sit." He patted the log bench as he picked up the plateful of cakes. She looked around quickly to be certain she wasn't being watched, and then complied. He picked up a still steaming cake and placed it on a small piece of bark, then added honey. He smiled as he handed it to her. "Today you eat with White Buffalo and the chief of your tribe."

Her eyes filled with tears, and both men knew it was partly due to constant hunger and partly because the two men praised her. She closed her eyes and slowly chewed the acorn cake. Long months had passed since she last tasted anything so wonderful.

Jesse saw everything but remained silent. These good people that he considered his new family had suffered so drastically that any words spoken would be meaningless. His thoughts, however, framed events that he would soon put into action. *These people have suffered enough. This is going to stop, and before winter sets in they are going to be eating healthy food again—regularly.*

Aleena McKannah

Aleena McKannah spotted the two men riding toward the log cabin that she and her two traveling companions had built after dropping out of the Donner Wagon Train. She was standing inside and back far enough from the doorway that the men outside didn't see her. Something about the bold way the two men rode toward her two friends, who were splitting wood while Aleena prepared a small lunch, caused her to step back further into the darkness of the windowless cabin.

Her friend's husband had worked tirelessly for days digging into the hard soil to create the root cellar so they could store their remaining food and other perishables. After everything was in the cellar the three of them constructed the small log cabin on top of it.

They all three knew that winter would soon be upon them and worked long hours to complete the ten feet wide by twelve feet long cabin. Once the four corner posts and two doorway posts were in the ground they secured the tops, so the roof could be completed.

After tying the front beam with rawhide strips they moved to the beam that would support the rear end of the roof. It was two feet lower than the front so when snow built up it could be easily removed. The pitch of the roof also made it much easier to secure to the rear corner posts.

With the roof beams all in place the man showed his wife and Aleena how to secure the first two roof logs in place. "Use these long rawhide strips to make a tight fit." He talked as he worked, "See how I tied this first one just beyond the front and rear of the corner posts that I cut off." He saw them nod, so continued, "I will now position the next roof log beside it, but by putting the larger end next to the small end of that first roof log, the roof will remain more or less square as you move toward the other end. I will cut and trim the roof logs and you can each drag one here so they can be put in place. Remember to pull every other log by the large end so you won't have to turn them when you get to the cabin." He pulled a cloth measuring tape from his pocket, "I will stop cutting after six logs and check to be sure the roof is moving evenly toward the other side, and adjust the gap if it is not. And then we can add a little more of the limbs that I will be cutting off before we cover it with sod."

He pulled a wad of chewing tobacco from his pocket and cut off a chunk by running it along the edge of the razor-sharp axe. "I will cut only saplings that are three inches at the large end, and then when the roof is finished, I will cut a larger log that will run across inside in the middle under them from one side to the other to keep the roof from sagging." He pulled a small file from his jacket's pocket, and in four strokes sharpened both edges of his double-edged axe. After the file was returned to his jacket he headed toward the thick stand of saplings less than twenty feet away, "Come," he said with a wave of his arm, "let us begin."

The following week the three of them had completed the roof and each was dragging big armloads of brush and limbs from the pile trimmed from the slender logs. While the two women used the ladder that he made to cover the saplings with the brush, the man was digging sod squares to cover them with.

"There's no more sod close to our cabin," he said after several hours of digging. "I will work with you to get these last squares up on the roof, but then we must go to that hillside," he pointed to a hill a quarter mile away. "I walked there last week when you two were butchering and salting the deer that I shot, and there is enough sod to complete the roof. But," he grinned wide, "you are going to need a two-girl sled to pull if here."

Aleena liked them both very much and grinned as she turned to her friend, "Now where in the world will we find two girls to pull a sled full of sod?"

"Hmmm," her friend mused, "maybe we will be visited by a group of energetic Indians that would like to earn a small parcel of our potatoes and apples."
No Indians, energetic or otherwise showed up, but three days and several trips later, with both women in harness at the front of a short sled, the roof was sodded.

"Before we begin on the walls," the man said, "I am going to construct a hatch that will allow entry into our root cellar. It will also be our refuge in the event that hostile Indians begin marauding in this area."

The following day it was completed. He used the small saw blade, which he guarded as though it was a treasure, to sever the saplings that would be used to cover the entry to the root cellar. Before beginning he used thick rawhide strips four inches wide to hold them together. The man was extremely frugal with the short nails that he brought on the trip for emergencies.

He then made a cut where rawhide hinges could be nailed in place, and then severed the logs on each side and the middle of the two hinges. Before severing the logs at the other end of the hatch he nailed a piece of the four inch wide rawhide in place so one of the women could keep the hatch from dropping in and destroying the hinges at the opposite end.

Once the last log was severed Aleena lifted the hatch and held it up. "Lay it down, Aleena, and I'll secure the logs by using these two cross pieces I cut this morning."

After attaching the two logs he had split for this hatch, by toe nailing them each on both ends with several of his valuable three inch nails, he turned to Aleena, "When I get down in there and the candle is lit I'll tell you to slowly lower the hatch and then hold it so I can attach this stop that I trimmed just for this."

When this was accomplished he came out and lowered it into place himself. "Now, let me show you what I decided to do so the entrance to our refuge won't be easily noticed." He put the hatch back down and then laid a small square rag rug that his wife had worked on during the past two days over it. He then carefully nailed the wooden box to the hatch through the rug. Standing back he looked at the rug and box. "Looks quite natural just sitting there beneath the kitchen counter where our meals are prepared." He turned his head and scanned the small room. "We'll keep two cabbages and a few apples in the box all the time and hopefully no one will ever think to look for a hatch beneath the box."

The three pioneers began putting the wall saplings up on the frame the following day. After chinking the many small cracks between the logs with mud and the hair that they all had been diligently collecting ever since entering the wilderness just west of Massachusetts, the husband began splitting small logs with which to build a door. Once the cabin was completed and the stove from their wagon was brought in and the pipe fit into a hole left in one end, they all worked on a lean-to at the end of the cabin where their two horses could push through a split in the canvas to get in out of the cold weather.

"We must hope and pray that there are breaks in the harsh weather so the horses can forage for grass." He looked out at the surrounding terrain and then shook his head, "I think we have stopped at a good area." He pointed to the hill where they had dug the final sod with which to cover the tiny roof, "There are several places up there where we can help them uncover small patches of grass. If we're not snowed in for long periods, then the six bales of hay that we bought in the last town we came through, plus the remaining grain we have, should be enough to get them to spring." Again he turned three hundred and sixty degrees to visually scour the surrounding landscape, "I don't know if we need go any farther to settle a homestead." He looked at Aleena, "I know you want to join your brother at his ranch outside Yerba Buena, and if we decide to remain here, my wife and I will see to it that you get into a good safe wagon train going in that direction."

The winter began setting in one week after Aleena and her two traveling companions got settled into their small cabin. An after-thought caused the husband to construct a wall of small saplings that would segregate him and his wife's bedroom from the rest of the cabin's interior. After measuring off five feet, he asked Aleena if that would still allow enough room for her to sleep comfortably on a small bunk he would build in the far corner next to the kitchen counter. "Oh yes," she said smiling, "even if I am taller than most men, I sleep curled up in a ball."

~

Spring had just begun peeking into the foothills east of the huge mountains to the west of where Aleena McKannah and her two friends had dropped out to build a winter cabin.

The cabin's door was tied open and Aleena was about ready to call her two friends to come inside and have lunch when she heard horses approaching and stepped back inside until she could see who it was.

She watched as the men brought their horses to a stop, but

the moment that Aleena saw them both reach for the long-barreled pistols hanging on their side, her mind reacted, *oh my God they're going to kill them.* As the first of several loud shots reverbrated through her head, she rushed toward the root cellar hatch in the corner of the floor. Within seconds she had entered it and eased the hatch down into its hidden position beneath the rug and wooden box, which was now half filled with cabbages and apples that she had planned to cook during the next few days. She stood in the dark trembling, as shots echoed through the cabin just above her head.

Aleena held her breath when she heard the men enter the cabin and begin ransacking it. Their harsh voices were barely muffled by the thin covering between her and them. Nothing was said for a few minutes as they tore apart the interior. Aleena barely breathed during their noisy decimation of Aleena's and her two dead friend's labor. When one stomped noisily toward the hatch, under which she cowered trembling with fright, her breathing stopped as she listened and waited for the hatch to rise. She had a mental picture of a long barrel with its black hole of death pointing at her face, and before it exploded she closed her eyes tightly and awaited her fate.

Aleena heard one speak to the other, "These dern pilgrims ain't been digging fer gold or panning thet thar river yonder neither. They must be part o' them Mormons a'headin t'ards Californy fer ta start up another one o' them churches what lets 'em have a hunert wifes t'diddle if they's got the money t'feed 'em with."

Trembling, Aleena opened her eyes as the other killer talked from across the room. "Well, let's git what food they has n' tie it on their horses to tote then toss them folks in here n' set 'er ablaze. I know where there's a cabin south o' here on the river. Saw a coupla wimmin an a real old man workin a small dredge right out in thet river. Betcha they's got a bag'r two o' gold dust n' nuggets." Aleena thought, *thank you God for not letting them go north to our neighbor's cabin.*

Hearing the bodies slammed down above her made Aleena want to scream, but she remained silent. Soon she could hear the fire crackling above as the dry walls and roof was embraced by the flames. She heard no more talking and never heard a sound as the two killers rode away. Long after the cabin burned to the ground, Aleena remained in the root cellar even though the hatch above her head was only smoldering charcoal.

A sliver of moon was the first thing she saw in the crack that Aleena now caused by pushing up on the hatch. Even though she saw nothing and heard not a single noise of any kind, she still silently lowered the remains of the charred hatch and sat back down on an empty crate. Her mind was abuzz with fear, *they might be camped up there, or they might have left a third man to see if anyone comes to see what the fire was all about, or they might . . .* these fears and others kept her cowering in the darkness as fear ate holes in her brain.

Daylight came and still she hesitated. Her tiredness and fear was beyond normal human endurance, but after the third time, she pushed the hatch cover open and slowly climbed the ladder; looking in every direction, much as a trapped animal does that watches while the door to their entrapment slowly swings open.

Standing half in and half out of the cellar, Aleena put a hand over her mouth, *oh dear God.* She averted her eyes then climbed out and past the burned remains of her two friends.

Finally outside the embers of their small cabin, Aleena turns completely around. She hears noises but sees nobody nearby. *I guess those're just animals foraging the forest. God,* she looks to the heavens, *I don't want to judge You, but why did You put horrible people like that on earth with the rest of us?*

Getting no answer did not surprise her at all, because He had seldom answered any of her prayers. *I'm sure you're just testing me, and I hope I pass, but I have to admit that I sure don't understand why You created bad people like that.*

Aleena took one last look at the cabin where her two friends lay in a charred heap, and then turned and headed north toward a bend in the river where a family of five had also stopped, but on a wagon train that was also heading toward California two years prior to the Donner Expedition.

Patrick McKannah

Patrick stood and walked very slowly toward the podium. His erect posture, trim physique, and graying hair made him appear very sophisticated, which indeed he was. San Francisco had blessed the day with perfect weather. Large green tents were assembled on the lawn of his mansion, hedging against rain, but the sky was clear. Three hundred affluent guests were invited to join the two dozen newsmen from across all of California. His campaign for Governor had been very intense, and everyone felt certain that he would soon be representing their state. After a lengthy applause, Patrick held both arms up. When there was silence he began speaking as women sipped Irish Cream Liqueur and men drank Irish whisky.

"During my recent trip aboard a very slow sailing vessel to the nation's capitol I was given new information that will alter my future, but I hope not the future of this wonderful state."

As though someone had laughed at a funeral, absolute silence crept across the sea of guests. Most lowered their drinks.

"I will not continue my pursuit for the office of governor of California." Once again he held up his arms to silence his guests. "I have no doubts whatsoever that John Bigler will win the seat in the governor's mansion and serve you Californians quite well." Before anyone could speak he yelled, "Now let's all enjoy some great barbecue and Irish whiskey."

"What in the hell do you think happened back east, Fent?"

"I haven't got the slightest idea, Parker, but we'd better keep a close eye on that slick Mick."

After his invited guests had all left the mansion's grounds, Patrick turned toward his valet, bodyguard, good friend and constant traveling companion, Aldo Calaveras. "Please meet me in the library at four o'clock, Aldo. I need to lay out my new plans before you to be certain that I'm plotting the correct course." He smiled at his most trusted friend, "You are the only one who I can rely on to give me your honest opinion."

~

Manollo Calaveras' oldest son, Aldo, was about the same age as Patrick's young brother, Jesse. When the four McKannah boys and their sister Aleena allowed their brother Jesse to sell the family ranch, so he could get away from the terrible memories of the fire and subsequent death of both parents, Aldo decided to ride to San Francisco to inquire about entering the new college there.

Aldo learned that with money Jesse had given him, he could get enrolled into a two-year-degree-course and learn business management, and still pay for all of the necessary books. He qualified for on-campus housing for married students, and would have enough money to buy food to last until he could find an after-class job. He paid the enrolment fee, which also included all of the necessary books, and then went to housing and paid two months rent. It was a small, three room bungalow and the nicest place he had ever seen, so he knew that his wife would love it. When he headed toward the McKannah ranch to get his wife, Aldo had five days to get set up and be in his first class.

Aldo returned home swiftly and together they began to load all their treasures and personal belongings up onto a two-mule-driven wagon. Before heading toward the coast, Aldo went to the barn to find Jesse. When he informed Jesse of his plans, Jesse hugged his young Mexican friend and wished him good luck. "You've been reading ever since I've known you Aldo, so a college education oughta open the way for a great life for you and Maria. I'll write down my brother Patrick's address in San Francisco so you can contact him if you ever need help with anything." He walked him to the mule-drawn cart and then held Maria's hand a moment as Aldo prepared to start the mules walking. He patted her tiny hand, "I promise to come visit you folks as soon as I get settled." Jesse stepped back and watched as the wagon began moving.

Halfway to the coast they were caught in a terrible thunder storm. While struggling with the stubborn mules to move the old wagon up the side of a shallow ravine, Aldo suddenly heard the roar of water. Before the young man could get to his wife and carry her up and out of the ravine, the wagon was hit broadside by a high wall of water rushing down from higher country.

Aldo had seen flash floods during rainstorms, but never anything like this. One moment he was about to grab his wife's arm to help her down, and the next he was slammed into the wagon. As the wagon rolled over he heard the screaming mules and then he was tumbling over and over as the water swept him up and away.

What seemed a long time was no doubt only minutes, but he later recalled being thrown up into a tree. He grabbed frantically at the limbs as he was first swept into and then flushed out of the limbs of the tree. Finally his arms went around a limb, and then he locked his legs around another. Gasping frantically as the rushing water intermittently allowed his head to rise briefly into the air, Aldo was able to keep enough air in his burning lungs to survive until the water rushed on without him.

The water moved on and soon there was only a trickle left in the ravine. The sun returned, briefly creating a surreal scene that caused him to look around as though he had just awakened from a horrible nightmare. Pain caused by being slammed into the wagon and others from being thrown against the limbs of the tree that he now looked down from, reminded Aldo that he was not dreaming or awakening from a nightmare. As the sun slipped into a cloud he noticed that the rain, which had stopped, was now beginning again. As quickly as possible he worked his way down to the lowest limb. The ground was fifteen feet below but it seemed much farther. *Another wall of water could come down this ravine any minute,* he thought. He searched the ground for the best place to land, so he wouldn't hit a large rock and break a leg or twist an ankle. *I've gotta land well or I'll never get out so I can find Maria.*

Aldo targeted a spot that had no rocks, and when he was hanging by his hands to shorten the distance, he glanced down and swung slightly ahead so he would hit it, and then let go. He was quickly on his feet and scrambling up the few feet to the top calling his wife. "Maria, Maria, Maria."

He half ran and half walked back the way he had been swept

down the ravine. When he spotted one of his wagon's wheels lodged in tree roots, he recognized the road ahead that they had been on when it crossed the ravine. *I wouldn't have missed Maria if she was somewhere along the way I just come from.* He looked up at the afternoon sky, which was allowing the sun to peek through occasionally. *I know I would have seen her, but I'll look on the way back anyway.* His eyes searched every spot where she might be lying unconscious or waiting for him to see her; too exhausted to yell or move.

Aldo walked slowly along until it was dark enough that he feared he might miss seeing Maria. He stopped beneath a huge tree and sat shivering in the rain. *Dear God,* he prayed, *please keep your eye on my lovely Maria until I find her tomorrow.*

He began walking again at dawn, but by noon the ravine had lost its banked sides and had leveled out into a flat surface that ran across the terrain toward a distant string of low mountains. He stood looking at the ravine he had just searched, and then at the landscape ahead and all around him. Finally Aldo wilted to the ground and just sat there. *Maria's gone,* he thought, *I will never see her sweet smile again.* Tears ran freely from his eyes as he shook his head slowly back and forth.

I have to walk back over the entire area again, Aldo thought, *because if she is lying somewhere injured I am her only hope.* Before dark, Aldo had retraced the steps of his search, but still found no sign of his wife. He crumpled wearily to the ground, and shivering from the cold he lay at the top of the ravine sobbing quietly until sleep relieved him of his misery.

By dawn he was walking west and continued long after it became too dark to see where he was putting his feet. He caught the glimpse of a fire somewhere ahead and moved toward it. As it became more distinct, he moved much more cautiously. Soon voices drifted across the damp air and he began putting each foot down carefully. Aldo crept through the forest until he was close enough to hear their voices clearly. *They're Mexicans,* he thought, *but what kind are they? Maybe banditos, desperadoes, or, or...* his mind was whirling as he watched their campfire, and then he heard them begin singing church songs he recognized.

He stood and walked slowly toward the campfire. When he was close enough for them to see him he spoke softly in Spanish. "I have lost my dear wife in a flash flood and need help. Please help me."

Two days later the small wagon train of Mexicans delivered him to the college campus. They had been fishermen along the coast near Santa Barbara but so much violence between rival fishing families caused them to decide on a move north. "Our young men are sailing the two boats and we are bringing everything we own in these wagons. God sent you to us so that we might save you. Please come one day to the waterfront and ask for the Hernandez family so we will know you are doing well."

~

During the two years that Aldo studied for his degree he did look up the Hernandez family and enjoyed their company, but their efforts to get him interested in one of the Hernandez girls was in vain. His heart was still grieving for Maria, and his mind was interested only in his education.

After receiving his degree, Aldo contacted Patrick and asked how he should go about securing a position in San Francisco. He had spent all of his life in rural California working for Sean and later Jesse. The big city did not frighten him, he told Patrick, but he felt lost among so many people.

Patrick inquired about Aldo's wife, and listened silently as the man explained. "Aldo, I am very saddened to learn about the terrible manner in which your wife lost her life, but am humbled by the tenacity you have exhibited in pressing on with your education." Patrick paused a moment as he looked directly into the man's eyes. "Your family is the reason that Jesse is still alive, because had your brother Miguelo not sounded the alarm when Jesse was grabbed by those gangsters who used to run this town, he would not be with us today," he paused as a frown pulled his eyebrows down, "if indeed, he is still alive." He saw concern spread across the man's face and smiled at the Mexican that he had not seen in many years, "Don't worry, amigo, he's out there somewhere in the wild, probably living with his Indian friends and enjoying life a lot more that most."

Patrick pursed his lips in thought a moment before speaking again. "Please stay here in my home as a guest and I will speak to businessmen that I know well and can trust. We will find you a good, suitable position with a reputable firm somewhere in this frantically growing city."

Aldo had grown from a small boy during his young years on

Sean McKannah's ranch, to a gangly, six foot tall young man when he married Maria. Standing in front of Patrick McKannah was a stoutly built man that worked diligently to keep his body trim and muscular. His jet black hair was always trimmed short and his brown face shaved daily. Aldo's alert eyes had small black pupils in the room lit brightly by the chandelier under which he stood.

Patrick looked directly at him, thinking, *he looks like an alert deer confronted by a human for the first time.* He smiled warmly at the young Mexican from his childhood, "So amigo, what do you think of my suggestion?"

Without hesitation, Aldo nodded and replied softly, "Yes, Señor McKannah, but only if you allow me to work for you until a suitable position for me is located."

"Very well," Patrick said, "but first I'll have my housekeeper get you settled into the small apartment that I had added onto the house to accommodate the occasional visits by my four brothers."

Simon McKannah

Simon McKannah waited until just after midnight to ride into Jackal Flat, Arizona. His Texas Ranger identification badge was pinned to the leather folder that had a warrant for the arrest of Bols Stedman.

A three-month search was finally ending in the small desert town. Simon reached inside his thick coat and touched the folder to be certain it was settled into the inner pocket. The November wind had teamed with an unusually low temperature, so he lifted slightly in the stirrups and pulled his vest down before settling back in the saddle. He urged his horse, Dragon, to move slowly along the dark deserted area behind the row of buildings; deceiving shadows dancing in the late evening twilight. He was here last year and recalled easily where the livery stable was. He planned to put his horse into the outside corral, and then slip inside to get some rest.

It had been a long hard chase and he figured nobody knew he was in this area, so it would be a good time to catch a little shuteye. *I don't think I've slept four hours in the last three days.* Simon's mind was fuzzy from lack of sleep as he headed toward the door. It didn't have a lock when he was here before, just a block of wood with a nail in the center. Simon was looking forward to lying down in the fresh hay that he knew was stacked up in the hayloft. *I'll find som'n to tie the door shut on the inside so nobody can slip in on me.*

The killing spree that Bols Stedman began, had left three men and two women dead, plus a young girl crippled for life. They were all working in Texas banks, except the girl, who was just standing out on the boardwalk outside the bank when the trapper turned lawman decided to get rich by robbing banks.

~

Two years earlier, Simon McKannah was tracking another man who had ambushed and killed a Texas Ranger. A short time later it was determined that the killer mistook the Ranger for another man—one who had sworn to kill Ellis Sidler on sight. It had something to do with a woman in Juarez. When told, Simon said, "Don't mean a thing to me. He killed a Texas Ranger and he's coming in—sitting on his horse," his hard black eyes bore into the bearer of the information, "or tied across the saddle on his horse."

Two months later, Simon hailed a camp very high up in the mountains above Yerba Buena, renamed San Francisco. "Hello the campfire."

"Yeah!"

"Can I come in?"

"How many are ya?"

"One riding and one across his horse's saddle."

"You a lawman?"

"Texas Ranger."

"C'mon in, but kinda slow like till I see what the deal is."

After entering the camp's firelight, Simon nodded saying, "I'll just hobble 'em both till we get t'know each other."

"Had anything t'eat, Ranger?"

"Not today." Simon continued at the two horse's front hoofs.

"I'll getcha a tin o' m'famous camp cuisine, and coffee that'll melt boot leather."

Fifteen silent minutes later, Simon laid the empty tin plate at his feet and continued sipping his coffee. "Best dern beans n' hardtack I've had all day." He smiled slightly adding, "I was starved as a drover lookin for a lost herd, and I appreciate the grub and this coffee, amigo." He lifted the tin cup and said, "Just the way I like it too, strong enough to keep m'guts squawking all night. I don't like t'sleep too sound when I'm out in the bush."

"That fella across the saddle a bad hombre?"

"Not any more." Simon sipped his coffee a moment then added, "he killed a Texas Ranger by mistake; thought he was somebody else."

"Wouldn't come with ya peaceful like, huh?"

Simon never felt very comfortable with anyone that tossed too many questions his way, but he understood a man being cautious in the wild when he was alone, and a stranger riding in like he just had. He wanted to know a little about this man, too. He seemed to be friendly and easy going, but Simon's natural caution often caused a small alarm to go off between his ears. *Y'never know about a fella till y'been with him a good while.* "Caught up with him in Nuevo Laredo, sittin with a coupla gals. Told him to stand and unbuckle his gunbelt n' put it on the table. While he was getting up he told me that he mistook the Ranger for someone else. I told him that if it was true, he'd probably do a few years in prison and then be a free man again. I turned slightly toward the gal on his left, who was twice as old as the other gal, and I was about to tell her to stay put with her hands on the table n' tell the girl t'keep her hands on the table too. Just as I turned, and was about to talk to her, he reached up like he was gonna smooth out his hair. He was a slicked-back hair kinda dude lookin fella," Simon sipped his coffee before continuing, "Last move he ever made."

"Have a gun tucked away back there?"

"Bowie knife in a sheath, but I already knew he was as good with it as ole Jim himself. Lotta fellas I talked to said he was always getting in it with local boys and had carved up a few, but as far's they knew had never killed anyone."

"The guy musta wanted t'die," the man commented, "going for a knife in a back sheath against a Texas Ranger holding a gun on him."

Simon finished getting a sip of the coffee then lowered his tin, "Wasn't in m'hand. I never pull out one of these guns till it's my time to kill someone."

The man's hand stopped half way to his mouth with the tin cup of coffee. He looked directly into Simon's eyes a moment before speaking—quietly, almost to himself. "I know another guy who carries a Bowie in a back-sheath up behind his neck between his shoulder blades, like that guy lying across his horse, and Ranger, that guy's so darn fast it seems like magic." He shook his head slowly, "Pheweee, you must be fast with them pistols. What kind are they?"

"Colt Dragoons, a matched pair. Bought 'em last year from a gun drummer that work's for a fella named Sam Colt." Simon pulled one out so the man could get a better look at the latest reliable revolver on the market. "Holds six, forty-four caliber loads, but it takes some gettin used to, cause it weighs about five pounds when she's full of powder, wadding, primer cap, and slug. Tell ya som'n though, Mister...uh, what's your name?"

"Bols Stedman, originally from New Orleans, but been s'long out here I don't reckon I'd recognize the place now."

"Well, Mister Stedman, my name's Simon McKannah, and I figure this gun's gonna change Texas, and maybe even the whole darn country." He eased the long barrel back into the holster, and then tuned back to the man. "This fella Colt has a gun factory som'rs in the east near that school named Harvard where two of my brothers went to learn how t'be lawyers."

"Only seen one other fella wearing a pair o' guns in them cross-draw holsters, like yours. I reckon they take a lotta gettin used to, huh?"

"Yeah, I s'pose they would, but they seemed natural t'me the first time I put 'em on, and that was a long time ago when I was still just a kid."

The man was silent for a few minutes as they both sipped coffee. He finally turned toward Simon, "I been fed up with trappin these damn mountains for a long time now, and was just thinking about checking out Yerba Buena and some other towns down yonder, t'see if I could get on as sheriff or a deputy." He stirred the fire then added a small log before continuing, "If a fella ain't ever done any of that kinda work, what's he hafta do to get a job?"

Simon sipped his coffee and looked at the man over the top. Finally he said, "A lotta towns'll hire a stout guy like you if he's carrying a gun and looks like he could handle a coupla rowdy cowpokes with their guts full o' likker, without havin to kill 'em." He reached for the pot sitting in the coals and filled his cup. "A lawman doesn't make much money, and he's always got a few people wanting t'kill him each time they get drunk, so it really ain't a hard sought after position. If you're serious, I know the sheriff in Yerba Buena, and..." Simon stopped and said, "I gotta stop calling it that, cause they made the town officially San Francisco in forty-eight. Anyway, he's always lookin for a big fella like you t'sign on as deputy. If you're serious, I'll send him a telegram n' tell him your name."

"I'd sure appreciate that, Simon."

"Okay Bols, consider it done, and I'll recommend to ya now that you order yourself one of these revolvers before you pin that badge on."

~

And that was how Simon McKannah met Bols Stedman. When he got down out of the mountains he stopped at the first trading post where he knew someone. He had them compare the body to the wanted poster, and showed them a letter that was addressed to the dead man. After paying a young man a dollar to bury him, Simon sent a telegram to his boss at the Ranger's headquarters to let him know he'd just buried the killer and was heading back home to Texas. He then sent one to the sheriff of San Francisco to introduce a man named Bols Stedman that he met in the high country, and who would be coming soon to sign on as deputy. Simon signed it, bought supplies, had himself a good hearty hot meal, and then headed southeast toward Texas and home.

Bols Stedman worked as a deputy in San Francisco until summer 1850. He had watched the mule-drawn wagons and sailing vessels bringing shipments of gold from the mines, and then depositing it in the local banks. He decided to make a career change, and handed the sheriff his resignation. Bols rode into the mountains he had trapped for several years, and then rode back down with three men who were also tired of trapping. With the Wilkinson brothers, Jeffrey and Percival, and a Frenchman he knew only as Black Ben, Bols Stedman had his gang, which he named X-trappers.

They successfully robbed their first bank and rode away with over nine thousand dollars in gold. By the time they'd ridden high into the mountains to their cabin, which the Wilkinson brothers had built years earlier, they realized that their haul of loot was too heavy to keep hauling it into the mountains. When they robbed the second bank, they headed south and didn't stop until they reached El Paso, where Black Ben said he had friends.

Their haul was even larger this time, but they had the foresight to have three mules stashed with a friend who had a ranch southeast of San Francisco. Bols paid him well to allow his gang to stay a week until the heat died down. It was a well rested gang that headed toward the Texas border town, leading mules carrying a fortune in gold.

El Paso's many brothels and cantinas kept Bols' new gang, X-trappers, occupied for a couple of months, but a conversation with a man running guns into Mexico changed everything. Bols sat up and paid attention when the man rambled on about what was going on in Brownsville. "We carry a load of rifles n' pistols into Brownsville and meet up with a big mule train that pays us in new gold ingots, and then they carry 'em over to the revolutionary rebels in Matamoros. Me and m'pal just carry a small load, but there's a coupla big outfits that carry two or three wagonloads. They git s'dern much gold for them rifles they gotta put it in the bank right there in Brownsville. We're thinkin about mebbe gittin us a wagon and go looking for a big batch o' rifles."

Bols kept rolling the info around inside his head all day, and that night he told Black Ben to have the other two ready to move at dawn. "We're gonna go have a look at that bank full o' gold in Brownsville."

He learned that there was a boat coming into Bagdad at about midnight, and the gun traders would be meeting the rebels. Bols and Black Ben sat by the fire outside of town and considered robbing the men with the wagons, after they had the gold but before they could get it into the bank.

"Sure sounds like a better idea t'me," Black Ben said, and then motioned with his chin toward the sleeping Wilkinson brothers, "and them two fellas there don't give a hoot what we rob, jist as long's there's drinkin money in it."

Everything changed when they sat in the shadow of a small abandoned house and watched as about a dozen hard-looking men escorted two wagons covered with tarpaulins toward the border.

When they returned several hours later, a dim gas streetlight provided enough light for Bols to see that the gold had been loaded into both wagons, because the springs were still down like they were when the rifles were in them. X-trappers watched as the men escorted the wagons to the rear of the bank. "We'll sit tight and see what these guys do once their gold's in the bank." Black Ben just nodded, and both Wilkinson brothers continued snoozing.

Less than two hours later, the large man that Bols could tell earlier was in charge, walked out of the bank's front door. He was accompanied by two rough looking men wearing leather holsters filled with revolvers and a huge knife in a sheath—each carrying a shotgun. He commented to Black Ben, "That's an outfit not to take any chances with."

"Yeah," Ben agreed quietly, "especially when all we've got are those two sorry bastards," with his long pointed chin he nodded at the Wilkinson brothers, "who only wanna drink whiskey n' sleep."

"Once we get as much of this gold as we can carry, I'm gonna get us a few more guns to ride with us."

"How much y'reckon we can each carry?"

"Well now," Bols said, "I once carried a trapper up behind me when his horse got et by a big grizzly, and that fella warn't no lightweight. We came all the way down to Yerba Buena where he could get hisself a good horse, and that big ole dun o' mine had no problem atol totin him all that way. I reckon we'll be able to stuff all that gold in them big saddlebags we bought, and get to Laredo okay."

"I reckon," Black Ben grinned, "that'll be enough t'keep us in side meat n' beans for a while."

Bols laughed heartily, "Let's go git us some tequila, and hash this over now that we know the gold's in there." Bols and the three men headed across the street.

When the two wagons quietly left town a little after dusk, with the men riding alongside, Bols and his three men were sitting in Jaime's Paradise Cantina—entertaining four ladies.

The following day at a few minutes before noon, Bols and his gang watched as two young tellers and a middle-aged lady left the bank. "That's the same three who went to get some lunch yesterday." Bols pulled out his pocket watch, "Same time too, and they'll stay gone for two hours, just like yesterday." He turned to the two brothers, "Get all four horses back behind the bank and one of you be ready to come in with them saddlebags when Ben opens the door."

Bols and Black Ben walked across the street toward the bank. "This noontime siesta thing's gonna work good for us."

"Yeah," Ben grinned adding, "might try it m'self, after we get this gold."

The two bandits walked through the door, and when they saw there were no customers inside, Ben turned the latch that locked the door, and then he turned the sign around to the side with SIESTA TIME facing out.

Bols pulled the Colt Dragoon out and walked swiftly to the

old bank president, who was preparing to close for the two hour lunch period. On Simon McKannah's advice, Bols bought the gun the same day he was hired as deputy in San Francisco. Black Ben liked the weapon so much that he bought one soon after joining X-trappers.

The aging, overweight banker was now looking into a black .44 caliber hole. "Wh, uh, is this, uh, I...

"Shuddup and git that there back door open." When Bols said loudly, "**Now**" the perspiring little man actually jumped, and rushed to the back door.

When Jeffrey and Percival started to enter, Bols snatched the two saddlebags from Percival, "Git back out there n' keep an eye on them horses, like I tole ya."

Bols shoved the barrel against the banker's protruding belly, "We want that gold them fellas brought in here yesterday, and make it snappy if y'wanna stay alive."

"Oh my God, oh lordy," he looked around in a panic as he continued, "oh my God, oh my G...The loud noise as Bols pulled the hammer back jarred the man out of his panic. "They didn't leave any gold here. They just stayed and asked me all kinds of questions about investing, interest on deposits, and uh, uh, property for sale, and uh, things like that, and then they left."

"Well I'll be damned," Bols glared at the banker, "you made a deal with 'em so it'd look like they was leaving all that gold in here, and then they took it with 'em, huh?"

"Nossir, I didn't make any deal at all with those men. They pulled out yesterday after it got dark and took whatever they had with them."

"You knew they was bringin guns to them Messikins?"

"Yessir, everyone knows everything happening in this little town, but I sure didn't make any deal with those men." Sweat ran freely down the banker's face and his shirt was already soaked. "If their gold was here I'd sure let you have it."

"Goddammit," Bols grumbled, "git that vault open and let's see what's in there."

"Yessir, oh my God." He had already locked the vault, and his hands were now shaking so bad he missed the numbers the first time. "Oh lordy."

Bols growled in his ear, "Git it open this time or I'll blow your brains all over the damn thing and then I'll go find m'self another bank t'rob."

The banker took a very deep breath and slowly turned the

dial from one number to the next—it clicked and opened.

A quick look and Bols could see that there was no gold in the vault. "Goddamn sneaky sons o' bitches just made it look like they put that damn gold in here, so nobody would follow 'em." He then spotted boxes that had both Mexican and American bills. He motioned with his head toward the boxes, "You guys stuff that money in the saddlebags while I keep the gun on this banker." Jeffrey and Ben began filling the saddlebags, which didn't take long, because there was less than a thousand dollars combined.

Bols prodded the banker out to the cashier's area, and while holding the gun to the banker's back Ben grabbed the bills in each teller's cage. He heard a noise and turned to see a man holding the door handle and pulling. He then placed his hands on each side of his eyes and pressed his face against the glass. Bols pointed the gun at him and the man ran.

"Gitcher fat ass inside that vault." The banker quickly did as Bols demanded, and was relieved when he heard the door click shut and the dial turned.

They tossed the filled but very light saddlebags behind their saddles and tied them with rawhide dangling from each. Just as they mounted their horses, a sheriff and a deputy stepped around the corner. Both had a gun in their hand but pointed down beside their leg, and before they could say a word, Bols and Black Ben drew their revolvers and cut both men down. A scream cut the air behind them, and Bols pulled his horse around and fired—a nine year old girl fell.

Both lawmen died on the spot, but the girl lived. She would however, spend the rest of her life in a wheelchair.

Broderick McKannah

Broderick McKannah smiled down at the man sitting in the defendant's box next to the judge. He continued smiling as the small round man with no hair on his head and more on his face than a grizzly bear, glared back. Broderick stood frozen to the spot directly in front of Reverend Jedediah Fenner. The more Broderick smiled, the more the reverend glared. Broderick finally stepped forward and spoke.

"I want the jury to be certain that they understand the statement you made earlier, so I'm going to ask the court to have it read for them." He leaned so far forward that the puffy little man leaned away from the railing. "I'm certain that you won't mind," he emphasized the next word with just a slight sarcastic tone, "**Reverend**. They are, after all, your own words."

Broderick turned to the judge. "Your honor, would you please have a sentence read to the jury; the one that the defendant mumbled directly after I asked if he killed Ms. Valdez."

The judge nodded toward the thin young man who had been frantically scribbling as the lawyers and defendant spoke. He stood and read from his sheet. "She warn't but a worthless damn messykin."

It came as no surprise to Broderick when the all male, white Anglo jury found the defendant not guilty of murder, but guilty of accidental homicide. Fine $20. He was prepared for it.

With his fat lawyer beside him on the way to pay his fine, the Reverend turned to Broderick. "The Lord always sees the truth." He grinned as he turned to follow his lawyer. *And when I look at you*, he thought, *I see a dead man standing there in your boots,*

Broderick McKannah.

Broderick turned and subtly nodded to the sheriff, who saw his deputy watching for his sign. He tucked his chin down and rolled his eyes at the reverend. The huge deputy stepped in front of the bald little man, thereby preventing him from leaving the boardwalk in front of the judge's courtroom. He spoke in a loud voice that all people, including those who were still inside the courtroom could hear, "Reverend Jedediah Fenner, I have here a warrant for your arrest on charges that you embezzled a large sum of money from the San Diego California Church of Christ, a house of Christian worship that entrusted you with the highest office in that organization." He stepped forward and glared down at the man he had, until recently, thought was going to be the best thing that had ever happened in the church where he and his entire family worshipped. "Hold out your hands so I can put these cuffs on them."

The man was now quite frightened and looked at his lawyer, and then at the huge deputy holding handcuffs out toward him. "I don't know wha...the deputy's eyes narrowed as he stepped toward the little man.

"Jedediah, if you don't do as I instructed you then I'm gonna hafta use force to get these on your wrists, and" he then leaned forward threateningly, "you will then wish you'd done as you were told. One last time, Jedediah, put out your hands so I can cuff you."

When the reverend turned toward his lawyer it could have been interpreted as a move to flee, which is exactly what the big man holding the cuffs had hoped he would do. The deputy plowed into the reverend so forcefully that the lawyer and two newspaper reporters were also flattened. The reverend ended up directly beneath the seven foot two inch tall, two hundred and seventy-five pound deputy, who swiftly rose from the reverend while holding tight to one of the little man's arms. With his size seventeen shoes firmly beneath him, the gigantic deputy swung the reverend around as if he was square dancing, and pulled both wrists together and then snapped on the steel cuffs.

The baldheaded little holy man began screaming the moment that Deputy Ernst Grunwald yanked him up off the boardwalk, and he was still crying loudly and yelling foul obsenities when the jailhouse door swung shut.

Broderick McKannah turned to the several members of the jury that were just exiting, "If you turn him loose this time, let's all hope he doesn't tire of young Mexican girls and decides to grab one of your daughters to play with for awhile before slitting her throat." He turned and walked toward the jail.

Broderick stood silently watching as three deputies checked the reverend's clothing, and removed everything that was in the pockets. They had the man remove his shoes and socks, and then a deputy removed the shoestrings before telling him to put the shoes back on.

During this entire booking sequence, the reverend glared at Broderick, while clutching his bible close to his breast. Broderick calmly gazed at the man with a look of complete disinterest. When the huge deputy who arrested the reverend moved to open the door leading to the cells, Broderick's eyes narrowed, and he said loudly, "Wait a minute, Ernst, why are you allowing him to keep his bible?"

The man looked at the reverend and then at the bible he had been clutching all through his trial and subsequent arrest for the embezzlement of church funds. "He's always carrying his bible."

"Yeah," Broderick said as he stepped toward them, "I never noticed that before now. Let me see that bible, Jedediah."

Quicker than it seemed possible for such a fat little man, the reverend twisted, and even with his cuffed wrists, he managed to get the bible open.

Broderick was much quicker. He pulled his revolver from the oiled leather holster and smacked the reverend on the side of his bald head with the barrel. The deputy didn't know what was happening, but when the Holy Bible dropped to the floor and a small loaded double-barreled derringer fell out of the cut away pages, he then placed a huge foot on the reverend's hands. He turned to Broderick, "How in the heck did you know he had a hidden gun in there?"

"I didn't, but he's always smelled like a polecat to me, and he never made a move without that bible clutched to his chest like it was one o' those lifesavers y'see hanging on ships."

"Boy," Ernst said, "he sure fooled all of us. We thought he was a man of God." He paused then added, "And he really was a good preacher."

~

Two months later the Reverend Jedediah Fenner's trial began. His bank account had been frozen until after his new trial, so a court appointed lawyer handled his defense. Inept at his own financial record keeping the charge against him of embezzlement was upheld. The amount he stole was much more than his bank balance, so what money he had left was awarded to the church that he had stolen it from. The reverend was sentenced to thirty years at hard labor without the possibility of parole until 1875.

Three days after the reverend was sentenced, Deputy Ernst Grunwald and a senior member of the San Diego Church of Christ entered Broderick McKannah's law office. His secretary asked them to have a seat while she informed her boss they were there to see him.

A short time later she returned and said, "He'll see you now, follow me."

Broderick stood when the two men entered. With his hand out he smiled saying, "Nice to see you Ernst, and if my memory is correct, this is your father-in-law, Franz Heinrick."

"Yes," the thick muscular man said pleasantly with a smile, "I must say, you have quite a memory."

Broderick shook the man's callused hand then said with a sly smile, "One trait that is an absolute must to get through the Harvard Law School or Medical School is a good memory." He waved at the two chairs in front of his huge mahogany desk, "Have a seat, gentlemen and tell me the reason for this visit."

Ernst sat quietly and listened as his father-in-law spoke.

"Mister McKannah, the money in Jedediah Fenner's account was without a doubt stolen from our church's funds. The amount totaled six thousand and ten dollars, and God only knows how much more he probably took from us. I discussed this with the congregation and we all agree that it's little compensation for a human life, but we want Jaramillo and Maria Valdez, the parents of Olivia, the young girl that Jedediah slaughtered, to have it. Perhaps it will allow them to move ahead during these stressful times between the Mexican Californios and white Californians. We've brought the cash with us in hopes that you will see to it that it gets to them."

Broderick sat motionless for several moments, then shook his head several times side-to-side. "Mister Heinrick," he turned toward the deputy, "Ernst, you will only understand how much this will help that family if I tell you about them. Jaramillo was injured severely when a stagecoach lost a wheel and crashed into him as he loaded supplies into a buckboard at the General Store where he's worked for many years. Maria was struck down with polio five years ago and has difficulty finding any kind of work, even though she gets around by walking on the side of her ankles with the use of crutches. Olivia dropped out of school to work so her two younger brothers could remain in school. She became Jedediah's housekeeper only six short months ago, and worked twelve hours a day, seven days a week, walking three miles each way morning and night."

He shook his head again, "Even though the jury let him off, the overwhelming evidence shows that he forcefully raped her, and then when she threatened to tell the sheriff, he cut her throat and claimed that she attacked him and so he simply defended himself."

This time his head nodded up and down. "This unusual act of kindness on the part of you and the congregation of your church will change their lives dramatically." He watched as the old man removed the canvas bag of money from his heavy coat's huge inside pocket.

Broderick shook both men's hands and then said, "Maybe this will be the beginning of better relations between these two ethnic groups." He remained standing and watched as the two men left his office.

After sitting, he reflected on what he'd just said. *Nah! Won't make a bit of difference. Hell, many of these new Californians want the Mexicans shipped back to Mexico and us Irish sent back to Ireland or Five Points in New York City.*

Broderick adjusted his time so he could be there when Jedediah Fenner was taken from jail in chains and placed in a stagecoach that was modified to haul prisoners. Once he was inside, a chain that was bolted to the steel frame of the coach was padlocked to the chain between his wrists and ankles cuffs. As the two tall, burley marshals climbed into the coach's control compartment, Jedediah turned toward Broderick and snarled, "This ain't over yet, y'goddamn Mick."

Broderick put one finger up to the rim of his Stetson and winked, "Enjoy the ride, Reverand." The first filthy epithet to leave the prisoner's mouth was easily heard by all who had gathered to see their once revered preacher depart in shame. A long rambling string of vulgar threats continued but they went unheard due to the noise made by the four horses and the rattling portable jail cell.

Ian McKannah

Ian McKannah looked straight at the sheriff for a moment before speaking. "You're telling me that I'm gonna be arrested on the basis of what that damned Judy Dancer said?"

"Ian, she did more than just say it, she filed a warrant for your arrest. She claims that you raped and beat her."

"For Christ's sake, Sheriff Blount, you know me better'n that." Ian glared at the sherrif, a man he'd known for many years, "At least y'damn sure oughta know it."

The sheriff glanced around before saying quietly, "Yeah Ian, I do, but these are tough times here in Carson City. Since that new vein of silver was discovered, there's about a dozen o' them darn city lawyers around here and people are suing their own kinfolk. Judy went n' got her one o' them snakes to fill out the papers." The tall, thin, middle-age sheriff shook his head slowly, "I gotta take you to the jail until Monday morning then you can get a lawyer to getcha out on bail."

On the third floor of the hotel across the street, Judy Dancer and her boyfriend, a gambler, con man, and hired killer, Jewel L'Grieu, watched Ian walk away with the sheriff.

"Wha'd I tell ya, Judy, worked like a charm, huh? But this guy's got a helluva lot more than the old hardware store owner in Sacramento, we fleeced. We're gonna own that nice gambling hall that half-pint little Mick built."

A frown crossed her face as she turned to her lover. "I know Ian well enough to know that you just might hafta kill him to do that."

Jewel then put his swarthy dark arms around Judy's waist and smiled crookedly. "Hey baby, that just ain't gonna be no problem atoll."

~

In less than two hours after being released from jail on Monday, Ian was on his horse and heading toward San Francisco. Good weather, a strong horse, and a determined man teamed up, and the two hundred and fifty mile trip ended seven days later at his brother's law office.

Patrick heard Ian's voice, and before his secretary had time to get to his door, Patrick was heading along the hall toward the huge lobby. "Hello little brother, y'sold out n' started your own pony express service, huh?" His grin gave away the serious tone he spoke with.

"Nope, just a nice ride through the wilderness to say 'ello to me aging Irish brother. Bloody awful I would feel, by Jesus, if you's to die of old age 'fore we 'ad a chance t'get together again, old man."

"Oh my God, and 'ere I am right away thinking that me baby brother had gotten 'imself into a jam, and was in need o' me legal wizardly wisdom." Patrick grinned, turning toward the older woman standing next to her desk. "Nancy, can y'believe how cynical I've become in me old age." She simply smiled and shook her head.

"Well, old man," Ian said, "now thacha mention it, I do 'ave a wee bit of a problem that could use yer attention." Ian kept the grin hidden and maintained his trademark poker face as he shook hands with the elder McKannah.

"Well then," Patrick said, "let's go t'me office n' see what must be done t'keep you free, so 'alf the politicians in my area n' yours don't come down with delirium tremors."

Half an hour later Patrick was still silently listening as his brother explained. When Ian stopped, his brother dropped the slang and said quietly, "I gather that this little chippie, uh," he looked at his notes, "Judy Dancer, isn't the brightest candle on the tree, so she must have a man somewhere assisting, and probably trying to get that casino and hotel that you've worked hard for, put into his name."

"Yeah," Ian answered with a frown, "and Jewel L'Grieu is his name. She used to be married to his brother but he was killed in a bank robbery up in Idaho, and my money says this guy, Jewel, was in on it too. But the sheriff in Carson City says he checked with his friend, the sheriff in the town where it happened, and there was not enough evidence to even hold Jewel, so he walked. A month or so later he showed up in Carson City, and wasn't but a month after that he was moved in with Judy."

"Ian," Patrick said in a serious tone of voice with a direct but not hostile stare, "did you have a personal relationship with this woman?"

"No Patrick, business only and she's not a woman. My guess is she's either just out of her teens or maybe still in 'em. I never get involved with any of my ladies unless they've been over the hill n' through the woods a few times." He shook his head and the blonde hair floated back and forth before settling in front of his blue eyes. Ian pushed it back and looked directly into his brother's deep sea-green eyes, "Judy's just a cute little gal from over in Wyoming somewhere." Ian raised his eyebrows, closed his eyes, and took a deep breath. After releasing it, he said quietly but with a sincere tone, "I have always preferred grown women with at least a wee bit of intelligence about 'em, and she's dumber'n that old mule that Jesse traded his tule reed-boat for when he decided he was gonna plow an acre to plant banana trees on."

"Oh yeah," Patrick said with a grin, "haven't thought about that for years. He wouldn't even listen to pa when he told him it's too cold to grow 'em that far up in California."

Ian chuckled, "Wouldn't listen when ma said those things in 'em didn't look like seeds. Jess just kept pickin 'em out and said we'd all be begging for bananas 'fore long, and he would be eatin 'em and daring us to sneak in n' grab a few."

"What was he, about twelve then?"

"Maybe thirteen," Ian smiled.

Patrick's grin widened, "It woulda taken all four of us boys and Aleena too t'grab a stalk if he actually grew some."

"Ha! Aleena woulda been on his side, as always." Ian bent his head down and raised his eyebrows.

"You're right," Patrick said and puckered his lips, "Jess could do no wrong in her eyes. God, how I wish she had survived that Donner Wagon Train tragedy." He shook his head slightly then looked at his young brother, "Ian, I'm glad you stayed away from that hustling little tart because this Jewel guy's probably gonna get one of those two-bit lawyers I've been hearing a lot about that attend a three week course and then get a law degree from a New York City school. He'll tell 'im to dig up anything he can about you."

Ian McKannah's grin caused his brother to also grin, "Won't take 'im long because all he's gotta do is serve the sheriff papers to allow access to my records. Killed two men in self defense, and also shot a thief in the ass when I caught the bugger inside my house with a bag filled with artwork, silverware, and my small gold Buddha, plus several brawls inside my casino that, thanks to my two burly floor-walkers, I came through without having to kill some likkered up cowboy."

Patrick pursed his lips and shook his head up and down, "I reckon that's not bad considering how many years you've put in places like that." His eyebrows went up and he chuckled, "Hell, I've defended Broderick on more charges than that and San Diego's a pretty sophisticated place compared to Carson City and that Five Points area in New York City." He opened a drawer, "Care for a glass of good Irish wiskey?"

"Sure, that was a tiring trip."

When Patrick handed him the small, cut-crystal glass filled to the brim he said, "You coulda sent a telegram, y'know. We're getting messages from all the major cities as far away as Kansas City."

"Yeah," Ian said after a sip, "but I thought it would be better if I came here and explained it to you in person, plus it'll give the private detective I hired a chance to snoop around without me being in the way. Those Pinkerton guys are good, so if that weasel, Jewel, has anything like this in his past we'll soon know all about it."

Patrick nodded, "Good thinking, Ian, you've used Pinkerton before, huh?"

"Yeah, once! Remember when that little chippie who danced in my Follies Review at The Shamrock in Five Points claimed she was pregnant with my child and wanted a ridiculous amount of money?"

"Yeah, did you use a Pinkerton man that time?"

Ian drained the small glass and grinned as he held it toward his brother, "Yes, I was number thirteen on her list." He sipped the whiskey before continuing. "They quickly learned that she had made so much money from a banker in Boston that she decided to make a full time career of fleecing businessmen." Ian grinned and took another sip, "That banker was Jewish, so I reckon she figured if she could suckerpunch a Jew, then a Mick oughta be easy." Patrick's grin widened when Ian burst out laughing, "She had the baby in prison, and it was black."

Patrick leaned forward to refill Ian's glass then filled his own before speaking. "Another lesson learned about dealing with the Irish."

"Remember, Stoop?" Ian said with a wide grin.

"Yeah," Patrick replied, "that young guy from the islands who worked for you, and was half again as tall as you."

"That's him. I was kidding Stoop after she was sentenced for extortion. Tulip, that's all I ever heard her called, asked me several times to have Stoop come down to her room and move a chair or something for her. I never thought a thing about it until she tried to milk me for a bundle, but when I jokingly asked ole Stoop if the baby was his he got nervous and kinda stuttered. I remembered then how a couple of the other dancers had asked me to send him to their room to fix this, or do that." Ian grinned as he lifted the glass, "Or move the bed, maybe?" His grin spread a bit wider, "So the bloody thing wouldn't make so much noise, I reckon, as it bumped against the wall."

"Ever hear from Tulip or the boy again?"

"Tulip returned to her parent's home in London wi' her little picaninny," Ian smiled as he finished the whiskey, "and Stoop is still with me. Best bloody all around man I've ever 'ad, an e's a good cook, deals cards wi' the best of 'em, an when 'e's wearin 'is coal-black tux 'e would impress the bleedin Queen 'erself wi' 'is polite manners."

Patrick got a kick from listening to his younger brother revert to the Irish slang whenever he had a few drinks under his belt. "I have some work that must be done today, so I'll have my driver bring the carriage around and take you to my house. Get some rest, and after dinner we'll go over a few things I'll need before you return to Carson City. By the time you notify me of the date for your trial, I'll have everything ready for my associates to take over here in San Francisco during my absence. I'll then head to Carson City and we'll send this pair up the river for a nice long vacation."

Ian was exhausted when he climbed into his brother's new carriage. Leaning back against the plush headrest of the velvet covered seat he scanned the luxurious interior while thinking, *Very nice, brother Patrick, I bet brother Broderick is working 'is bloody arse off tryin t'keep up.* Ian closed his eyes and smiled as he thought, *or working 'ard to keep you workin yer own arse off t'keep up wi' 'im.* He chuckled quietly and dozed off.

~

Less than three weeks after Ian returned to his casino he was notified that his trial date had been set for August 15ᵗʰ, two months away. Ian sent Patrick a telegram on the afternoon of the day he was notified.

The day after Patrick received Ian's telegram he also received one from the Pinkerton Detective Agency's San Francisco office. It was less than 10 blocks from Patrick's office, but everyone was so caught up with the revolutionary means of communication that the new telegrams were being used by businesses that could have delivered them quicker by hand.

> **TO:** Patrick McKannah ... attorney at law.
> **REFERENCE:** Ian McKannah ... casino owner.
> **FROM:** James McKinnick: District Supervisor
>
> Field agents have acquired significant information concerning Jewel L'Grieu ... STOP ... will deliver same to you after business hours at SFBC ... STOP

Patrick handed the young Mexican delivery boy a coin and asked him to wait a moment. After reading the telegram he put a brief reply on the back.

> **TO:** James McKinnick
> **FROM:** Patrick McKannah
>
> Thanks for making this a priority, James ... STOP ... will see you at club around 6:00 ... STOP ... drinks are on Ian.

Patrick's private coach slowed and then stopped in front of the San Francisco Businessman's Club at exactly six o'clock that afternoon. After stepping out, he turned and looked up at his driver. "Mister Gonzalez, you can go and do your shopping for the weekend, and then return for us in about two hours. We'll have dinner here so we can get right to work when you take us home."

Patrick waited until Aldo Calaveras closed the coach door and then the two men approached the club's huge ornate door. After a solid rapping of Patrick's knuckles a small sliding door slid back revealing two scrutinizing eyes. The hand-carved laminated oak door opened inward on six silent one inch thick wrought iron hinges.

The two scrutinizing eyes were now softened as a broad white smile erupted on the coal-black face of the seven foot tall giant that shook both Patrick's hand and the hand of his companion and protégé, Aldo. A voice too deep for definition spoke. "Good evening, Mister McKannah. I'm pleased to see you up and about, Mister Calaveras."

Aldo smiled, "Thank you, Gwadon. That was the worst of all the colds I have ever had."

The huge black man in a stork-white tux stepped back and motioned with a hand the size of a skillet, "Mister McCluskey requested a private table, Mister McKannah." He turned and snapped his fingers at a young man standing nearby. Turning back he said, "Warren will escort you to the table, sir."

"Thank you, Gwadon. Mister Gonzalez will return in a couple of hours, so please call me when he does, because we have a lot of work to do at home."

"Yessir." The giant turned to greet the next arrival knocking.

One hour later the agent from the Pinkerton office gathered up the papers he had been discussing with Patrick and Aldo. As the waiter cleared the table in preparation to serve their meal, James McCluskey placed the documents into a thin leather briefcase and handed it to Patrick. "I have an appointment, so I'll leave you gentlemen to your meal. If you have any questions I will be home by nine and will remain there all weekend, so do not hesitate to come by if necessary."

Both men were hungry and remained silent until each had eaten a few bites. After sipping his wine Patrick asked, "So, what do you think, Aldo?"

After swallowing the bite of sirloin, Aldo answered. "I'm very impressed with the thorough investigations that these men conduct. I'd say this Jewel L'Grieu is going to wish he had never chosen a McKannah as his next victim."

"I wholeheartedly concur, amigo." He then motioned for the waiter, "I'm going to have one brandy before Gonzalez arrives, which should be soon. I want you rested so this cold you had is completely gone by the time we must head toward Carson City."

Once they were in the coach Aldo leaned back and closed his eyes. *What a lucky break,* he thought, *that I grew up among the McKannah family. Few men ever have friends like these. Thank You, God. I hope I am deserving of their friendship and Your love.*

Jesse McKannah

Jesse allowed his horse to move along slowly as they headed toward the distant mountain. The earlier teachings of his father and his childhood Indian friends allowed him to maintain a course that would take him through the narrow canyon leading around the mountain on the north side. Jesse looked up at the group of stars that Lame Wolverine had pointed to before he left the camp. "When I was younger, Jesse, a group of us went through the canyon in search of mustangs. There was no town there then, but a short time after you left I led a group of braves through there again, hoping to find a few buffalo. We found no buffalo but we saw the town in the distance. It is set back against the western side of the mountain. We first saw it as the sun began chasing stars from the sky. If we had let our horses walk slowly we would have been there long before the sun was above our heads. All white men except you, Jesse, have been bad medicine for us, so we returned here and have not been there again."

Jesse pulled out the pocket watch that his father gave him on the day he headed into the mountains on his first trapping trip. He'd just turned thirteen that day and was already anxious to explore the mysteries of the undeveloped wilderness.

He arrived at the base of the mountain and hunched over to prevent light from the match being seen. As soon as he saw the dial, his leather glove closed on the flame. *About three hours before daylight,* he thought, *took a bit longer than I figured it would. I still oughta be able to get within a mile or so of the town before sunrise, and find a place for me and Shadow to hide until dark.*

Judging by the faint light of a full moon, plus the glow of a candle in several of the town's windows, Jesse was as close as he wanted to get. He climbed from the saddle and cautiously led Shadow along the base of the mountain. The trail that he'd been following snaked along between a thick forest on the west and the trees running up the mountain on his left. *Whoever cleared this trail musta wanted badly to get to that canyon I came through.* His thoughts were still on the trail as he walked slowly along, leading Shadow. *Wide enough for half a dozen riders and must be close to fifteen miles from town to the canyon; phew, heck of a big job.*

With only an hour of darkness remaining Jesse located a good place to head up the mountain through the trees. *Musta been an earthquake here a long time ago that caused this chunk of the mountain to fall off.* His eyes scanned back and forth across the area as Shadow climbed. The horse stopped after reaching a reasonably level area that was surrounded by trees. Jesse looked ahead at a small indented area and nudged Shadow toward it. "That's an Indian firepit," he said quietly as he patted Shadow's neck, "and there musta been a family living here not too long ago, because all that's growing on this five or so acres are small saplings." *This'll make a good place to hide Shadow,* he thought, *while I'm scanning this town through the telescope. After that maybe I can get m'self a little rest before scouting that town tonight.*

During the morning Jesse quietly moved several of the larger stones so Shadow could move around easier. He also cut a limb and probed any holes that might house rattlesnakes. He then hollowed out an area to line with his canvas poncho and poured water from one of the two canteens and led Shadow to it.

After attaching the hobbles to Shadow, Jesse slung the leather pouch holding the telescope across his back. He moved slowly across the mountaintop while keeping an eye on the trees down the side of the mountain between him and the town. Once he spotted the first cabin through the trees, he slowed his advance across the top and began cautiously working his way down. Even though the trees were so close together that he could only see a glimpse of an occasional small cabin, he knew it would be possible for someone to spot him if he got careless and made noise.

Being careful to place his boots where a stone wouldn't begin a loud journey down through the trees, Jesse worked his way across. Every few yards he set his boot against a tree and pulled the telescope out. Remaining behind a huge tree, he rested the scope against first one side of the tree and then the other. In this manner he was able to see that the small cabins were all on the west side of a wide dirt road and on the east side, which was the side he was looking down from, there were only two structures.

One was a single story building that was narrow but very deep. Judging by the people entering empty-handed and leaving with a sack or some other type of container, Jesse figured it was either a general merchandise store or something similar.

The other building on the east side was a double-wagon width from the first one, and was two stories tall. It was about four times wider than the first and even deeper. *That building must be a hotel*, he thought, *and the way some men come out wobbling, I betcha it has a likker bar too.* He slowly moved the scope from front to rear before lowering it. *That building's bigger'n pa's barn, and that sucker was at least a hunert feet deep n' over half that wide.*

Lifting the scope back to his eye, Jesse held it on the lone window that was positioned in the rear quarter of the structure. *I can see in where somebody wiped a spot clean up near the top. Musta wanted t'look out n' see how hard it was rainin or snowin.* Jesse lowered the scope to carefully scan every area around him, even up the mountain behind. Satisfied, he brought the scope to his eye again. *Yep, just what I figured, that window's in the bar area, probably so the cigar smoke can be let out when it gets too thick.*

It was well into the afternoon by the time he was pouring water into his leather hat for Shadow to drink. Before lying down to sleep a while, he removed the hobbles from the horse and led it to an area where the grass was a bit thicker, and then put them back on.

Jesse slept well, considering the circumstances, and now sat in the dark chewing jerky and watching lights of the small town below begin blinking on. He removed the hobbles and tied Shadow's reins to a slender limb that the horse could pull away from if threatened by a grizzly or a wolf. He knew that either might take the horse down, *but*, he thought, *at least you'll have a chance.*

While chewing the last chunk of jerky, he opened the left

saddlebag and got the horse's feed. After replacing the bag he rubbed Shadow's neck while talking softly, "I hate leaving that saddle on you but I might be in a hurry getting outa here later tonight, big fella." When Shadow's neck came up, Jesse leaned down and filled the lined hole with water. He continued talking softly and rubbing the horse's neck as it drank. "You ain't been through a lot with me, Shadow, but you're a smart boy, so we'll be seeing a lot of adventures together."

He wasn't surprised when the horse didn't blow noisily through his lips, but simply rubbed his wet nose along Jesse's cheek and then stood silently as Jesse rubbed the side of his huge head, "I'll be back in a few hours and we'll head home."

It took Jesse a little over an hour to move from his hideout to the fringes of the small town. Once he gathered several landmarks in his head, he removed his boots and hung them over a low limb. After pulling on the knee-length moccasins that Ruben, the Negro lawyer-shoemaker tossed in free when he bought two new pairs of boots, he counted the steps required to reach the building that he'd earlier decided was a merchandise store. *Sixty steps from this corner'll get me back to my boots*, he thought, *unless I hafta run for it.*

Moving silently by the rear of the single-story building, Jesse paused twice to look in all directions, and then listen for noise. Standing at the corner he looked at the lone window twenty feet away. Looking up at the small area that had been wiped clean he could see only shadows of movement inside. After looking in all directions he moved across the alley and pressed his body close to the wall beside the window.

Listening at the edge of the closed window he could hear two people talking, but after half an hour he realized that it was two cooks discussing what and how much they were going to cook for breakfast.

Staying in the shadows and moving as though he was in a Blackfoot war camp, Jesse moved along the side of the large building that had several lighted windows. *Looks like I was right, it's a saloon and a hotel that serves food.* He had darkened his face with streaks of black festival paint that Lame Wolverine had given him. Moving very cautiously, Jesse looked at every possible place along both buildings where someone might step out.

The moon would eventually cast light into the alley, but for now it was so dark that he was forced to move at a snail's pace for fear of stumbling into a mislaid pail or something else that would sound in the silent alley like a tin pantry falling off the roof.

Back at the window the two cooks were still talking. "C'mon Toad, less go back to the kitchen with these beers afore tonight's taters boil away to starch agin n' ole man Kellerman has another shitfit." Jesse watched through the soot clouded panes as two shadows, one tall the other very short, stood and moved away.

Other voices were loud and also sounded like several men were discussing something. He knew there wasn't a door along either wall of the two buildings that someone might step out of, but realized that there was always a chance that someone might turn into the alley to use as a shortcut or to empty their kidneys. *The main door's on that end facing west and there's no door in the rear of either building, except maybe this one on the other side.* Once he was back beside the window where he could hear the men inside talking, he took a moment to orient himself to the path back to his boots. *Don't wanna press m'luck too far, so I'll get outa here before that moon gets too high.* He glanced up through the trees that were shielding the moon's light, *and that ain't gonna be but a few minutes.*

"**I don't give a rat's ass who it was**," the loud voice boomed, "**how big he was, how goddamn fast he was going, or any of that shit**." Jesse was alert as the man paused. *I wish he'd keep talking so I wouldn't hafta worry about someone inside spotting som'n and pointing at this window.* He breathed easier as the booming voice inside continued.

The voice was calmer now, "I sent thirty of my so-called best men to wipe out a handful of those damn savages, and what I got was two of you shot in the ass and the rest returned with shit in your britches."

"Boss, we was...

The man who had been speaking screamed, "**Don't you say another damn word, Larson, or I'll put a bullet in you that'll still be hurtin long after the one that went through the cheek of your sorry ass is healed**."

Larson, Jesse thought, *I'll remember that.*

"We're gonna do some checking to find out who blew the whistle on your little morning party with the Flatheads, and then I'll see to it that he's no longer a problem. What I want,

Larson, is for you and some of these guys to get all the gear ready to head to Texas when they send word that the herd's ready, and then you can help the men I hired to drive 'em here." There was a long pause, but Jesse heard the clinking of glass and figured he was pouring a drink before continuing, so he scanned the darkness around him and waited.

The tone of the man's voice had changed, and Jesse could hear slurring, as though he'd been drinking during the day. "I can't figure out why this g'ment gave those damn Flatheads the forest and half the damn lake. Coulda stuck 'em out on a plateau and they woulda been glad to get it. They live like cattle anyway, but hell no, they gave the bastards a forest that I planned to cut down for fence posts and I need that lake if I'm gonna put a few hundred thousand head of cattle on this land. Stupid damn politicians ain't got brains enough not to piss into a hard wind. I paid Soderman enough money to choke a damn mule, and what's he do, huh, what's he do? Gave me the same kinda crap you guys did. Gonna be some changes around here, and unless my orders are carried out, there's gonna be some new names at roll call and some of you are gonna be soldiering again or loafing around waiting for leftovers like y'was when I hired you."

Jesse had the information he came for and had a hunch there was going to be men coming outside soon. He backtracked to the boots and put them on before heading toward his horse.

He made better time returning than he did heading toward the town, so it was still dark when he approached the Flathead camp. His trilling signals were picked up immediately, and before he could even see the shimmering surface of the lake, a voice startled him. "Still remember the signals, huh?"

He looked down to see a smiling Lame Wolverine walking beside him.

~

Unknown to Jesse, dark eyes had watched as he moved from one building to the next in the small town of Burgess Montana that he had just exited. Crazy Joe Flambert actually was crazy, but he wasn't stupid—he knew how to take good care of himself. *Burgess Kellerman,* Joe thought, *will pay a bundle one o' these days to know about that feller what was snoopin around here tonight.*

~

Jesse spent the next day looking around the small settlement of Polson. A small group of Irish people in six wagons heading to California was led by a man named Polson. They were from New York City but stopped, liked what they saw, and decided to stay in northern Montana.

While having lunch at O'Hannahan's Diner, a huge man with rusty red hair similar to Jesse's two older brothers and wearing a white apron came walking out of the kitchen through a pair of swinging batwing doors. He approached Jesse with a small clay plate, on which sat a huge slice of the most scrumptious apple pie he'd seen since the last his mother had placed before him. "'Ow bout a slice o' me best efforts wi' the gorgeous apples fallin t'the ground outside me kitchen window, lad." A friendly smile was spreading across his round red face, "An' lad, it's a courtesy slice from Michael O'Hannahan 'imself."

Jesse swallowed the last of the tastiest and most tender meat he'd ever chewed, and began sopping up the remaining gravy with bread. "If I was to turn away from a slice of free apple pie, Mister O'Hannahan, me dear ole father, God rest 'is Irish soul, would spin about in 'is grave n' not catch a wink in a fortnight."

Sitting the saucer on the counter, the smiling Irishman said, "If an Irishman turns down anything free 'e'll not sleep a wee wink for a bloody month as Leprecauns run about in the attic a'rattlin chains n' stomping their three-toed feet." He held out his hand, "Michael O'Hannahan."

Gripping it firmly, Jesse smiled, "Jesse McKannah."

"By Jesus, it's good t'be speakin wi' me own people fer a change. "'Ow long've y'been 'ere in this wild new country?"

"All me life, and m'four brothers n' one sister too. M'father came when 'e was still a wee lad."

"That was good thinking on 'is part, by Jesus, 'e came to a better land to start 'is own family. We, that's me n' m'wife and two boys, came to New York City two years ago, and as bad's things are back 'ome I reckon there's no bloody place's bad as New York, at least where we 'ad t'settle. That place called Five Points is an Irishman's bloody 'ell on earth, it is by Jesus. Those dregs that've been there a while treat the Irish worse than dogs n' pigs. Even the newspapers slander the Irish." He looked hard at Jesse before adding, "Tis true, lad, seen the cartoons m'self. They make us look like bloody cavemen, they do, by Jesus. An ugly old woman sellin wormy corn an 'alf rotten t'maters once lifted her walking stick to me after I pointed n' called 'er stuff garbage to be fed to hogs." He chuckled at the memory, "Swung the damned stick t'knock me 'ead off, but I ducked n' jumped back. Screaming 'er bloody lungs out; she said, "that's why we save it for you Irish."

While the owner of the café stood talking to the tall thin man sitting at the counter, Crazy Joe Flambert sat at a small table next to a front window. To a casual observer it would appear that the stout, scruffily-garbed man was absorbed in the meal he was consuming. He was bent over the plate while picking at the individual chunks of vegetables and meat, but his extraordinary hearing was missing nothing communicated between the two men at the counter. He plucked a chunk of meat from the stew with his fork and chewed as his ears tuned in their talk.

"An she was so dark," Michael O'Hannahan continued, "an 'ad a big red nose so hooked that a kettle coulda been 'ung from it to swing into that 'uge toothless mouth. I reckon she musta come from Africa or somewhere in that part o' the world." He shook his head while mumbling in the Gaelic language that Jesse didn't understand.

"I've 'eard similar stories, Michael, and 'ave no plans to ever go visit that part of this country."

"By the way, Jesse, if that fella in Missoula changes 'is mind about selling the cattle, then stop back 'ere and by then I'll 'ave located the name of another fella in Idaho what stopped 'ere last month. Said 'e was sellin out n' movin to San Francisco, where 'tis not so bloody cold, were 'is own words. An' I also 'eard there's a Mormon over that way sellin a big herd so 'e can move 'is family down by that big salty lake that a big buncha Mormons took over." A customer entered and Michael headed back into the kitchen.

Jesse spoke as he soaked up the second chunk of bread with the gravy on his plate. "He better go farther south than San Francisco if it's warm he wants, because it gets pretty darn cold there and rains all the time." After one last swipe across the plate, Jesse tossed the wet bread in his mouth and shoved the plate aside. Speaking around the bread he said, "Can't wait to get m'teeth into this pie."

When he finished, Jesse said loud enough that Michael could hear from the kitchen, "I'm certain that you've got an award winning pie if ever you find a pie contest. An' Michael, that was the tenderest beef I ever chewed and also the tastiest."

Michael O'Hannahan came from the kitchen with a sly smile, "Beef y'say lad, ah yes, beef."

Jesse raised an eyebrow as he paid him. He thought about all the meat he'd eaten without knowing for certain what animal it was cut from. He grinned then added, "Tastiest meat I ever et."

Jesse covered the eighty miles to Missoula Montana without an incident and arrived a couple of hours before noon the following day. He'd stopped in a clearing atop a hill to feed Shadow and eat some jerky himself. After removing the horse's tack he rubbed his back briskly before hobbling him on a grassy area. Jesse spread the horse blanket on top of some pine needles he gathered, and then rolled up in his own heavy blanket—hand resting on his pistol.

The following day he easily located the small restaurant that his new friend, Michael O'Hannahan had told him about. After ordering a bowl of stew, Jesse asked to speak to Paddy. A moment after the young waitress placed coffee and fresh rolls in front of him, he watched as a small man walked through the opening to the kitchen with a bowl of stew. Neither smiling nor frowning, the man said, "I'm Paddy McGill, wha' kin I do f'ya, lad?"

After explaining, Jesse gripped the offered hand as the man smiled. "I 'aven't been up to Polson in a month, 'ow's Michael doin these days?"

"He seems t'be doing well," Jesse replied. "One thing I know he's doing very well is making apple pies. Best I've had since my mom passed away."

"I 'ad a slice m'self, an' it was better'n mine, so he offered t'show me 'ow he makes 'em." He finally smiled, "Few cooks'll ever let a recipe like that git away, not even one Irishman to another."

"If my sister was still alive I'd ask him for it, but I don't cook good or very often." Jesse grinned, "Gotta wait'll I'm starving to be able to eat what I cook."

The man said, "Scuse me while I get m'self a cup o' coffee." He returned and sat with the cup beside Jesse. "Joe Furnt is the fella wants t'sell 'is bloody cattle. Says 'e wants t'go where it don't get so dern cold in winter, but there's other reasons 'e wants t'get away from this area. Still 'as 'em he does, because nobody 'ere has a spare bit o' cash or gold, so I reckon y'oughta be able to get the entire 'erd fer a nice price."

Jesse sat his coffee cup down, "How many head does he have?"

"Last tally was two hundred and thirty and all nice n' fat. I can tell ya how t'get to 'is ranch if ya wanna go look at 'em. Ain't but a short 'alf hour ride, I reckon."

Forty-five minutes later Jesse rode into Joe Furnt's ranch. He could tell immediately that it was built by a man who knew how to work with wood, stones, and mortar. It reminded him of his own ranch that he and Arliss O'Reilly had built. The memory of what the men that he'd killed had done to his foreman, who had become his best friend, plus his entire crew cast a dark shadow across his mind for a brief moment. It returned to the depths of his memory when a huge man stepped from the doorway with a big smile. "Howdy friend, what brings you this way?"

Jesse remained in the saddle and said, "A restaurant owner in Polson named Michael O'Hannahan told me you had a herd of cattle to sell, and his friend, Paddy McGill told me how to get here."

"Sure do, climb down and let's have a cup of coffee and talk about it."

During two cups of strong black coffee Jesse listened as Joe Furnt explained what type of cattle he had and how he cleared the land and built the small homestead for him and his wife and two sons. "Jed and Luke were good, God fearing boys, Jesse. They worked beside me since they were old enough to sit a horse or handle a hoe in the garden." The thick skin surrounding his eyes seemed to soften and his eyes misted with melancholy when he continued, "Jed was fifteen and Luke was a month from turning seventeen when they both took sick. Julie, that's my wife, knows about as much as any doctor we've met and tried everything she could think of when the boys took sick. Jed was a stout young fella and didn't get knocked down right away, but Luke seemed to simply wither like a bean vine attacked by voles or gophers." The huge man had to stand and walk to a window to continue. "Luke died on a Monday morning last June and Jed passed a week after on a Sunday."

A long silence allowed Jesse to imagine his mother and father being forced to endure a similar twist of fate. He set his jaw and remained silent.

Finally, Joe returned to the table as Julie Furnt, a rail-thin but attractive woman silently poured both men another cup of coffee. After the coffee Jesse said, "The price seems fair, Joe, and looking at your herd as I rode in, they appear to be in good shape. I brought gold to pay for 'em but was hoping you'd have a couple of hands that I could hire for a few days to get 'em home."

"Jesse, we can ride to the Henderson Ranch, which ain't but five miles, and see if their two boys wanna make a few dollars. I'm sure they will, because spending money ain't a'hanging on trees in this part o' the country. When you wanna head back home?"

"Tomorrow wouldn't be too soon for me, Joe."

"Fine, I'll saddle m'horse n' we'll ride next door and see what they say."

The two Henderson boys, both stout teenagers, rode in at dawn the following morning. Julie fixed a breakfast of flapjacks, fried hog side meat, and a dozen hard-fried eggs. Once everything was washed down with coffee, Jesse thanked her and then held his hand out to Joe. "I'll make a point to get back up here fore y'leave, Joe."

"Hope y'do, Jesse, but we ain't parting yet. I'm gonna ride along with you n' help keep those critters calm, cause the only voice they've heard lately has been mine." He smiled broadly as he pulled his leather hat down and tied it beneath his chin. "I've another reason for going. Been thinking about that apple pie of Michael O'Hannahan's you told me about, and if it's better'n Julie's, then I'm gonna keep eating it till I figure out what he's doing different from her."

As Jesse saddled Shadow and checked his tack, he thought, *Joe's comin along to help me get 'em home, but he's also keeping an eye on these two boys. Darn good man, shame he lost his two sons.*

The two men and two boys drove the herd around the west side of Polson and straight on to the Flathead Reservation. Jesse had spoken to Lame Wolverine two days before leaving, so he wasn't surprised to see him leading a herd of cattle. He had already selected the men who would ride guard on the herd and called the braves now to lead them to a good grazing area.

Jesse was surprised when Joe greeted his friend in their dialect of the Salish language. Later, as both men and the boys sat at the fire sipping sassafras tea, Joe said, "I was a trapper before meeting Julie, and traded a lot with the Flatheads back west of here, and never met a better buncha people. Makes sense now why you paid me for the branding irons. Circle F, will be the Flathead brand now instead of the Circle F, Furnt brand."

"Just a coincidence, Joe, but it sures saves us a lotta time registering a new brand."

"Yep, same ole Circle F, but it just means som'n different now. I reckon this's the most decent thing anyone's ever done for these people."

Jesse grit his teeth as he thought of his friend's thin starving wife, but then relaxed, "Soon's I get these people eating regular again, I'm gonna try to learn why this new government ain't keeping their end of the bargain. And a tidy bargain it was for 'em too, all of the Flathead land around here for this small chunk that's half lake."

"Mister McKannah." Jesse turned toward the older of the two Henderson boys. "Sir, if you ever go lookin to get another herd o' cows, me n' m'brother would sure like to hire on again."

"How old are you fellas?"

"I'm sixteen gonna be seventeen in four months, and Johnny will be sixteen next May. We done finished our schooling and ain't gonna leave ma n' pa, but it sure would be great to get away for a while."

Jesse didn't have to think about it. "Robert, you n' Johnny did as good as any drover I ever saw, so if I go som'rs to get more cattle, and if your folks say okay, then you can count on riding with me for the Circle F again."

Don Christ

Aleena

Aleena McKannah trudged along beside the river. It was still early fall but there was a chill in the air and she was glad to be wearing a warm coat. Moments before the two killers rode in she had put on the heavy wool coat that hung to midway between her knees and feet. Almost two hours after leaving the charred remains of the cabin, she rounded a bend and climbed a slight rise that she had climbed several times to visit during the year she spent at the Green River cabin.

Seeing the burned heap where her new friends' cabin once stood caused a weakness in her legs and she slowly collapsed to the ground. Silent tears began running down her cheeks until the cabin's remains and everything surrounding it was nothing more than a blur.

Aleena remained on the ground until her knees began aching, but before struggling to her feet she looked up through tear-filled eyes and spoke quietly. "Dear God, please don't make any more good people suffer like this just to teach me a lesson. Whatever I've done, please forgive me and just strike me down with a bolt of lightning and send me to Hell, but please don't kill any more people because of something I've done."

After wiping her eyes with one of the two large blue hanker-chiefs that she carried in the pockets of her hardy Levi Strauss pants, Aleena got her bearings from the sun and headed south. She had found the floppy canvas hat that she had rolled up and shoved into the pocket of her jacket the previous day once the warm spring sun ended its journey across the sky. She pulled it down over her big ears, and as the sun began dropping below the western mountains she sat beneath the tiny leanto she had just completed. She silently thanked a friend back in Boston for the folding knife and sharpening stone she gave her as a gift before setting out to join the Donner Party to head home to California.

Before it was too dark she spread one of the hankerchiefs and placed on it all of her possessions and silently listed them. *A box of matches, spare rawhide shoestrings for my brogans, knife and stone, six potatoes and four carrots from the root cellar, and one shriveled up apple.* "Dear God," Aleena prayed softly, "I thank You for giving me the wisdom to bring these meager supplies with me. I'm sure it's a lot more than Joshua had with him when he first ventured into the wilderness to serve Moses." She shivered a little and looked at the matches. *Better forget about a fire until I get away from this area.* She glanced up at the clear sky. *Not gonna be too cold tonight anyway, and the farther north I go the colder it'll be, so I'd better save 'em.*

Aleena pulled the pile of brush she had cut and gathered over her, and while slowly eating half of a carrot, she thought, *it'll get warm quick if I head south, but Jesse said to find a Flathead camp if I'm ever in trouble, and there won't be any Flatheads south of here.* Before Aleena went to sleep, she thought, *and Lord, I'm sure in trouble, so help me if You think I'm worth it.*

She was still sleeping soundly when the sun peeked over the mountain tops to begin its journey across the eastern sky again. She finally opened both eyes and through slits viewed the area surrounding her.

Mental exhaustion had carried Aleena into a deep sleep. The door to her mind snapped shut the moment she fell asleep, but it was now open and the reality of the previous day's events were rushing through. She clamped both eyes shut and tried to flush the horror out. Moments later she shoved the brush aside and sat up to look at the terrain around her.

After wiping the sleep from her eyes, Aleena leaned forward and stretched the stiffness from her back then slowly stood. Scanning the area she was momentarily frightened by the silence of the vast area surrounding her. Aleena stood beside the tree she had slept beneath and leaned wearily against it as her head rotated from right to left and then back again. *How can such a vast area be so silent?* She moved to the other side of the tree and then scanned back and forth again. *Oh my, I could be the last living thing on earth for all the movement I can see out there.*

After he carefully checked the ground to be certain nothing

had fallen from her coat pockets during the night, she began walking north. She soon noticed that birds and small animals were out of their night burrows and moving about. "Well," she said with a smile, "guess I'm not alone after all."

The second day ended like the first with Aleena sitting against a large tree after and gathering a pile of brush as a cover while sleeping. She had sliced one of the six potatoes in half and ate the smaller chunk for her lunch. As she chewed the remaining bits she realized that it added to her thirst. Stretched out beneath the brush, her last thoughts prior to dropping off into the blessed abyss of sleep were, *I must find water tomorrow.*

Two hours of walking the following morning brought Aleena to a small creek running down from the western mountains and disappearing into a wooded area to her east. After drinking her fill she thought, *why didn't I think to look for a container to carry water?* A glance back in the direction of the nightmare she had survived, Aleena realized that it was a miracle she had survived it at all.

She followed the stream and crossed where the water barely covered the stones and continued for an hour, hoping to find a container of some kind to fill with water. Stopping in the shade of a tree she glanced up at the sun then said aloud, "I must keep moving north toward Flathead country." Realizing what she just said, Aleena's thoughts clouded; *if I'm going to survive I must learn how to trap small animals and birds. What will I do if I'm confronted by a grizzly bear? There must be wolves in this part of the country, too.* Looking behind her she recalled the bear they had all seen while still with the Donner party. *I don't know what kind of bear that was but it was big enough to eat a scrawny old woman like me.*

She took a deep breath and continued walking. *Gotta stop being frightened and concentrate on surviving. Maybe I should cut back toward that creek so I'll at least have water.* She took another bite of the potato she'd halved. *Nope,* Aleena thought, *that's right where bears and wolves would be if there are some around here. Keep moving north girl, and think about a future with Jesse.* She closed her eyes and trudged along, but after a while stopped and looked ahead. Closing her eyes tightly her thoughts turned to her brothers. *Jesse you and me gotta go visit Patrick, Ian, Broderick, and Simon, no matter where they are.*

An involuntary sigh flowed from her lips, but she tightened

her jaw and trudged steadily on. Two hours before sundown she thought certain she was watching a mirage. A single wagon pulled by a horse was moving west at a very slow pace. She continues walking, certain that the mirage would soon disappear, but after several steps it was still there. Aleena began walking faster and finally broke into a run while waving her long skinny arms.

Nearing the wagon, she saw that it was following an old wagon trail. An aged man with a long white beard sat on a seat in front of a narrow door leading into the wooden wagon. It was similar to the wagon that a tinker came to her parent's house in and sharpened knives, axes, or anything else that had an edge in need of work. He also sold ready-made knives or took orders for a specific knife, and would have it on his return trip, which might be several months later. As she stood in the middle of the road waving and yelling for him to please stop; she wondered, *maybe he's the same tinker, just older, like me.*

Aleena breathed a sigh of relief when she saw him pulling back on the reins. She stepped back so the horse wouldn't be so apt to spook and begin running. As the side of the old wooden wagon stopped beside her she read the faded sign. *Reverend Isaiah Shepherd.* She tilted her head momentarily toward Heaven and whispered, *Thanks, God for sending me some help.* Aleena heard the old man say something, so she stepped toward the front. "Excuse me sir, I didn't hear what you said."

"What in the world are you doing out here in the middle of this wilderness, lady?"

She forced a weak smile to spread across her plain face and said, "It's a long story but if I can ride with you I'll tell you what happened."

His cloudy grey eyes narrowed as he looked down at Aleena. After what seemed a very long time to her, the old man nodded toward the other side, "Go around n' climb up here."

He slapped the reins against the horse's rump once she was seated and the wagon began slowly moving ahead. An hour later, Aleena had told him the entire story, from going east to attend a teacher's college, to her career teaching young men and women who also wanted to become teachers. She passed over her sad love affair that ended with the suicide of her fiancé and continued with the trip home as a paying member of the Donner Wagon Train. He only grunted when she told about the killers that burned her cabin after shooting the man and woman she had traveled west with. When she explained about her neighbors farther along the Green River he spoke for the first time after she began her sad story.

He turned to her and stared hard before speaking. "What for you people stopped along the way? Should orta stayed with them wagon trains. Thar's injuns n' killers along all the routes y'might take so y'gotta stay together." When Aleena looked into his eyes she felt a shiver travel up her spine. "Them folks is over there in Californy now all settled in an startin a new life, n' here you are all alone ouchere in the middle o' nowere."

They moved on slowly, and for an hour neither said a word. Finally Aleena turned toward the old preacher. "Are you going over the mountains and on to San Francisco?"

"Don't know izactly where ahm a'headin," he grumbled, "the Lord ain't been treatin me very good, lately."

Another hour passed by in silence, and she felt as though her dry mouth had been stuffed full of cotton. "Could I go inside and get myself a drink of water, Reverend Shepherd?"

His head swiveled quickly and he stared at her for a moment, "Whaju call me?"

"Reverend Shepherd," Aleena said softly.

His eyes peered at her through very thin slits as he said softly, almost to himself, "Oh, Yeah! Reverend Shepherd." But Aleena heard it clearly. He continued staring at her for a long moment, and then nodded at the narrow door behind him, "Yeah, there's water in there. Gitcherself a drink and then rest up a bit, cause it's a purdy good ride afore nightfall an som'n t'eat."

Aleena stood and made her way toward the door that was behind the Reverend. There was little room between the wall and the bench that she had been sitting beside him on, so she was careful not to rub against him. Turning the knob on the door it opened and she said quietly, "Thank you, Reverend Shepherd, I'll lie down and rest a while because these past few days have left me pretty exhausted."

The man was silent a moment thinking, *ain't one damned thing purdy abouchew gal,* but then replied curtly, "Suit yerself."

Aleena stood looking down at him for several seconds before entering the wagon. Once inside she closed the door and looked to see if there was an inside latch. Finding none, she shook her head very briskly as if to flush images from her mind, but then thought *something's odd about the Reverend. Most men of God that I've met have been kind and thoughtful, and if not, then at least courteous and polite, especially to women.* She stood holding the knob a moment. *Maybe I'm just being too critical. After all, these last few days have been stressful to say the very least.* She looked around the small room, and for the first time noticed that it also had a rear door. Three steps and she had the knob in her hand. *If it's not locked then at least I'm not trapped inside here.* She turned the knob and the door opened. Quietly closing it she turned and surveyed the entire room, mentally checking off what she saw. *A bunk with drawers above and below, a small closet on one end and book shelves from floor to ceiling on the other end.* She turned toward the opposite wall. *A small counter to put together something to eat, I reckon, and more storage drawers below. A seat built in at the end with a holder for a kerosene lamp. That must be where he sits and reads the bible.*

Standing beside the door at the rear, she noticed a square area on the wall beside the door she'd entered through. It was a little lighter in color than the wall. *Must have been a poster hanging there recently.* Her brow furrowed as she advanced to see the area better. *Mighta been one of those new photographs that have been popping up all around Boston.* She reached up and ran her fingers across the area. Looking at the tips she saw nothing, so she then ran them across the wall beside the faded square area. *Dust and grime,* she thought, *whatever was hanging here has recently been taken down.*

Aleena sat on the bunk looking at the wall. She let her eyes roam all around the small room, and then leaned out and looked down between her long skinny legs. Reaching down she gripped the two handles on the front of a drawer and spread her legs enough to let the drawer slide forward. Glancing up at the door behind the Reverend, she quickly rifled through the contents. Finding nothing that might have been on the wall recently she closed it and scooted over so she could open one of the other two.

There, upside down but lying on the top was one of the new collodian process photographs. She turned it over and saw a tall thin man standing behind a plain but attractive woman. She was seated on a small chair almost exactly the same that Aleena had sat upon when she had her picture taken in a photo studio in downtown Boston. That was just shortly before her departure on the doomed Donner Wagon Train for her dreamed-of return to California and her brother Jesse. *The man in this picture is obviously a preacher because of the collar he's wearing.* The furrows returned to Aleena's brow as she stared at the picture.

At the deep end of the drawer she noticed a sheath of papers protruding up above the rest of the contents. Pulling one up and out, she gasped slightly when she saw the same man's face. The woman wasn't in the picture and he now had a small wooden cross hanging around his neck. She silently read the words that had been written below his picture in a beautiful scroll. *My dear husband, Reverend Shepherd, carrying the word of our savior, Jesus Christ, to the pioneering pilgrims of this glorious new country. Your donations will help us spread the Holy Gospel to our brothers and sisters.* Aleena read two words to herself again...*help us...and* again...*help us.*

Aleena sat staring at the picture a moment and then she returned the poster with the others and closed the drawer. She placed her bony elbows on still-swollen knees and held her head in her hands. *Oh my God,* she thought, *that man driving this wagon must have killed the Reverend Shepherd, and...*she paused a second then closed her eyes, remembering the words his wife wrote on the poster...*donations will help us spread the Holy Gospel...*tears ran freely from her eyes as she thought, *he must have killed them both. Oh sweet Jesus, what am I to do?*

She wiped her eyes and looked into a small mirror on the wall above the food preparation shelf. Holding a small cloth lying there she poured on it a few drops of water from a hide bladder hanging above the shelf and wiped the tear streaks from her face. When she finished, Aleena stared at herself in the mirror. *I'm not a pretty woman but when that man stops this wagon I know what he's gonna want from me. I've gotta find a weapon to hold him off. Oh Lord,* she thought, *please forgive me but I know he's gonna kill me when he gets what he wants, so if he comes after me I'm gonna try to kill him.*

Still looking at herself in the mirror she noticed the amulet that her brother, Jesse, had sent her. It took the trapper almost six months to return home to Boston, but as soon as he arrived he went to the teacher's college where Aleena was a professor. She recalled being momentarily speechless when he handed it to her. Aleena remembered that day as though it was yesterday. *He saved my life, ma'am. A bull moose attacked and busted me all up, so your brother rigged a travois and dragged me all the way to a Flathead Indian camp. Took us three days but them Flatheads cleaned all the infection outa the wounds then put Indian medicine on 'em and me n' your brother stayed there till I could get around okay. He told me his name was Jesse, but I speak their language well, and them Indians called him White Buffalo. They treated him like he was special.* She recalled the man pointing at the amulet and saying, *see that white buffalo that someone carved on the amulet? He asked me to tell you that when you get with a wagon train to come home, keep that around your neck. If you ever need some help, try to find a Flathead camp and they'll do whatever needs doing to see to it that you get home.*

Aleena now stood looking at the amulet that she put around her neck later that same day by braiding good rawhide through holes in it then joining the braid and making it too small to get off. *And I remember the letter Jesse sent with another man,* she thought. *Jesse told me about Prairie Rose getting killed, and his Indian friends saying he was White Buffalo, but he said that's just the way Indians are.* She ran her long spidery fingers across the buffalo and wondered, *what could they have used to make it stay so white?*

She shoved the amulet back inside the top of her shirt and began looking for a weapon. *There's gotta be some kind of knife here somewhere.* She opened each drawer as quietly as possible, and after finding nothing that might serve her as a weapon, she went to the closet, but still nothing.

Aleena sat on the bunk again and looked through the third drawer. Lying along the side of the drawer and covered with hand made doilies was a knife in a leather sheath. Glancing at the door that she knew he would eventually come through, she quietly pulled the sheath out. Pulling out the blade she saw that it was short. Testing it on her arm's hairs as she'd seen her brothers do many times, she realized that it was razor sharp. *The real Reverend Shepherd musta used this to skin animals to cook.*

Aleena cut off a piece of the rawhide lace on one of her boots. She tied it to the belt loop on the sheath, and then attached it to the braided rawhide that held the amulet around her neck. She worked the sheathed knife around back so it hung unseen down inside the rear of her shirt between her shoulder blades.

Just after she had checked to be sure she could easily reach the knife, Aleena felt both legs tense to maintain her balance inside the wobbly wagon. "Oh my God," she said softly aloud, almost to herself, "he's slowing down." Looking around, Aleena thought; *settle down, girl, getting all panicky will not help you a bit.* She grabbed a clean rag lying on the small counter and wiped her face. After taking a deep breath, she moved away from the small narrow door behind the driver's seat and waited for the old man to open it.

Patrick

Aldo was so efficient at the tasks given to him that it quickly became apparent to Patrick that he was getting much more work done than ever before. Efforts to secure a job elsewhere for Aldo were ceased. Patrick informed him that he would be extremely pleased if he would accept a position with him as, he stopped talking and mused momentarily as he gazed at the wall behind Aldo, "As what, though?" he asked, not expecting an answer. "Hmmmmm," he mused again briefly, "how about this; as my chauffeur, valet, secretary, bodyguard, all around number one man, and traveling companion?" Patrick smiled and held out his hand saying, "And," he paused, "I believe, based on what I've seen these past few months that it would be appropriate to add, confidant and friend."

Aldo took Patrick's hand and said, "You humble me sir, with such praise, and I will do my very best to justify it."

Patrick walked to a walnut replica half-barrel attached to the wall of the room they were in. Placing a finger of each hand under the lower edge he pulled the two sides open to reveal a selection of several bottles of fine imported Irish and Scottish whiskey. Removing a short round bottle and two small, cut crystal glasses, which he placed on the round oak table beneath the chandelier, he turned to Aldo. "Shall we toast my luck at securing the assistance of an honest and diligently intrepid man, and your luck at following an unclear path to my door that I may assist you in your search for a toehold in this ever-changing, but most wonderful and exciting new country."

Before he began pouring the cognac, Aldo said, "I will be very happy to toast my great good fortune in finding someone such as you to offer my services to, but sir, I do not partake of spirits, so please just a dash of water will do me fine."

His good natured smile warmed Patrick. He replaced the cognac bottle and brought the water bottle to the two glasses. "I forgot, in that case, amigo, we will toast this allegiance with the finest of beverages, and given freely to us by God himself." He poured water into each glasss and handed one to Aldo. "Here's to a long and very fruitful relationship, my friend."

~

Now, many years later, Patrick glanced at the tall grandfather's clock standing beside the hallway leading to the library. Seeing both hands standing straight up he moved swiftly toward the library. Upon opening the huge hardwood door, he saw Aldo standing in the center of the room looking up at one of the many shelves full of books. Aldo turned toward him and smiled. "In my old age I plan to read all of these wonderful books, Patrick."

"My friend," Patrick said, "they will always be here awaiting the touch of your hands." He stopped in the middle of the room and turned slowly around until he was again facing Aldo. "I am often saddened when I see how many volumes have never been opened since I placed them on these shelves."

"You're had a very busy career, Patrick."

"Yes Aldo, but there really is no valid excuse not to enjoy the many books that these brilliant authors have left for us." He looked up at the row of books that Aldo had been staring at when he entered. In a barely audible voice he added, "Perhaps some distant day." He motioned with his hand, "Please have a seat Aldo, and I will explain."

Even before Aldo was seated, Patrick began. "During my last year at Harvard I attended a lecture by James Buchanan, Jr. At that time he was a lawyer by trade, but also the Chairman of the House Committee on the Judiciary. He is a fellow Democrat that made his first bid for the presidency in 1844, and again in 1848, then finally in 1852. Aldo," he looked at his friend, "I was very impressed with his sincere dedication to this new country when I first met Mister Buchanan, and am even more so now. Like me, and unfortunately it seems, like you too, he is a lifelong bachelor, so he is free to devote a large portion of his life to serving his country." At this point, Patrick's courtroom habits took over and he stood to begin pacing the floor as though a jury sat where his friend leaned on the armrest and silently listened.

After a sip of water, Patrick McKannah continued. "We have become close friends over the years, and he has even visited me here in San Francisco twice." He paused a moment and looked directly at Aldo. "James Buchanan has asked me to move temporarily to The Capitol and take charge of his last campaign to become President of the United States."

Without a moments hesitation, Aldo replied, "That is quite an honor, Patrick."

Patrick looked at him a moment then turned to watch the birds flying into and out of the huge gazebo feeder he had his gardener build in the center of his walled-in backyard. Aldo remained silent but noticed his friend's contemplative mood as his lips remained pursed, his head nodding slightly.

Directly, he turned toward Aldo and spoke quietly, almost reverently. "I have spent most of my fifty-three years here in California, and have devoted a significant amount of time and energy making it into a better place for all kinds of people to live, including the tribes of Native Americans that were here when we arrived." He remained standing a moment then sat down beside Aldo. "There is still so much that I want to do for California." He turned to his friend and exhaled a long sigh, "I feel as though I'm abandoning her to go to the aid of a friend." He looked at Aldo, "Does that make sense?"

After a long silent moment, Aldo said, "No it doesn't but I understand. Every time I see an attractive young woman and think it would be nice to have someone like her waiting at home for me, I feel guilty for weeks. It doesn't make sense, because I was a good and faithful husband to Maria, but I still miss her so bad that I feel guilty thinking about another woman." He looked at Patrick and smiled, "Does that make sense?" He lowered his head slightly and rolled his eyes up, "No, of course it doesn't, but I understand." Aldo grinned, "Didn't I just say that?"

~

Kenneth and Seamus Kavanaugh had been with Patrick for almost twenty years. Both men were born in Ireland and had lived near the waterfront a stone's throw from the apartment building where Patrick's grandparents had died in a fire that consumed the building. Arriving in America on the California coast with their parents, both men were still boys, but worked hard to help their parents begin a new life.

Their new life began with the same occupation—fishing. The boat their father bought was larger and better than the one they made their living with in Ireland, so they did well all working as one family unit.

When the boys were 19 and 20 their father bought a very large fish market on the San Francisco waterfront. Seamus Kavanaugh's 24th birthday turned sour when he and his older brother Kenneth returned to the dock behind the market. The dock was all that remained. The huge wooden building had burned to the ground during the day while their parents and three Chinese workers were up in the attic selecting cardboard boxes for the day's business. They all lost their lives that day.

Kenneth and Seamus Kavanaugh continued fishing for their living, but sold their catch to another fish house. One afternoon a year later, Patrick McKannah was sitting with the owner of the Blue Pacific Mermaid, a San Francisco waterfront bar and restaurant. An argument between the Kavanaugh brothers and six Italian fishermen who had been drinking at the bar erupted.

Patrick and the owner stopped talking, to watch and see if it was going to be settled peaceably. The bar owner, Liam Bellamy, whispered to Patrick, "Those six Italians are always looking for a way to impress the girls in here with their muscles and fighting skills."

A moment later the largest of the six Italians threw a punch at Seamus while he was arguing with another of the six. He was not facing the man that threw the punch so it caught him behind the ear. When he staggered slightly forward, the man that he had just been arguing with took advantage of the moment and fired a right fist into Seamus' face—and the fight was on.

Almost simultaneously Kenneth hit the big one who punched Seamus from behind, in the gut, and Seamus hit the man he'd been arguing with in the stomach too. Both men doubled over as air rushed out and then saw stars when the Kavanaugh brothers brought huge Irish fists in contact with two Italian jaws. The two Italians were knocked out while still upright, and before they hit the floor, two more Italians were semi-conscious and going to the floor to join their friends. Before the remaining two Italians had time to get their feet set and square off with the two *Micks* as they had refered to them a moment earlier, they absorbed blows to the solarplexes, jaws and eyes. They lay groaning on the floor among their friends as Seamus and Kenneth stood and looked down at the pile of once, tough young Italians.

The two brothers moved to the bar and emptied their bottles of Guiness Stout. When Kenneth lifted his empty bottle toward the bartender, Patrick McKannah stepped forward and said, "I'd like to buy you two Irish gentlemen a drink and talk to you a moment if you have time."

They accepted his offer and followed him to the table where the owner still sat watching. After they were all seated, he said, "I'd like to thank you fellas for not breaking anything." He let his eyes scan the six men who were struggling to get back on their feet, and then added, "Except half a dozen egos and maybe a coupla jaws." He turned to Patrick, "The rest o' these drinks're on the house."

The owner finished his glass of scotch and stood. "I gotta get back in the kitchen t'keep an eye on things." He nodded at the two men, "Thanks very much for all that entertainment, lads; bloody good show it was, by Jesus." He turned to Patrick, "I'll tell Orin that these drinks're on me, and we'll talk further about the legal contract we were discussing."

Patrick turned to the two men, "I'm a lawyer here in town, and I've been looking for two men who can operate my private coach and be my bodyguards too." He paused a moment before continuing. "I'll pay you good, because there'll be times we will go on long trips to a trial and maybe stay a week or two, so your families will have to understand and also agree."

Both men turned and looked at each other and smiled, and then Kenneth spoke. "We've been fishing since we were kids and we're fed up with it. If you'd like to give us a try we won't hafta ask anyone, because we're not married and our folks are dead."

One month later they sold the boat and the property the fish house had once sat on. That was almost twenty years before they were told to rig the coach for a three thousand mile trip to the east coast. Now, with six stout horses in harness and the coach all checked out, they were anxious to get the rest of Patrick's gear loaded and begin the trip.

Simon

When word reached the Texas Rangers, they put Bols and his gang's pictures on walls everywhere. Simon worked with the artist that created the poster, as they were carefully described by the bank president and other witnesses. When he looked at the final sketch before creating the poster, Simon said, "Good work, Roggespierre, that's Bols." The bank employees confirmed that all three sketches looked just like the gang. They were at the top of the list of Most Wanted. Word had reached Simon that Bols shot a little girl because she was screaming as he left the bank, so after the sketch was completed; he wired his boss that he was going after Bols and whoever was with him.

I'm the one that's responsible for bringin him down outa those mountains, he thought, *so I'll try to be the one who brings him in to face a judge n' jury—or over his saddle to face his maker.*

A Tonto Apache reservation tracker, known among local Indians as Kawevikopaya Yavapai, led Simon to Jackal Flat, the town where the trackers' Indian informers had spotted Bols and Ben two days earlier. The Apache took his pay and departed. Simon knew that he could catch both men and their gang now.

With his horse settled inside the corral and unsaddled, Simon walked noiselessly toward the door. Always cautious, a pistol was in his hand as he eased it open and was about to step in. That's when the shotgun exploded. The blast knocked Simon backwards, landing hard on his back against the packed dirt.

The shotgun pellets struck Simon in the left shoulder, but it wasn't a direct hit, because his survival sixth sense screamed a split second prior to the blast. He was already lunging to the right, which was the closest wall to provide him with protection.

Simon had his right, butt-forward pistol still gripped firmly in his left hand, but he knew it was useless.

When Simon hit the dirt he rolled a little to the right and was pulling his left pistol out of the holster with his right hand, when the young man inside began screaming.

"I got him. I shot that damned ranger, pa." When he pulled the door open and looked toward the man that he was certain he'd just killed, his eyes didn't have time to focus on the large black hole.

Simon carefully aimed and from the large black hole in the end of his pistol roared the last sound that the young shooter would ever hear.

Simon knew that whoever the boy was yelling at, he was nearby, so he scrambled to his feet. On the way inside he shoved his right-hand pistol back into the left holster then reached down and grabbed the shotgun from the dead boy's hand.

As he searched the walls in the moonlight coming through the window, Simon could hear the man calling. He opened the double-barrel ten gauge shotgun to be certain there was another shell, and breathed easier when he saw it.

"Hey Percy, you all right, boy?"

Simon heard the man repeat it twice before yelling, "We're a'comin boy, you hold on, we're a'comin."

We're comin? Hmmm, wonder how many are out there? Simon finally spotted what he'd hoped was there. Lined up nicely on the windowsill like ducks, were six shotgun shells. He held the weapon between his knees and pulled out the spent shell, and then shoved another one into the barrel. He leaned it against the wall and began an inspection of his wound. After picking at the lump on his neck he finally retrieved one of the pellets. *Small birdshot* he thought as he rolled the lead ball around between his fingertips.

"Hey Percy, where y'at, boy?" The whispering voice was now close. When the other man spoke, Simon knew who had set the ambush.

"Y,y,y,ya,a,a, b,b,b,b,b,better b,b,be k,k,k,keerful p,p,p,pa, c,c,c,c,c,cause, t,t,that ranger is a sn,sn,sn,sneaky d,d,d,devil."

"Shut up Lemuel," his father yelled.

Bols must be tied in with old man Schultz and his two boys. He thought a moment as he listened for movement, *only one boy now and that stupid Lem can't get out of his own way.*

Simon continued his inspection. *Ain't anything busted badly or I couldn't move the arm like this.* He felt the ragged area where the pellets hit. *Sure glad I had this old saddle blanket vest made and that stupid kid bought birdshot instead of double-ought buckshot.* He felt inside and found very little blood. *I think my arm n' shoulder both were more stunned by the blast than received any real damage.* He began opening and closing his left fist, then a while later started moving his arm up and down.

A short time later he was still exercising his arm when he heard the sound of horses departing. *Just like ole Schultz to run when things get hot or don't go his way. I'll just stay put till dawn anyway. He might be a bit cagier that I give him credit, and hard tellin where that damn Bols might be.*

A bell rang inside his head and jolted Simon awake. His left pistol was in his right hand as he struggled to locate where the noise in his subconscious mind came from. His head slowly followed his eyes when he heard the voice.

Softly, almost indistinguishable, the voice drifted across the room again. "Macanner, it is I, Naiche." The voice could belong to only one man that Simon knew, because the Tonto Apache scout was the only person who ever called him that.

Simon moved silently to the rear where the soft voice said, "Here, near the corner."

Simon finally saw a shaft of moonlight cut through the hardwood boards and he eased his way toward it. "What're you doin back here, Naiche?"

"I was with a woman I know, and later when I headed north, I saw two men leave this horse-house soon after the gunshots. I watched and they met two other men, and have now returned. A dark evil cloud crossed the moon, so I came back to warn you."

"Thanks Naiche, I owe y'one."

"They might be close enough to see me if I come in, so I will stay outside and watch."

"Yeah, I think they're gonna slip into position and try to flush me outa here before daybreak." Simon moved to a new area in case Bols or one of the other two had heard them talking. He leaned back against the wall and rested the shotgun across his legs. He patted his jacket pocket to be certain the shotgun shells were still there, then turned and looked hard at the rear door that led to the corral. He recalled the liveryman saying when he stopped here a year earlier that it was nailed shut, "To keep kids and bums," the man said, "from sneaking in while I'm busy with a customer."

Next he looked up at the loft. He could see the sliver of moon through the open hay door. *Ain't a far drop to the ground, but if I broke m'leg they'd sure kill me before I could hobble away.* His eyes were adjusted to the darkness, so he scanned the interior of the tack area. *A good strong rope or lariat might get me down to the ground.* He saw something that caught his eye, and eased up to the toes of his boots. He put his hand on it and smiled, *must be a spare rope for the pulley to hoist the hay up.* Easing the rope off the hook, Simon returned to the wall, but in a different spot.

Once he'd pulled the rope through his hands to be certain it wasn't old and rotten and forgotten about years earlier, he stood again. As quietly as possible he climbed the stairs to the hayloft, and after removing the coiled rope from around his neck and left shoulder, Simon laid it down. He picked up a bale of hay and moved it a few feet so it was below one of the timbers, which were nailed between the rafters about half way down from the peak of the roof and the top of the wall, to keep the rafters from sagging in. It was the last one before the opening where the hay was hoisted in, and he could move around without being seen by someone outside watching.

After tossing the end of the rope over the timber, he climbed down and pulled about half of the rope across it. First he tied a knot in the end and pulled it tight, and then tied one every three feet until there were five knots. He could barely make out the timber in the dark loft, so he knew he was not visible to Bols, Black Ben, old man Schultz, or any other members of Bols' gang that were still with him. He thought, *Lem's too stupid to look up, but I'll keep an eye out for him anyway if I get outa here.* Simon gathered both pieces of the rope and wrapped them around his right hand. *Better be sure that timber's not rotten before I step out of that hayloft door.* He carefully eased all of his weight on the rope for a moment after his boots left the floor. *Good, that timber's cured and probably stronger'n the day it was put up.*

After lowering the rope out of the opening until the knot in the end was six feet from the ground, Simon stood on the bale of hay again and wrapped the other end around the timber several times before tying it off. Just as he was stepping down from the bale, he was startled momentarily when the lights went out. He froze in the pitch-black loft for a split second, and then grinned as the cloud passed and allowed moonlight in again. *Lord, I'm sure glad to see that you're on my team tonight; gonna need all the help I can get. Naiche, I hope you're still out there watching.*

Simon pulled out his Bowie knife and cut off several feet of rope, and returned to the tack room. He sat down and leaned against the wall so he could lay the old double-barrel shotgun across his legs. Once the rope was attached to the barrel and stock, he stood and slung the weapon over his shoulder and headed back up the stairs. With his back against the wall next to the open hayloft door, Simon scanned as much of the sky as he dared; *sure don't wanna get spotted by one o' those devils before I get outa here n' m'feet're on the ground.* When he saw how many clouds were passing overhead he knew it would be a short wait.

He held tightly to the rope and waited. A few minutes later everything went black again and Simon eased his large body out of the opening. Seconds later his feet were on the ground and he was moving swiftly but silently toward the corral. He was slowly moving along the corral planks to get away from the building, when a small light next to the wall caught his attention. It soon became obvious that he got out of the building just in time. *Figured those rotten bastards were gonna torch the place.* He counted two people working on the fire, but then he thought, *hard to see, so those other two might be right there in the shadows, but I can't let 'em burn that old fella's building.*

Simon had worked his left arm regularly and now realized that it hardly hurt. *Ain't anything busted in there. Thank You, Lord.* He removed the shotgun from his shoulder, and after muffling the noise with his bandana, cocked both barrels. Rather than follow the fence planks around to the building, Simon went straight across the corral toward the two men who were still trying to get a fire going. He heard old man Schultz fussing.

"Lem I tole ya t'git only dry wood, dammit. You ignoramus, this here green stuff ain't never gonna ketch fire."

Still not certain where Bols and Ben were, Simon decided not to risk losing anyone involved in shooting that little girl. A split finger-pulling second before the double blasts, he said, "Maybe this'll help." With the sound still ringing in his ears, he dropped the shotgun and pulled both Colt Dragoon revolvers out, and ducked down to move swiftly away from where he had fired the shotgun. When the ringing in his ears stopped he heard both of the men screaming in agony. *That's old man Schultz and his moron; wonder where Bols and Ben are?*

Daylight arrived soon and answered Simon's question. Schultz and his son were still alive, but filled with lead shot. The doctor would have a long enjoyable task removing them from two of the three members of the Schultz gang that had caused everyone in the area so much misery and grief for several years. They would both live—to die at the end of a hangman's rope.

Simon leaned down to handcuff Shultz's right wrist to his son Lemuel's right ankle and then removed all of their weapons. He very cautiously began looking for a sign to indicate which way Bols and Ben had gone.

He found Black Ben first—in a heap atop a pool of dried blood. His throat had been cut from ear to ear.

A young Mexican man came running, "Señor, there is a dead man by that tree." Simon followed his pointing finger.

Simon said softly, "Espera," and the young man waited while he went to see if the body was Bols. He didn't have to roll Bols over to see what happened, because the wound was exactly the same as the one on Ben's neck—ear to ear. He looked out across the terrain in the direction where Naiche lived with his wife and several children, when not working as a scout for the Rangers. *Can't blame ya for not sticking around, Naiche. Lotta folks think it ain't right for a colored man or an Indian to kill a white man; regardless what they've done. Thanks, amigo, I owe you, cause y'saved m'life again.*

Broderick

Broderick learned that his brother Patrick, after returning from Carson City, upon completion of Ian's trial was going east to New York City to take charge of James Buchanan's campaign to become the 15th President of the United States of America.

Broderick learned too from reliable resources that Patrick was unknowingly stepping head-on straight into a hornet's nest. Broderick's sources informed him that there was going to be an assassination attempt on Buchanan and his entire entourage.

After receiving this information he sent a telegram hoping to delay Patrick just long enough for him to travel north to San Francisco and warn his brother by stressing that his source of information has always been reliable.

Patrick and Aldo had already left San Francisco in his private coach. Patrick's friend at the telegraph office informed Broderick that Patrick had advanced his junior partner to full partner and sold him half of his very successful law firm. He would be in charge until Patrick returned.

Having no idea which route Patrick would take, Broderick advanced his associate of fifteen years to office manager, and instructed him to take charge of his San Diego law firm and guide the eight young lawyers until he returned. "Do a good job," Broderick said with a wink, "and when I return we'll sit down over a good bottle of brandy and see if we can come to a mutually agreeable contract to make you half owner."

The lawyer was eleven years older than Broderick. He started his legal career with two well-used books, about ten years prior to Broderick's entry into the Harvard School of Law. David Engels II was Jewish and arrived in San Diego with his Jewish mother and English father. His father, David, was a solicitor that received his law degree from Oxford, but after embracing his wife's religion he was ostracized so thoroughly by his peers and British business associates that he booked passage to the burgeoning new country across the Atlantic Ocean that he'd been hearing so much about.

Like his father, David II took no guff from anyone and never appeared to be in a hurry about anything—both traits that were admired by Broderick.

After so many years working together in the same building that went from a wooden one-room law office to a three-story law firm, Broderick understood David. He especially liked the way that he never got upset or in a hurry, so he just smiled when David looked up from the dossier on his desk. "Half owner, eh?" he reached up and removed his thick glasses and shoved one of the wire half-circles against his chin and scratched with it. "You do understand why I've been perfectly content working for you rather than being your partner, Brod?"

Broderick walked to one of the wooden chairs in David's office and sat down. "Well," he said as his eyes scanned the ceiling while he also scratched his neck, "I reckon," his eyes were back on David now and a sly smile was about to contort his handsome, but angular face, "it's because I do all the worrying about all the cases we handle."

"Correct, and now you're going to allow me to hoist half of that load to my bent and aching old back, which, as you well know is more than ten years older than yours." Before Broderick could answer, David lowered the eye glasses and continued, "And for this additional load I will have my business cards changed and my name painted on the sign on the front of the building." He smiled at Broderick, who was enjoying his friend's spiel, but was holding a smile inside. "Ah yes," he continued, "I can see it all quite clearly now, 'David Engels of Engels and McKannah—lawyers for hire'." He tugged the wires behind his big ears and then folded his arms across his enormous belly and let himself float back in his modern new springloaded chair that was covered in kangaroo hide shipped in from Australia.

Broderick contained his smile and replied with a look of complete confusion, emphasized by his rusty red eyebrows. "I was thinking 'McKannah and Engels—lawyers extraordinaire'." His smile could no longer stay hidden as he added, "Perhaps adding, 'serving the citizens of San Diego'." Before David could speak, he added, "Well, counselor, whadaya think?"

With his lips pursed, he looked over his glasses, "I think you and I should walk around the corner to Ryan's Pub and have a drink. While there you can tell me the specifics of what must be handled during your absence, and I will make notes. When you return we will continue as we have these many years together.

That same evening he instructed his two drivers to add two horses and then hitch all six to the coach in the morning and be ready to leave at dawn. The two men had served him loyaly as bodyguards and coachmen. They were Irishmen and brothers and had been with Broderick for many years. Both men were also accustomed to being told that they would be on the road for a period of time, so they told their wives to spread the word that their Irish friends should keep an eye on Broderick's office building and his home too until they returned.

That night after all harnessing had been checked and the coach was loaded, the two men selected two stout coach horses from the group that Broderick had begun breeding soon after his new ranch was completed. They were led to stalls directly across from the four horses that were currently being used to pull the coach. Broderick and his crew had learned that adding a couple of horses to a team adapted quicker and worked better together if they spent some time in each others presence, even if they had been raised together. Once the horses became familier with the scent of new team-mates they settled down and accepted them as part of the team.

At bedtime that night Liam Beckett hugged both of his daughters before tucking them in. He hugged his youngest child, 12 year old Brien, and then held him close briefly before firmly gripping the youth's hand. Brien had heard the same spiel several times in the past couple of years but he never tired of listening to it—his father was his idol.

The stout boy, already almost six feet tall, strained against his emotions and maintained a somber face as his father spoke. "I'm leaving with Mister McKannah in the morning, lad, and until I return you'll be second in command," Liam grinned, "just as I am when yer ma's around. Treat her n' yer older sisters as though they're the most prescious things on this earth, just as I do." He hugged the boy again before sending him upstairs to his room.

Liam returned to the living room and sat in the chair beside the one that his wife, Maureen, sat in as she continued kniting a hat for Liam. "I'm gonna miss you all som'n terrible, Maury."

When she turned toward him, her long red hair caught the glow cast by the fireplace and made it look even redder and her pretty face more beautiful. "We'll be thinking about you every day until you return, Liam."

When she smiled before returning to her knitting, Liam had to take a long deep breath and he closed his eyes while doing it. *I don't know why You blessed me with this lovely woman, Lord, but thanks very much.*

In the house sitting on the second half of the ten acres that Broderick gave them, Aidan Beckett had his fifteen year old twin daughters sitting on the couch with him, one on each side with a huge muscular arm holding them tightly. After finishing their favorite story about the leprechauns in the old country, both girls kissed his cheek and went upstairs.

He went into the kitchen where his wife, Allison, was just finishing the dishes. Aidan put his arms around her and held her tight with his head buried in her long, coal black hair. "This'll be the longest trip we've made, darlin, and I'm gonna miss me three ladies."

She turned around and put her arms around his waist, which was just below her breasts, and held him tight. "Both girls gone to bed, are they?"

"Yeah," he answered, "tole 'em a story n' off they went."

"My turn," she said, looking up into his eyes, "an' laddy it's not a story I'm wanting."

Aidan scooped her up as though she was light as a feather and climbed the stairs toward their bedroom. *I'm a very lucky man,* he thought as he neared the top step.

~

After leaving his office Broderick walked the few blocks to the telegraph office and sent three telegrams: one each to Salt Lake City, Utah; Julesburg, Colorado; Independence, Missouri. Each was the same.

TO: Patrick McKannah.
FROM: Broderick McKannah.

Danger awaits you ... STOP ... Wait for me ... STOP ... I am enroute to Salt Lake City, then

Julesburg Colorado, then Independence Missouri
... STOP ... Sit tight and trust me ... I'll find you.

Five miles southwest of Salt Lake City a young rider approached Broderick's coach. When close enough to be heard he yelled, "I was sent by Patrick McKannah. Are you his brother?"

Broderick shoved the pistol back into the holster, but one of the drivers kept the shotgun pointed in the general direction of the rider.

Broderick leaned out the window and yelled back, "Yes, I'm his brother."

"He received your telegram and is waiting at the Main Street Hotel."

"Please tell him that you found me and I'll be there as soon as possible."

"Yessir." The young man then wheeled the horse around, and galloped away.

Broderick leaned way out to yell to the drivers. "Sure glad I got that telegram off in a hurry. Probably saved us a lotta lookin huh, Liam?"

"Yep! Reckon yer right, Brod, cause Patrick don't let no grass grow under 'is bloody feet. Always on the move, 'at bugger is, by Jesus."

Broderick leaned back on the seat smiling and thought to himself, *mighta had to chase him all the way to the capitol.*

Before dinner was brought for the four driver-bodyguards at one table and the two brothers and Aldo at the other, Broderick had explained the situation.

Patrick stood, "I'll send a telegram right now to a friend I can trust and have him explain the situation to James Buchanan."

Patrick returned to the table just as their meal was being served. "Brother," Broderick said with a smile, "your timing is as good as ever."

"Inspired by my desire not to starve." Patrick grinned, "Last good meal we had was in San Francisco, and so we've all been anxiously looking forward to this feed. Didn't you notice that Kenneth had his napkin tucked beneath his chin before he even ordered, and Seamus Kavanaugh had his knife n' fork in hand while he was ordering." Patrick chuckled, "You might think the poor lads never get a full meal, but look at the size of meals they order."

"I recall what those two brothers ate when I worked with you on that Kennelman case back in forty or forty-one, and I think they were just boys then."

"Late summer of forty-one," Patrick said, "and yes, they were both just boys in their early twenties." He looked at his two men for a moment before turning back to his brother. "How long since you've been here in Salt Lake City?"

After swallowing the food that he was chewing, Broderick answered, "I was here two years ago to defend a Mormon that was accused of deserting a wife and coming out here to join their church." He sipped his water then added, "Grown quite a lot in those two years."

"Certainly has," Patrick agreed with a sly grin, "did you get the poor bugger off the hook?"

Broderick washed down a bite before answering, "Like my older brother, I don't take cases that I think I'll lose."

After dinner the four drivers left the hotel to check on their horses. They never completely trusted livery stable employees to attend to them properly. Kenneth and Seamus brushed all six of Patrick's horses even though they had already been tended to. They called each by name and spoke soothingly to each horse as they worked. After checking each hoof for unseen stones or cracks, they pulled carrots and apples from a bag they'd asked the hotel cook for and slowly fed them to the six horses. Both men knew that these six horses wouldn't be getting the same tender care in the future, since they were going to be changing to fresh horses as often as possible on the long trip to the east coast, so they spent an extra hour with them.

Liam and Aidan did the same with Broderick's team, but knowing that these six horses would be the same ones they'd go home to San Diego with, they finished checking them and then left the livery.

While the drivers tended to the horses both McKannah men ordered cognac, and Aldo asked for a small pot of tea. While waiting for the drinks, a young man walked slowly through the dining room ringing a small bell while calling out in a soft voice as he moved past each table, "Telegram for Patrick McKannah."

Aldo was first to hear him and motioned with his raised arm. "Over here, boy," he waved, "that's Mister McKannah," he said, nodding toward Patrick.

The boy handed Patrick the telegram, and then smiled as he pocketed a coin, "Thank you, sir."

After carefully reading it, Patrick looked up, "This is from the personal aide to James Buchanan. I sent a telegram when we first arrived." He placed it on the table and remained silent for a few moments before speaking.

"A few minor but important changes have occurred that will enhance Mister Buchanan's situation. No mention of what that is, but he asked if I could possibly arrive by the end of this month. "Patrick picked up the pencil and began doodling; a habit that his brother and Aldo both knew was caused by intense concentration on a very important matter.

Aldo sipped tea as Broderick lifted his snifter. After a few moments of silence Patrick laid the pencil down in front of him and looked at Aldo and then his brother.

"Today's the ninth, which leaves us about three weeks to get there. Kenneth calculated before we left that if it ever became necessary we could average ten miles an hour by changing horses as regular as possible along the trail. I reckon we could rotate two of us up top driving while one sleeps inside the coach and get there by the end o' the month." He glanced from one to the other, then pursed his lips and ran his finger back and forth under his lower lip.

"There are enough stage coach stops along the way now," Broderick said, "to change horses, so I reckon you could do it, but by Jesus you'll all be worthless for a spell once y'git outa that bloody coach."

"I wouldn't even consider it for anyone but James, but if he thinks it would help his final bid for the presidency, then I'll do my best to be there in time."

Patrick looked up and the other two men did too when a man walked up and asked Patrick, "Do one of you gentlemen have a brother named Jesse?"

"Yes," Patrick and Broderick said simultaneously.

"My name is Filbert Hanly Prescott. I overheard the name of McKannah and I just spent a week up in Traveler's Rest where a big, loud, overstuffed Texan was shootin his mouth off about a squawman named Jesse McKannah. Said he was gonna put him in the ground and then run those Flatheads outa the area.

Patrick stood and held out his hand, "He's our brother." He pulled a chair out, "Please sit with us and tell us all you can."

While the man was still standing, Broderick leaned across the table with his hand out to introduce himself. Once they were all seated again, the man said, "I made a point of hearing all I could, because I was married to a Flathead for almost twenty years until she died a few months ago. Settled up all m'business and gonna go to New Orleans n' buy m'self a boat." He smiled when Patrick poured cognac in the snifter the waiter placed in front of the man.

After a sip he said, "Always enjoyed fishing, so I'm gonna try m'hand at doin it for a livin."

Sitting the glass down he said, "I've met few people that I admired as much as the Flatheads I lived among, and nary a one was a Texan. This blowhard said he was gonna have the biggest dadburn cattle ranch in Montana once that squawman, McKannah, was buried and all them damn savages was back in California on a reservation where they belonged."

"Were you able to get this guy's name?" Broderick asked.

"Yeah, I did," he said as he fished for a chunk of paper in his jacket pocket. "Wrote it down so I wouldn't forget, because he sure struck me as a guy up to no good." He straightened out the crumpled paper. "Here it is, called himself Burgess Kellerman, and acted like we all shoulda known who he was." He laughed and picked up his cognac. After a sip he chuckled again, "Must be som'n in the water."

After a silence, Aldo asked, "How's that?"

The man turned toward him and smiled, "Bout all of 'em I've met are that way, Texans, I mean. Must be som'n in the water down there."

Patrick laughed, "Was this guy still there when you left Traveler's Rest?"

"Yeah he was, but said he was leaving for Burgess Montana as soon as his foreman and crew showed up." When he saw the look on Broderick's face, he turned to Patrick and Aldo and saw the same look. "What?"

"Burgess Montana?" All three said the same thing.

"Oh! Yeah, that's what he called it. Said he built the town a while back and named it Burgess and said it was gonna be the largest cattle ranch outside of Texas." He shook his head, "Texans." The man stood after draining his glass. "Well, I'm gonna turn in now. I hope what I've told you helps stave off any problems this guy from Texas is planning for your brother."

"Mister Prescott," Patrick said as he held out his hand, "I appreciate you taking time to talk to us. It might very well save our brother, Jesse's, life."

Broderick's eyes narrowed to slits when he said, "Or the lives of that Texan and whoever's riding with him."

After they sat back down, Broderick spoke to his brother. "Patrick, you go ahead east and get your pal elected. Me n' the boys'll head on up to Traveler's Rest and see what information we can get about this guy that's planning to get rid o' Jesse."

After only a brief pause, Patrick agreed. "You'll be able to locate Jesse once you learn where this Burgess Montana is. You can get a telegram to me at either of those places I wrote down for you, so keep in touch when you can, and lemme know what's going on."

"You got it, brother. Good luck with this project to get Mister Buchanan in the White House."

Aidan and Liam were at the livery stable about two hours before sunrise. The old blacksmith was already there firing his kiln. "How long ago did my boss's brother leave?"

"Bout half an hour. Them fellas with him was already here when I showed up, and they had the six new horses all rigged n' ready to go."

When Broderick walked in, Aidan had four of their horses hitched to the coach, and Liam was getting the harnesses on the other two, so they could be towed. "You fellas about ready for a big breakfast before we go lookin for m'brother Jesse?"

"About hell," Aidan said, grinning broadly, "we was both ready for breakfast before we went t'bed last night."

"Well," Broderick chuckled, "let's go see if the hotel has a steer left." He grinned, "After seeing those steaks on the plates in front of Patrick's boys last night there might be a need for a herd of cattle in this town."

"No problem atoll m'Lord," Liam said softly, with a sly grin spreading across his face, "if they 'ave n'got any cows left I spotted a corral that 'as so dern many sheep in it they can 'ardly move around."

"I don't like the taste of that greasy sheep meat," his brother Aidan said with a scowl.

"Well," Liam replied with a straight face, but he winked at Broderick, "then you kin 'av a plate o' taters, n' I'll 'ave meself a nice big bloody plate o' greasy sheep meat, by Jesus."

Aidan grumbled, "Let's go see what the bloody 'ell they 'ave in the kitchen fer three growin lads 'eadin into the wilderness t'find a wee Irish lad that chose the beasts and savages over the likes of us t'live among."

"By Jesus," Liam said as he turned to Broderick, "been livin wi' a bloody Jonathan Swift all these years n' never 'ad a clue."

Ian

Jewel L'Grieu leaned back in the chair and looked hard at Judy Dancer—so hard in fact that she nervously asked him, "Why are you looking at me like that, Jewel?"

"Like what, darlin?"

"Like, well, like you're appraising me," she replied nervously as she twisted her long hair between her fingers, "or like maybe you're trying to figure out something."

"Darling, I've been a gambler for twenty of my thirty-five years, and believe me I already know everything there is to know about you." He stood and approached the seventeen year old girl. His long fingers almost touched as they encircled her slender waist. "I was just trying to figure out if you'll be able to stand up under interrogation in a courtroom." He twisted his mouth as he held her away from him, and one dark eyebrow lifted as the other went down. "All the others settled with us to keep from going to trial, but I have a feeling that this damn Mick is not about to pay for something he didn't do, so you're gonna be put on the stand and cross-examined by his lawyer." He held her at arm's length a moment then pulled her to him. After kissing her forehead, he spoke softly into her ear in the smooth language of manipulation, which had been his trademark and calling card for two decades of cons, crooked cardgames, and killings. "Do you think you can handle it, sweetheart?"

"You think Ian will have a lawyer?" Her small voice came out soft and tinny with fright.

Jewel shoved her away so suddenly that she nearly fell, but caught her footing and leaned against the wall. It was not the first time she had seen his temper. "Of course he'll have a lawyer to give his side of the story to the jury." His voice was not loud but was cutting in its unveiled ferocity.

Judy Dancer stared out the window and trembled when she asked, "There's gonna be a jury there just to hear me say what happened?"

Jewel L'Grieu held his temper in check, knowing that his plan to own Ian McKannah's casino hinged on Judy's ability to pull the wool over the eyes of a jury. His dark eyes icily closed to slits as they bored into the back of Judy's head, but by the time she had turned toward him they were softened. When she looked up into them, his eyes were open and smiling; one of many weapons in a con man's arsenal.

"Yes, darling," he crooned softly into her ear as he put his arms around her, "but with me coaching you they'll be eating out of your hand like sheep when they look into these innocent blue eyes." He kissed each of her eyes before whispering, "It'll be like taking candy from a baby."

Judy closed her eyes and lay against his shoulder thinking, *I'd squawk like hell when I was a kid if anybody took candy from me.*

Patrick timed his arrival carefully, knowing that it never pays to allow the enemy to prepare for an impending attack. At a little past midnight on January 14th his private coach pulled quietly into Carson City, Nevada. His two drivers had brought him to visit Ian several times during the past few years, so they drove on through town to Ian McKannah's sprawling ranch two miles north of his casino.

When the coach entered the long road approaching the high steel gate, it appeared that they were alone, but a dozen pairs of eyes watched. The gate was attached to the ten foot tall adobe wall surrounding the five acres on which sat Ian's single-story fifteen room stone and adobe home.

The coach stopped and the four armed guards, two from each side, stepped out of two small rooms, cleverly built into the wall and concealed by vines, shrubs, and small trees.

Patrick leaned out and spoke, "Patrick McKannah here, is that you, Jorge?"

"Si, Señor McKannah, I have been looking for you to arrive in the night. Ian is awake and waiting in the library. My son, Grego has already gone to tell him of your arrival."

"Thank you, Jorge, I'm lookin forward to spending some time

with all of you when we put this mess behind us."

On the short trip to the house, Aldo said, "Ian surrounds himself with good people that he can trust."

"As do I and all of my brothers." Patrick spoke to his friend sitting across from him in the darkness. "These men have all become family to Ian just as you have become family to me."

"And we are all fortunate for it, Patrick."

"No more so than we are to have men like you and these at our side."

Patrick stepped down and waited until Aldo was beside him, and then both walked up onto the porch. Ian stood beside an elderly Mexican who had opened the front door. "Hello Juan," Patrick said, "how is Matilda?"

"Very good, sir. We are all doing quite well." The old man nodded at Aldo, "Very nice to see you again, Aldo."

"Juan," Aldo said in Spanish while smiling wide, "you never age; what is your secret?"

"Tequila, cigars, and wild women." The old man's face broke open into a wide weathered grin.

"Well spoken," Ian said, "for a man that has never tasted the tears of cactus or the heavenly scent of good tobacco, and has the same woman at eighty that he married at twenty."

As the old man closed the huge door he shook his grey haired head, "He gives away all of my secrets, I can hide nothing from him."

Both brothers laughed as Aldo just smiled and watched the old man shuffle toward the kitchen. All three turned and moved toward the huge library.

By dawn they had extracted every ounce of information from the papers relevant to the investigation that was conducted by the Pinkerton Detective Agency.

At 9:00 AM the following day the jury was seated and waiting for the judge to enter the courtroom. Ian sat between his brother, Patrick, and one of his childhood friends from long ago, Aldo Calaveras.

Ian leaned toward his brother and whispered, "Who was the fella that spoke to you just before we came in, and said it was going to turn out to be a very nice day?"

"An Irishman that I met with in San Francisco." Patrick then turned toward Ian and smiled, "He's sort of a weatherman." He looked out of one of the windows lining two of the walls, "I certainly hope he's right." Turning his eyes back to his brother, he winked.

Ian was about to say something when they heard the double doors open. The three men turned to watch as Judy Dancer, Jewel L'Grieu, and two men that were dressed as though they had just stepped off a riverboat casino, entered the courtroom.

Patrick watched as all four entered the swinging gate that separated the public spectators from the trial participants. He spoke only loud enough that Ian alone heard him, "I love it when the first thing the enemy does in court is piss off the judge."

Ian was about to ask what he meant, when a booming baritone voice said loudly, **"All rise for the Honorable Judge Elijah Worthington."** Once the grey-haired elderly judge was in his seat, the same baritone voice said less dramatically, "This court is in session. Be seated."

The judge's deep-set eyes narrowed as he scanned the entire courtroom. His voice was an octave lower than the one that had just announced his entry. "For those among you who are in my court for the first time I will explain my rules of behavior. Number one, no outbursts at any time or the public will be barred from this trial. Number two, no speaking among yourselves while you are in this room. Number three, if you must use the toilet, then stand and quietly leave and do not return. Nothing will be allowed to interfere with attention that should be concentrated on the issues in question.

The judge and his wife lived on a lake in Northwest Nevada but he presided over trials in Carson City often, and had been a guest of Ian McKannah several times at the casino. Neither he nor his wife used alcohol to excess, and they never gambled, but they found his establishment a relaxing event in a tiring schedule and both praised his food to all they met.

Patrick and his date, a young countess from Spain touring California, had spent an evening at Ian's casino with the judge and his wife. Judge Worthington began his legal career in Los Angeles after almost twenty years in Great Britain as primary legal council to the Duke of Wellington. He and Patrick enjoyed each other's company and talked far into the night.

"Patrick," the judge said, "you are the legal council to Ian." He turned his cold gray eyes toward Aldo, "And Mister Calaveras is your associate?"

"Yessir, Your Honor." Patrick's voice rang strong with the tone of absolute confidence.

"Duly noted." The judge then looked directly at Judy Dancer. "I believe you are the plaintiff, Judy Dancer."

"Yessir, but that's not my real name."

After looking over his bifocals at her for a moment he spoke softly, "Then for the court's record, what is your real name, miss, and where are you from?"

"Millicence Pratt from Pratt Wyoming."

The judge could tell by her body language and demeanor that she was not comfortable being in court, so he thanked her and turned to the two men dressed like riverboat gamblers.

"Joseph Gandova." The judge looked from one to the other.

"Yessir, Your Honor." The taller of the two men raised his arm. The judge looked at the red ruffled shirt sleeve protruding from a nearly flashing blue jacket and wondered if the man was moonlighting as a pimp.

"You are council for the plaintiff?"

"Yessir."

"Duly noted." His eyes went to the rotund man sitting beside Judy. "Arnold Presscott."

A thick arm enclosed in a yellow sleeve went up displaying even gaudier, frilly, ruffles. "Yessir, I am the co-council for Miss Dancer." He paused to look again at his sheet of notes, "Uh, Miss Pratt."

The judge mumbled, "Duly noted," and then wondered, *do the pimps in Carson City work in pairs?* He then let his icy stare fall on Jewel. After a moment he said, "And you are?"

"Jewel L'Grieu, judge." He smiled amiably, "We's gonna be married in a coupla months. Me n' Judy, that is."

Without smiling, the judge said, "Congratulations, Mister L'Grieu, however you must sit on the other side of the gate. Only client and counsel are allowed on this side." When Jewel just sat there looking confused, the judge pointed at the gate, "Please go to a seat on the other side, so this trial can begin."

The old judge had a stare that few men could challenge. Jewel stood and moved to the gate being held open by the court bailiff. He stood a moment at the end of the front bench and stared at an old man sitting on the bench next to the isle. The old man nudged the man next to him and scooted over to make room for Jewel.

Patrick looked at Jewel when he eased his lean swarthy body down onto the bench. He then turned back and whispered to Ian, "There's something evil and malignant about that man."

"Yes," Ian whispered back, "that describes him perfectly."

Judge Elijah Worthington explained the duties, responsibilities, and perjury penalties to the jury, and then called the primary attorney for the prosecution, Joseph Gandova, to the floor. "You will please explain the charges lodged against Ian McKannah by Miss Millicence Pratt to the jury."

Patrick, Ian, and Aldo listened as the lawyer in pimp garb explained in detail the events that led up to the trial. Patrick only glanced casually at Judy Dancer and saw that she was sitting in such extreme rigidity while staring straight ahead, that she could appear catatonic except for the sweat flowing profusely down her face.

A subtle smile crossed Patrick's face when he turned back and thought, *yes, it's going to turn out to be a very nice day.*

After speaking to the jury, the pimp called his client to the witness chair. Judy Dancer walked like a person that had just received a blast of Haitian voodoo zombie dust. She stepped into the witness box and placed her hand on the back of the chair. Frozen in place momentarily she stared out across the heads of the fifty spectators who had come to watch her perform in a court of law for the first time during her brief criminal career. When her eyes moved they did so without moving her head.

It struck Ian as if she was searching for a way out and might bolt at any moment. He leaned toward his brother whispering, "I've never seen her like this."

Patrick didn't move a muscle, but with his eyes still on Judy he whispered, "She's never been caught before."

Ian continued staring at Judy while his eyebrows furrowed down toward his tightly pinched lips.

Judy Dancer shook off all of the dark thoughts that had completely taken possession of her mind for a moment when she heard the bailiff say, "Place your hand on this Holy Bible and repeat after me. Do you, Millicence Pratt, also known as Judy Dancer, swear in this courtroom to tell the truth, the whole truth, and nothing but the truth, so help you, God?"

The "I do" came from a voice that Ian had never heard. It was not the confident lilting voice of the pretty young teenager from Wyoming that he had hired to sing and dance on stage for his customers. It was the voice of defeat preceeding doom, and he knew at that moment that his brother had somehow been pulling strings in the background, even though they had spent nearly every waking moment together since Patrick's arrival from San Francisco.

Judy Dancer sat down as her lawyer returned from his table with a sheet of paper. "I have here your sworn statement, which describes the actions of the defendant, Ian McKannah, against you." His voice was filled with the confidence of a gambler that knew he was the only one at the table who knew that it was a stacked deck.

He held up the paper and strutted across in front of the jury as tacky as a court-dressed stork delivering the King's first son. Upon returning he held it out toward Judy, "Would you please look at this and tell the courtroom that it is your statement and is all true."

The stork froze in his tracks and looked first at his client and then at the paper he held. Disbelief was painted on his face when he looked back at Judy. "But, but," he stuttered, "I, uh we...

Judy cut him off by saying loudly in her newfound confident voice, "I said it's the statement that I made but it ain't true. I lied because my boyfriend, Jewel," she pointed straight at him, "said he'd kill me if I didn't. We was...

Jewel was temporally stunned to hear her lie in court with him sitting only fifteen feet from her. He was already gripping the pistol as he stood to shout, "You lying hillbilly bitch." His voice betrayed the inbred ruthlessness that drove him to some day reach the top of the pile where stood only men of vast wealth. His voice was as harsh as his attitude toward all men who worked. He had exploited women from the west coast to the east coast and from the frozen lands north into the hot deserts of Mexico. With his extra inches of height and coal black eyes, both gifts from his Portuguese and French ancestors he had often backed down men who could have easily overpowered him. Jewel was also a man of immediate action and never once considered failing as he pulled the gun from its holster beneath his right armpit. He knew that once his bullet found its mark in Judy's brain, a fact he accepted since no man had ever been faster on the draw or more accurate with a shot, he would easily escape to search for a new, and perhaps prettier young associate to assist in his schemes.

One fact of his undoing was being born left-handed. That and the fact that there was another man in the courtroom who was also driven by immediate action whenever a situation involving him was presented.

Patrick McKannah had killed only four men in his fifty-three years, and all had departed earth long after he had honed all of his skills with a pistol. Since opening his private law practice he spent more money on ammunition for paper target shooting than most spent for their horse, saddle, rifle, and pistol. The first of the four was a lone bandit that held up his private coach when he was heading to a small town south of San Francisco. A friend of the Mexican family brought their plight to Patrick's attention.

"This family," he said to his friend, Patrick, one evening at the club they each held membership in, SFBC, shortened from the San Francisco Businessman's Club, "does excellent work at reasonable prices, but has been slandered by another saddle maker that wants a monopoly on all phases of saddlery."

When the coach suddenly rolled to an unscheduled stop on a barren area between San Francisco and Overlook, a small town on the coastal trail overlooking the Pacific Ocean, Patrick swung the door out and stepped down to find himself looking at the barrel of a pistol being held by a lone man wearing a dirty blue bandana across the lower half of his face.

Patrick glanced up at his lone driver and nodded slightly. As he predicted it would happen, the bandit thought it was a signal and began turning his gun's barrel from the man in fancy clothes to the coach's driver.

His gunbarrel's movement halted a lifetime from the point at which he could shoot the driver and then continue dealing with the ritzy dude standing in front of him. In that span of time Patrick pulled his small, five shot pistol from the custom-built holster beneath his left armpit. As the bandit's pistol was still following a trajectory to align on the unfortunate driver's head, his own head was in the sights of Patrick's pistol.

The bandit's gun hand trembled when the lead slug entered his brain. The fingers released their tension on the pistolgrip and the gun dropped from his hand. Before it was halfway to the ground, Patrick's free hand revolved the cylinder so a fresh shell was aligned with the barrel. Never one to do things halfway in an emergency, Patrick then put a second lead slug into the bandit's head. His outstretched arm placed the barrel less than two feet from the man's face, so the bullet entered just beneath the left eye and exited above his right ear, taking a significant portion of the brain and right side of his head with it.

The cadaver hit the ground, and again, Patrick revolved the

Cylinder, and then wheeled around in a crouch to scan the area on his side, alert for any movement. His driver had a short 10 guage shotgun hand-loaded with lead shot and small chunks of glass. His hands held the shotgun as his huge boot held the brake to prevent the four horses from bolting. He scanned the area ahead and to his left, knowing that Patrick would be doing the same on his side.

Satisfied that the bandit either had no backup or they had fled when the shooting began, Patrick climbed back in, saying to his driver who had been with him several years, "Seamus, I do believe that young man chose the wrong career. Let's get on the way so the animals can begin cleaning up the mess before a passenger coach rolls through here.

The second and third witnessed first hand the speed with which Patrick McKannah deals with men on the San Francisco waterfront who believe that all of the well-dressed gentlemen in the area are easy pickings for tough men who do not engage in manual labor. Patrick believed it was his civic duty to help keep his chosen city tidy. The sharks that are always nearby respond to all splashes along the wharfs of the growing new city, never knowing when they might get lucky. They did on this evening.

The fourth man, an Irishman himself, learned the hardest way possible that the well-dressed Irish lawyer was not one of the soft pampered children of the privileged rich that were fast filling the area.

After a long and fruitless search for the man that his wife had been seen swimming nude with by a private detective, David O'Shaunessay entered The Boar's Heart Saloon on Bay Street. His muscular three hundred pounds were evenly spread over a nearly seven foot tall frame. He could normally absorb whiskey and keep a cool head while doing his job as foreman of a twenty man crew of bricklayers. There was however nothing normal in his life on this day as he staggered into the waterfront bar.

Patrick sat at a huge round table with several men celebrating his friend and fellow lawyer's sixtieth birthday.

The drunken Irishman shoved two men aside as he placed his huge hands on their table and leaned forward. His eyes scanned back and forth until stopping on Patrick McKannah. "There y'are y'rotten bastard," David O'Shaunessay thundered, "play me for a bloody fool n' think y'kin 'ide among us real men, eh." He put a hand on the back of a chair to steady his wavering body.

"Y've soiled yer last maiden, y'bloody rooster." He pulled an extraordinarily long knife from a leather sheath and took a step that placed him in an unobstructed isle. He was now facing Patrick, a few feet away, who had stood and turned toward the man when he first began his drunken tirade.

"You've got the wrong man," Patrick said. "Let's go stand at the bar and I'll buy us a drink and introduce myself."

"Me bloody arse." He was swaying left and right like a giant tree about to fall, and holding the long blade out in front. "I was told by friends that m'wife's lover was 'ere, an by Jesus there y'are in the fancy pants n' blue jacket they said y'd be wearin."

Patrick knew he could drop the man before he closed the distance separating them, but he didn't want to kill a man that had been given bad information. "Go home, lad, and meet me here tomorrow with your wife so she can tell you that she's never laid eyes on me."

The man screamed incoherently and began his rush. It seemed to Patrick and by later testimony of the many spectators too, that he would fall due to his drunkenness before reaching his target.

Before the man barely shortened the distance by half, Patrick had his short-barrel pistol out of a shoulder holster. His brother Ian bought the latest pistols on the market, and then designed the holsters and had one made for both of his lawyer brothers as a gift. The gun was aimed at his adversary's head.

As David O'Shaunessay's hand was raising the knife, Patrick thumbed back the lever with the attached firing pin. The blade was straight up when the huge lead bullet plowed through his forehead. As it tore through his brain, the lead slug canceled all messages to the body's limbs. The hand holding up the knife released its grip, and the legs holding up the body folded as though they were made from paper. David O'Shaunessay fell at Patrick's feet with his left pinkie finger resting on the toe of his boot. Patrick looked down and thought about a game he and his siblings played when they were children. *That's last touch, so I guess that means I'm it.*

Jesse

Burgess Kellerman sat at one of the poker tables in his saloon and gambling hall. It was situated exactly in the center of town on Kellerman Boulevard and served as the hub of all business activity in the city of Burgess Montana. Burgess was a Texan with an ego as big as the state he was born in and harbored impossible dreams of grandeur that few ancient kings could surpass. The chair he sat in was positioned against the wall and was but a few feet from the very window that Jesse had stood next to listening only a few days earlier.

Geoff Colter and Jiggs Hathaway sat facing each other, one on each side of their boss. They tossed down a shot of whiskey then turned toward Burgess as he spoke. "So, this guy's a damn Mick that's in love with these stinkin savages, eh?"

"Yeah, boss." Geoff spoke quietly, glancing nervously at the occupied tables, a cautious habit developed during half of his forty years in jails and prisons; the other half spent weaseling for men like Burgess Kellerman. "That squaw in Polson what thinks she's married to me says he's some kind of medicine man. Came here from som'rs back west, and she says he usta live with 'em a coupla years ago."

"Musta been that big tall guy I saw up in Polson t'other day," Jiggs said as he poured himself another shot of whiskey.

Geoff turned to him, "Gray beard and hard gray eyes?"

"Yeah."

"That's him, alright. He looks real hard right atcha, like he'd stick that big knife in ya fer just bumping into him or som'n."

Burgess leaned back in his chair and sipped whiskey while he rolled thoughts through his dark scheming mind. He finally leaned forward after glancing around his gambling hall and said quietly, "Lean in and listen to me." Once both men did as he said, Burgess spoke in an even softer voice, "Keep an eye on that troublemaker, and the first chance y'git scratch his name off m'list of people that I don't want hanging around this area causing me trouble." His black pupils floated in the center of a clabbered sea of yellow cream. The eyes narrowed to oriental-like slits as he glanced first at Geoff, who he knew was the leader of the two killers he'd brought from Texas with him two years earlier, then at Jiggs. "Once he's no longer around here to cause me problems there'll be a hundred in gold for each of you."

"Keep it handy, boss," Geoff's grin bared rotting teeth with a covering of fiber-like green hair, "cause he ain't gonna be aroun' here much longer." Jiggs just snorted softly and poured his shot glass full.

~

After seeing that Lame Wolverine had the cattle well guarded, Jesse explained to his friend what he hoped to do, and headed south. "I'll be back tomorrow."

His friend had patted Shadow's neck and looked up at Jesse, "Watch your back because you probably made enemies bringing these cattle here to feed us."

"This horse's the first since Paloma that let's me know when som'n ain't right or there's something or someone nearby. His head rises a bit and both ears lay back n' stay there till I pat his neck." Jesse nodded at his friend, "But thanks for remining me not to let my mind wander." He touched the horse's flanks with his heels and headed south into the trees.

Lame Wolverine's eyes went to the colt revolver that Angus gave his friend when they last met. He knew Jesse always had the small pistol in a shoulder holster, and he could see the knife and tomahawk hanging from the wide leather belt around his slender waist. *He will be a hard man for even three to take down.* He caught a glimpse of Jesse as he disappeared into the forest, and thought, *ride with caution, White Buffalo, in case you actually are not immortal.*

~

Geoff Colter and Jiggs Hathaway were on top of the only saloon in the small town of Polson and had been camping there for two days. It was a three-story rooming house, casino and saloon owned by Rose MacAllister. She was a tough six foot tall Irish woman who arrived in a covered wagon with three young women soon after the first group that settled the small mountain town.

Rose had rigid rules and unbendable policies. Rule #1 was that any man who ever got rough with one of her girls would not return for two months, and the second time he did it was his last trip into Rose's Rose Garden. Rule #2 was any man hoping to spend time with one of her girls had to bathe first. Policy #1 was every one of her girls must clean up thoroughly after spending time with a customer—"Any girl that doesn't take time to clean their bodies after being with one of my customers will learn first hand why I carry this riding crop." Policy #2 was any of her girls caught stealing even a small amount of money or anything else from one of her customers will have her head shaved and she'll be tossed out to fend for herself.

Not surprisingly, none of her rules or policies had ever been broken in the two years since she arrived and had the building constructed. Her girls were always clean, as were most of her customers, her games were fair, and the whiskey was top shelf brought across the border from Canada.

Had she known about the two men camping on her roof she would have thrown them off, just like she'd thrown them both through the front batwing doors and threatened to shoot one or both if they ever returned. Had she somehow known of their evil intent she would have stormed up the stairs and promptly shot both where they lay atop her building.

Geoff lifted Jiggs' small telescope, similar to the one that Burgess had once loaned him. "I want it back in the same shape or you'll wish you'd been careful with it. Took a long time to get m'self one, an then I had to pay the trapper a fistful of gold nuggets fer the dern thing." He paused a moment before adding, "Took pert near two months t'steal thet much gold."

Jiggs watched as Geoff moved it slowly to keep it on Jesse as he waved at Lone Wolverine and headed up the mountain and through the forest. "He's headin toward Missoula, so let's get the horses and pick up his trail."

Jiggs followed him to the door leading to the stairs and down to the rear entrance. Few people used the rear stairs but they still moved cautiously until they were outside. Geoff had heard stories about Rose MacAllister and feared her, so he used his tool to lock the door after them. The two men hurried to the livery stable to saddle their horses. Fifteen minutes after spotting Jesse leaving the Flathead camp they were moving toward the last place that Geoff had seen him.

Jiggs Hathaway was the better tracker, so Geoff Colter stayed back as Jiggs moved slowly ahead. When his partner's hand was waving, Geoff moved up the mountain toward him. "Heading towards Missoula, juss like y'figgered he would." The two men began moving along with greater caution after Geoff reminded his friend, "He's gotta be the same guy that squaw of mine says her people call White Buffalo. I reckon he's some kinda medicine man to them simple-minded savages."

"Probably the same guy ole Crazy Joe Flambert was tellin me about t'other night when he drank too much o' the panther piss that boss makes in the cellar."

"What did he say about 'im?"

"Didn't say it was him, Crazy Joe just mumbled about seeing somebody sneaking around outside the boss's gambling hall. Said boss will pay him good once he figured out what the guy was up to."

"Ole Joe," Geoff said, "is way too far gone to do anything except talk about what he's gonna do." He rode along behind Jiggs who was following Jesse's trail. *When we get rid of this Indian lovin guy that's messing up Boss Kellerman's plans I'll get with Crazy Joe and find out if he's just mumbling or really has some information what I kin use.*

~

Jesse remained vigilant as he moved toward Missoula, watching the forest ahead for movement, and regularly seeking a high spot from which he could observe his back trail for ten minutes to see if he was being followed. He would normally have stopped before dark to make coffee and boil some jerked meat, but an uneasy feeling, which he never ignored, caused him to continue on until after it was dark.

He then stopped Shadow, and after hanging his boots from the pommel, put on his moccasins and put padded bags on all four of Shadow's hoofs. He tied them in place with rawhide, and then led him into the forest ninety degrees from his trail.

About 100 yards later he turned Shadow back toward Missoula, and climbed into the saddle again to walk the horse slowly ahead for half a mile. Jesse climbed down then and removed the padded shoes from the horse's hoofs. A sliver of moon allowed him to see the small cleared area well enough to locate a patch of scrub grass that would let his horse graze contentedly while Jesse slept a few hours.

After hobbling Shadow and removing the tack, Jesse dug in his saddlebags until he located the carrots. After digging a shallow hole and lining it with a corner of his canvas poncho he poured water into it and waited while his horse drank. Refreshed, the horse greedily munched down two of the carrots, and then used his huge muzzle to coax another two from his master. Holding his hands open in front of Shadow, Jesse said quietly, "That's all for now, big fella, but I promise to getcha an apple or two while we're in Missoula." He stroked the side of the horse's long head and then patted its neck.

After spreading his horse's blanket on the ground only a few feet from where he was already nibbling at the sparse grass, Jesse rolled up in his own blanket on top of it, his pistol, as always near his hand. Jesse wanted to be close to Shadow so the horse could easily get to him in the event he sensed danger nearby.

An hour before dawn, Jesse was once again in the saddle and heading toward Missoula Montana.

One hour after dawn, Geoff Colter and Jiggs Hathaway were squatting in a very small clearing a short distance from where Jesse had placed the shoes on Shadow. "What in the goldang hell d'ya mean his tracks just disappeared. Is he some kinda ghost or som'n?" Geoff Colter had very little understanding of tracking, or for that matter, anything to do with survival in the wilderness. He was good at what he did, which was killing from the nighttime shadows of dark alleys, brothels, and apartment buildings.

Jiggs Hathaway had once been a scout for the U.S. Army and could move close enough to an apache guard to slit his throat. A run-in with a colonel over some traveling prostitute ended his career with the Army. The colonel's career ended too as Jiggs cut the officer's throat while atop the young prostitute that the argument was about. She refused to run away with Jiggs and swore she wouldn't say a word to anyone, because if they left together, she argued, then the Army would know it was Jiggs that killed the colonel.

He watched as she bathed the blood from her body, and was considering what she'd said. After deciding that regardless, they would be certain it was him that killed their fancy colonel that everyone was saying would soon be a general, Jiggs stood when Rosalee turned her back to him and began dressing.

The young girl had a split second to realize that she should never have turned her back to Jiggs, but as the knife bit into her slim neck it no longer mattered.

He leaned down and picked up the towel still clutched in her lifeless hand. After wiping her blood from the blade he looked down at her one last time, "Shoulda done like I tole ya, Rosalee, and made that fancy-dressed sojer leave ya alone. We coulda run off down t'Mexico an done real good with me a'lookin after ya."

Jiggs looked at Geoff a moment then said, "He didn't disappear anywhere, and he's a smart som'bitch." He used a thin stick to move a few leaves in front of them before speaking again. "See that flat kinda print there?" He waited as Geoff leaned forward to look.

"Don't look like no horse print I ever saw." Geoff leaned back on his heels but continued looking at the end of Jiggs' stick.

"Well, that's sure as hell what it is. That guy's probably as much savage as them stinkin injuns, and betcha he's been a squaw man since he 's big enough to climb up on one of 'em." He leaned way forward and rested his weight on his free hand to place his stick on some dry leaves. "See how the horse with bags on his hoofs smashed down the leaves, kinda like an injun walkin in moccasins. That feller's been through the woods n' over the hill a few times, and best we pick up his trail again this morning, and then wait outside Missoula. When we see him move toward Polson and that reservation, then we'll pick us a place to ambush him."

Geoff looked hard at his partner then asked, "Y'sure we can pick up his trail again in the morning?"

"Of course I'm sure, cause he can't let that horse walk holes through them things when he figures he'll probably need 'em again fore he gets back to his squaw."

"Okay," Geoff said, "y'wanna wait here or go on up aways?"

"Here's fine, cause ain't no way o' tellin what a savvy guy like that'll be doin, and we dern sure don't wanna tangle with him till we got everthang in our favor."

"I'll get us a fire going while you hobble these horses." Geoff dropped his reins and began picking up dry twigs for tinder to get a fire going so they could have coffee and jerked beef.

Jiggs just shook his head as he led the two horses toward a grassy area to hobble them. *That damn fool'd give his scalp to the Apache before he'd go without a fire and his dern coffee.* He looked south toward Missoula Montana, *and that feller we gotta kill's probably good as any damned Apache what ever lived.*

Aleena

Aleena sat on the bunk and steadied her nerves; knowing that the old man would soon come through the door. A few minutes later the door opened and there he stood. She had not noticed before now that he was a very short man with thin skeletal arms and small child-like hands at the end of them. His Adam's apple bounced up and down in the center of a scrawny neck that reminded her of a pet banty rooster she had named Squawk the day her father, Sean, gave it to her on Christmas when she was a young girl. The old man's white beard was parted and appeared to Aleena that it had been constantly twisted into points. *Probably uses bacon grease*, she thought as his Adam's apple bounced, *like that old Tinker that came to daddy's ranch used to do with his long beard.*

The bouncing Adam's apple had kept her from seeing the bottle in his hand for a moment. When she looked down from his rheumy eyes to the bottle in his hand her heart skipped a beat. *I was so exhausted when I climbed up beside him all I could think of was I've been saved, but he's probably had that bottle to his lips on and off all day.*

He hadn't said a word since entering; wobbling slightly back and forth, his eyes roamed up and down Aleena's body, making her shiver inside. She stood exactly where she was when he entered and continued staring into his cloudy grey irises floating in what looked to her like muddy water. He finally spoke when his roaming eyes ended their journey across her body. Through thin slits he stared into her eyes and said, "Missy, I ain't had no woman in so long I can hardly remember, and I aim to have you now." He lifted the bottle to his lips but turned his head slightly so he could still see Aleena. Lowering his arm, he grinned and for the first time she saw the few remaining rotted stumps that were covered with hairy moss that looked to her like the slippery rocks along the edge of a stream that ran into the lake on her parent's property in Northern California.

Aleena knew that she would soon be fighting for her life so she concentrated and gained control of her breathing. *If I lose my temper he'll probably stab me then take what he wants and kill me. I've gotta keep myself calm and get control before he makes a move.*

Just as Aleena decided to move toward the old man he did the last thing she thought he would. He drained the very last of the whiskey and then threw the bottle straight at her face. The blue quart bottle struck her forehead and shattered. Through a sheet of her own blood she saw him rushing at her.

Aleena's legs wobbled but she managed to get both hands on him and before he could hit her she threw him against the rear wall of the trailer. His back slammed against the top of the three shelves beside the rear door that ran from the floor up to about three feet. The back of his head hit the wall with a solid sound, and for a second, one that she badly needed, he was dazed. She used that moment to grab a cloth that she had just used to wipe her face before he came in. Wiping the blood from her eyes let her see him struggling to get back on his feet.

Before she could get her hands on him though, he sprung up on his palms and toes. His small body shot straight at her like a rocket. Both fists landed blows on her already bloodied and swelling face. Aleena managed to get her arms around him, but she was weakening fast and felt her legs giving out. She attempted to roll his small body beneath her hoping to knock the air from his lungs, but he sensed what she was doing and used his short legs to keep her beneath him. The tables turned as air rush from her own lungs as he hit her face and neck repeatedly.

Aleena was panting like a dog giving birth to a huge litter. He held a roll of her neck flesh as he fumbled with the other hand to get his pants unbuttoned. *My God*, she thought, *what a way to lose my virginity, middle aged and raped by a lecherous old man who is probably a murderer too.*

He tugged his stiffened member out of his pants and was on top of Aleena trying to get her heavy Levi Strauss pants down. She had been fumbling with the braided rawhide that held the amulet and small knife. She felt him rip her underpants off then felt his hand parting her pubic hair as the handle of the knife came into her hand. The old man was trying to get her pants a little further down when he felt a hot pain rushing through his neck.

His eyes were wide with fear and panic as he grabbed her hand holding the knife. She yanked so hard that the knife blade almost severed his fingers. She slammed the blade into his side repeatedly as he screamed and scrambled away from her. She was still trying to get her breath when she lunged to her feet. On wobbly legs Aleena pulled up her pants and flung her body at the rear door. Just as she hit it a loud sound was accompanied by a searing pain in her head.

As Aleena crashed through the door to the dirt trail below, a second gunshot rang out and she glimpsed splinters flying from the edge of the door, now hanging from one hinge. It was the last thing she saw before a black shroud was pulled over her face.

The gunfire spooked the horse and it began trudging along the trail once again. Inside the trailer the old man had struggled to the bunk and managed to climb half in by the time his severed carotid artery had allowed his life's blood to redecorate the rug and bedspread. The small two-barrel .40 caliber Derringer was still clamped in his tiny gnarled hand as his body was carried west toward the mountains in Reverand Shepherd's wagon.

~

Five days later Aleena McKannah's eyes opened and she looked around. There was an old Indian woman sitting on the floor beside her, so a faint smile crossed Aleena's face. But when she tried to speak her head felt as though it was going to burst. Closing her eyes she waited until the pain eased a little and then turned very slowly toward the Indian woman again and spoke very softly. "Drink," she smiled and repeated, "agua." Aleena tried to remember the word the Indians near her parents home used for water but couldn't.

Aleena was running her dry tongue across even drier lips, and tried to smack both her lips together so the old woman would understand, but they were simply too dry. Exhausted from the effort, and with her head pounding again, she closed her eyes while thinking, *I hope this pain between my ears stops soon.* Hearing the skins of the tepee she was in rustling, she opened her eyes and saw an old Indian man entering.

He stopped beside her and squat. Reaching out to place his thumb on top of her wrist and his first two fingers on the other side he then closed his eyes, obviously checking her pulse. "Got good blood moving now, miss, so you soon feel plenty good."

When Aleena tried to speak, her eyes showed the degree of pain she felt, so he patted her hand and pursed his lips, "Shhh, shhh, no talk now. You be good soon. You are in Flathead camp. Bullet hit you on head but not go in." He grinned wide and his eyes twinkled, "You got very Ironhead, just like all Flathead women." He saw the desperate plea in her eyes, so when she ran her tongue rapidly back and forth across her lips, he said, "Want water?" She strained to open her eyes wide and nodded slightly.

He said something to the old woman who quickly stood and retrieved a rawhide waterbag from a rock-lined hole near the entrance flap and replaced the flat stone cover. Handing it to the man, she sat back down to watch.

Placing the narrow spout in her mouth he said, "Only little now, more soon." He tilted the bag up and let a small amount trickle across her parched lips and into her desert-dry mouth.

It felt to Aleena as though a cool spring rain had rushed into mouth and then across her body. She opened her eyes and tried to say thank you, but eyelids again became heavy, and a moment later darkness swept her away again in its protective embrace.

How much later she had no idea, but it was dark outside and she could see some stars through the open flap. Tilting her head slightly she could see a small fire glowing inside the tepee and a few people sitting around it talking quietly. When she tried to speak only a grunt passed across her lips but instantly a hand was softly patting her shoulder and a voice said, "All is good, I here with you again." The voice sounded like a young girl's when she spoke louder in her native tongue. Aleena heard someone moving and a moment later another voice spoke to her while holding a small torch. "It is I again, Doctor Caruthers, or as my people refers to me, Chief Bonesetter."

Two days later Aleena was being held up by two young Indian women as she walked slowly out through the tepee's entrance flap. Doctor Caruthers walked behind, giving Aleena encouragement as she moved toward a group of Indians sitting around a fire pit. A tall old Indian stood just beyond them. He was dressed in a very elaborate costume, which caused Aleena to think, *he looks like that friend of Jesse's who was the Medicine Man for the tribe that lived on mom and daddy's property several miles from our ranch.* As Aleena neared the group she realized that the tall man was staring intently at her. *I hope these Flathead Indians are as friendly as Jesse told me in his letter.* She smiled at him, *of course they are, my God they brought me here and saved my life.*

The two women guided her to a huge round log that had long ago been carved out to create a seat. From behind, a voice said, "It is me, Doctor Caruthers, sit outside now and when you tire we will take you back in and lay you down."

Aleena was aware that it was getting lighter by the minute so she turned her head carefully and saw that the sun was coming up. "It is early morning," she said softly, "so I must have slept all night." Doctor Caruthers sat on a smaller log next to her and repeated what she said, but in his language. The people around her chuckled, and a young girl held up both hands with all five digits on each spread out.

One month later, the concussion that Aleena had received from a bullet striking her head had almost healed and she was feeling good again.

Aleena sat at the evening cooking fire as Doctor Caruthers explained all of the events leading to the Flathead hunting party finding her. Meanwhile, his wife added cama and bitterroot to the huge iron pot hanging above a glowing cooking fire.

"My oldest son, Silent Stalker, and ten Flathead braves were returning to our camp with two deer carcasses when he spotted a very large elk grazing on the side of a hill. He and his hunting partner moved toward it while the others waited. Halfway to the elk they crossed a small trail used by white traders, and my son, who never misses any signs, spotted you in the distance lying on the ground. While checking to see if you were still alive he saw the amulet with a white buffalo on it. There is only one amulet like it and it was made for the white man that all Flatheads call White Buffalo. The chief, whose life he saved from Bad Wolf, a Flathead brave that turned evil, made it himself for the white man to wear so that all Flathead Indians would know he is our friend."

He paused, knowing that Aleena's brain was still healing and needed time to absorb new information. "What is your name?"

"Aleena McKannah."

"I am very happy to hear that, because often a bad blow to the head causes people to forget many things."

She turned enough to be able to see his face and asked, "How did your son and his friends get a big woman like me all the way here to your camp?" Aleena slowly turned her head to scan the terrain, and before he could answer, she spoke again. "Or is this camp near where they found me?"

"No," the doctor smiled, "our camp is two days away when you are pulling a travois full of meat behind a horse."

Aleena smiled when she turned toward him again, "I've seen our Indian friends that daddy allowed to live on his ranch, come back from hunting with meat and skins piled on a travois. I sure hope your son didn't have to leave any of that meat behind to get me here."

"After seeing the amulet he would have, but he moved all the meat over so he could use the skins to make a comfortable place for you to lie between the meat."

After a dinner of venison stew, Aleena turned to the doctor, "How did you become a doctor?"

He held his palm to her then pointed to his full mouth and continued chewing. After swallowing and a drink of sassafrass tea he answered her. "When I was seven years a Blackfoot war party attacked our small village. Two of us survived, but none of the adults. I and a boy younger than me were gathering berries a long distance away when we heard gunfire. We lay quietly under the bushes until long after dark. When we returned everyone had been killed and the village destroyed, so we gathered a few potatoes that the Blackfoot had either missed or dropped, and a sheep bladder full of water. With those few supplies we began walking toward where the sun sleeps. We came to a trail like the one my son found you on and followed it. Three days later we had only a few drops of water left and the summer sun was very hot. A short time before the sun left for the day, we saw a small wagon, very much like the one you were in when the old white man shot you. God was looking out for us because it was Doctor Caruthers and his wife, Katherine.

His eyes were almost closed and his head was back slightly as he shook it slowly up and down; no doubt replaying those days, six decades later, that changed the course of his life.

"Doctor," Aleena said softly, "you mentioned the wagon I was in when that old man tried to rape me then shot me as I was crashing out. How do you know what it looked like?"

"My son sent three of his hunting party along the tracks left by the wheels. The horse was old and stopped before the sun went behind the mountains, so the three braves came to it while they could still see inside. It was easy they said to see what had happened, so they tossed him out and turned the wagon around. They knew it would be bad to be confronted by white men while one of the braves was driving the wagon, but there were many things that could be made from the wagon once it was taken apart. They decided to drive through the night and hope they did not come upon any white men." He smiled, "It has now been taken apart and already we have made things from it that will make all our lives better," he grinned at Aleena, "and the young children enjoy riding the old horse inside our camp."

Aleena sat quietly for several minutes. The elderly Flathead knew that she was replaying those tragic events, just as he had done regarding events that happened to him many years earlier, so he sat beside her and said nothing.

Finely Aleena turned toward him and asked, "How did you become a doctor?"

He paused a moment after she spoke, and then said, "On my twelfth birthday in seventeen ninety-five my new father gave me a small leather bag filled with tool of the medical profession." He stood slowly saying, "Wait here a moment please."

Aleena turned and watched as the old man entered their tepee. *I had no idea,* she thought, *that he was that old. I would have guessed sixty, but he's seventy-two. My goodness, I've been feeling old at forty-eight.* She shook her head side to side, *no more, by golly, I feel like a girl again after talking to him.*

Doctor Caruthers, who he had told her earlier, was also the tribe's leader, Chief Bonesetter, returned carrying a bag made of doeskin and a wooden box. He sat beside her and opened the bag. "These are the surgical tools that my father gave me that day." He retrieved a thin wooden box and opened it, "I have used this scalpel many times and it is still sharp, because I put it and all the others to the leather strop regularly," he grinned at her, "Just like my barber taught me."

He took several others out and showed them to her, one-by-one, obviously very proud of them. After returning them to the

bag he said, "It is a shame that white men have never learned how to treat the hides of animals so they would last many years.
I made this bag when I was thirty, after the other one fell apart."

Aleena felt it and said, "It feels like it was made recently, it's so soft and pliable." She pointed down at the wooden box, "Are there more medical tools in there?"

"Ah yes," he said, grinning while glancing over his shoulder, "there are small tools, bandages, suturing equipment and medicines," he glanced around again, "that my brother, the tribe's Medicine Man does not like to see." His grin widened, "He says my medicine bottles all have evil spirits in them." He made a funny face by twisting his mouth up and closing one eye as he looked at her, "Perhaps it is best to let him use the old methods on our people because I fear he will not see many more passings of the full moon. He is over ninety and is no longer enjoying good health."

Aleena chuckled, "Can you not help him?"

"Yes, I believe I could, because I feel certain that it is his liver. He has always eaten many hot peppers with his food, and I have medicine that would make his liver function better but he would never allow me to treat his illness." He opened the box and let Aleena see all of his medical supplies.

She ran her hand along the edge of the box's lid. "This box must have been built long after you began practicing medicine." Before he could speak, she added, "Where did you go to medical school, and when did you start working as a doctor?" She smiled at him saying, "I hope I'm not being too nosy, but I've never met an Indian that is a real medical doctor."

The old Indian chuckled softly, "I have been asked those very same questions by many white people. My father taught me all that I needed to know so I could begin practicing. He studied medicine in London, and then came to this country with several of his friends, who were also doctors. Like my father, they did not like the way the government in England was treating its citizens. I was his assistant and student for ten years, and after we worked together to remove a tumor on the brain of the mayor of Yerba Buena, father told me that I was ready to begin treating my tribal people." He turned to look at Aleena, "I told him when I was still very young that I wanted to be a good doctor for my people because they have many health problems and have no trained doctors to help them. I traveled throughout Flathead country trying to help my people have a better life and better health until five years ago. I knew that it was becoming much too difficult to go from one village to another, so I settled here with old friends. This village is near the center of Flathead territory, now that the white men have cheated us out of much of our land." He paused a moment, but then turned toward Aleena again and smiled. "I have no bad feelings toward white men because I have seen the exact same things going on amongst Indians: Flatheads and other tribes. White men do not hold monopoly on greed; it is a disease that can affect all humans, male or female."

"You are a very extraordinary man," Doctor Caruthers," and I hope you can meet my brother, Jesse, when I learn where he is living now."

The old chief turned toward her again to ask, "Is he the only brother that you have?"

"Oh, goodness no, I have five wonderful brothers, but Jesse and I were always very close."

"Is Jesse the brother that gave you the amulet with the white buffalo on it?"

"Yes, he told me to always wear it while I was traveling home from the east where I was a school teacher. He said that if I was ever in need of help, to find a Flathead village and show it to the chief." She smiled broadly at the old Indian doctor, "But when I was in really serious trouble the Flatheads came and found me and then their chief made me well." Aleena took the old man's hand in hers and gently squeezed it, "Thank you, Doctor Caruthers." She looked around the small villiage before saying, "When I'm feeling strong again, I want to thank everyone here in your village, because if they hadn't allowed me to be brought here I would have been buzzard bait."

He laughed heartily, "Aleena you have a very funny way of expressing your feelings."

"I probably got that from my brother, Broderick. He's a very successful Lawyer in San Diego, California but I'm sure he has not changed. He always had funny things to say when faced with a tough situation or something dangerous was about to happen. I hope you meet them all one day."

"Aleena, when the amulet was found on a cord woven too close around your neck to be removed, my son knew that you were someone that White Buffalo cared very much for or he would not have removed it from his own neck. My son, Silent

Stalker, and two of his best friends have left here to locate your brother, who they believe to be the legendary White Buffalo."

Aleena took hold of his arm before speaking, "I believe I will have to go back to my bed now, doctor, I'm feeing weak and shaky."

After the chief and his wife had helped her back to the pallet of furs that she'd been lying on since they brought her to the village, she said, "When I'm a bit stronger I'd love to hear about White Buffalo."

"Have some of my wife's wonderful woodchuck stew now, and then rest. Next time we sit outside I will tell you all that I have heard about White Buffalo."

Doctor Caruthers looked up two mornings later to see a sleepy-eyed Aleena coming out through the flap in his tepee. "Good morning," he said, "may I assume that you are ready for a cup of coffee?"

"Good morning to you too, doctor, and yes, I begin each day with a hot cup of black coffee." She sat down beside the old man on the wide split log that had been worn smooth during the decades that this Flathead Indian village had been home to his extended family.

"And," she added smiling, "when there's no coffee or tea, then a cup of hot water will do just fine."

After pouring Aleena a fire-hardened clay cup full of strong coffee, Chief Bonesetter then topped off his own clay cup and returned to the log. "Is the dizziness from the concussion still bothering you, Aleena?"

"I almost hate to say it for fear it'll bring a hex to me," Aleena said and then laughed, "but I feel as though I'm almost back to where I was before those men rode into our camp." She reached out with her free hand and gently squeezed the elderly doctor's arm, "And I will never forget you and the wonderful people who brought me here so you could help me."

"The Flathead people have always tried to get along with their neighbors, Aleena, but there have been times when it simply was not possible." His tired old eyes scanned the distant mountains above the fire's smoke, "We tried many times to get along with the Blackfoot too, but sometimes I believe they would rather fight than eat." His gray-haired head shook slowly side-to-side as he stared into the distance. "I saw that the white men were moving into our lands in great numbers, and encouraged my people to accept them as neighbors and learn their ways. They always did as I said," he turned a grin toward her, "well, not always but on most things they did as I said, and as a result we have always treated white people well and in return have usually enjoyed a good relationship with your people."

"My brother Jesse, who your people call White Buffalo, wrote me letters when I was a teacher. I could tell that he was very happy among the Flathead people." She turned toward him, "Doctor, I'll never be able to thank your son enough for going into the wilderness to locate the tribe that Jesse is living with." A melancholy sigh passed across her lips, "If indeed he is still alive."

The Chief turned toward her, "He is alive, Aleena, because if White Buffalo was dead all Flathead people would know it."

"Oh my God, doctor, I hope and pray that he is."

The Chief was a man of positive convictions, so when he said softly, "He is still alive, Aleena, and living with my people," she immediately felt better.

~

It was a very hard winter snowfall that announced the arrival of winter in the Indian village where Aleena was recovering from the beating and gunshot wound. Hunting had been good during fall and an abundance of meat had been cured and stored. Wild vegetables that grew in the area had been placed in root cellars carved into the hillside. Cama, bitterroot, onions, apples and nuts were in abundance, so everyone was cheerful and happy as winter passed leaving full bellies and smiling faces in its wake.

Spring was announced with the arrival of Silent Stalker and his two companions. The Chief hugged his son and asked that they all sit at his fire and drink coffee until Aleena came outside for her morning coffee.

The three young braves were all very tired and welcomed the invitation. Before they had even finished their first cup, Aleena stooped beneath the tepee flap and approached the fire.

Before she reached the sitting log, the chief's son stood and spoke. "Your brother, White Buffalo, is living in a village with my people near Flathead Lake. It is far away, so we will need to be many people when we go so that you will be safe."

Tears burst from her eyes as she said softly, "Thank you, Silent Stalker, and thank both of you too," she closed her eyes and nodded at the two young men sitting on the log.

Aleena had learned many words in the Flathead dialect of the Salish language from the women who allowed her to live in their tepee. She nodded her head and repeated "thank you" in their language.

Barely a week after Chief Bonesetter's son had returned with the information that Jesse was living in a Flathead village near a lake in northern Montana, the entire village was prepared to leave.

"We must go north in very large numbers in case we are confronted by the Blackfoot." Doctor Caruthers looked at Aleena and could tell that she was perplexed. "Do not feel as though it will be a hardship on my people, Aleena." Before she could speak he continued, "For centuries my people have been moving across the land like the wind," he paused a moment when he noticed the doubt on Aleena's face. "Aleena, it will help my people more than you can understand if we are able to reunite you with your brother, because he is to them the legendary White Buffalo." His weathered face softened and his smile was grandfatherly. "My people are in need of a light to guide them to better times. Our partners in life, the buffalo, are no longer abundant, and your people are moving into our land in very large numbers, so it is very important that they have something to believe in, if only for a while until they can adjust to all of these changes. Your brother, Jesse, will be White Buffalo to the Flathead people long after he has passed from this life to the next. Young children today will be old people sitting at a fire many years from now waiting for White Buffalo to lead the large herds of buffalo back to them." Doctor Caruthers looked deeply into Aleena's eyes and spoke softly, "That hope is what will keep them alive until they become used to their new lives."

Three mornings later a little before dawn Chief Bonesetter sat on his beautiful palomino horse at the head of his tribe of over three hundred as they began moving north.

Behind him walked the women, including Aleena. Behind the women, old men sat on horses that pulled the travois rigs that carried the hides, which would once again cover the lodgepoles and become their tepees. Children too young to walk rode atop the hides, as did the old people who could not walk all day.

Armed warriors were mounted on horses along both sides of the human caravan. A dozen warriors were spread out a quarter mile to the rear and another dozen were spread out ahead.

Twenty scouts were divided into five groups that moved with the caravan, but at a mile distant, and with the point of a star being directly ahead.

Aleena could hear the warriors along the edge of the caravan making sounds that Chief Bonesetter had explained to her were answers to signals made by the distant scouts at all five points of the star.

After a few difficult days of walking, Aleena finally began to feel invigorated. Chief Bonesetter regularly brought his horse close enough to talk to her. "I've noticed a new bounce in your step, Aleena," he said one afternoon a week after they began.

"Yes," she answered, "this has done me a lot of good, and I feel certain that I'm now back to my old self."

"Sometimes," the old chief said with a wry smile, "even when wounded, we need to get back on our feet to properly mend."

Aleena watched him right ahead of her and marveled that he always rode erect, never slouching, and remained ever alert. *Extraordinary man,* she thought, *and I must never forget how very fortunate I was to be taken in by his wonderful people.*

Chief Bonesetter led his people north from the Great Salt Lake area, but remained east of Fort Hall. He knew that many white pioneers were moving west along the trail that John Fremont blazed a few years earlier in 1843. He wanted no problems with the white men and figured the best way to accomplish that was to keep his tribe away from the trails they might use.

After crossing Jedediah Smith's old 1824 trail he kept them west of Pierre's Hole and Fort Henry until they crossed Smith's later trail, created in 1829, to end at Pierre's Hole.

When they passed by Fort Henry he changed direction and headed them northeast across the Continental Divide to a valley he knew of that was west of Yellowstone Lake.

Several weeks later they located the Madison River, which he knew joined the Missouri River that Lewis and Clark used in 1805. The chief's love of history, and his acquired ability to read books written in English, was now helping his tribe to avoid any confrontations with white men.

Five weeks later Chief Bonesetter turned them northwest into a valley that would pass north of Traveler's Rest. The valley was reasonably free of obstructions and would be much easier traveling.

"Flathead Lake," the chief said to Aleena as they sat near the cooking fire one night, "is about two weeks north of here, so you should be with your brother soon."

Aleena sipped from her clay cup of sassafrass tea, and then it was lowered, and she closed her eyes tight to pray. *Oh sweet Jesus, if only my dream will come true.* She turned a smile toward the chief, "Doctor Caruthers, I have dreamed of seeing my brothers again for so very long now that it actually happening hardly seems possible."

~

As Chief Bonesetter led his huge tribe, which now also included Aleena, on into the valley north of Traveler's Rest, four white trappers were also moving north a half mile west of them.

The tallest of the four men was also half again as heavy as any of the other three. Because of his size and aggressive attitude he became the leader of the small group. All any of them knew him by was Big John. When he spoke, his words came out as though they had been mixed with gravel. Twenty-five miles north of Traveler's Rest he raised his huge arm and spoke, "Hold up." He sat for a short time saying nothing as his dark eyes scanned the terrain ahead.

The other three sat silently in their saddles and waited. They had seen a fifth member of their group beaten almost to death by Big John for refusing to obey him when he told them all to stop and stay in the saddle.

Pepper, which is what the man that was beaten was known as due to the hot peppers he was constantly slicing over everything that he ate, climbed down from his saddle saying, "I gotta walk a little of this damned stiffness outa my bones."

When Big John wheeled his horse around and climbed down, the other three men stayed in the saddle. He walked to Pepper and hit him in the face so hard that Rupert, the short fat one, later said that both of Pepper's feet came off the ground from the one blow, and even though Big John continued to hold him by the collar of his jacket and beat him bloody, the fight went out of him after that first blow. Stick, the tall thin one confirmed it and said he was certain that Big John meant to kill Pepper.

Big John then climbed back up into the saddle and wheeled his horse around to face Pepper, who was slowly climbing into his saddle. He waited until the man was in the saddle with both boots in the stirrups, and then raised his huge arm to point one finger back in the direction they had come from. He growled only two words—"Pepper, git." Big John then reined his horse around and continued scanning the terrain ahead as though nothing unusual had just happened. Without saying a word, or turning to watch Pepper ride slowly away, each of Big John's remaining three men decided right then and there to get away from the man at the first opportunity.

Big John finally motioned with his arm, and the four of them moved on. After three hours he turned to the short muscular man riding closest, "Bud, they's plenty who'll say I'm a mean ole bastard but thet juss ain't really so. Ever buncha men what gits together gotta have one leader and they's gotta do whatever he tells 'em to do."

Bud was older than he appeared and had been across the oceans a few times before tying in with the three men he was riding with. He had seen the man's temper get out of control once before, so after the beating of Pepper he said nothing, and like the other two, decided to get away from him at the first opportunity. For now though, he knew it would be wise to go along with the big man's plans.

"Yeah, boss," Bud replied, "you decide what needs doin and we do it."

The other two men were near enough to hear, so they agreed. "Yep," Rupert said, "one man's gotta be the boss."

"That's the way it works best," Stick said loud enough that he was sure Big John heard.

"See thet rise there up ahead," Big John said while pointing, "we'll make camp rot thar."

~

At the first opportunity for them to talk about the incident when

Big John couldn't be listening, they each agreed to head west together toward the coast and get back on a boat and remain there to minimize the possibility of running into Big John again. They had all worked together as deck hands on a sailing freighter before signing off in San Diego to see what this new country looked like.

While Big John and his three men were setting up their camp, Chief Bonesetter and his tribe, a short distance away, were busy preparing their own camp for the night.

Patrick

Seamus nudged his brother Kenneth and motioned ahead with his chin. Less than a hundred feet ahead of their coach stood three men. A slight pull on the reins slowed the six horses down. Kenneth had already yanked the short alert-bell-cord that went down to the stagecoach's passenger compartment, so Patrick and Aldo already had a weapon in hand. Aldo held his pistol confidently due to an enormous amount of practice with it, and Patrick held a shotgun and was looking into a small mirror that Seamus had attached to the rear window frame. He bumped the gun's barrel against the oak wall right behind the driver's bench so his men would know that they heard the alert and was ready.

Seamus held all the reins tight in both hands, and without turning to his brother said, "When we're right on top of 'em I'm gonna let the horses give it all they've got."

All Kenneth said was "Give 'em hell, brother."

The taller of the three road bandits stepped away from the other two and stood in the center of the dirt trail with both thumbs hooked in his belt.

One of the other two men was holding a shotgun, but much too casually. One gloved hand was on the short barrel and the other gripped the wooden stock, so Patrick figured the man was an amateur, and knew Kenneth would too. He concentrated on the short man standing beside the amateur. Shorty's right hand was staying close to the grip of his pistol and Patrick noticed that the man's eyes kept shifting from the driver's bench where Seamus and Kenneth sat, and the coach's passenger area. *I better take that guy out first,* Patrick thought, *because he acts like this is his main line of work.* Patrick took one last glance at the amateur with the shotgun. *He looks scared to death so will probably be a little slow when the shootin begins, so I oughta have plenty of time to get lined up on him after I send Shorty to hell if Kenneth hasn't already taken care of him.* Patrick cocked both hammers and waited.

A moment before he knew Seamus would slap the horses to get then running, Patrick quickly moved to the other seat, and Aldo did the same. At the same split second that the coach lunged forward, Patrick leveled the shotgun at Shorty and pulled the trigger.

A fraction of a second later Patrick registered the expression of dread and horror on the amateur bandit's face before Kenneth blasted it and the head it was pasted to off the body from a short distance. Patrick also noticed that the gloved hands still held the shotgun in the same casual manner as the cadaver crumpled to the ground.

A loud unmistakable bump causes Patrick some concern. Aldo was also concerned, so by using the hand mirror resting in a sleeve on the door he looked at the trail behind the coach. "That third bandit," he said to Patrick, "was apparently caught off guard by the swiftness of our four horses being slapped by leather reins and couldn't get out of the path in time."

Patrick leaned far out the window and yelled up at Seamus, "You're sure gettin good at saving ammunition."

"Well boss," he yelled back, "didn't wanna chance clippin an ear on one o' these 'orses, cause this team's workin dern good together."

A very uneventful thousand miles later they drove into the town of Independence Missouri. It was settled in 1827, but had been occupied by Osage Indians prior to the Louisiana Purchase in 1803. Before becoming part of the United States it was occupied by a few Spaniards and Frenchmen. A hardwood plaque carving was nailed to the wall of the boardwalk that testified to the 1804 visit by Lewis and Clark when they stopped to pick some plums, apples, and raspberries.

The Kavanaugh brothers stopped the coach in front of the Independence Hotel so Patrick could look for a telegraph office and Aldo could make arrangements for their stay. The coach rumbled away toward the livery stable they were directed to by the sheriff, who accompanied Partick to the telegraph office. "Yessiree," the elderly lawman answered, "we have our own telegraph office, a small but efficient hospital, one dentist but another one's comin here t'live and pull teeth, a fine school with three teachers, and," he looked up at Patrick and grinned, "since Independence was declared the very hub of the central route to Californy, we got ourselves the best mail delivery in this here new country." He opened the door to the telegraph office and waited until Patrick entered, and then continued. "Word is that rails for a train to go all the way from one coast to the other are gonna be laid purdy dern soon."

"Sheriff," Patrick said as he put one hand on the old man's shoulder and held out his other, which the lawman took, "I must get this telegram sent right now, but if you're gonna be in your office, I'll stop by, because I have some questions that I'm sure you can answer."

The sheriff touched the edge of his Stetson, "Mister, uhh" he paused and Patrick told him his last name, "McKannah, ain't a thing goin on in this entire area that I ain't aware of, so you just c'mon by and we'll have us a coffee and chat a bit." He wheeled around too fast and almost fell, but Patrick steadied him a little, and then opened the door.

"Can I help you, sir?"

Patrick turned from watching the old sheriff wobble along the boardwalk, "Yes, I'd like to send a couple of telegrams."

By the time he got the telegrams sent to Broderick's office in San Diego and his contact in New York City, who was also James Buchanan's press agent, and a short one to his new law partner in San Francisco, Seamus and Kenneth had already returned from the livery and were waiting in rocking chairs beside Aldo on the hotel porch.

Patrick smiled as he approached the porch, "How does a pint of cold beer sound t'you boys?"

"Like bloody 'eaven," Seamus answered as he leaped up and out of the wooden rocker. Aldo's weary, tired smile was noted by Patrick, "How does a fresh cup o' coffee sound, amigo?"

"Wonderful." Aldo smiled and stepped toward the door.

Kenneth was already on his feet and opening it. "I'll buy the first round," he said as he stepped back and with a slow wave of his arm added, "after you, gentlemen."

Before stepping into the lobby, Patrick looked at Seamus, "I reckon we oughta check the coach t'see where he's been hiding the pantherpiss he's been drinking."

Seamus smiled and said, "Likker 'as always brought out the

silly side o' that bugger." He walked on through, followed by Kenneth.

Kenneth entered and let the door close. "It just doesn't pay to behave like a gentleman around blokes the likes o' you fellas."

Aldo grinned when Seamus said, "Is that whacher bumpin yer lips about, lad? An I thought sure that this fine 'otel must 'ave 'ired you to be the boardwalk jester to coax sophisticated clientele such as Aldo, Mister McKannah 'ere, and meself into their establishment."

"By Jesus," Kenneth mumbled, "me dear old mum n' pop, God rest their souls, must 'ave bought this babbling ape from a tribe of passing gypsies."

"Come," Patrick said quietly to Kenneth, "and walk between us or they might not letcha in the bar."

Seamus skipped ahead and looped his arms through theirs as the foursome walked through the swinging batwing doors. He tried to keep a frown on his face, but when Patrick burst out laughing so did he and his brother. A tired Aldo laughed too.

The three ordered beer and Aldo a coffee. While they waited each plucked a boiled egg from the huge glass bowl sitting on the bar and began peeling them. The plump bartender delivered the three mugs of cool draft beer and a huge slice of cheese that he was carrying on a plate in his free hand.

"Welcome to Independence, gentlemen," His friendly smile raised his bushy handlebar mustache. "I don't recollect seeing you fellas before, first time in Independence?"

Patrick, always aware of the value attached to making friends in new places, held out his hand. "Patrick McKannah, lawyer in San Francisco and Irishman wherever I go.

"Lawyer huh," the man said, "are you planning to set up a practice here in Independence?"

"No," Patrick said with a wide smile, "at least not at this time," he pulled out his leather cigar case to pluck out a hand-rolled Havana Ambassador. After clipping the end he put the cigar in his mouth and prepared to light it, he saw the hungry look on the bartender's face. "Care for rum-soaked cigar direct from Cuba?" Patrick smiled and shoved one forward and held out the case. He smiled when he noticed the look of pure pleasure crossing the man's face after taking a draw on the cigar, while closing his eyes. When he opened them he exhaled the smoke slowly and nearly crooned, "Mmmm, boy." He looked at Patrick, "Heard about 'em but never had the opportunity to try one, but I can tell anyone who asks me now that there's not a better cigar on this earth. He held out his hand and spoke around the cigar, "Thanks, Mister McKannah, and I don't even wanna know how much these beauties cost you."

"They were a gift from James Buchanan, soon, I hope, to be the fifteenth President of the United States."

"Hey," the bartender said excitedly, "I met Mister Buchanan last year when he came here to visit a friend. I've been a democrat all m'life, so he n' I talked quite a bit and got along splendidly."

"Well," Patrick said, "I hope you'll be able to shake his hand again as the new president."

A group of customers entered the bar and sat at one of the varnished white oak tables, so the bartender said, "I'll be looking forward to seeing him again." He moved swiftly to the table, and spoke loud enough for Patrick and his men to hear him speak—around his cigar. "My hostess hasn't arrived yet, so I'll be taking your orders."

Kenneth took a sip of his beer before commenting, "Friendly fella, that barman, wonder if 'e owns the place?"

"Nah," Seamus said, "if 'e was a republican maybe, but a lazy democrat, never. If 'e owned the place y'd n'er see 'im be'ind the bloody bar servin drinks."

Aldo smiled and sipped his coffee.

"Didja 'ear yer bloody republican coachman, Patrick? Thinks 'e can...Patrick cut him off in mid sentence.

"Better bottle up the polital scuffling gentlemen, till we reach Mister Buchanan's headquarters. We're pulling outa here early, so let's finish these and have dinner then get a good night's sleep to head east on."

"I do agree," Kenneth said in an exaggerated tone of voice, "that's the democratic thing t'do."

Seamus drained his glass and walked toward the dining room mumbling, "Crossing the country with a pair o' democrats I am; musta been outa me mind."

Several pounds of freshly butchered, prime, corn-fed beef, accompanied by garden grown potatos and vegetables sent the four men off to bed early.

The next morning, long before daylight, a fresh team pulled the coach out with Seamus on the reins and Kenneth holding the shotgun. Aldo leaned his head back against the padded headboard and thought about finally seeing the nation's capitol. Patrick sat on the other side looking up through the window at the stars. His thoughts turned to the coming campaign to get his friend elected. *The nation's divided*, he thought, *on the issue about our treatment of the Indians, but I'm convinced that the tide of public opinion is turning in favor of the Indians.*

He stared at the unseen wall ahead for several minutes of deep thought. Finally, looking back up at the stars, Patrick's mind clicked into the correct notch. *I'll use that*, he thought, *as a base to rally support for James and the Indians; both underdogs battling a government that wants them to disappear.*

Two days later the coach rumbled along with Kenneth at the reins and Seamus holding the shotgun. Patrick sat beside Aldo as both looked at the map he was given by an old friend. "Crude as it is," his friend had told him, "it's quite an accurate map, Patrick, and will keep you knowledgable as to your whereabouts during this epic adventure that you've undertaken."

After using his pencil to compute the approximate miles they had covered since leaving Independence, Patrick pursed his lips while shaking his head slowly up and down, *better than I hoped for,* he thought, *even stopping every four hours to rest the horses and check the harness.* He spread out the crude map again and studied it a moment before using his calipers' pointed tips to walk across the map from Independence to St. Louis again. After folding it up he looked back at the western sky behind them as the falling sun closed the gap to the tips of the Rocky Mountains.

He leaned out and yelled at his two men, "We've been doing pretty well since leaving Independence. We're averaging about a hundred miles every twenty-four hours, so we oughta be eating breakfast in St. Louis."

Kenneth was now riding shotgun, and leaned over to answer, "Figured we were doin pretty good, cause the trail's been a bit better since we pulled out of Independence."

Patrick returned to his map and began to estimate when they would arrive in the nation's capitol. As the interior of his coach began getting dark he carefully folded the map and replaced it to the leather pouch that his friend asked a leather-smith to make, before giving it to him.

He leaned back and lit a cigar, then closed his eyes to let his mind retrace the trip. After running the past few weeks through his thoughts he opened his eyes and watched as the smoke he exhaled drifted up and then out the window. *We've come about twenty-five hundred miles and still have a good nine hundred to go before we're in Washington DC.* He turned to look at the terrain as it flowed past his window and thought, *wherever you are, Jesse, I hope all is well and we're together again soon.*

Patrick heard Aldo snoring gently and smiled. *I must never lose sight,* he thought, *of how fortunate I am to have loyal friends like these men to work with me on any plan I lay before them.*

Simon

Simon McKannah rode slowly out of Jackal Flat two days later heading toward El Paso Texas to visit with an old Texas Ranger friend, Sammy Hawkins. The man had fought with him in three battles against Apache Indians during 1840. The Council House Fight in San Antonio was the toughest, but Sammy took a bullet in the raid on Linnville, and then lost a leg at the Battle of Plum Creek. When Sammy shoved Simon out of the way, an Apache shoved the spear through his hip instead. Simon had been firing at a group of Apache Indians trying to sneak up on them from behind.

When he heard the war cry he turned and put a .44 caliber slug from one of his Colts into the Indian's head. But the lance meant for him had been coated with feces, and before they could get Sammy to a doctor, the infection had already spread out of control—amputation was inevitable.

As Simon rode along the narrow trail, he remained observant of the terrain ahead and to both sides, glancing often to his rear. His vision was unobstructed and he could see over a mile in any direction. Confidant that he would spot anything unusual, he let his mind wander back to the last time he visited his one legged friend.

Sammy Hawkins never let his spirit fall into a slump, but on the last visit, Simon realized that Sammy's age was causing him problems. *Ole Sammy's getting on in age,* Simon thought, *and that oak peg for a leg that he made himself sure ain't helped.* His brow furrowed as he thought about his friend's age. *I'm almost fifty and I reckon ole Sammy's ten, or mebbe more, years older'n me.* "Dern," he said quietly aloud, "musta been three or mebbe four years since I last saw him." He reached inside his coat and pulled a plug of black chewing tobacco from his shirt pocket.

After biting off a chunk, he replaced the wad and began working on the chunk with his teeth. As he worked the chew into the corner of his mouth he thought, *gotta make a point of visiting Sammy more often.* His brow rippled with furrows again, *I sure hope t'heck he ain't up n' kicked the bucket on me.* A wide smile spread across his bearded face causing his black eyes to sparkle brightly, *nah, that old man's tougher'n a wild hog's hide.*

Simon looked behind and realized that a storm was catching up with him. He reached back and loosened the rawhide strings that held his waterproof pancho to the saddle. After buttoning it he pulled the chin strap on his hat down and snugged it beneath his beared. He gently slapped his horse's neck saying, "Might as well keep on goin, Dragon, cause there ain't no way I'd get any rest with it pouring." He shifted sideways to look back, then slapped Dragon on the neck again, "And ole pal, sure's hell it's gonna pour, but ain't no worry about flashfloods in this flat country though, cause it'll soak it up fast as it comes down."

Simon slouched on Dragon as the horse plodded slowly on through the rain. By dawn the rain had stopped and a clear sky was beginning to warm the two old friends. Simon had already removed the pancho and placed it over the saddle horn. Patting Dragon's neck he spoke softly, "You're a good boy, amigo, never once hesitated. Y'just kept your nose pointed toward El Paso and kept on puttin one hoof in front of the other." The horse shook his huge head and snorted. "Yeah, okay," Simon said, "we'll stop up ahead in that small stand o' trees."

Two hours later Simon had removed the tack, and then fed, watered, and rubbed down Dragon before hobbling the horse on a thick patch of grass. He fed the small smokeless fire with dry sticks that he always carried in the center of his canvas-covered bedroll. While the water in his small pot heated, he crushed coffee beans with the steel butt of his Bowie knife.

With his pot of hot coffee in hand Simon moved to the ebony tree three feet from his fire. Leaning against it he pulled from his shirt pocket the last of the jerked beef he'd been chewing on through the long night, once gagging when he mistook the last thin piece of tobacco in the other pocket for the jerked meat. When the coffee was gone, he stood and hooked his bedroll to a pair of pointed spines on two of the tree's nodes so the light breeze would dry the dampness in it. After spreading the waterproof canvas bedroll cover, he put the brim of his huge hat down close to his eyes to avoid the glare of the morning sun. Leaning against the tree he scanned slowly from left to right and then moved to the other side and repeated his surveillance. Satisfied that he was alone within his eyesight's distance he lay down on the canvas. His pistols remained in their holsters, but his new Jennings lever action rifle was at his side when he let his head fall back onto the saddle. After one final glance at Dragon, Simon placed the hat on his face and was asleep in minutes.

~

Three days later Simon rode into the outskirts of the small Texas border town. When he rode into Sammy Hawkins' small ranch he expected to see Madonna Echiaveria walking out through the open doorway with her usual friendly smile.

She had moved in when Sammy married her only child in 1830, twenty years prior to El Paso becoming part of Texas. Her husband was killed by Mescalero Apache Indians while raiding to steal horses. Before daylight Madonna bundled up her twelve year old daughter and began walking north. A month later they arrived in El Paso, where mother and daughter worked together cleaning houses for the American soldiers that Stephen F. Austin was already referring to as Texas Rangers.

Sammy Hawkins had already achieved the rank of second lieutenant and his pay was over twice the $1.25 per day paid to privates. He was living in a small adobe house he built himself on twenty acres he bought on the outskirts of town.

When Mrs. Echiaveria and her young daughter Lucinda first began cleaning his house twice weekly, Sammy could not believe it was the same house. His home quickly became an example the senior officers used to encourage the other officers to upgrade their living quarters.

Three months later he approached her. "Madonna," he said in the perfect Spanish he'd learned as a child, "I reckon this house is cleaner than even the commander's." He grinned wide and Madonna did too, which caused young Lucinda to giggle. "I have not been in it but four times in all the days I've spent in this town since January. And here it is already August and I'm heading off again toward North Texas to recruit a bunch of young rangers. I would feel better if you and Lucinda would move in and make this your home, so nobody will steal or damage it while I'm gone."

Several months later Sammy returned and added a room so Madonna and Lucinda would be more comfortable. Five years later Sammy married Lucinda. Ten years after that he buried his pretty young wife. A virulent strain of influenza came through the area and killed hundreds, including her and some of the new Texas Rangers.

Madonna Echiaveria remained as his housekeeper and friend but Sammy spent almost all of his time in the saddle. Simon sat on Dragon and looked around, but hearing a noise coming from his friend's house caused him to turn back toward the open doorway.

Simon was shocked to see how frail Madonna looked while putting one foot slowly ahead of the other as she made her way through the doorway to the covered porch and sat in her rocker.

By the time she was settled into one of the two old wooden rocking chairs that Simon had bought for her and his friend, he was off of Dragon and standing beside the old woman.

Her voice was as frail sounding as she looked. "You're too late Simon, that crazy old man climbed up on that old horse of his and headed north." She looked up at him, "What day is it?"

"It's Monday, ma'am."

"Been gone three days then," she rattled. "I thought sure he'd come to his senses and turn back, but should have known better because he never turned back once he rode out of here." She shook her grey-haired head and kept on wringing her hands together nervously.

Simon sat in the other rocker and reached out and took one of the old woman's sun-dried hands in his. "Why did he ride north, Madonna?"

She turned slowly toward him and shook her head briskly. "I saw three young boys following a grown man with the biggest head I ever saw on a human. Well, they looked like young boys to me but I reckon they were men. Anyway, I saw them ride on by and they were looking real hard at Sammy's herd of cows." She turned and looked at Simon, "He'd built that herd up to nearly a hundred all by hisself." She took a deep breath and when she let it out her head slumped against her bony chest. "I guess maybe I should have said something to Sammy when I saw them same fellers come riding by again the next day, but he was napping and I didn't want to get him riled up." She tried to smile but tears came to her eyes instead. "You know how vile Sammy gets when he thinks someone is crowding him." Tears were flowing when she tried to speak, "I didn't think those boys would...

Simon patted her hand, "Madonna you did the right thing by not saying anything to Sammy. Tell me what those three guys looked like and I'll follow the trail and see where they went." He smiled at her, "I'll probably run into Sammy on his way back."

"I sure hope you do, Simon." She pulled a small delicate silk hankie from her sleeve and dabbed at her eyes. "Two were tall in the saddle and the third was a real little fella that looked like he must have been helped up onto the saddle. His horse was one of those paints like the Apache seem to favor and the tall ones were riding big ole grays that looked more like working farm horses than riding stock. That big man with the big head was riding the biggest horse I ever saw."

Simon stood and looked down while still holding her frail hand. "You take it easy Madonna, and I'll go get on that trail fore it gets too cold." He gently squeezed her hand and stepped off the porch. Once settled in the saddle he headed toward the north end of the ranch where he figured they had cut the wire so they could slip away unheard with his friend's small herd. A short time later Simon McKannah was on their trail.

Broderick

The three men pulled out of Salt Lake City at the crack of dawn the next morning and by noon their coach was rumbling along on Fremont's 1843 trail. Seven days later, where Fremont's trail cut west at Fort Hall to follow the Snake River toward Fort Boise, Liam pulled the coach into Fort Hall. Their intentions had been to continue north following Jedediah Smith's old 1825 trail, but a cracked wheel rim spotted by Aidan prompted an immediate change of plans.

Broderick had been riding shotgun so Aidan could get some rest, and when Liam began talking, he listened carefully. "I had a few beers with a teamster that's been carrying supplies up to a place that Lewis and Clark made mention of in that journal they wrote after returning. It's called Traveler's Rest and is about four hundred miles north o' here. He said it's a pretty good trail that this new government's trying to keep in good repair by paying men to move big boulders and fill in where it gets washed out."

"Did he say what's up there?"

"A coupla places t'get a bite t'eat, and several stores that were well stocked with trapping supplies," Liam responded, and then turned a smiled toward Broderick, "and three beeeyoutyful gals t'spend a few minutes with."

Broderick laughed hard, "I'll bet they were beeeyoutyful."

"Probably were t'him, cause he said he hadn't seen a white woman in three years."

Broderick laughed again, "Did he have enough money left to get som'n to eat and a little grub for the ride ahead?"

"Dunno," Liam turned and answered, "but he did say he was leavin Traveler's Rest three or four dollars lighter than when he pulled in.

"Tried all three of 'em while he was there, huh?"

"Twice."

"Phreeeee," Broderick whistled, "musta been some sho nuff classy maidens."

"Dunno," Liam said and shook his head, "an sure as hell ain't plannin to find out."

Broderick nodded, "Good idea. Hope brother Aidan feels the same as you do."

"He will," Liam answered with a grin, "Allison's a wee bit of a woman, but she's got a temper that few 'ave seen n' lived to tell others about. If 'e brought 'ome a surprise for her, 'e'd be sleepin in the wood shed long after those darling twins were outa the school 'ouse n' livin wi' their own 'usbands.

Just before Aidan climbed up to relieve Broderick, Liam asked if he'd heard anything about the Reverend. "Did they get him to the prison okay?"

"Yeah," Broderick replied, "I got a telegram from one of the officers that accompanied him. Said he ranted and cussed all the way to the new prison."

"That new one up near Yerba Buena that the g'ment opened in fifty-two?"

"Yeah," Broderick replied, turning toward Liam, "but it's not Yerba Buena. The name was changed to San Francisco a while back. I wrote a few briefs for the state in forty-five when they were conducting a survey to determine public opinion regarding a maximum security prison in Northern California. Looks like San Quintin will be the end of the line for a lotta bad guys that thought they could keep killing as long as they wanted and never get caught."

"Like that preacher?"

"Nah, he'll do his time and probably find a town that needs a preacher and milk 'em for all he can then move on to another town." Broderick stood when Aidan moved forward and held to the brass rail beside the seat. "But," he added, "if it had been a white girl that he raped and killed, he'd get a close look at the gallows they're now using regularly in San Quintin."

"Quite the devout holy man 'e was, eh!" Liam watched as Broderick prepared to climb down into the passenger area once Aidan was seated. "Takes all kinds," Liam said.

Before slipping down through the windowframe, Broderick

nodded, "Sure does, but the fewer of those the better this world will be."

Once he was settled back into the coach seat, Broderick began thinking about the Reverand Jedediah Fenner. *I wonder if there's any real hope for someone like him. Maybe this long prison sentence will make him see a new path.* Broderick leaned back against the plush seat and closed his eyes a moment. A few seconds later he thought, *I don't believe those kind ever change. Nah, he'll keep being exactly what he is, a worthless piece o' shit, until someone's had enough of him.*

~

As it turned out, the long sentence that the reverend received was shortened considerably.

During the first month that Jedediah was in prison he was so frightened that he didn't associate with anyone. Beginning the second month he slowly became his same cocky, self-centered, egotistical self.

Unknown to Jedediah, an Irishman serving a long sentence after he was caught in the process of robbing a San Diego bank, was not finding anything that came out of the short, fat, bald little man even remotely funny.

Jake Maguire listened as the fat preacher entertained a young thief named Edwin Haven and several of his younger criminal friends. When he heard Jedediah ask if any of them knew how an Irish lawyer pulled up his sagging socks before approaching the jury, Jake's cruel eyes narrowed beneath bushy black eyebrows.

Jedediah stood and unbuttoned his trousers and let them drop to the ground around his pudgy ankles. His audience grinned when he bent down to pull up both socks, and then pulled up his grey trousers and rebuttoned them. Had Jedediah or any of the young men seen the murderous look that crossed Jake's face their laughter would have stopped in mid giggle.

Over the next month Jedediah cultivated Edwin Haven, who was serving five years for robbery, not his first, but the first time he was ever caught. Jedediah saw the opportunity that he figured would take a great deal longer to materialize, but Edwin

Haven unknowingly handed it to him on a silver platter.

"So," Jedediah said to Edwin one afternoon in the exercise yard, "you're being released next month."

"Yeah, Preach," he replied using the nickname he and his friends had given the little man, "served m'time and heading back to San Diego."

"Got anything going when you get back home?"

"Ever heard of the Brass Balls Boys?" Edwin unbuttoned his left sleeve and pulled his blue denim shirt up a bit.

Jedediah had never heard of them but said, "Sure," when he looked at the BBB tattoo on the young man's wrist.

"I did several jobs with Ivan Vidivitch, the boss of BBB, and he let me join his gang."

After several days of joining Edwin whenever possible when there was nobody else around, Jedediah asked him quietly, "Can you kill a guy if the money is right?"

The young man looked intently into Jedediah's eyes for a few seconds before answering softly, "What kinda dough we talking about, Preach?"

"Ten thousand bucks. I've got a wad stashed at my woman's place, and I'll write and tell her to leave a thousand somewhere for you when you get out, and then to give you the other nine after he's dead." Jedediah stared into Edwin's eyes intently as he considered what he'd just heard.

Finally he asked, "What's the guy's name and where does he live?"

"Broderick McKannah, and he's a stinking damned lawyer in San Diego."

By the time Edwin was ready to leave San Quintin they had put everything together. "I got a note back from my gal and she'll be at Gallagher's Bar near the big fish market next to the city dock on the second Sunday after you're outa here. She'll have the thousand wrapped up in brown paper like a fish."

"Okay, Preach, the guy's as good as dead."

~

Edwin walked into Gallagher's Bar right on schedule and picked up the money from Jedediah's girlfriend. Moments after he left the bar, she stepped into the sunlight and opened her parasol. Neither she nor Edwin had any idea that they were both being followed by men with a BBB tattoo on their left wrist. As her Chinese rickshaw driver padded the street with his feet, a young man with a BBB tattoo pedaled a bicycle along behind, but a block away. Once he had discovered where she lived he turned around and headed back toward his gang's warehouse where Ivan Vidivitch waited.

The following day when Edwin entered the dumpy rundown hotel where he had a room, the young man who had been following him all of the previous day hid his bike and waited. Twenty minutes later Edwin came out, looked around, and then began walking toward the waterfront.

Before he was a block away the young spy was inside his room searching.

Half an hour after the bicycle spy entered the warehouse, in walked Edwin. "Hey, boss," he said while nodding at Ivan, "You left a message that you wanted to see me?"

"Yeah, Eddy, c'mon in the office." Edwin followed his boss and never noticed that the two men standing next to the big door had closed it and were following.

The moment that Edwin entered the big warehouse, which was also used as the gang's office and headquarters, one of the men who were behind him followed very close. A moment after Edwin stepped inside the office, the man whipped out a leather belt and pulled it down over Edwin's arms.

The belt was pulled tight and buckled, making both his arms unusable. The huge man behind him held the belt tight as the other men pulled Edwin's pants down. After they removed his shoes and socks they pulled his pants off of his legs. He then slammed Edwin into an iron chair that sat in a steel pan so Jocko could strap the boy's legs to the chair. Before he could scream or say a word, a rag was pulled across his open mouth and around behind his head then tied.

"What's this?" Ivan tossed ten, one-hundred-dollar bills on the table. Edwin's eyes bugged out when he looked at the money and then at Ivan, who pulled his somewhat oriental eyes closed into almost slits, giving his gaunt face an even more evil cast. "I heard about your little deal with that preacher up in the can, so we've been keeping an eye on you." When Edwin's eyes pulled down in obvious confusion, Ivan smiled, "Jake Maguire and I go way back." His heinous grin caused Edwin's stomach to quiver. "He always keeps me informed about whatever my boys're doing up there." He motioned with his chin at a thin young man with an odd shaped head sitting on a stool, "Yesterday, Jocko followed you to that shithole you live in, and today he went back inside after you left n' found this." With his sharp chin he motioned again toward the money.

Ivan leaned back in his padded chair and smiled. "Edwin," he said in his accented English, "you have never seen the buzzbox that I found in a back room after buying this old building. Truly a very unusual device created by a brilliant man named Michael Faraday." He grinned and leaned forward, "I know that because his name is on the machine, but it was useless until ole Jocko did a little messing around on it." He turned toward the bicycle spy, "Who woulda thought that deformed head had a genius brain in it? The current generator produced a small jolt until Jocko worked on it." Ivan turned again to the deformed young man, "What did you do Jocko that the brilliant Mister Faraday couldn't figure out?"

"Wrapped more copper wire around the coil."

Turning back to a now terrified Edwin, Ivan pulled a very serious frown across his pockmarked face. "I have used it many times to get information, now that it does more than put out a small jolt." His severely scarred face became an evil mask that Edwin had never seen as Ivan's laughter filled the small office. "Especially," he gasped while recovering from his outburst of laughter, "since Bobo," he nodded at the huge man who had pulled the belt down over his arms, "suggested salty water." The pox-crater deformed face twisted into what only a sick mind would refer to as a smile. Ivan chuckled as he stood and moved forward until he was almost nose-to-nose with the unfortunate young man. "As you are now about to understand."

Edwin shook his head back and forth, and wanted to scream but all that came through the filthy rag were guttural grunts that sounded like a stuck pig—he had indeed heard of the buzzbox.

When Ivan spoke again, Edwin lost control of his kidneys and bowels. All the Russian had said was, "Get my buzzbox."

After Jocko placed another leather belt across Edwin's lap to secure him in the steel chair, he put two small clamps on the boy's ears. Ivan stepped back to make room for Bobo to pour salt water into the steel tray that Edwin's feet were secured in with another belt. Ivan nodded toward his second-in-command, Agga Villichenko, a fellow Russian.

Ivan's cruel face was so close to Edwin's that his foul breath overpowered even the smell of urine and feces coming up from the boy's bottom. Bile began rising up into Edwin's throat when Ivan said, "You'll understand now what I meant when I said that nobody ever cuts me out of my share of their action."

Agga's eyes also had a slight oriental slant, genetically passed on by his Mongolian ancestors. His somewhat flattened face had a perpetual sneer, which now broadened as he began cranking the handle of the modified generator.

Each time Agga stopped cranking, Ivan asked Edwin another question. The young man shook his head violently up and down to indicate yes and sideways for no. His responses followed a pattern of truth, but Ivan continued asking the same or similar questions until he was finally satisfied.

Fortunately for Broderick McKannah, Ivan never thought to ask Edwin for specifics about the job that the money was for. Once the three Bs were tattooed on a new gang member's left wrist, withholding a fee for a job was a death sentence.

After torturing him for less than half an hour with his bare feet in the shallow tin pan full of heavily salted water and the wires clamped first to his ears and later his testicles, Ivan was certain that nothing of importance about his gang's operation had been passed on during Edwin's stay in San Quintin, which was his main concern. The boy was not the first ex-con with three Bs tattooed on his wrist to be interrogated by use of the buzzbox—and would not be the last.

Ivan turned toward two burly gang members that had been standing near several dozen steel shipping drums with Apple Cider labels on them. "Pack our young traitor and send him out with this shipment."

Ivan sat back down and watched as Agga cranked the handle a last few times until Edwin's eyeballs almost burst from their sockets and foam gushed from around the rag in his mouth. When the boy's body went limp, Agga stopped cranking and removed the clamps from his testicles. Ivan sat in his chair eating sardines on crackers and watched as his men lifted Edwin from the steel chair.

Two men lifted Edwin and carried him to the drum. When his feet went into the drum, which was half full of cider, Edwin's eyes popped open, but the only sounds he made were muffled by the foam still gushing from around the rag.

His eyeballs still appeared to be about to burst from his face, and when one of the men sliced through a rope holding Edwin's hands together and maneuvered his limp arms into the drum, he began shaking and shoving against the bottom with his bare feet. When his body rose up slightly, one man kept his hand clamped to Edwin's arm as he retrieved a leather-bound lead slapjack from his rear pocket. Two hard blows with the deadly weapon caved in the boy's skull and he went limp.

Ivan watched as the cider that had been removed was poured back into Edwin's wet coffin. After the steel ring had been bolted to the top of the drum, Ivan turned toward Agga, who had put away the buzbox and was standing in the entrance to the glass enclosed office. "Be sure," Ivan said, "to put a California's Best label upsidedown on that one so the boys in New Orleans will know which one to pour into the bay."

"Gotcha, boss." His cruel grin spread across his flat face as he said, "He oughta be pickled good by then." His guttural laugh would have made anyone but Ivan shudder.

Ivan just smiled, "The sharks'll enjoy having another pickled cadaver for dinner." His smile widened when Agga laughed.

Edwin's girlfriend finally told the two cruel young men with BBB tattoos where Jedediah's money was hidden. After the boards in the closet were removed and a large leather bag containing forty thousand dollars was pulled out, a sharp blade crossed her throat and the house was set ablaze. Every dollar of the forty thousand was there when the leather satchel was handed to Ivan.

Jake Maguire took great pleasure in beating Jedediah to death with a large ham bone. Everyone in San Quintin knew that it was not worth the consequences to get involved with Jake Maguire in any way. Twelve years later he was released, and went back to work robbing banks, but this time he had three Bs tattooed on his left wrist.

Broderick McKannah was never to learn about the deal that Jedediah Fenner had made with Edwin Haven to end his life.

Ian

Being left-handed, Jewel L'Grieu lifted his right arm slightly to open a path to the pistol resting in a shoulder holster under his right armpit. A great many gamblers, private detectives, and professional men too, living in the larger cities such as New York and San Francisco adopted the new device. They saw those used by other men and had leather shops create one to accommodate their pistol, often a small derringer, to conceal the fact that they were armed. Leather shops were soon creating shoulder holsters to fit a variety of small pistols.

Jewel was one of the first to purchase a custombuilt shoulder holster. He practiced until he could not only pull his pistol out fast, but also hit what he aimed at. Three men had died trying to prove that they could draw quicker and fire the holstered pistol resting on their hip in plain sight.

Jewel had however developed a habit that put him in a casket on the day he went to court with Judy Dancer to separate her employer, Ian McKannah, from his casino and bank account.

While she was still pointing her red, long-nailed, manicured, finger at him, Jewel turned slightly to the right as his left arm and elbow rose in preparation for the lightning fast move that would put the gun in his hand.

That raised elbow blocked his peripheral vision just enough to prevent him from seeing Patrick's right hand heading toward his left armpit. A split second prior to Patrick's finger pulling the trigger; Jewel had already aligned the barrel of his pistol on the forehead of his young girlfriend, Judy Dancer. The moment that Jewel pulled the trigger he heard the second explosion—a noise that would send him straight into eternity. He was already on his way when the third expolsion erupted.

As Jewel raised his pistol, the judge, a known marksman, not knowing who Jewel was going to shoot, grabbed the long-barrel pistol lying in a nearby and opened drawer. A mili-second after Patrick's slug passed through Jewel's brain, a larger chunk of lead hit Jewel a few inches below the left corner of his dark dimpled chin.

That slight turn to the right was still working against Jewel. The judge's .44 caliber lead slug exited the heart and flattened against the spine. The lead slug instantly shut down all electrical signals remaining. The gambler, killer, wannabe casino owner's cadaver wilted to the floor.

A reporter for the Carson City Gazette described the scene for the newspaper readers.

> The quiet courtroom of Judge Worthington was thrown into mayhem and murder today as the trial of local casino owner, Ian McKannah, began.
>
> Plaintiff, Judy Dancer, had just rebutted her previous testimony against Ian when her lover and apparent co-conspirator, Mr. Jewel L'Grieu, pulled a small pistol from a shoulder holster, and from a distance of fifteen feet put a bullet between and slightly above her blue eyes.
>
> Sitting directly behind Ian I watched as his brother and chief legal council, Patrick McKannah, pulled a slightly larger pistol from his armpit holster and fired at Mr. L'Grieu.
>
> This reporter watched in awe as yet another bullet hit Jewel in the chest. A quick glance and I saw the judge holding a long-barreled revolver straight out and pointing at Jewel.
>
> I stepped over to look down at Jewel, who only a moment earlier had been smiling very confidently at his girlfriend, Judy Dancer, who I had noticed was not returning his smile.
>
> Jewel now lay in a heap between his seat and a barrier wall. His dark good looks that we have seen about town these past few months were now hidden among a pile of his blood-soaked clothes and one protruding red leather boot.
>
> Judy Dancer's body hung down from the wall in front of the witness seat. The small size of the lead bullet that ended her life did not propel her back. She seemed to

simply be laying her head down to rest a moment, but the blood soaking her blonde hair quickly dispeled that notion as it steadily pooled beneath her on the floor.

Pictures will join a more in-depth description of today's drama in a special evening edition.

That same evening, Patrick, Aldo, Ian, and Pinkerton Detective Lon Garrett, sat at a huge round table inside Ian's walled garden. Imported Irish whiskey was sipped by all but Aldo, who had a tall glass of iced tea in front of him.

"So," Ian said, turning to his brother, "before entering the courtroom you knew that Judy was going to turn on Jewel."

"Not really," Patrick replied, "but after hearing what Mister Garrett had to say to her yesterday evening after Jewel was lured away to a supposedly lucrative poker game, I figured we had a very good chance of seeing the case thrown out and a new one against Jewel initiated."

Patrick watched as Ian's eyes turned toward the agent that Patrick had hired to investigate both Jewel and Judy.

Lon Garrett watched as his glass was being filled. After a sip, he spoke. "I let Ms. Dancer leaf through the case files pertaining to Ian's trial. Evidence that she conspired with Jewel and his brother, her dead husband, to fleece several men that she lured into her bed was indisputable. When I explained that there are now several prisons that have the facilities to also house female criminals for lengthly sentences, although not altogether secure and certainly not comfortable, she paled dramatically. She was very obviously frightened. Her shaking hand that lit a fresh cigarette calmed considerably when I explained that all charges against her would be dropped if she was willing to testify that she had been coerced by Jewel with a promise of severe beatings if she refused his offer." After a sip he added, "I must add that I sympathized with her." He looked around before taking another sip, "She was, after all, just a child."

Gloom palled over the foursome momentarily until Ian said, "I'll always feel bad that she got mixed up with those two guys. You're right Mister Garrett; she was just a kid with stars in her eyes and got into something that she didn't know how to get out of or away from."

Before Patrick and his men headed back to California, where his home and legal career awaited his attention, he spent the evening with his younger brother, Ian. After a few drinks Patrick asked Ian how long it had been since he had seen their brother Jesse.

The glass in Ian's hand stopped halfway to his lips. He frowned as he looked at his brother, and then twisted his mouth and squinted as if to look back into the past. Ian finally set the glass back down on the table and looked into Patrick's deep sea-green eyes. His brows pulled down and he finally answered softly, "Jesus," his head shook back and forth, "I really don't know, Patrick, but it's sure been quite a while." He lifted both eyebrows when he spoke. "I gotta say though, too bloody long." He took a deep breath before repeating, "Too bloody long."

"I had this same conversation with Broderick," Patrick said, "earlier this year when I was in San Diego." He put his hand on the glass of Irish whiskey but didn't lift it from the table. Ian watched as his oldest brother turned the small glass but remained silent. When Patrick finally spoke it was in a soft hollow voice that Ian had heard only twice before; once when their father died and again when their mother died.

"We are all far beyond the halfway point of any reasonable expectation about the length of our lives." Patrick picked up the glass and sipped, then replaced it to the table and looked at Ian. "Brod and I were planning a short visit to surprise Aleena before we boarded the sailing vessel that returned us to California." Ian saw the pain in his brother's eyes as his lips pinched over tightly clamped teeth. Patrick sucked in a deep breath through his nose and released it the same way. "We have both regretted not going to see her all our lives." He sipped from the glass then continued in a stronger voice, "We both agreed to send a telegram to Simon and ask him to contact Jesse's Indian friends and see if they can locate his whereabouts. When we know where Jesse is, let's all arrange our current schedules and meet there for a long overdue family reunion."

Patrick drained the glass and poured in another three fingers of whiskey, but before bringing it to his lips he grinned and lowered his head to look at Ian over the top of his glasses, "I'm the bloody worst about keeping too much on my plate, but regardless, I promise to shove it all aside and be there."

Ian raised his own glass high, "'Ow can I not pledge me own attendance," Ian said through a wide grin, "when the future governor o' the 'ole bloody state o' Callyforny, will be there—and 'e bein me very own brother." Ian's smile was sincere but his voice abruptly lost the Irish lilt when he added, "It's a terrific idea, Patrick, and after that let's not allow so much sand to run through the hourglass before we all gather again."

"I'll send a telegram," Patrick said, "as soon as I get home and request that the Texas Ranger office send Simon a telegram and ask him to get in touch with one of us." He was standing beside his coach while he spoke to Ian. "I'll give them your address and Broderick's too so they can pass it on to Simon when he finally checks in with the Rangers."

A while later Patrick climbed into his coach, and after closing the door, looked down at Ian. "Take care, brother, and I'll see you at Jesse's camp one of these days," he grinned, "soon I hope, wherever that camp might be."

Before the driver released the brake Ian said, "It'll be among good people wherever it is." The coach lurched ahead and Ian stood watching it leave a trail of dust as it headed west toward San Francisco.

~

Two months after the trial, Ian was in his casino office talking to a stage show promoter and dance choreographer. Ian's strategy for success had always been to stay a step or two ahead of his competition, whether it was the type of gambling games or the quality of the stage shows that encouraged families to book rooms and spend their vacations in his hotel and casino. Semi-nude dancers were still seen in the MEN ONLY section of the casino, but a new 40 room addition now had its own stage, and booked only the professional acts that toured the western casinos and advertised themselves as fully dressed professional dancers and actors.

The other casino owners in Carson City laughed when told that Ian McKannah was advertising in newspapers throughout the western cities that his stageshows were designed to entertain entire families. Inside information let Ian know that a railroad to Carson City was inevitable in the very near future, so he began planning to accommodate larger crowds—entire families.

Stagecoach companies were quickly created that cut the trip to Carson City down to a 48 hour ride by changing horses and drivers four times. It not only kept the passengers anticipating a good hot meal stop, but also a brief period to walk out the kinks while their drivers and horses were being changed.

Ian met with these companies and offered to subsidize the coach fare for families who stayed at his resort for one full, seven-day week.

When his new addition began filling with families who were taken on tours through Indian villages, gold mining camps, and roaming buffalo herds aboard custom-built carriages driven by knowledgeable guides and guarded by reliable men on Ian McKannahs payroll, the other casino operators began offering a variety of gimmicks, but Ian's imaginative mind had gotten a big jump on them—they would still be trying to catch up when he retired many years later.

The casino and the Family-Fun addition, which is what the new section became known as, were full and running smoothly when the boy from the telegraph office rode in and stopped at the casino with a telegram for Ian. Ian asked the boy to wait while he read it, so if an immediate answer was needed he could send it with him.

After reading the telegram he handed the boy a coin and thanked him. "Stoop," Ian called when he saw his black friend and all-around man enter the front patio where the boy had delivered the telegram, "do you have a spare minute?" The tall Bahamian had been with him for many years and now occupied a position of absolute trust with Ian. He ducked under the rose arch that few heads ever came closer than a few inches, and headed toward Ian. "Yessir boss, sure do, what's up?"

Ian handed the telegram to Stoop without saying a word. Stoop began reading to himself.

TO: Ian McKannah.
SUBJECT: Jesse.
FROM: Broderick McKannah.

Received telegram from Simon ... STOP ... Located Jesse ... STOP ... Simon is with him ... STOP ... Possible war zone ... STOP ... Time to close ranks ... STOP ... Leaving now for Flathead Lake in northern Montana ... STOP ... Beware when nearing small town of Burgess Montana ... OCCUPIED BY ENEMY ... STOP.

By sunset on the day the telegram arrived, Ian and his two men had four of the best horses hitched to the coach and were in the process of stocking it with everything needed for an extended trip.

Lon MacKandle and his brother Solomon had worked for Ian while he still owned the gambling casino near Five Points in New York City. When he sold it, many of his employees came west with him. Shea MacHue and Ian began working together in the San Francisco casino where Ian first began his gambling career, many years earlier. Shea also came west with Ian, but three years after Ian's new resort and casino were completed Shea MacHue suffered a heart attack and died soon after.

Lon and Solomon would share the driving and were also used to dealing with all manner of firearms, and were familiar with most, especially the pair of eight gauge double-barrel shotguns, one of which was carried in a scabbard up above.

Ian knew he was fortunate to have men like them and also a reliable man like Stoop who could manage every phase of the business during Ian's absence.

When everything was checked out and declared functional, Ian climbed in while his two men climbed up top. The brake was released and the reins lightly slapped the rumps of the horses. The coach rumbled smoothly through the gate as his Mexican foreman waved his sombrero, and then coaxed his palomino to nudge the gate closed.

Stoop had supervised the gathering of supplies needed for the trip to Montana, so when the coach pulled into the casino's loading area everything had been assembled and was ready to be loaded.

An hour later Ian shook Stoop's hand, "See you when we get back, amigo."

"Yes mon," Stoop replied, "I see to it dis place do juss like it posed to while you gone." He waved and watched as the coach rumbled off into the night.

Soon after leaving the casino, Lon and Solomon had the coach on the trail that Joseph Walker's expedition located in 1833 to get through the Sierra Nevada Range. Since then many wagon trains had used it, and as often happened the route was made more useable by the removal of large boulders and trees. Slight changes in the direction that the trail took were made by men with knowledge of the wilderness, and the many pioneers who followed them benefited enormously.

Ian knew that his two drivers were constantly talking to passing pioneers and were now using the knowledge they learned to make this trip as easy on the horses and coach as possible. When faced with doubt about the trail ahead they stopped the coach and locked the brake. While one scouted the trail ahead the other thoroughly checked the coach for needed maintenance. Ian always took the opportunity to stretch and then assist with maintenance of his coach. Ian would also relieve one of his men, which allowed him to rest while Ian either held the reins or the shotgun. Their system actually kept the three men reasonably well rested and alert during the long difficult trip across the rugged terrain in search of Ian's younger brother, Jesse.

Their rotating system paid off on the thirteenth day on the trail. Lon had the reins and Solomon held the shotgun as the coach rounded a huge boulder. The trail was well maintained all the way across the Yosemite Valley because many coaches and smaller groups of wagons used Walker's trail that Ian's men decided to use rather than Peter Ogden's trail, which cut north toward Fort Boise and was used primarily by large wagon trains.

No sooner had the coach rounded the boulder when Lon spotted three men a short distance ahead. He eased back on the reins as Solomon yanked a small rope that made a hinged paddle smack against the ceiling above Ian.

Ian's fast reflexes were still as good as ever, because his pistol was in his hand and cocked before the paddle hit the ceiling the third time.

Solomon didn't like the posture of the three men ahead and said to Lon in a calm voice, "Do not stop."

Lon gently slapped the reins against the horse's back to get them moving faster. Solomon had both hammers on the shotgun pulled back as they neared the three men standing shoulder to shoulder in the middle of the trail almost touching each other. Ian sat with his back forward and held a small mirror outside far enough to see what was in the trail ahead.

When it was obvious that the coach was not going to stop, the skeletal-thin man in the middle that had been holding his hand up, let it drop to a pistol in a leather holster at his side.

The men on each side of the skeleton also went for their own pistols, which were shoved behind their belted trousers.

The skeleton's gun was almost up and in the firing position when Ian's team of horses hit him head on. A second later Solomon's first barrel was only a short distance from the fat man whose gun's hammer had snagged against his shirt. The blast that hit him in the chest, they learned later, had also dislodged the hammer and allowed fatso's death-reflexes to pull the trigger and blow off most of one kneecap.

As his partners in their grand holdup scheme were dying, the bearded man was frantically trying to cock his old single-shot pistol when Ian put two bullets in his head.

Lon stopped the coach when it was out of pistol range. All three men surveyed the area and finally decided that there were no other bandits. "There are no others," Ian said, "or they've all hauled ass outa here."

"No wonder," Solomon said, as he replaced the spent shell with another load of buckshot, "after the reception we gave 'em." He leaned over to smile at Ian. "Rowdy buncha Micks we are, by Jesus."

Ian and Solomon walked back cautiously, each holding his gun ready. After determining that all three men were dead they pulled the skeleton out of the trail and headed back to the coach.

They enventually approached the area just beyond the Ruby Mountains where Walker's 1834 trail headed north and his other, the 1833 trail, headed toward the northern tip of the Great Salt Lake.

For some reason, something that Ian never figured out, he said they were going to take Fremont's new 1844 trail down around the southern tip of the Great Salt Lake and stop in the city to see if there was a telegram. "We'll get us a room and some fresh clothes while we are there." Ian smiled when both of them yelled loudly, **"Hell yes**."

Lon and Solomon took the coach to a livery they were told was at the far eastern end of the main street. Ian was told that there was usually someone at the telegraph office in the hotel a few doors down, so he headed that way to see if there was a telegram for him.

On the way to the hotel Ian passed a store that had a sign in the window. He read it to himself, *tinned fruit*. He entered and headed toward the counter where a gray-haired old man was wrapping something for a youngster. When the boy left the store

Ian asked about the tinned fruit. "Yessir," the old man said, "got peaches, pears, and apples."

"Let me see how big the tins are," Ian said, "so I know how many we have room for." The man reached beneath the counter and brought up a can that had PCH painted on top. "How much they cost?" Ian asked as he picked it up.

"You carrying gold?" the proprieter asked.

"We carry mostly silver coin to pay for what we need along the way," Ian replied, "but I always carry a wee bit o' the yellow stuff t'git what we need if silver won't do."

"Silver'll do just fine," the man said smiling, "so you just tell me what y'want n' I'll stack it on the counter and then tell ya how much silver it'll cost."

Ian left the store an hour later with a gunnysack slung over his shoulder. It was almost too heavy to carry, but the thought of tinned fruit lightened the load a bit.

A while earlier Solomon said, "Lon, let's go see if Ian needs some 'elp. We'll come back 'ere n' check on the 'orses later when we know 'ow long we'll be 'ere."

The two men found Ian entering the hotel with a sack over his shoulder. They sat in the lobby eating canned pears and peaches while Ian opened a door with a sign stating TELEGRAPH on it. A few minutes later he came out reading a telegram. After finishing it he looked first at Lon and then Solomon, but remained staring at Solomon for several long moments until he finally asked, "What's 'appenin, Ian?"

Ian shook his head slowly saying, "You were right all along, Sol."

"Ain't I always?" He replied with a grin. "But about what this time?"

"That was from Broderick." Ian glanced at the telegram again before looking up at Solomon and Lon. "He says don't go any further with the coach. 'E tried it n' 'ad t'come back n' get ridin 'orses n' saddles."

Both men had thought it was not practical when the trip was first planned and had talked between themselves. But knowing Ian so well they decided that he would have to try it anyway, regardless of any warnings from them.

Two days and several cans of fruit later, Ian had bought three good riding horses, tack, weather gear and ponchos for all three, plus a matched pair of pack-mules to carry the food and camp gear he also bought.

While the two men sorted through the new gear and decided how to pack it and the remaining cans of fruit on the mules, Ian made arrangements to board his horses and have the coach tended to and put in dry storage until they returned.

Jesse

The following day Jesse returned to the same office that he had stopped into when he was in Missoula to get the herd of cattle. Before going inside he pulled a piece of paper from his jacket's pocket. *Ben Brack, esq: Land Agent.* He returned it to his pocket and entered.

The same man he had spoken to earlier looked up from the desk he sat at writing in a ledger. He stood and came around to Jesse. With his hand out he said, "Mister McKannah, Ben Brack, glad to see you back so soon."

Jesse shook the man's hand as he spoke. "I've made up my mind to stay here, Ben, and forget all about California, so I'm gonna buy land before the price goes way up, like it did back there.

An hour later they were still standing in front of the huge map that covered an entire wall. "It's just a rough outline," Ben said, "but it's quite accurate, and it's only for sales purposes, because the actual land survey that was done a few months ago will determine exactly where the boundaries are."

"So this section," Jesse said as he moved the wooden pointer across the map, "borders the eastern side of the Flathead Indian Reservation and then goes east to the Swan River and north to Swan Lake's southern tip."

"Yes, Ben said, "and then your boundary runs north right to Swan Lake before cutting west to end at the very northern tip of Flathead Lake." He moved his pointer and then pulled it down through the center of the lake and stopped. "You'll own the eastern half of Flathead Lake, and your friends, the Flathead Indians, will own the western half."

"That's exactally what I want, Ben. Your new telegraph in operation yet?"

"Sure is. I sent several messages with it since last Monday when it was officially opened for use. It's just a trial, but I think it will speed business transactions significantly, and if it does then the men who are in charge of developing this area will see to it that the telegraph becomes an integral part of their efforts."

Jesse pulled a pad from his pocket and handed it to Ben. "My bank is in Yerb...I mean San Francisco," he grinned, "I keep forgetting that it's not Yerba Buena now." His brow wrinkled as he looked at the land agent, "How do you and the bank work it so the money will be sent here to pay for my land?"

"You give me your full name, something that few people will know, and then your account number. I'll send the telegram and when the bank has been notified, they'll send me a telegram to let me know that the money will be sent to our New York City office by ship or stage coach. My office will notify me when it arrives and I'll get a message to you at Michael O'Hannahan's Diner in Polson. You can then come up here and pick up your deed to the land." He smiled, "Pretty easy and very efficient."

Jesse shook his head slightly, saying with a grin, "Sure is, and it causes me to wonder just what's comin next into this wilderness?"

"I can tell you the answer to that, Jesse, the railroad. There's already talk about a railroad straight across this country to link the west coast with New York City."

Jesse laughed before asking, "Y'ever been across the Rocky Mountains, Ben?"

"Nope, spent most of my life back east in New York City after I left Harvard."

"Well, Ben, I can assure you that we'll both be in our graves a long time before they figure out how to get them trains over the mountains."

"I don't know, Jesse, seems like everything is moving ahead faster than I would have thought possible just a short time ago."

"I can tell you one thing that ain't movin very fast, Ben, those Rockies. I reckon the fellas running stagecoach lines are gonna be busy carrying folks east and west for a hundred years or so before them railroad folks figure out how to get over those high mountains."

Ben walked around his old desk to the new teletype. "Well, Jesse you're probably right, but nothing surprises me any more about progress." He looked up at Jesse, "Wanna watch me send this telegraph?"

"Yeah, is that funny lookin thing it?"

"Yep, this's what I meant by progress. It's the very latest one that they're trying out here in the west. It's called a European Camelback Key," he pointed to the arching metal that had the sending key on the end. "I had to close up here and go to school in Helena to learn how to use it." He laid the paper that Jesse had just given him in front of the odd looking little rig. "Jesse Devon McKannah, correct?"

"Yep."

"And you're absolutely certain Mister McKannah, that this is the correct account number?"

"Only one I got."

"Okay, here we go." Jesse was very impressed at how fast the man's finger pressed the key up and down. Thirty minutes later Ben shoved his chair back and looked at his fingertips, "Phewee, that was the longest telegram I've sent. Had to relay all the info about the land parcel's two hundred and thirty thousand acres including half of the lake and all of those preliminary survey markers, so there's no problem later in case people have been squatting on the land."

"What'll happen to 'em if there are some folks that've been livin on m'land?"

"They'll be notified that they'll have to move off it."

"That won't be until after I actually own the land, right?"

"Yes."

"Don't notify anyone you learn about that's livin on land that belongs to me. Notify me and then I'll talk to 'em. Might be som'n we can work out to let 'em stay there."

The land agent looked at Jesse for a very long moment before speaking. "Well, Mister McKannah, that land'll be yours to do with as you see fit," he coughed to clear his throat and paused momentarily when he realized that Jesse was staring at him through unblinkling, cold hard eyes, "but I, uh, feel it's my duty to warn you that something like that could get out of hand very quickly."

"Ben, just do your job and get that land in my name as quick as you can and let me worry about the folks that might be living on my land, and if there are some, what I might work out with 'em," Jesse's eyes narrowed, "okay?"

The small frail land agent's words caught in his throat as he tried to answer. After a cough and another pause, he said quietly "Uh, yessir, Mister McKannah. I'll do my very best to have everything settled soon." A weak nervous smile followed, "And I'll see to it that you're notified promptly so you can come on up and finalize the paperwork."

"Good." Jesse turned and headed toward the door, but he stopped and faced the nervous little man. "Ben, I keep all of my business dealings to m'self, and I don't wanna hear about this transaction from anyone except you, understood?"

The tomahawk, large knife, and revolver on his belt, plus the small pistol in the shoulder holster had been covered by the long coat that he unbuttoned when he first stepped into the cool room. But when Jesse turned it fell open slightly and Ben now saw the entire arsenal that included the revolver's long barrel protruding from the leather holster on the wide leather belt. Nearly everyone he had dealt with after being transferred from New York City to Missoula Montana carried or wore a gun, so it didn't concern him. Now however, after seeing the weaponry carried by this lone man standing before him, he found it difficult to maintain eye contact.

"Always maintain direct eye contact with any customer."

That salesman's 'tool' was stressed by every professor in all of the Harvard sales courses he had taken concerning sales and business dealings with the public.

He now stammered badly and his weak voice, once it found its way out of his pinched mouth, squeaked like a panicked mouse confronting his first tomcat. "I, uh, I'll, I'll, uh, will do, uuuh, my very best, uh, Mister McKannah."

Jesse stared hard at the pitiful little man's reddening face for a moment, and then smiled, "Can't ask for more'n that, Ben. I'll be seein ya soon."

During the trip to Missoula to get the herd of cattle, Jesse had to inquire where the land office he'd heard about was located. One of the places he'd stopped in was a restaurant specializing in German food. He'd eaten in one when he was buying supplies in San Francisco and enjoyed the food very much. The noon lunch hour was still a couple of hours away, so when he stepped into the restaurant he was the only customer.

After placing his leather hat on the stool beside him, Jesse laid his forearms on the counter and looked around at the fancy drinking vessels sitting on a shelf that went all the way around the ceiling. When he heard the door to the kitchen open he turned back to see a tall stout woman wearing a colorful apron over an even more colorful dress. Her hair was done in braids so carefully that there didn't appear to be one hair out of place.

Her smile was sincere and friendly. "Guten tag," it widened, "means good day in my language. You have eat German food before?"

"Yes, and I enjoyed it."

"Vo...oops, I forget that we serve mostly German people and I must remember to use English, where did you dine on German food?"

"In Yerba Buena before they renamed it San Francisco. I had a great dinner and I don't remember what it was called, but the thing I do remember is a big potato dumpling called a noodle, or nerdle, or som'n like that, and it was delicious."

"Kartoffel knodel."

"Yeah," Jesse said enthusiastically, "that's what I think it was called."

"Potato dumpling," she said. "It serve in thin broth?"

"Sure was, and I can still remember that it tasted just like my mother's chicken soup."

She liked the tall enthusiastic man. "What your name?"

"Jesse McKannah." He held out his hand.

She took it and replied, "Gunhilde Geisinger." Her kind blue eyes sparkled as she asked, "How hungry you are, Chessie?"

He grinned, "Half a cow or a whole hog hungry. Ain't had no time t'git a real meal for a few days."

He sipped coffee as she worked in the kitchen, only peeking in to reassure him that his meal was progressing.

Half an hour later she brought a bowl and placed it in front of him. It made his stomach rumble. It was a chicken broth that had a large potato dumpling in the middle, and another plate with two big thick slices of fresh jet-black pumpernickel bread. "Eat," she said, "I be back with more food."

Jesse sliced the dumpling and chewed on it a moment before spooning in some of the broth. After swallowing he closed his eyes for a moment and took a deep satisfying breath before attacking the dumpling. He laid the spoon down and picked up the bowl to finish off the broth.

Hilde's big arm was loaded when she said, "Wienerschnitzel" and grinned when Jesse moved the bowl so she could place the plate in front of him, "veal cutlet, red cabbage, und kase-spatzle." She frowned for a brief moment and then grinned again, "Kase-spatzle is cheese-noodle. I make them fresh every morning before open for customer." She turned to the coffeepot, "More?" She picked up his cup when Jesse nodded.

After swallowing, he said, "Gun...uh...

She smiled, "Juss, Hilde ist okay, Chessie."

"Hilde, this is even better than that German dinner I had in San Francisco, and it was pretty darn good."

"Gute...ah, good. I go in kitchen now to work. You finish, yell for me und I get you apfel-kuchen...ah, umm, apple pastry."

Through a mouthful he mumbled, "I'll save room for it."

He ate the dessert and paid for the meal then said, "Hilde, that was as good a meal as ever I had, and every time I come back down to Missoula I'll stop by for another one."

"Gute," she grinned self-consciously, "ah, good. You fine me here seven days every week."

Before high noon Jesse was walking Shadow out of Missoula toward Polson. His mind had been on the land he just bought, but as he entered the forest, Jesse's mind severed all thoughts except those concerned with the wilderness he was entering and the dangers he might encounter therein.

~

"That's him, Geoff." Jiggs moved the telescope and looked at his partner, "Leavin at noon like he is, I reckon he'll be lookin for a place to rest just about where I tole ya we can jump 'im."

"Let him get ahead of us a good ways," Geoff said as he kept the telescope on Jesse, "but this time don't let him get ahead so far that he can slip off the trail like he did."

Jiggs glanced back at him but kept his mouth shut, *damn fool couldn't track a gutshot moose across a prairie, but he's gotta tell me how t'do it.*

The two killers let Jesse get a half mile ahead before they got on his trail and followed.

The thin slice of moon offered little light as Geoff and Jiggs rode cautiously through the dark forest. Half an hour later Jiggs held out his hand and stopped Geoff. "What," Geoff whispered.

Jiggs was pulling the telescope from his saddlebag, so didn't answer until he had it up to his eye. "That squaw man's already got a small fire agoin, so won't be no trouble sneakin in n' earnin thet gold what ole man Kellerman promised us."

Geoff said softly, "Let's give him time to get comfortable and asleep fore we go in."

Jiggs had the telescope back to his eye as he thought, *mebbe we should go galloping in n' see if he'll invite us t'dinner.* He shook his head in the darkness, *how'd I ever git involved with this stupid damned idjut?*

Jesse's fire had burned down to a small pile of glowing coals by the time Geoff and Jiggs slipped silently into the cover of trees surrounding his camp.

The two men stood motionless, each peering cautiously at the sleeping man from behind a tree. Geoff used the barrel of his old cavalry pistol to motion at Jiggs, who also had his revolver in hand. It was a Colt similar to the one Jesse carried, and a better weapon than Geoff now held pointing at the hat covering their sleeping quarry's head.

After carefully stepping into the clearing, Jiggs motioned to Geoff with his pistol's long barrel. Geoff looked at the horse that stood at the edge of the cleared area, its eyes fixed on Geoff and his long ears lying back, almost flat against his head. *That horse is hobbled, so he can't run when we shoot this squaw man. I'll use him to carry the saddle back to town, and then I'll sell him and keep that fancy saddle. To hell with Burgess Kellerman,* he thought with disgust, *I ain't givin that big windbag none of this shit.* He glanced at Jiggs, *I might juss shoot him n' tell Kellerman thet he run off skeered.*

Geoff's eyes were on the sleeping man, but his thoughts were about Jiggs, *Betcha he's gonna try to take that nice pistol for hisself. Yeah, I'll reload and shoot him too.* He watched as Jiggs raised the barrel and pointed it at the hat. Geoff raised his too and pointed it where he figured the man's neck would be.

As Jiggs leaned forward and began putting pressure on the trigger. Geoff did the same. When the loud explosion was still ringing in his ears, Geoff heard a second explosion. He turned a bit and saw Jiggs' body being slammed to the ground as though a gigantic hand had come crashing down on him. For a brief split moment Geoff was confused, but before his slow mind could sort it all out, a third explosion took off his hat, which was filled with part of his small brain.

Jesse stepped out into the clearing after he had revolved the

Colt's cylinder to align a fresh cartridge with the long barrel. He looked at the two men a moment before picking up his hat. Poking a finger through the bullet hole, he just shook his head. After gathering his horse blanket and canvas poncho he dropped the poncho near Shadow, then saddled the horse. Climbing tiredly into the saddle, he glanced again at the two cadavers, *two less worthless men to be taking up space that good honest men can use.*

Jesse rode to their horses and removed the hobbles, and then took the bridles off and tied them to the saddle horn. After smacking them both on the rump with a switch to get them moving, he nudged Shadow, saying softly, "Might's well head on home cause ain't no way I'd sleep tonight."

~

After explaining his land purchase to Lame Wolverine, Jesse put his coffee cup down and turned toward the lake behind them. "I had been thinking about my land back in California, but since I came back here to be with your people," his emotions produced a shy grin, "our people, I decided this is where I plan to stay." He turned back to his friend, "This part of the country is still wild and undeveloped, sorta like California was when I was a kid. But after the gold peters out I'm sure a lotta the people are gonna stay there, or come back once they see how things have changed back home, wherever they came from." Jesse scanned the terrain, "We sometimes gotta lose som'n t'make us realize how much we really loved it," he paused to look deeply into his friend's eyes, "or them. I'd give all the gold I got and all I'll get till it's gone, if I could have Rose and my sister Aleena back."

Aleena

Aleena had gained back all of her strength and felt as though she had been reborn as she marched along the trail leading north toward where her brother, Jesse, lived with his Indian friends.

Chief Bonesetter was aware that the Blackfoot Indians, their immortal enemy, was known to roam as far south as Flathead Lake, and had been observed one time by trappers as far south as the valley they were now in.

He called his head scout and told him to have his braves do a thorough search of the surrounding area to determine if there were signs of other people, especially the Blackfoot. "Go out," the chief said, "three miles in every direction. If there are fresh tracks of any kind we will continue ahead, but with greater caution. I will stop here to give the old ones a rest, and will also tell my war chief to position his braves on the outer perimeter."

Without a word or hesitation the stout middle-aged Chief of Scouts trotted off to get his horse while sending out the trilling sounds that would alert his men and bring them to him.

Chief Bonesetter's alert eyes watched as two dozen young scouts gathered around their leader, Eye of Hawk. Two minutes later the young scouts had paired off and were moving out away from the tribe as though following the spokes of a huge wagon. Chief Bonesetter nodded his head in satisfaction and headed toward Aleena.

"You sent out the scouts?" Aleena asked.

The chief stopped in front of her. "Yes, but not because I have seen something," he smiled at his new white friend, "I just have a hunch. Blackfoot warriors," he continued, "have been seen in this valley, because there is an abundance of deer and it's not too far from their camps in Canada."

"Is that why you asked the other two larger tribes to join us on this trip to where my brother is?"

"Yes," the chief said, "but also because I've known for some time that both of those tribes are also struggling and together we can all do better, plus I can provide them with better medical service. If the tribe where your brother is will agree to it we will join them and become even stronger."

"Oh," Aleena said, "I would really love that, because I have made such good friends among your people, Doctor Caruthers."

He smiled warmly at Aleena, "And they have learned that you are a good friend to The People by the way you have gathered the young ones to you and have taught them words in English that will help them understand white people better in the coming years as we merge together."

Aleena smiled, "I have never taught young people so anxious to learn. Not just a new language but everything. They all want to learn about mathematics, geography, history," she spread her long gangly arms wide, "they just want to learn, learn, learn."

"Perhaps," the chief said in a sincere voice, "you can create a school and teach the young how to better understand the new future they will be facing." He paused a brief moment to look out across his tribe before adding, "And to understand more about white people so the tensions between them will be less with each generation."

She placed her hand on the old Indian's shoulder, "You are such a wise man, Doctor Caruthers. It is inevitable that there will be more and more white people coming west as this new country grows, and as sad as it is there will be less and less Indians."

He had been looking directly at her as she spoke, and now shook his grey haired head up and down slowly. "I began several years ago telling my people that the white people are here to stay and that they all must learn to get along with them and to try and understand all of the ways they do things because they are much different than how we do many of the same things."

"Yes," Aleena agreed, nodding her head, "my people are not blessed with patience or tolerance of other people's habits and methods of doing things, so it will be the responsibility of your people to adapt to the white man's ways."

An hour later the scouts began returning two-by-two, and ten minutes later they were all accounted for. Chief Bonesetter leaned against a shade tree and listened to the scouts sitting in a semi-circle in front of him.

"There are signs that Blackfoot warriors have recently been in this valley." The old chief looked down at the young scout and nodded his head slightly. The scout beside him that had been a short distance away when the young Indian saw the sign, spoke.

"Yes my chief, there were nine warriors riding ponies, but we saw no sign that they had extra ponies to carry meat.

The chief's brow furrowed momentarily, and then he said, "Sounds like Blackfoot scouts are moving through this area to see how many Flatheads and white men are here."

"Should we continue tracking them?" The leader of the scouts spoke and then remained silent until his chief had time to think about what he'd said.

"No," Chief Bonesetter finally stood and answered, "I have been in council with the chiefs of the other tribes that joined us, and we all agree that it is in the best interest of this new large tribe to continue on toward Flathead Lake. You and your scouts plus those from the other tribes must continue to keep our perimeter under watch as the tribe moves ahead. In the event we are attacked by Blackfoot warriors you will be nearby to aid us."

Without a word the Chief of Scouts stood and walked toward his horse while sending out the trilling whistle that would summon his braves and the scouts from the other tribes that had joined them.

Chief Bonesetter rode through the huge encampment calling out a command in his loud voice and the tribe began preparing to move ahead. Only an hour later more than four hundred and fifty people, including Aleena, marched ahead surrounding forty travois rigs being pulled by the stoutest horses the tribes had. They carried their tepee coverings and poles, plus all the elderly and the children too young to walk. Simon was on Dragon, following in the rear and constantly scanning behind.

When they crossed Jedediah Smith's 1829 trail that Chief Bonesetter knew would lead them to the northeastern corner of Flathead Lake, he led his tribe deeper into the valley.

~

While Chief Bonesetter was closing the twenty mile gap between his tribe and Lame Wolverine's people camped near the lake, scouts rode into camp and stopped at Lame Wolverine's tepee.

Jesse had been listening to his friend reminisce about the buffalo hunts when the scouts rode up. His friend stood and approached the brave still sitting astraddle the small horse.

"Hola," the chief said loudly, "what new information does my Chief of Scouts bring?"

"There are Blackfoot braves in the valley," he pointed south, "on the other side of Fat Woman Walks Mountain."

Chief Lame Wolverine remained silent for a moment, but then spoke with severity, "Assemble your men and tell them to use extreme caution not to be observed, but when you find those Blackfoot again observe them at close range and determine what they're up to."

"We will do as you command, my chief."

"I had the same dream two nights in a row." He looked off into the distance beyond the mountains between his camp and the valley that Chief Bonesetter was traveling through. "A large camp of Blackfoot across those mountains to the north of us was dancing and putting on war paint."

Jesse saw the expression on the scouts's face and understood why he was concerned. Lame Wolverine's dreams had often been a glimpse of events to come true.

Before the scout could swing his horse around and go to his men, Lame Wolverine spoke again, "I have already ordered all braves to carry a full pouch of arrows and I told those who have guns to carry them, and to have good ammunition at all times until further notice." He patted the scout's horse on the side of the neck and added, "If the Blackfoot come to attack us they will not find a sleeping village. We will be prepared."

"We will return with the information you seek as quickly as we can, my chief."

Lame Wolverine heard the trilling signals that would call his men as his head scout rode away. Jesse walked to him and spoke quietly, "Too Tall is a good scout and will soon return to let us know what those Blackfoot are doing."

"Yes," the chief said, still watching the scout, "he was a good tracker even before he was big enough to mount a pony."

By noon the following day Too Tall and his scouts had covered over twenty miles and were well spread out across the valley searching for tracks that would indicate where the Blackfoot were.

An hour later they were gathered together and following Blackfoot tracks heading south. One mile along the trail and their tracks turned east then headed into the mountains.

Too Tall sent out trilling signals that his scouts heard and mimicked, so they'd reach the next pair of scouts. Half an hour later the last pair galloped into the temporary camp where the others sat drinking sasafrass tea and chewing dried venison.

This last pair had been farther south than the rest, and told Too Tall about a large tribe of Flathead Indians they had seen. "We decided to come quickly and tell you about them."

"That is good thinking Quiet Wolf," Too Tall said, "because we still do not know what those Blackfoot are planning to do." He paused a moment to think. Still looking into his scout's eyes he said, "Are you two able to head right back to that tribe of our people?"

"Yes," both men spoke almost simultaneously.

"Get some food in you to keep your strength up, and then ride swiftly to them. I will send two scouts back to our camp to tell Chief Lame Wolverine about the Flathead tribe that is now heading toward us up the valley, and the rest of us will track the Blackfoot.

When the two scouts returned with the news that a large tribe of their people were heading toward them, Lame Wolverine said, "I will choose fifty warriors to go back with you. Lead them to the tribe so they can help the Flatheads if there are more Blackfoot than we are aware of. If you come to more of our scouts tell them to go with you to the travelers and help if there is trouble, but now go to my lodge, and Gentle Breeze will feed you both before leaving.

The two young scouts rode off to get a hot meal. The chief, accompanied by Jesse, mounted their horses and went to locate the warriors that would go with the scouts. Less than half an hour later the two scouts left camp followed by fifty warriors and Jesse, who insisted that he go along to help his people.

Lame Wolverine stood with Gentle Breeze and watched them head toward the south pass through the mountains that would lead them to the valley.

"If all white men were like him we would all be living better." He spoke softly, but loud enough that his wife heard.

Gentle Breeze touched his hand and said softly, "All men wise like you and everyone have full belly and good life."

Patrick

Patrick, his two men, and Aldo were completely exhausted when their coach finally came to a full stop inside of James Buchanan's campaign compound. Patrick had been in the new nation's capitol once before when he and his brother Broderick were studying law at Harvard, but it was a new experience for Aldo Calaveras and the two Kavanaugh brothers.

Patrick was immediately taken inside and introduced to Joseph Alderman, Mr. Buchanan's campaign coordinator. After shaking hands with Patrick, he explained why Mr. Buchanan wasn't able to be there to personally thank him. "Mister McKannah, we are all very grateful to you for coming all the way from California to take charge of this campaign for his final bid to be elected President of the United States. He has been working out of this compound for a month, and has also been living here, hoping to be able to meet the arrival of your coach himself, but a republican debate was scheduled in Baltimore that he had to attend. I put him on the B & O rail line myself along with two aides and a Pinkerton bodyguard."

Before the man could continue, Patrick smiled to set him at ease, and then said, "Mister Alderman, my men and I are all so exhausted that it would have been a waste of time for anyone to have gone out of their way to meet us." He turned toward his men, who were watching as six black men from the livery stable unhitch the horses. "I can hardly believe my eyes when I see those two men of mine watching as others tend to the horses and coach, because they've been with me for over twenty years and it has never before happened." He gave the man a tired smile before continuing, "That's a very good indication of how tired we all are."

"Twenty years with you, huh." He nodded his head slowly up and down, "Says a lot for them and you, Mister McKannah."

"Twenty-two for the Kavanaugh brothers I believe, Mister Alderman, and Aldo Calaveras, my personal aide and assistant has been with me eleven years." Through a tired smile he added, "And from here on it's just Joseph and Patrick."

The tall thin man smiled and pointed at a huge ornate door on a covered porch of the gigantic two-story house at the rear of the compound, "Let's get your men and go look at the rooms we've set aside for you, and while you bathe I'll have the chef send food to your rooms so you can get some needed sleep after eating."

Patrick glanced up at the western horizon that the sun was rapidly approaching. "Joseph, that sounds great, and by the looks of the low sun in that sky," he smiled and looked at the sun almost touching the trees in the distance, "I doubt you'll see any of us again until tomorrow."

The next morning at a little past seven, Patrick was shaving when he heard noise in the adjoining room. When he finished, Patrick went into the hall and tapped lightly on the door, "You up, Aldo?"

The door opened and a smiling Aldo stood there. "Up and I can't wait to get a cup of coffee in my hand."

Patrick nodded at the door on the other side of his, "I'll see if the boys're ready for breakfast?"

Aldo pulled the door to his room closed saying over his shoulder, "I'll be on the front steps sucking in some of this fresh morning air."

Patrick went to the other door and knocked. A completely dressed Seamus opened the door, "We thought you were gonna sleep the day away, Patrick." He grinned, "We've not made a sound since dawn for fear o' wakin you."

Kenneth opened the bathroom door and stepped into the living room. "We've not made a sound since dawn, because until thirty minutes ago we've both been sound asleep."

"By Jesus," Seamus exclaimed, "times flies doesn't it, seems like we've been up for hours." He grinned again as his stomach growled.

Kenneth nodded at his brother's stomach, "An we'd both be still sawin logs if not for that built-in alarm clock 'e has be'ind 'is bellybutton."

After a breakfast that would fill eight normal men, Patrick said, "You fellas check on the coach and gather up everything of any value and stash it in our rooms," his eyebrows raised and he smiled, "we're back in civilation now. I'll tell Joseph that we'll be seeing the city today." Aldo followed Patrick out the door.

Three days later James Buchanan's private coach pulled in about an hour before dark. Joseph Alderman had received a telegram at noon letting him know that he would arrive before dark and was looking forward to dining with Patrick. Joseph had sent him a telegram from Baltimore as soon as Patrick and his men were settled into their rooms.

Joseph Alderman had the chef prepare dinner for the four of them, so he and James could bring Patrick up to date on their campaign plans.

Patrick handed Seamus and Kenneth each a small roll of money to enjoy a night out while he and Aldo dined with his friend. It didn't surprise Patrick in the slightest when the older Kavanaugh, Kenneth, pulled out one bill and handed the rest back, saying, "I reckon this'll get me all the grog n' sausage I need at McElroy's Pub a short walk down the street, but thank you anyway." He was not surprised to see his brother, Seamus, do the exact same.

Before they turned to head toward the pub they had found the second day, Kenneth said, "Patrick, you'll be able t'do a better job of gettin your friend into the White House if you know that we'll always be but a shout away. I've already let everyone in this compound know that when we're not 'ere, then we'll be playin cards or tossin darts wi' the boys at McElroy's." He motioned with chin toward Patrick, "Go do wha' y'do best and we'll be available to follow your orders, whatever they be." He noded at Aldo and said, "We'll see you fellas at breakfast."

Patrick stood watching as the two men headed south on the boardwalk. He replaced the bills with the rest and then shoved the leather pouch back into the inside pocket of his coat. Smiling to himself he walked toward the entrance to the dining room. *I'm a very lucky man to have two loyal men like that beside me.*

Walking beside him, Aldo said quietly, "No man could ask for better men than those two."

Patrick grinned, "I do believe you're learning to read my mind, Aldo." His friend just smiled.

~

Two weeks later, Patrick returned to the campaign headquarters with Aldo, Joseph Alderman and Mr. Buchanan. Kenneth was heading toward his room, but changed course when he spotted the coach pull in. He arrived as a fourth man climbed out.

"Kenneth," Patrick said, "I'd like you t'meet Devin Quinn," he nodded toward the tall dapper man beside him, "he's with the Pinkerton Detective Agency."

After shaking the man's hand, Kenneth asked, "Are you n' your boys gonna be lookin out for Patrick t'see nothin 'appens to 'im?"

"Yes," the man replied with a friendly smile, "me and six highly trained men are gonna do our very best to see that not only Mister McKannah comes through this campaign safely and in one piece, but also Mister Buchannan as well."

"Good t'ear that," Kenneth commented as his head nodded up and down, "I've 'eard that you fellas are good at whacha do, n' don't pussyfoot around."

"I appreciate the compliment Mister Kavanaugh."

Kenneth's brow furrowed a bit at hearing his last name. He turned when the Pinkerton agent said, "Here comes one of my men now." He nodded with his chin.

Kenneth looked at the man and then turned back to the agent. "I been tossin the darts wi' that fella all week down at McElroy's." He grinned when the muscular young man joined them. "I like yer style very much, Quinn. Take nothin fer granted n' check out everyone."

"Even grandma whenever we think it's necessary," the agent answered with a wide grin.

"Good." Kenneth looked at Patrick, "I reckon you're in purdy good hands, boss."

"Kenneth," Patrick said, "I've told Devin about the run-ins we had with some of the crud along the trail to here, and he's convinced that you and Seamus will be an asset to have along during the campaign." He smiled when he added, "You boys game?"

"Does a Pommy piss into the wind?"

"Good, where's Seamus?"

"Still at McElroy's tossin darts," he nodded toward the agent and grinned, "probably wi' one o' his men."

"He is." Devin Quinn grinned.

Later that same evening, Patrick and his three men joined the Pinkerton agent and his six hand-picked men; two of which the Kavanaugh brothers knew quite well by now. To remain as low key as was possible under the circumstances, they dined in the campaign headquarters cafeteria.

After getting acquainted through small talk and stories about their lengthy trip from the west coast, Devin nodded toward one of his agents. "Detective Cronin suggested that we supply you three men with the latest Colt revolver and holster, and then give you men some training." He turned to look at Kenneth, then Seamus, and Aldo. "Would that be agreeable with you fellas?"

Aldo spoke first. "I would certainly enjoy some tutoring by a professional, but the pistol that Patrick supplied me with a long time ago," he patted his left armpit, "feels like a part of my anatomy after these many years."

After a brief pause Kenneth said, "Sure! If we're gonna be in the area where Patrick's promotin 'is plan t'git Mr. Buchanan elected then we oughta blend in n' 'elp keep an eye out f'trouble."

"I think," Seamus added, "it's a good idea, and we'll certainly need a bit o' training t'get used to 'em," he grinned, "since the common shotgun is all we've used, and even a Pom can 'andle one o' those as long as the barrel is painted white so 'e don't point the wrong end at the enemy."

"No problem atol, Seamus. Detective Homeier," he laughed, "the man you've been tossing darts with all week is also the Pinkerton Agency's leading weapons expert." His Irish eyes had a twinkle when he added, "He's also a Pommy."

"Oh damn," Seamus said with a grin.

Devin laughed, "He came here from London as an infant with his mum n' pop, who had moved there from Limerick to find work."

The small, almost delicate, middle-aged man with grey hair chuckled then spoke softly, "If Seamus' brother is as adept with darts as he is then I seriously doubt it'll require more than a day at the gun range downstairs to get them used to working with a pistol instead of a shotgun."

"You'll 'ave no problem there," Seamus said, "that old man is still able t'pin me arse t'the board regularly."

"Tryin praise again, 'e is," Kenneth said, "t'git 'imself a slight edge." He shook his head and grinned, "Y'would think a bright fella like 'im woulda learned by now, eh."

"Settled then," Devin said, "we'll stop by the new Colt store right here in the Capitol tomorrow and pick up a couple of pistols and plenty of ammo for practice. The best leather man I've yet used is at a farm about ten miles from here, so once we have the pistols we'll ride out there and get you boys fitted." He turned to Aldo, "You can get all the ammo you need while we're there.

Aldo smiled, "Patrick and I make our own, but thank you just the same."

Devin's eyebrows went up and he just shook his head.

That same evening all of the men got to know each other better over several pitchers of cold draft beer. They mutually agreed to call it a night by eleven o'clock and headed toward their individual sleeping quarters.

By noon the following day Devin and the two Kavanaugh brothers were in the Pinkerton private coach heading toward the farm of the man who had made holsters for the Pinkertons since they put an office in the nation's capitol. Rumors had spread that William McCoo, this leathersmith, had also made a custom holster for James Butler Hickok three years earlier when the soon-to-be legendary lawman that became known as Wild Bill, was only fifteen years old. When Detective Devin Quinn heard that, he located the old man and had him custom design a new holster for him. Since then many detectives who joined the firm had their holsters and even saddles made by McCoo.

The leathersmith took all of the measurements needed to make a custom-fit holster for Kenneth and Seamus. Three days later the two brothers rode horses loaned to them by Ian McElroy, the pub owner, to pick up their new holsters. By this time both men were familiar with their new Colt Model 1855 sidehammer revolvers. They were available in 28 & 31 caliber and offered three barrel lengths, 3½, 4, and 4½ inch. Both men decided that the larger caliber with the shortest barrel would best suit their needs.

They fired more than fifty of the paper-cartridge-wrapped bullets, and after only a few, both men were hitting what they aimed at. When they returned to the indoor firing range with

Lon Homeier to become accustomed to the new holsters, they listened intently when he demonstrated how to make their own precision paper cartridges. "I picked up these loading kits for you. It'll allow you to carefully measure the amount of gunpowder, and there are also over one hundred papers soaked in potassium nitrate, plus a hundred lead slugs."

After demonstrating the paper-cartridge-making process, the agent watched carefully as both men used the wooden dowel to wrap the paper around the lead slug, and then carefully measure the amount of gunpowder to go into the paper shell.

Homeier was impressed when both men ignored the boxes of factory-made paper cartridges and carefully made their own. After filling the five holes in their cylinders and firing at the targets many times, he knew they were both men that he could rely on to be ready at all times and handle whatever came up. He later relayed that information to his boss, Devin Quinn.

After the brothers left the firing range to shower and dress for dinner at McElroy's Pub, Homeier turned to Aldo who was in the process of cleaning his weapon. "You're quite a marksman, Mister Calaveras. Been shooting all your life?"

"Never fired a gun," Aldo said looking up from his pistol, "until I went to work for Mister McKannah."

"I've noticed that he's not self-conscious about the shoulder-holster, as many who wear one are. I assume that he's also very good with the pistol in it."

"The best I've ever seen," Aldo replied matter-of-factly.

Both men completed what they were doing and headed toward the stairs. On the way up Homeier said, "Aldo, now that I've seen how all of you handle your weapon, and shoot with a deadly accurate aim, I feel much better concerning the safety of Mister Buchanan."

Aldo waited at the top until Homeier locked the door leading down to the indoor shooting range. He then said, "We all plan to do everything we can to see to it that we all come through this alive." He smiled and held out his hand, "Thank you for all that you've taught me and the Kavanaugh brothers, might save a life or two."

"That's m'job, Aldo." He shook his hand, "Good night."

"See you tomorrow."

Simon

A few weeks before Broderick and his two men headed north in the coach to locate Jesse, Simon was on Dragon and steadily moving northward toward Traveler's Rest. He had made a brief stop in Salt Lake City for supplies to carry him into northern Montana, where trappers had told him Jesse was living with a tribe of Flathead Indians.

While browsing through the dry goods and supplies in Emil Gustafson's Mercantile Store, Simon heard the now-familiar name Kellerman.

He slowly worked his way toward the two men that were talking about cattle. Simon lifted up a pair of leather gloves and tried them on as the two men talked. After hearing the name Burgess Kellerman again, he replaced the gloves and walked toward them. Bringing out his badge, he introduced himself. "I'm Texas Ranger, Simon McKannah, and I've been tracking a fella that killed one of our rangers a while back. What I've been able to learn so far about a man named Burgess Kellerman makes me think he's probably the killer." Simon looked intently at each man before speaking again.

"I couldn't help overhearing, when one of you mentioned the name Kellerman. Did either of you men speak to him when he stopped here?"

"We both did," the shorter of the two said.

"Yeah," the other man offered, "kept telling us about this big herd of cattle he was gonna put together in a town north of here in Montana, over east of Idaho a ways. Said he started the town hisself a few years ago and named it Burgess."

"Big bag o' hot air," the short man said, "I bet he didn't have enough coin in his pocket to jingle. Never saw him buy a drink, but he never turned down one he was offered, neither." The tall thin man in bib overalls waved his arm as though dismissing someone, "Big bag o' Texas hot air if y'ask me."

"How about describing him to me," Simon said. "We'll all go to that saloon I saw next door, and I'll set you boys up a round o' drinks."

After a second round of whiskey was put on the bar in front of the two men, the tall thin one asked, "You don't drink likker?"

"Not when I'm tracking a polecat. Puts a slight curve in my aiming eye and I like t'hit what I aim at."

"Well," the short one said with a grin, "reckon I'd feel the same if I was a lawman, but I don't even carry a gun, so here's to you." With that he bolted down the shot of rye.

After listening while the two older men took turns describing Burgess, Simon returned to the mercantile store to get a couple of things that he'd forgotten, and then headed toward the stables. He felt a bit better now that he had a good description of Kellerman.

Broderick

Since pulling out of Salt Lake City they regularly alternated one man down into the stagecoach's compartment so he could rest. Broderick's coach was making remarkable time, and even though he knew that Liam and Aidan were expert teamsters that could feel their horse's moods concerning the trail through the reins, Broderick still had an uneasy feeling that crossing the mountains in a coach was asking for trouble.

Their knowledge of horses, he thought, *allows them to be prepared for difficult turns and twists ahead so they can slow the team down a bit until we're safely beyond the worst of these rough trails,* Broderick let his head rest against the window post as his gaze passed across the distant mountaintops, *but damned if I don't think those trails are a wee bit small and much too rough for a coach.*

The brothers, Liam & Aidan Beckett, were both knowledge-able hands-on maintenance men that looked at every one of the many possible problem areas each time the coach stopped to rest the horses and check them for harness abrasions. By their routine of regularly tightening bolts and greasing movable parts, the group proceeded along the crude trails with a minimum of repair stops.

Several months prior to this coach trip, Aidan, who was a lifelong tinkerer with anything mechanical, had acquired an English-made lamp named after the inventor. "That's a funny lookin lil bugger," his wife said, "what's it used for?"

"Coal miners use 'em," Aidan replied, "because the Pommy that invented it," he pulled a small piece of paper from his shirt pocket and read, "Sir Humphry Davy," he grinned at his wife, "a Knight no less," he then returned the paper to his shirt pocket and turned it around to point, "figured out that by enclosing the flame in this fine gauze-like wire mesh the flame wouldn't ignite the coal dust or gases that's always in those mines." He moved it into more light so she could see what he pointed at. "I learned the mesh also prevents the flame from easily being extinguished outside in an area like this."

When Aidan pulled out a match she stepped back saying, "I think it would be better to light it outside."

"I've lit the thing dozens o' times while trying to figure out 'ow t'make the light reach beyond the bloody lead 'orse's head." He turned toward her and smiled, "I just filled the tank wi' oil, so watch 'ow well it lights up the area ahead when I light it."

He lit the lamp then picked it up and swung is back and forth briskly before he put it back on the bench and pointed. "See this small mirror that I placed be'ine the area where the flame is?" He turned to see if she was watching, "It makes the light reach out much farther."

When the small workshop beneath their house was suddenly lit up completely, she gasped. Seeing the small lantern glowing brightly, Allison said in a half-jokingly voice, "Yer not plannin t'quit Mister McKannah t'go down in the mines, are ye?"

Aidan laughed hard and looked up from the flame he had adjusted. Straightening to his full height and stretching his back, he looked down at his tiny wife of twenty years. "No sooner than I'd trade you n' me two darlin twin girls for a mountain o' gold. I am a very lucky Irishman, luv, an I'm makin no changes atol in me charmed life." He stepped around the wooden bench to pull her to him. Holding her tight he kissed the top of her black hair covered head.

After releasing Allison, he picked up the glowing lantern and moved it across Broderick's coach that was sitting in the distance beside their house. "See 'ow much better this light is?"

"No doubt atol about that, darlin."

"Remember a while back when we brought Brod 'ome from a meeting one night near the waterfront, an I tole ya we almost ran over a wee lad out lookin for 'is dog?"

"Yeah, you were still mumblin about it the next day."

"Darlin, we woulda crippled the lad if not kilt 'im on the spot, and would 'ave been the fault o' those sorry lanterns. They only let others see ya comin, but don't light the way ahead atol."

Allison shook her head slowly up and down. "You're gonna 'ang one o' those," nodding at the lantern he was holding, "on the coach."

"Righto, lass." He grinned wide, "Always said, I did by Jesus, that you were the brightest o' that 'uge litter yer mum n' pappy donated to this marvelous new country."

"Yer only sayin that, lad," her grin widened, "because I was the only one of nine girls that gave ya a second glance."

"Sorry they were, I've 'eard, that each 'ad already chosen her mate fer life."

"Wouldn't 'ave made a bit o' difference, luv, b'cause even as the youngest at fifteen they'd all seen me temper."

"Y'mean t'tell me tha' y'woulda fought yer own littermates to keep me?"

"Not that first month, old man, but after y'kissed me, yes."

"By Jesus, I finally understand why I can't get away from the kissin booth at the church bazzar."

"Y've noticed, I reckon, that I'm always close by?"

"Why do ya think I always 'ave me 'ands in the pockets o' me trousers?"

Allison chuckled, "T'keep that stallion in there from rearin 'is 'uge 'ead an runnin wild amongst all the ladies, I reckon." Her laughter bounced off the walls as she left the workshop, "I'm gonna see if the girls're asleep."

"At fifteen," Aidan said, "I doubt very much they'll be at this early hour."

Allison turned her head toward Aidan and then wobbled her black eyebrows, "We've got all night, lad."

As the coach moved ahead, the lantern mounted on a removable pole between them against the backrest, illuminated the trail but did not hinder the horse's or the driver's night vision.

The coach was stopped twice before midnight and twice after to allow two of the six horses that they all decided to remove from the coach harness and lead on a tether behind, to replace two of the four horses that would then be pulling the coach. It was Liam who suggested it after they left Salt Lake City. "Broderick, now that we're not in such a big 'urry, I believe we'll make much better time goin up through the mountains wi' four pullin an two tethered be'ine an trotin along easy wi'out a load. It might not seem that way, but pullin this bugger's no walk in the park, even for these rugged fellas we're raisin. We can stop regular n' pull a pair out to give 'em a break from the 'arness so they kin trot along behind on a rope. I reckon we'll all benefit a wee bit of a regular break too."

He was correct, and unfortunately for only a few days, their midnight break was a lengthy pit stop anticipated by all. While Broderick prepared supper, and chose an assortment of tinned food easily reached to carry the men toward dawn and breakfast, one of the Beckett brothers serviced all six horses while the other stood watch in the dark—a double-barrel shotgun in his hands, another hanging from his shoulder, and a long-barrel pistol tucked beneath his belt.

Proof soon appeared that Liam Beckett's idea had merit. The value of switching to four horses pulling the coach and two on tethers behind was apparent when they made a brief stop before noon to look for a noise that Aidan said was driving him nuts. While the two men searched for the cause of the odd noise, Broderick calculated their progress since pulling out of Salt Lake City. "Boys," he said cheerfully, "you'll 'ave a 'ard time believing 'ow far we've come since leavin the lake."

Two mountain men had made a temporary camp there before heading on toward the Salmon River up in Shoshone country to put out their beaver traps. After putting away his maps and caliper, Broderick invited them to share a dinner of salted tripe mixed with onion and sun-dried tomatoes that he'd purchased at the new Mormon store in Salt Lake City. Broderick added, "I'm also making a fresh hoecake," when he saw the enthusian spread across the two trapper's faces. The pot of tripe and tomatoes was simmering and Broderick had just flipped the hoecake when his two men working on the coach yelled out almost simultaneously, "Found it!"

After all five men had a tin bowl of tripe stew and a chunk of hoecake, Liam explained. "The left rear rim is cracked, Brod, so we're gonna put on the spare. We can then git on into that fort the Mormon livery owner tole us about an 'ave it fixed good as new. We oughta be on our way t'that Traveler's Rest place in the mornin if they can git right on it."

The larger of the two old trappers stopped his wooden spoon halfway to his mouth and stared at Liam and then Broderick, who they could easily see was in charge. Before he could speak, the short thin man swallowed before shaking his head. "You fellas ain't gonna try to go up n' across them Bitterroots in thet bloody bit of a wagon are ye?"

Before either of his drivers could speak, Broderick answered.

"I must admit that I've been wondering if it's wise to attempt it in a coach such as that." He nodded toward his.

"Ah've seen it tried," the large one said around a mouthful of stew, "but ain't heared o' any what ever made it across."

"Y'ain't goin back t'thet Mormon town lookin for a livery, are ye?" The short one kept shoveling more stew in and looked at Broderick.

"There a livery at the fort," Broderich asked, "that sells horses and tack?"

"Yeah," the large man answered, "and he ain't no Mormon." He grinned showing only a couple of remaining teeth, "I heard them folks are purdy good people, but ah also heard thet they'll skin ya quick if y'let 'em."

The small one added, "I been knowin MacHandy, the feller at the fort, several year an he knows his horses. Never give me no special deal but he never took the lint n' sand outa m'pocket neither."

"Boys," Broderick smiled when he turned toward his men, "I reckon we oughta go shoppin for some ridin horses over at Fort Hall."

It was long after sunset when they approached the fort. In the glow of Aidan's lantern, the two brothers sitting up top could see the two men ahead holding rifles. The shotgun had been placed in the leather scabbard by the time the coach was close enough to the fort to speak in a normal voice.

"Who are you?" the heavy man in front asked, "and where y'comin from?"

Before the men up on top could answer, Broderick leaned his head out. "Broderick McKannah from San Diego California and the two men up top have been my drivers, assistants, and very good friends for over twenty years. We need to buy horses to continue our search for my brother, and were told to see a man at this fort named MacHandy. By the sound of 'is name, another Irishman like we three."

"We five, Mister McKannah," the large man said, "an more'n a few like us inside." His thundering voice had mellowed when he said, "Pull 'er in, lad, an I'll post a guard t'see nothin is taken or touched while we go to the pub n' see wha' ole Tommy might 'ave for ye." He motioned them forward until the coach was all the way inside and the huge gate had been closed again. "That'll be fine, lad, setcher brake n' c'mon down."

188 The McKannahs ~together again~

He yelled for someone named O'reilly to come on the run, which he did, and out of breath said, "Whacha need, sarge?"

"You take the first watch on this coach, me lad, and I'll 'ave someone relieve you at midnight. I don't want a bloody thing on 'er or in 'er touched."

"Righto, Sergeant." The young man immediately walked all the way around before saying, "Nice rig. Shall I have a couple of loafers unhitch the horses and take 'em to Tommy's livery?"

The huge sergeant abruptly turned to Broderick, who was by now outside and standing beside him, "Whadaya think, sir?"

"Yes," Broderick said, "and I'll be more than happy to pay them, because it's been a long and difficult run to here." He turned toward the lighted compound, "A pub, you said."

"Yes by golly, wi' earthen-cooled beer n' good Irish whiskey too. C'mon lads, n' y'll be glad t'know that Missus Behan," his grin was wide and friendly, "me wife, will be glad t'fix all of ye a plate o' whatever she 'as leftover from supper."

When they entered the small building they saw that it was not only a pub, but also the post office, and had a small counter with food condiments on it, plus a barber chair sat near one of the large front windows.

"By the way, lads," he held out a huge hand to Broderick, "me name is Eavan Behan." After shaking Broderick's hand, he called a young man sitting nearby. "Bruce, c'mere willya."

The young man sat his pewter mug down and walked over, "Yessir, sergeant, wha' kin I do for ya?"

"Wouldya please go ask Mabel t'fix three plates o' food for our travelin guests?"

"Sure will, an mebbe she'll 'ave one o' those fried doughballs she made yesterday, left." He turned and went through a narrow door in the corner behind the food counter.

The sergeant yelled at the retreating young man, "An tell 'er that they're all 'uge, 'ungry, an Irish." He laughed and headed toward the bar.

The three men sat at a small round table while the sergeant walked behind the bar and began filling a tin bucket with beer from a spigot in a large crock that was wrapped in wet burlap. As he was doing this, the old man that was pouring whiskey into the glasses of two of his customers put down the bottle and carried three pewter mugs to their table.

"Sarge'll be right here with the beer," he said and returned to his two customers.

Eavan held the bucket of beer near their table, but before he could pour, the front door opened and a tall thin man entered.

"Tommy," he said looking at the thin man, "come sitcher arse down n' I'll getcha a mug." He gestured with his thick arm, "Irismen all, by Jesus." Placing the bucket on the table he turned to go behind the bar for another pewter mug. "They'll introduce themselves."

"Broderick McKannah," he said while holding out his hand.

"Pleased t'meetcha, Tommy MacHandy."

Liam and Aidan introduced themselves and the man pulled a chair out and sat down. Eavan placed the mug he brought in front of Tommy and began pouring beer into all four. After pouring he sat the bucket down and remained standing. "While you fellas talk 'orses I'll go see if Mabel needs 'elp wi' them dinners."

After each had taken a sip from their mug, Broderick spoke. "I believe an error was made when I decided we could cross these mountains in my coach to search for my brother." He paused and picked up his mug for a sip, allowing the thin man to speak—which he did.

"Where you fellas 'eadin?"

Knowing Broderick's negotiating skills well after being with him for so many years, both of his men remained silent and held up their mugs.

After a brief explanation, Broderick lifted his pewter vessel to sip his beer. He was relieved to hear the man begin speaking in a very casual tone. "You're not the first and probably not the last to underestimate the trails through these mountains," he smiled before sipping from his mug, "an that's all they are, gentlemen, just trails. A wee bit better than Lewis n' Clark, Ogden, and ole Jedediah Smith left 'em, but 'orse trails is all they are, an by Jesus if the bloody 'orses 'ad a say in it, y'd all be 'iking across on the leather soles o' yer boots." He chuckled softly and sipped from his mug again.

"That bad, eh?"

The thin man looked at Broderick and smiled. "Truth or fable, there'll be no turnin y'back, so it's the truth I say, an like always, I say that only men cross these mountains."

Before Broderick could even reply, the old sergeant and his wife arrived with three plates of food. After placing them in front of the three travelers he pulled three pewter spoons from his shirt pocket and laid one by each man. After filling all four mugs he lifted the nearly empty bucket and headed toward the bar, "I'll fill 'er again b'fore 'elpin Mable fix up a room wi' three stout beds for you lads."

Tommy continued while the three ate. "I 'ave a dozen'r so to choose from, an it's good stout 'orses y'll need." He paused to let Broderick speak, but when he just kept chewing, Tommy asked, "y'plan t'swap that old coach for 'orses?"

Broderick wiped his mouth slowly while thinking. Finally he spoke, "I've done business wi' the Mormon wha' 'as the livery, an I noticed the telegraph in the post office," he nodded, so 'e can send a coupla fellas t'git m'coach back to Salt Lake City. If I ca'no make a decent swap f'three 'orses t'continue m'search for me youngest brother, then I'll pay gold for 'em an then send 'im a telegram."

"Mmm, gold, eh" Tommy mumbled, "an tha' desent swap y'juss spoke of would include those six old nags y'come in wi', eh?"

"Th' two nags tethered t'the rear'll serve us as pack 'orses, an th'four, five year geldings th' we raised at 'ome will go wi' that custom built coach." Broderick paused a moment before adding, "But only if three fine an 'ealthy 'orses come dressed in the very best saddles n' bridles n' shoes too."

The two brothers got a good lesson in Irish negotiations as the two men sipped beer and haggled. When the sergeant returned to say the room was ready anytime the three travelers wanted to retire, Broderick turned to them and spoke in an exasperated tone. "Boys, I'm thinkin mebbe we oughta juss turn back in the morning an consider locating me brother, Jesse, at a later date." Nothing had been settled but he knew that Tommy wanted the coach, so he stood and yawned wide. "Let's hit the sack n' let tomorrow take care of itself."

Both brothers stood and yawned while leaning their heads on back and stretching both arms out wide. "Yessir," Aidan said softly and yawned again, "before I'm asleep wi' me 'ead in the plate."

"Lead me to the bunk 'ouse, Sarge." Liam was exhausted and did not have to force a wide yawn.

A somewhat surprised Tommy remained seated and said, "I feel certain Broderick that we can come to a mutually agreeable swap in the morning."

"See you for breakfast then." Broderick just waved without turning.

By noon the following day the three men rode out on three stout horses and were leading their two spares with bundles of food and supplies strapped to them.

"Y'reckon," Aidan asked, "that telegram y'sent will get to Ian in time?"

"Yeah," Broderick replied, "sent a copy of it to the casino, 'is ranch and one to that 'otel in Salt Lake City we ate at, because he'll be there lookin for one if 'e hasn't 'eard from me."

"Yeah," Liam interjected, "like me n' 'im," he nodded toward his brother, "we usually know wh' t'other is thinkin."

Aidan just nodded.

Broderick said, "Patrick and Ian's guys too. Like you two they usually know wha' th'ell we're thinkin too." He grinned at both men before adding, "Gonna take a while for me arse t'git used t'this saddle."

"Aye, lad," Aidan replied with a short laugh, "y'been livin it up like a real dandy lately."

Liam added, "It'll do ya good, Brod, an probably give you a few extra years."

Without looking back at him, Broderick said, "Tell me arse that tonight when we stop."

"Stop?" Aidan withheld the grin that wanted to burst out, and turned with a frown, "We'll 'afta keep a brisk pace if we're t'find Jesse in these mountains."

Broderick just looked hard at him and remained silent.

Ian

Both Lon and Solomon MacKandle rode a horse wherever they had to go while at home. But Ian almost always had a sachel full of papers, memos, notes, and drawings for improvements on his establishment, so he used the small horse-drawn buggy to move back and forth between his business and ranch.

Knowing that many less-desirable characters were following the hords of people moving into Carson City and the lake area nearby, Ian always traveled with four armed men; two on horseback ahead and two behind. He always traveled this way whether in the coach with Lon and Solomon or by himself in the buggy—lessons learned years earlier in Five Points.

Now, moving into the mountains above Salt Lake City sitting in a leather saddle made Ian wish he had ridden his horse more often. "Reminds me," he grinned at Lon, "of my first saddle horse. Pa gave each of us, including my sister, Aleena, a horse n' saddle of our own on our tenth birthday. We all rode a horse now n' then but never in a saddle; always bareback and usually didn't go far. I loved that beautiful leather saddle n' went everywhere there was t'go those first two'r three days," he grinned at Lon and then turned and grinned wider at Solomon, "then ate standing up n' slept on m'belly for a week."

"Figured as much," Solomon said with a sly grin, "so I bought a bottle o' witch hazel an a tin o' cornhusker's salve." He bit off a chunk of tobacco and after working it into position in his jaw he turned toward Ian, "Mind you though, I'm not rubbing it on laddie, you will 'afta take care o' that yer ownself."

Ten days later the men rode into Fort Hall, Nathaniel Wyeth's first American settlement west of the Continental Divide. Each night they stopped for five hours rest and also tend to the horses. As soon as Ian had taken care of his horse and hobbled it on grass, he began rubbing on the witch hazel and when it was dry, he rubbed in the cornhusker's salve. On the third morning he asked Solomon, "Where didja hear about that witch hazel stuff?"

"From them Chinamen that work on the roads b'tween us n' the coast. Brung it 'ere from China an swore it'd take away the pain in m'back that time I cricked it gittin the cracked wheel off the coach n' the spare back on." He grinned, "An by Jesus it sure did."

"I didn't know y'buggered up your back that time," Ian said turning in the saddle to look at him.

"Whadaya reckon I shoulda done," Solomon said sarcasticly, "some girlie squealin an cryin?"

"Well," Ian said, "I mighta told you to slow down a wee bit n' take it easy."

"We were 'eadin to th' lake about Jacob Gonzalez."

Ian remained silent for a moment. "Oh yeah, I remember now. We just barely got there in time, but we did and it kept him from being hung."

"Yep! An I been keepin a bottle o' witch hazel around ever since. Meant t'bring it but forgot, so was 'appy t'see it an the cornhusker's salve b'ind the counter in that store."

"Me too," Ian McKannah said with a grin, "cause I'm gonna ride into Fort Hall like a man born on a horse's saddle."

Seeing a livery stable at the edge of the small settlement, Ian suggested they board the animals overnight if there was a hotel where they could bathe and get a good night's rest.

"Ain a hotel," the old man fitting new shoes to a horse said, "but Evelyn Swift rents some bunks by the night since Otto, her husband, died." He drove in a last nail and placed the horse's hoof down. Patting the side of its neck he said, "Hope them suits ya big fella, an ole Emma doan wait s'long next time."

He nodded with his bearded chin, "Evelyn's house is at the end o' the street. Big ole sprawling place b'tween Roddy Endel's saddlery n' leather shop, and the mercantile store. She keeps letters left by folks thet wanna let their families back home know how everthang's a'goin, so when a mule train brings supplies, she has 'em tote the letters back down to civilization." He spit out a stream of tobacco juice and laughed, "Betcha lots of 'em wished they had tossed them letters and went back down to civilization their own damn self."

"Can we board these animals here overnight if she has three bunks available?"

"Bring 'em on in the corral," he said while walking to the gate. "Ain't been no travelers lately, so she'll be right happy t'rencha some bunks." After closing the gate behind their horses and two mules, he added, "She also cooks the best dern food I ever et, an don't charge no more'n it's worth." After spitting tobacco juice on the dirt road he shook his head up and down, "You fellas'll see what I mean at five o'clock. There'll be about twenty of us what ain't got no woman, lined up in front waitin for her t'open up an hand us a tin plate o' vittles n' bread."

At a little after 5:00 while Lon and Solomon ate, Ian read the letter that Broderick had left with Evelyn Swift. After handing it to Lon, Ian began working on his plate of food, which was the best he had seen in a long time. After Solomon read it, Ian said, "Brod and his boys're not too far ahead of us, so we all oughta be able to get together to deal with this guy from Texas."

The next morning Ian heard the door to the bunkroom open and eased his pistol out from under his pillow. When his sleep-filled eyes tuned in the faint light of the candle he relaxed. As he swung his legs out from under the light blanket, Evelyn Swift's voice cut through the darkness, "Mister McKannah, the coffee's ready and I'll have breakfast on the table time you fellas get up."

"Thanks, Missus Swift, we'll be there directly."

A bit after noon the three men were in the saddle and moving on Jedediah Smith's 1825 trail and were heading north toward the Bitterroot Range. When Solomon finally got the fresh chunk of chewing tobacco into position he spit on the ground then turned to Ian and asked, "Missus Swift remind you of anyone?"

"Molly MacHue," Ian answered without pause.

"Yeah, by golly she does." Lon turned in the saddle, "Hadn't thought o' her or ole Shea in years."

"Me neither," Solomon said and shook his head, "kinda sad 'ow quick yer pals fergit all aboutcha, eh."

"Ah well," Lon said and chuckled, "we'll all git t'gether roun' the big bonfire."

"Not a saintly fella like meself." Solomon grinned at Ian, "I'll be flappin me angel wings from cloud t'cloud n' lookin down at you sinners."

Ian smiled and thought, *couldn't be on the trail with a better couple o' guys.*

On the ninth day after riding out of Fort Hall they were climbing toward the 7,000 foot high Lemhi Pass that was mentioned in the Lewis & Clark chronicles.

"Where y'reckon we'd be," Lon said, "if you 'adn't stopped at the salty lake n' read the telegram from Broderick?"

Ian laughed hard, "Ridin those coach horses bareback n' not sittin down to eat." He turned to Lon, "At least, not me."

"Y'reckon anyone'll ever get across 'ere in a coach?" Solomon looked around and nodded his head.

"Probably." Ian turned to look back down the mountain. "By the time we're old men there'll be good trails going over all of these mountains and stagecoaches will be carrying people to the west coast like sailin ships're carrying people from Europe to the east coast now."

"Well," Solomon grinned at Ian, "that's in th' future, lad. This is t'day, an I'm bloody well 'appy as a pig in shit thacha stopped like y'did n' we're ridin these nice 'orses over these 'ills."

"Hills," Lon said loudly and looked at Ian, "this 'igh altitude is makin 'im daffy."

"Callin 'em 'ills makes 'em seem smaller t'me."

"Betcha that 'orse'd toss yer arse off 'is back if 'e knew wha' y'juss said." Lon shook his head and mumbled, "Hills."

~

As Ian and his two men approached Lemhi Pass, two young men rode into Fort Hall and began asking about a large Texan with a huge head—named Kellerman.

Jesse

Jesse awoke early and carefully slipped from the tepee so he wouldn't disturb Lone Wolverine and his wife, Gentle Breeze. He added several small logs to the hot coals and then walked the short distance to the lake and rinsed out the coffee pot. After returning he eased the filled pot onto the flat stone that had been placed there for that purpose. He watched the fire burn high before it began settling down into brilliantly glowing logs. After he positioned several of the smaller logs around the coffee stone, Jesse lay down and stretched out on the long flat sitting board to watch the stars.

"Spot any shooting stars?" Lone Wolverine carried two clay cups with him and sat them on the plank after Jesse sat up. Jesse stood saying, "Nope! The shootin will probably begin about time we go inside to sleep." He grinned at his Indian friend, "Coffee oughta be ready by now." He leaned down and picked up the old pewter pot and sniffed the pouring spout.

Jesse's friend leaned forward to sniff the aroma too, "Ahh yes, and smells like someone added a few beans to it."

"Yeah, I brought a pound of beans from Missoula." His grin widened, "Figured it was time to retire those old grounds."

"Oh no," the Indian growled, "don't tell me you tossed out those grounds." He turned a scowling face to Jesse and said, "I just got those broke in and adjusted to the pot last week." He tried to maintain a stoic face but laughed so hard he had to stop while Jesse poured his cup full. After Jesse returned the pot to the stone and sat beside him, the Indian said, "You're going to spoil us if this continues." His eyebrows wobbled as he added, "but me n' Gentle Breeze are really enjoying it while it lasts."

As the two men drank coffee, Jesse explained his plans. "I

bought a good, strong-looking mule from that German fella who built that sawmill over to the west of Polson, and some tools at the general store. I'm gonna build m'self a small log house right at the south end of the lake." He swiveled around and pointed through the trees, "Right about there, on the other side of those two big boulders."

"That's a nice place to have a house Jesse, and we couldn't ask for a better neighbor."

"Ain't gonna be a big house," Jesse continued, "like the one I had in California, but I'm gonna put two big bedrooms in it so when one of my brothers comes to visit they'll have plenty of room." He pulled a folded paper from his jacket pocket and laid it on the plank between them. After unfolding it he pointed, "I been sketching how I want it ever since I decided to stay here."

Lame Wolverine leaned down to better see the sketch. "This is a place to build a fire, right?" He looked up.

"Yeah, it's called a chimney. Ain't never built one m'self, but I watched as my friend," he looked at Lame Wolverine, "the one I told you those men killed, built the one in my cabin. We could put two big logs on the coals before going to bed, and close the damper to the hole going up the chimney a little bit, and in the morning that cabin was still warm, even during the cold winter. Whoever got outa bed first put a coupla logs on the coals then opened the chimney damper, and in no time at all we'd have a nice fire going."

"What is this?" His friend pointed to the sketch.

"That's what I'm gonna build first. It's a small barn where the horse and mule will be able to get outa the cold during the bad months of winter. There'll be room up in the hayloft for me to live while I'm building my cabin, and still be room enough to store hay for 'em."

"Are you still planning to put a big herd of cattle on your property?"

"Sure am," Jesse said as he folded the sketch and returned it to his pocket, "because until we get this new government to honor those promises that are in the treaty they made when they cheated you out of your land, that herd is what'll keep the Flathead people from starving." Jesse looked into his friend's eyes, "They gettin use to the taste of beef, yet?"

Lame Wolverine chuckled, "Some of the old people are still complaining that it doesn't taste as good as buffalo, but as you can see everyone is putting on weight."

"Yeah, I've noticed and that's good, because it will probably be a long time until those government people start sending you the supplies they promised. That's why I said we've gotta start turning the Flathead braves into Flathead cowboys and Flathead gardeners."

Jesse sipped his cup of coffee and remained silent for a while. "Before I start building the cabin I'm gonna take those two boys that helped me bring the herd of cattle down from Missoula and go over to Idaho and see if the herd that I told you about is worth bringing back here through those Bitterroot Mountains."

"You said it's Mormons who want to sell the herd, right?"

"Yeah," Jesse answered, "they wanna move down to Utah and be closer to that big group of Mormons that took over the entire area around a big lake."

"There's five hundred head in the herd?"

"Yeah, that's what I heard, and the tinker that stopped here last week told me the same thing."

"If you get them all, you'll need more than a couple of kids to get them back here. It might be better if you take a dozen of my young braves."

"I'm sure they could do a good job of herding 'em back here, but we still don't know what those folks in that new town over on the other side of the canyon are up to. You might need every brave you have if they decide to get tough and come at your village again." Jesse laid his hand on his friend's shoulder, "You must always put your people first, because without you they will be lost. If I buy the herd, I'm certain I can hire a few men to ride with us and bring them here."

Lone Wolverine looked worried when he asked, "When are you leaving?"

"I sent a message to the boys through Michael, the owner of O'Hannahan's Diner in Polson. If Robert and Johnny, the two Henderson boys, can't join me, then they'll send word back with Michael's man who goes to Missoula for supplies. But if they do return with him, then we're gonna head west toward Idaho the following morning."

"Okay," Lame Wolverine reluctantly said, "but take the time to tell me what size logs you'll need to begin your cabin, and how many. My braves will begin dragging them to wherever you say they should be pilled."

"You don't hafta ask them to do that, old friend."

The Indian smiled, "I will ask for volunteers, and every brave will step forward to help White Buffalo build his home near our village."

Jesse was embarrassed but smiled, "Okay, the first logs will be for the foundation. They'll hafta be a foot thick at the butt end and fifteen feet long. I'll make a marker stick for you to show them. The cabin's gonna be twenty feet wide and thirty feet long and there'll be a foundation post every five feet both ways, so it will take thirty-five, fifteen footers that are a foot thick at the butt."

Lame Wolverine turned and looked toward the end of the lake where Jesse planned to build his cabin. "The land slopes down to the edge of the lake. Are you going to make it all level before you begin?"

"No," Jesse said, "I don't like to disturb the lay of the land, so I'll dig and bury all of the foundation poles, which I'll smear tar on where they go in the soil, and then fill the holes with lake gravel, so they won't rot. Once they're all in and sticking straight up, then I'll cut them all off at the same height. Then I'll begin nailing on those stringers that Mister Heimler, the man who built that sawmill, will have already cut and racked for me so they'll cure."

Lame Wolverine pursed his lips and shook his head, but grinned when he spoke. "Why do you not build a simple tepee that can be moved?"

Jesse chuckled, "Old friend, I thought very hard about that and almost decided to do exactly as you just suggested, but," he grinned, "my Irish daddy would have leprechauns stomping on the ground inside and outside until I tore it down and built a house or cabin."

"Those are the little people you told me about who live in the forests and make mischief."

"Yes, so the story goes." Jesse grinned and winked.

"We have them too," the Indian said with a somber face, "but ours are mean little devils, and they just might start nailing your doors and windows shut or stuffing things in your chimney so the smoke stays inside the house." He grinned at Jesse, and then said, "I've been talking to my people about building traditional cedar log and bark lodges now that we have a permanent camp. We know now that the buffalo were all killed by white men and will never return, so there is no need of tepees or the small shacks we covered with straw mats in summer. The young braves have never seen a Flathead cedar lodge, so I will tell them to help you build your cabin and to learn how to make their own so it will be strong and will last." The chief's face broke open into a wide grin when he added, "Maybe they will put chimneys in too so the smoke goes outside."

~

Jesse stopped at O'Hannahan's Diner in Polson to say hello to Michael and ask when his man, Leon, might return. The huge Irishman shook Jesse's hand then removed his grease-stained white chef hat to run his fingers through the twisted mass of red hair. "I reckon 'e'll be back tomorrow, Jesse. If those two young fellows come with him, y'leaving right away t'go 'ave a look at that 'erd of cattle over in Idaho?"

"Yep," Jesse said, "wanna get back with 'em as soon's I can if I swing the deal, so I can get started on m'cabin."

"Ever dealt with those Mormons?"

"Nope, never even met one, why?"

"Crafty buncha folks, they are, by Jesus," he answered then pulled the chef hat back over the red forest. "They seem like purdy good folks, but in my dealings with 'em, which 'as been a right smart amount, they sure like to come out on the better end of a deal, so you keep yer wits honed sharp n' act as though y've got another deal just down the trail a wee bit that might be more t'yer likin." He winked at Jesse, "I'll get a message to you as soon as Leon returns."

The very next day while Jesse and Lame Wolverine were sipping a coffee in front of the chief's tepee, Leon Small rode into the Flathead camp without the two young men. "Hi, Jesse," he waved then dismounted. After hobbling his horse and getting a tin cup from his saddlebag, the extremely tall man walked to Lame Wolverine, "Hello, chief, got another cup o' that stuff?"

"For you, my friend," the chief said with a smile, "I would make another pot if there was none left, but we started this day with a big one."

Jesse's eyebrows lifted as his eyes opened wide, "You fellas know each other, huh."

"All his life," the chief said.

"My mother was orphaned when she was ten." Leon said. "Her folks were moving west to get away from the cold weather, wherever they had been living. Don't know exactly where that was, cause all I know is what the Flatheads learned from mom. She died of influenza when I was three years old."

Lame Wolverine continued when Leon lifted his tin cup of coffee to his lips. "War Eagle and Leon's mother, Rachael, were like you and Desert Rose, good people that the Great Spirit put together. But like you and Rose, their happiness did not last."

Jesse looked at Leon, "You live with the tribe all your life?"

"Just till I was fifteen. My dad, War Eagle, was killed during a battle with the Blackfoot, so when a group of cowboys moving a big herd stopped near our camp to ask about the best trail to take through the Bitterroot Mountains into Idaho, I joined 'em. I was fifteen then and stayed with 'em fourteen years."

"Y'musta liked wrangling cows," Jesse said.

"Nope!" Leon grinned, "Never even tried it. I learned to cook by watching the Flathead wimmin, so they hired me to drive the chuckwagon."

"Howja end up workin for Michael?" Jesse asked.

The tall young man grinned, "Broke m'leg and couldn't git on n' off the darn chuckwagon. We was all movin a real big herd through this area when it happened, so they brought me on a travois to Polson where they knew a tooth puller, who also did some doctoring, had set up a little clinic." Leon pulled up the leg of his pants and showed Jesse the long scars. "One of them dern cows went nuts and run me over. He durn near ruint that nice chuckwagon too. Busted up m'leg som'n awful, but ole Doc Rock got everything back where it belonged and ain't had no trouble with it since, and that was almost two years ago."

Jesse thought, *He's over thirty, but looks about twenty.* He asked Leon, "Y'been workin for Michael ever since, huh?"

"Yeah, while m'leg was all wrapped up with sticks holding the bones in the right place till they healed, I was able t'help Michael in the kitchen, but since Doc Rock took all that stuff off, I'm able to do anything that Michael asks me t'do."

"Like go down to Missoula for supplies, n' stuff like that."

"Yeah, and when he wants t'go som'rs I can open up the restaurant and keep everything running till he returns."

"Well," Jesse said somewhat dejected, "since the boys aren't with you, I reckon I'll be heading toward Idaho alone."

"Nah, they're at Michael's filling their gut. Told 'em I'd ride on out here n' letcha know they're ready t'go when you are." He smiled, "I met 'em about a year ago, and liked both those boys.

Good workers and smart as a whip, both of 'em."

Jesse grinned, "That's the kinda news that makes a guy's day. I'm going to need a couple of guys that I can rely on t'help those cowboys I hire t'help me git that herd back here."

Lame Wolverine said, "Sure you don't wanna take a few of my braves with you, Jesse?"

"I'd like to, but as I said, you've gotta look after the welfare of your tribe until we see what that bunch over on the other side of the mountain plans t'do."

Leon turned to Jesse, "What bunch is that?"

After Jesse and Lone Wolverine explained, Leon said, "That Burgess Kellerman is a fella to keep an eye on, Jesse. He was run outa Texas while we were gettin ready to move a big herd west. A small rancher disappeared and Kellerman tried to move in and take his ranch away from the guy's three boys. Lotsa folks down there still think he musta killed old man Brasco and was probably gonna kill them boys too. Somehow he got word that a group of vigilantes were comin out t'get him, and he hauled ass. Them boys're about growed up now, cause that was near three years ago, so one o' these days he might look up n' see them standin there with shotguns. Serve him right if them boys cut him down, cause tough ole ranchers like ole Brasco don't never just up n' disappear."

The next day, Jesse was busy getting everything set up for the Flatheads to position the logs near where he would eventually place them, and was explaining again to his friend how many and how long they should be. He and Lame Wolverine had decided that it was a waste of time and energy to use the same length throughout and then cut them off later. The Indian Chief had suggested it to Jesse, earlier. "My braves are smart and learn quick when it's something like trees or building on the land." He grinned at his white friend, "Some of the young braves are saying they might build a wooden tepee for their wife like yours after they see what it looks like." The smile vanished and he explained, "You decide how far into the ground you will put the foundation poles, and we will measure the slope of the land to determine how long each row of poles must be."

Jesse agreed with him. "That will not only speed things up, it will also make the foundation posts much easier to stand upright into the holes."

Lame Wolverine shook his head and smiled, "They are now

cutting our winter wood with the two-man crosscut saw you bought, and can use the file to sharpen it as good as you. You are forcing them to adapt to this changing new world, and it is a very good thing, because we must change or be left behind."

It was late afternoon by the time he and the two Henderson boys, Robert and Johnny, rode out of Polson Montana heading toward a small cattle ranch in Idaho on the western side of the Bitterroot Mountains.

~

Unknown to Jesse, Crazy Joe Flambert had been watching him closely for several days. Months ealier when Crazy Joe witnessed Jesse as he stealthily observed Burgess Kellerman that night in his hotel and casino, he convinced himself that he was going to somehow make the fortune he needed to return to Mexico and live like a king—if he kept a close eye on Jesse.

Confident that he could pick up the trail left behind by the three men, Crazy Joe repeatedly shoved his spurs into the horse as he headed toward a hidden canyon that ran directly into the new town of Burgess Montana. *I hope Cecil and Goat did like I tole 'em and stayed sober.*

He was relieved to see his two sidekicks squatting in front of a small fire near the leanto that the three men shared. Crazy Joe remained in the saddle and said, "Squash that fire, we got things t'do, boys." A minute later Crazy Joe and the two escaped killers were moving south along the edge of the low hills. "We'll take it easy," Joe said, "and let 'em get on over these hills. Won't be no trouble atol pickin up their trail."

"We gonna kill 'em?" Cecil said in his high feminine voice.

"No," Joe answered in an aggravated tone of voice, "what the hell good would that do us, you damn moron?"

Before Cecil could think of a suitable reply, the one Joe called Goat, because he ate anything lying around, spoke in his deep southern drawl, "We gonna foller 'em all the way to New York?"

Joe turned toward the little man that caused many who saw him astride a horse, even a small one, to laugh. "New York ain't nowhere near where there a'headin, you simpleton." He shook his head and chuckled, "You'll both die out here if anything ever happens to me, because New York is about ten thousand miles south o' here."

Cecil frowned, "We gonna foller 'em all day?"

In the same aggravated tone, Joe said, "Just till they camp tonight. Then we're gonna grab 'em and take all three back to Burgess so old man Kellerman can find out what that tall skinny, injun lover's up to."

~

Johnny Henderson had turned in the saddle several times to let his eyes scan the area behind them. Very few things went unseen around Jesse, so when he noticed the boy checking their back-trail again he nudged his horse close to Johnny's. "Y'got a feelin we're being followed?"

The youth turned toward him, "Yessir, for an hour or so the hair on m'neck's been standing up like the hackles on that old huntin hound o' pa's."

"Mine too," Jesse said quietly, "ever since we got on through that canyon." He casually turned in the saddle and scanned the trail behind, then turning back said quietly, "We've only got an hour of daylight left, so we'll make camp up ahead soon's we find a leveled off spot."

By the time darkness had spread across the area, Jesse and the two boys were hunched over and sipping coffee as their fire burned down. Once the tack had been removed from the horses and they were fed and cared for, the boys hobbled them, as Jesse worked his way back down their trail to see if he could spot the cause of him and Johnny's uneasiness.

Later, as he approached the camp, Jesse was impressed to see that a fire was already burning and the coffeepot sat on a rock at the edge. He had told them that coffee and the biscuits Michael sent with Leon would be dinner until they learned who, if anyone was following them. "You boys check them shotguns your pa let you bring, and be certain they're loaded with dry shells full o' buckshot. Lay the muzzle at your feet and have your hand near the trigger. If that fella Kellerman sent some guys to waylay us things might get dern hot, so I'm gonna be up on that big boulder watching," Jesse said while pointing at a spot a hundred feet back down the trail. He then added, "If you guys hear gunfire, git to your horses pronto, snatch off the hobbles, and bareback it outa here. I'll fire my Colt twice in the air and call to you if everything's okay."

The boys were uneasy, but by their very nature, as children of pioneers, each was calm and prepared. They silently watched as Jesse headed toward the boulder.

Jesse had told them to keep the fire low, so it was a glowing bed of coals when they heard Jesse call to someone in a loud voice, "Who are you and why are you riding into my camp so slow and silent?"

The next sound the boys heard was a man screaming. They realized that he was very close, so they stood and moved behind the big boulder that Jesse had set up their camp next to. While the man's screams continued they heard gunfire from the direction they knew Jesse had gone. Simultaneously both boys bolted, and in a flash they had pulled the hobbles from the front hoofs of their mounts. With a shotgun in one hand and a handful of mane in the other each was pressed close to their horse as the distance between them and the screaming man and the gunfire widened.

A few moments later they each heard the report of a gun, and then another followed by Jesse yelling their names loudly and saying everything is okay.

Johnny yelled loud and asked if they should return, and Jesse answered by yelling, "Yes, c'mon back."

The boys rode back slowly. Robert, at sixteen, was the older of the two and took more time than his brother Johnny to think a situation through thoroughly before acting. He turned to Johnny as they approached the foot of the hill leading up to the boulders where Jesse had decided to camp. "Y'don't s'pose some o' them bad fellas that Leon told us about could be holding Jesse and making him call us in, do you?"

Without hesitating Johnny answered, "Nope, ain't no way a man's gonna get Jesse McKannah to say som'n he don't think is right."

After a moment Robert agreed with him and the two boys continued on up the hill. They rounded the north end of the big boulder and the first thing they saw was a dead man with several arrows in him. Three Flathead Indians and Jesse stood beside the body while a fourth Flathead retrieved their arrows. Jesse heard the horses and looked up, "Hi boys, I'm sure glad t'see you did what I tole ya n' cut outa here when you heard my gunshot." Jesse pointed down at the body, "Looks like this one was gonna slip in and either shoot both of you or tie you up n' then take me down." He motioned with his arm, "C'mon, let's get some coffee and build up that fire a bit."

Two more Flatheads entered the camp while Robert was pouring the three tins of coffee. One was dragging Cecil by his big feet and the other Flathead had tiny Goat up on his shoulder. Cecil's legs were unceremoniously dropped next to the fire and Goat was dumped on the ground like a sack of feed. The hole from the gunshot had bled profusely so it was obvious that Jesse had hit each man in the heart. The gift from his friend, Angus McDonald, was still working well.

Jesse was speaking to the Flatheads in their language, so both Henderson boys remained silent. They watched as Jesse stood and embraced each Indian. All three men watched as the Indians vanished into the night.

Before either boy asked what had happened, Jesse spoke. "I didn't know that my friend, Lone Wolverine, had sent a scouting party to keep an eye on us." He shook his head then sipped the hot coffee before continuing, "Seems he spotted that one," he nodded toward Crazy Joe Flambert, "moving about in a sneaky way trying to keep an eye on me. He called in his best trackers and told 'em to watch our trail to see if we were being followed.

Thank God he didn't pay attention when I refused his offer of help, or we all might be dead.

Johnny blurted out loud, "We thought sure somebody killed you when we heard them shots."

"Coulda happened, but when the Flatheads saw that creepy guy," he pointed at Flambert, "sneaking up on you two with his pistol in his hand they put a few arrows in him. When he started screaming like a fat squaw with a scorpion caught in a fold of her blubber, them two," he motioned at Cecil and Goat, "turned when I told 'em to put their hands on their head. But instead of doin it they pulled their pistols out of their pants pocket, so I shot 'em both."

"Purdy good shootin' Jesse," Robert said.

"Especially bein dark," Johnny added.

Jesse pulled out his Colt revolver and held it so the boys could see what he was pointing at. "See this white paint on the rear vee sight?"

Both boys answered yes.

"These are tiny diamonds on the front sight, see 'em?" Jesse held it close to each boy. "A friend showed me how well they worked by saving my life and the life of a good friend who was with me. They were on a long-barrel rifle he had, but I learned to use 'em on this Colt." He looked up through the trees to a star-filled full-moon sky. "On a night like this the starlight will make them twinkle, so all I had to do was learn how to quickly get 'em lined up with the white vee in front of the hammer."

Jesse returned his Colt revolver to the holster, and then after finishing his coffee with a couple of biscuits and a slice of cured ham sent by Michael O'Hannahan, he stood. "Boys, Let's get a grave dug for these three while there's still light." Jesse walked to his horse and removed his bedroll. After unrolling it he held up a small narrow shovel, "I'll get a hole dug while you boys get enough stones to cover it."

Robert returned fifteen minutes later with a big load of rocks inside his poncho. After removing the poncho from his shoulder he dumped them in a pile just as Johnny arrived with his load; a poncho over his shouldfer with five boulders. Jesse continued digging as Johnny added his to the pile then stepped closer to look at the shovel.

"Never saw a shovel that small, Jesse."

Jesse straightened up and turned it over. "I'd sure carry a bigger one if I thought there'd be a lotta guys like those three out here tryin t'kill us," he said, nodding toward the three bodies. He ran his glove across the blade, "I use this to dig wild sweet taters n' cama root when I'm on the trail for long periods of time." He dropped the shovel and placed both hands against his lower back then bent backward and side-to-side a few times. "When there's only bitterroot, then it's really a handy tool." He picked up the small shovel and returned to his digging as the Henderson brothers went looking for more small bolders and big rocks to pile atop the grave.

Before the sun began dropping into the western mountains the grave was deep enough to hold all three cadavers. Jesse positioned the three bodies so there would be as much dirt over them as possible, and the large rocks and small boulders would keep hungry predators from easily digging them up.

Jesse and the two Henderson boys rode west toward the Idaho border until almost midnight. Feeling that they had put enough distance between them and the grave of Crazy Joe, Cecil, and Goat, they stopped and made camp. All it amounted to was a small smokeless fire to warm jerky and make coffee. Jesse's mind was ablase and he wasn't tired so he stood watch while the boys slept.

One hour before dawn he had a small smokeless fire going and the pot filled with water sat on a flat rock at the edge of it.

He nudged both boys with the toe of his boot, "Coffee'll be ready time you lighten your load."

A short time later both boys came from the bushes buttoning their pants and tightening their belts. "Any o' them biscuits left that Michael gave us?"

"Yep," Jesse said as he poured water into a small tin can, "enough for all three of us, and they'll go right good with the cougar jerky that Gentle Breeze sent with us." He used a stick to move the strips around in the hot water, and then added coffee beans that he'd already pounded to the remaining water in the pot.

Twenty minutes later Jesse was sipping his hot coffee after chewing a bite of hard but tasty biscuit. After swallowing he said, "You're both good men on a trail." He looked from one to the other then smiled, "I'm fortunate t'have a coupla fellas like you with me."

Both boys felt as though they had grown into men during the trip with Jesse bringing the small herd of cattle from Missoula to the Flathead reservation. Hearing this from a man they admired as much as their father reinforced their belief that they had stepped beyond childhood in the last few weeks.

Robert moved up and rode beside Jesse to ask, "What's the name of that river at the halfway point?"

"Clark Fork River," Jesse said. "It runs into Lake Pend Oriell as the Pend Oriell River and comes out as the Clark Fork River."

"Pretty big river, that Clark Fork?"

"Only been across it twice," Jesse said, "and it was shallow enough t'walk a horse across both times, but it was a dry period each time."

"We sure ain't had much rain lately," Robert said, "so it's probably pretty shallow."

"That's what I've been thinking." Jesse looked up at the sky, "Hope it lasts till we get that herd across and we're on our way home."

The sun warmed the backs of all three as they moved toward the Clark Fork River. A brief stop in the early afternoon allowed the horses to graze and the men to have hot coffee and boiled cougar jerky. Half an hour later they were back in the saddle and kept moving until near midnight.

Eighteen hours in the saddle with one mid-afternoon stop paid off for them the way Jesse hoped it would. His calculations indicated that they could be at the river in three days of hard riding.

It was late afternoon on the fourth day, but considering the delay to deal with four killers who never expected Jesse and his boys to go farther than where they caught up with them, he figured they'd made good time reaching the halfway point.

After walking their horses across the slow moving river, Jesse pointed toward a hill with a copse of trees on the top. "Let's get on up there and get the tack off the horses. After giving them a good rubdown we'll let 'em graze while we have some side meat and hoecake."

"Hotdamn," Robert yelled, "we was both hopin you'd make s'more o' that," he turned in the saddle toward his brother, "huh Johnny?"

"Yeah boy, we sure was." He grinned, turning almost all the way around as his horse kept heading up the hill at a walk. He untied the rawhide tongs on his saddlebags as he said, "And I brought som'n that's gonna make 'em even better."

When Jesse saw the small jar of honey he grinned wide, "Now that boy knows how to gear up good for a trail drive."

The second half of the trip took a day longer because of the Bitterroot Mountains. Jesse had trapped in the area many years earlier and, thanks to a memory inherited from his father, he recalled a pass through that they could drive the herd across on the return trip.

Halfway through the pass Jesse caught a brief glimpse of movement up ahead and to his left. As Shadow walked forward Jesse eased his Jennings rifle out of the leather scabbard attached to his saddle, all the while keeping his eyes on the area where he saw movement.

He knew the boys were always alert so he didn't take his eyes off of the area ahead to warn them. *Surely,* he thought, *those damn Blackfoot ain't raiding this far down.*

A moment after that random thought ran through his mind, Jesse spotted the wolf. It was about a hundred yards ahead and sitting on top of a large boulder. Easing the rifle back into the scabbard he kept his eyes on the wolf while untying the rawhide tongs that kept the telescope in the leather tube attached to the rear of his saddle.

A quiet "Whoa Shadow" stopped his horse so he could get a better look at the wolf. By this time both boys were beside him as he focused the telescope. A minute later he handed it to Robert.

After handing it to his brother, Robert leaned toward Jesse and whispered, "I think it's only got three legs."

"Nope," Jesse replied, "the right rear leg must be injured because he's keeping it up so he can run without bumping it."

"Yeah," Johnny whispered as he handed the telescope back to Jesse, "I just saw it hang down for a second before he yanked it back up against his belly."

"Boy oh boy," Jesse said softly, "that poor thing's ribs are really showing." He slid the telescope back into its tube and then secured it. "Probably ain't had meat since he lost the use o' that leg." He nudged Shadow, and all three men continued west through the pass.

Several times Jesse spotted the wolf. "He's staying way off but that wolf is moving along with us." Both boys said they'd also spotted it.

Jesse stopped Shadow again and quickly brought out the rifle. Before the boys could speak, Jesse took careful aim and fired. By that time Robert had spotted the small group of goats on the side of the pass ahead.

When one of the goats fell and bounced off a boulder to land on top of a flat boulder below, Johnny said quietly, "Wow, Jesse that was good shootin cause them goats was a good hunert yards off."

"Jennings gets most of the credit for a shot like that," he said while replacing the rifle, "helluva good rifle he built." He turned toward Johnny, "All y'gotta do is learn which way the bullet is gonna be pushed by the wind, rain, snow, or whatever else is out there."

Robert asked, "How many bullets didja go through, Jesse, before you had it all figured out?"

"Hmmm, never thought about that, Robert, but musta been at least a hundred." Jesse wrinkled his eyebrows down and looked at him, "Mighta been twice that many."

Before they passed that boulder where the goat had landed the wolf was dragging it off and down into the caves and cubby holes, which were formed over the centuries by the constantly moving terrain.

The three men rode into the sprawling ranch on the south end of Coeur d'Alene Lake in early afternoon on the fourth day after crossing the river.

At two hundred yards from the small group of men that Jesse had looked at through his folding telescope he told the boys to stop and get off the horses. "Let 'em graze while I ride in, but keep the reins in your hand and watch for me to signal by waving my hat." He handed Robert the telescope, "I wave it in m'left hand c'mon in, but if I wave it in m'right, haul on outa here in a hurry."

"Y'recon they might be rustlers?"

"Nope, I could tell by lookin close at what they's wearin that they're probably Mormons, but I've heard stories that makes me think it's a good idea to be careful when dealing with 'em."

"Left hand we ride in," Robert said, "and right hand we head for home."

"Yep!" Jesse headed toward the group at an easy trot.

As Jesse got close enough to see the three men clearly, he saw that they each had an old muzzleloader leaning against the split-rail corral. Glancing toward the huge house beyond what was obviously the bunkhouse for hired help, Jesse saw about a dozen men dressed almost exactly the same as the three he was heading toward. It appeared that each of them also had a rifle close at hand. Since they didn't actually have the rifles in their hands he figured they were simply being cautious. He also figured they were probably hoping he was there to make an offer for the herd he saw in the fenced pastures beyond the huge corral.

"Howdy, name's Jesse McKannah from over east o' here, and I was told that you have a herd o' cows for sale."

After listening to the old Mormon that seemed to be the man in charge, Jesse waved his hat with his left hand and watched as both boys rode in. After introducing them to the old man, who said his name was Jonah Beecher, but did not introduce any of the others, Jesse, both boys, and Jonah headed toward the herd.

After learning that the herd was not as large as he expected, but might still be more than they could handle, he turned to Jonah with a little white lie. "I brought only these here two boys because I was told that the herd was less than a hundred head."

"It was a hundred and seven," Jonah said, "until a few days ago when our neighbors decided to come along with us down to the salt lake." The old man continued looking at the distant herd a moment before turning back to Jesse. "We told him to put 'em in with ours and we'd try to get a fair price for all hundred and seventy head."

Jesse just looked at the old man for a long silent moment before nudging Shadow to move, "Well, let's go take a look at 'em."

The next two hours was spent moving through the herd looking at the condition of the cows and the four bulls that came with them.

Back at Jonah's house they sat on the porch beneath the huge overhanging roof. Jesse could tell that Jonah was ready to close the deal with a family from nearby Spokane that planned to create a new town on the edge of the lake and name it Mackensie.

"Joel Mackenzie plans to move his entire family from Canada and grow vegetables." He turned in the rocker, "I ain't never before heard bout anyone what don't eat meat, but ain't a soul in thet Mackenzie bunch what does." The old man shook his head, "Reckon the good Lord knows what He's doin, but I sure don't know how a man gets up much energy from corn n' taters."

Jonah knew that Jesse wanted the herd, even though he said he'd go south to look at another herd if he couldn't afford this one. The only hangup, as far as Jonah was concerned, was getting it back to Flathead Lake.

"How big a spread y'got?" Jonah asked. He intended to sell Jesse the entire herd and was feeling around for leverage.

"Two hundred and thirty thousand acres, but that includes half the lake."

Jonah paused a moment while his mind considered all of the options, "That's a good size spread, just t'put a small herd of cattle on."

Jesse didn't want anyone beyond their area to know that he was helping the Flathead Indians get settled on their small chunk of reservation land adjacent to his property. By the time that information became public knowledge, all of the lake and the land around it would belong to Jesse McKannah and the tribe of Flathead Indians living on it.

"Mostly lake," Jesse said, "but there is enough pasture for

this herd, and mebbe a few more later, and that'll be enough for me to live out my time on." He wasn't about to tell Jonah that his share of the gold mine was putting more money in the San Diego bank than he would ever need, but he had to convince the old man that he could afford to pay for these cattle, and make him believe that he was going to be shopping for a more in the near future.

"My brother, Broderick Luis McKannah, owns a big law firm in San Diego, California." Jesse locked his steel gray eyes on the old man, and continued. "If you and me come to a price we both agree on he'll send the entire payment in gold to you, your bank, church, or wherever you want it sent." He fished out a folded piece of paper to hand to Jonah. "That's his name and the name of his law firm. He's got about a dozen lawyers workin for him, so a telegram will always get there even if he's off somewhere in a court tryin t'keep an innocent man from goin to jail or getting his neck stretched."

He watched as Jonah acted as if he was reading. By the look on his whiskered face, Jesse knew that Jonah wanted to sell the herd. *Jonah probably wants to get 'em sold,* Jesse thought, *before his neighbor gets back so he can pocket a chunk.* "I don't think your price is too high," Jesse said, "but if it costs me too much to hire four hands to help get the herd to my spread, then," he shook his head of rusty red hair that had gone to rusty redish-gray during the past few years, "I reckon I'm whupped before I ever start home."

Jonah only paused a moment before speaking, "Whadaya say about five dollars a head with four of my boys going all the way back with ya?" Jesse knew he'd have the herd and wanted to smile, but kept it locked inside his face. "Them boys have all herded cows before and know what hard work is all about." It was his turn to stare at Jesse. "I reckon five dollars a head in gold is a fair price, Mister McKannah."

When he heard the word mister, Jesse knew he would be heading home with the herd the following day.

All four of the *men* that Jonah sent to ride with Jesse and the two Henderson boys looked a bit younger than Robert or Johnny. However before the herd was a full day away from Jonah's spread, Jesse saw nothing to make him think that this was their first cowboy job.

Jesse watched as the herd passed the area where he had felt

certain they would make their first camp. It was still two hours before sundown, so he began to question the uneasiness he had felt about moving a herd of cattle three hundred miles, even a small herd like this with half a dozen men who were actually still boys. His anxiety then melted a little with each mile covered.

After locating an area where they could graze, the four bulls were hobbled so they wouldn't attempt to return to the only home they'd known. "If they did," Jesse said, "I think every cow would follow, and we'd have a helluva time turning them."

Once the cows were grazing with the bulls in the center, Jesse said, "Two men'll be able to keep an eye on the herd. I'm still not sure about your names, so Johnny and Robert," he nodded at the Hendersons, "will take the first two hours while you fellas and me set up camp n' get t'know each other."

Once the coffee water was in the pot near the coals, a larger tin pot than the one he'd been soaking the jerked cougar in was filled with fourteen slices of dried meat and then filled with water.

Once the water was hot Jesse and the four cowboys ate their allotted two slices and had two biscuits each, slathered with butter and plum jam.

Jesse poured a quart of coffee into a tin pot that had a lid and handle, and with two tin cups in his other hand he walked down toward the grazing herd. They were quietly enjoying the tender grass a hundred yards away. The downhill walk from camp was under a full moon, so he could see both riders while walking toward the herd. He could also hear both boys either singing softly or talking quietly to the herd so they would know that someone was nearby.

When Robert spotted Jesse he walked his horse toward him. "I won't be sleepin much tonight, Robert, so I'll be out here again later. You n' Johnny are gonna love them biscuits that Jonah's older wife sent, and there's plum jam too." He watched as Robert wrapped the reins around the pommel so he could carry both cups and the pot.

Before Robert thanked Jesse and nudged his horse toward Johnny, his eyebrows furrowed down as he asked, "Older wife! How many has he got?"

"I've heard that Mormons can have as many as they can feed and clothe." Jesse's eyes roamed across the herd and then slowly scanned the entire area before speaking. "It ain't the way

I was raised, Robert, and the bible says 'judge not lest ye be judged' so I reckon I'll just pay attention to my business and let them do as they see fit." He then turned and headed back up the hill toward camp. After sitting on his bedrole and leaning against the saddle, Jesse thanked the young man who handed him a cup of coffee. "You're Otis, aincha?"

"Yessir." The boy smiled and nodded at the three boys sitting next to Jesse. "I'm the oldest of us four brothers. That's Ode, and the one next to him is Omar, and that one still nibbling on his second biscuit is Othelo." He grinned wide, making his pimple-pocked face resemble a Jack-O-Lantern, overly carved by a drunken celebrator. "His mama was in a college learning to be a stage actress when she met our pa and decided to be his sixth wife." He wheeled around and went to his bedroll. "I got second watch with Omar, so g'nite, and Jesse," he looked over at him, "thanks for fixin the coffee and warmin up them biscuits in that tin thing you have. They taste a whole lot better warm." He rolled over and was asleep and snoring so fast that Jesse didn't have time to formulate an answer.

The second day they entered the pass at noon, so they had made very good time. At the same boulder where the wolf grabbed the carcass of the sheep and carried it out of sight, Jesse kept running his eyes back and forth. He was certain that the wolf had moved on but he felt a buzz or a clicking inside his head. He closed his eyes and shook his head slightly side-to-side. When he opened his eyes Jesse was looking straight at the wolf.

The wolf was on top of a large boulder a hundred feet south at the edge of the pass through the Bitterroot Range. Jesse looked to see if any of his six men had seen it, but they were all so busy keeping the herd moving forward he knew they hadn't. When he looked back the wolf was gone.

That night at the fire he told the four new cowboys about the wolf. He was the only one that had a rifle, but he didn't want one of them to be startled and shoot at it with their ancient single shot muzzle loading pistol. "He has a damaged right rear leg or foot. I couldn't tell which when we came through. He holds it up close to his belly so it can heal and won't bump som'n if he hasta run. I reckon he feels like he needs some help is why he's following us, so don't take a shot at him if he pops up, cause he sure's hell ain't gonna be a problem to us. He's havin a hard time just staying alive and movin along with us, I reckon."

While the cowboys not on the first watch sat by the fire sipping coffee, Jesse used strips of rawhide to make three snares. When he gathered them and stood, Robert asked, "Need a hand setting those snares, Jesse?"

He smiled at the elder Henderson boy, "Sure, c'mon."

Back at the fire a few minutes later, Johnny and two of the Mormon boys were asleep as Jesse and Robert rolled up in their bedrolls. "I been seein lots of fat rabbits along the way, Jesse. Bet that wolf could handle three of 'em."

"He wouldn't turn down just one I'm sure, cause he probably ain't et no meat since that sheep I told you about."

Jesse slept three good uninterrupted hours, and after a cup of strong coffee that had simmered all night he felt rested. He sat the empty cup down and headed toward the snares. The first one was as they had left it, but the second one had a small but plump rabbit hanging by the neck, and the last one had a huge fat rabbit, also hanging by the neck.

He carried the rabbits to the fire and placed them on the ground. Dawn would soon be erasing the darkness, so he swung the saddle up on his shoulder and headed toward Shadow. After the saddle was cinched, he put on the harness then brought the reins back and wrapped them around the pommel. He still used a soft Indian harness rather than a traditional one that required a steel bit in the horse's mouth.

When asked about it by white men he said, "I would not want one in my mouth so I won't put one in my horse's mouth. I train my horse to the touch of my knees and hands or what I say."

He walked Shadow to the fire and picked up the two dead rabbits and then climbed into the saddle. Before he went to the herd Jesse rode to a large flat boulder and put both rabbits down.

He always remained behind to be certain that no cow was left because it had simply wandered off during the night. Once he'd checked the area, Jesse easily caught up with the herd. As he neared the area they had spent the night at he looked toward the flat boulder.

The wolf was standing in the shadows beneath a huge round boulder and was looking straight into Jesse's eyes. When Jesse and Shadow were almost to the flat rock Jesse glanced back at the boulder and saw that the wolf had disappeared. As they walked slowly past, the wolf leaped up on the flat boulder and moved to the two rabbits. Jesse watched as it let the left leg come slowly down until it was standing on all four—all the while looking into Jesse's eyes.

Before nudging Shadow to catch up with the herd, he watched as the wolf picked up both rabbits in its mouth, and then lifted the injured leg back up and jumped down behind the rocks.

Jesse smiled as he nudged Shadow ahead, *ain't all healed up but gettin better. Glad I could help, amigo.*

They made it to the river in record time considering the fact that they were driving one hundred and seventy head of cattle and three bulls, which at times were more mule than bull.

There were clouds in the sky but no rain had fallen since they had been on the west side of the river. As the herd moved across, Jesse kept scanning the area with his eyes in hopes of spotting the wolf.

He gently nudged Shadow to climb back up the bank when he noticed gaps in the herd. Jesse patted the horse's neck and spoke softly, "Let's go see if there are any stragglers."

He saw one young cow that had stopped to graze on a small patch of grass a few yards off the trail.

With no signal from Jesse, Shadow stayed on the trail and continued west for a dozen yards. He then moved into the trees on carefully placed hoofs and advanced toward the contentedly grazing cow. When he was still a few feet away Shadow snorted and lunged toward it.

Jesse had been twisting back and forth in the saddle looking for the wolf. With the terrified cow back on the trail and running toward the river, Jesse leaned forward and spoke, "She'll sure's hell have some stories to tell her friends back at camp tonight." He chuckled when Shadow snorted while shaking his head.

The first thing that Jesse noticed when he followed the cow up the farther bank toward the herd was the wolf. It was sitting on a small boulder a hundred yards south on the east side of the river. Jesse had the telescope out in seconds and was adjusting it. When Shadow felt the telescope being pulled out of the tube that rested on his rump behind the saddle, he stopped. Jesse shook his head as he replaced it, "Yep, that's the same guy we been seeing along the trail." After nudging him to get them closer to the herd, Shadow turned to look directly at the wolf. He walked at a fast pace but turned twice to look at the wolf, and each time *whoofed* softly. Jesse patted him on the neck each time, and the last time said, "Amigo, I'm glad you approve because I reckon he's gonna be with us a while."

They moved steadily toward Flathead Lake, and made camp twenty-five miles west of Burgess Kellerman's new town, Burgess Montana, a day earlier than Jesse expected. The weather had been phenomenally clear until the last night they set up camp.

Heavy rain began falling soon after the fire was started. Jesse had been watching the sky, and had rigged his poncho to spread out over the top of several sticks. It kept the rain from extinguishing the fire long enough to heat two pots of water, one for coffee and the other to soften the remaining cougar jerky.

The night passed miserably as the seven men remained in the saddle circling the herd singing or humming to reassure the cows during the lightning flashes and relentless rain.

Dawn broke on a disgruntled group of cowboys that were still being pummeld by raindrops the size of grapes. Jesse rode from one to the other saying the same thing. "Let's get that herd moving toward home because it doesn't look like this rain's gonna stop any time soon."

Once the herd was moving steadily along the trail, Jesse then pulled up beside Robert and explained what he planned to do.

Robert grinned when Jesse asked him to tell Johnny where they were headed and what they were going to do.

At almost exactly high noon the herd was turned by Jesse and Robert onto Main Street in Burgess Montana. The rain was still coming down and was still in droplets the size of small grapes. Jesse pulled Shadow over to the side and waited until the entire herd was heading north—right down the center of town. As the last few stragglers turned onto the hard-packed dirt road running through Burgess Kellerman's town, Jesse pulled out his pistol and fired twice straight up into the clouds. He hadn't said anything to the four Mormon boys, but when the gunshot rang through the trees, that herd began running, and the boys encouraged their horses to run along with them.

As they roared past the same saloon and gambling casino that Jesse had earlier eavedropped on Kellerman's plans, men began staggering out to see the show. Several loud drunken "Yeeeeehaaaaws" came from wobbling men waving tattered old hats while others stood with gaping mouths as cattle passed by a few feet away.

A few minutes after entering town the herd was back on the trail at the north end of Burgess Montana. They were once again walking, and heading toward the pass through the hills that Jesse used when he came to find out why the men from this town attacked his Flathead Indian friends.

Jesse was in the rear when the herd turned into the pass. He followed to be certain that a few didn't miss the entrance and stray into the surrounding forest.

After the last cow entered and was scrambling to catch up with the herd, Jesse saw movement off to his left. There, standing on the top of a huge boulder was the wolf. Jesse didn't need to pull out the small telescope to know it was him. The right rear leg wasn't pulled all the way up but still wasn't being used to hold up the body. It touched down momentarily but then was up again, as though the wolf was testing it.

Jesse smiled and turned to follow the herd. He then reached forward and patted Shadow's neck, "Looks like we've got us a new mouth t'feed." Shadow shook his head up and down while blowing through his lips. Jesse shook his head, "Big fella, you're gonna say som'n one day and I'll probably fall outa this saddle."

The herd had only been out of the pass one mile when Lame Wolverine led a band of a dozen Flatheads toward it. Jesse was still bringing up the rear, but when he saw his friend he nudged Shadow into a full gallop and headed toward the small band of Indians.

He reached them at the same time the herd did, and Jesse watched as the Indians spread out to cover both sides and the rear.

The four Mormon boys had never been so close to a group of any tribe of Indians and they were more than a bit apprehensive when the young warriors moved in among them and began whooping and yelling to get the herd moving a little faster.

Jesse knew it wasn't good to run a herd like they were, but he decided to wait and explain it to them later.

"It's only a mile or so," he said to Robert Henderson, "to the area they've fenced off to let these cows become used to livin here, so it won't hurt 'em none to run a bit." Robert, wise for his age, smiled and shook his head up and down slightly.

The following morning Jesse approached the six boys. "I have som'n for each of you t'letcha know that I think you all did a great job o' helpin me git this herd back here." He held a gold coin out and placed it in each boy's hand as he held it out. "Ain't a fortune, but it'll gitcha som'n y'probably been wantin for a while."

They were all very surprised and thanked him repeatedly then mounted their horses and headed home.

A few days later Jesse was sitting with Lone Wolverine while Gentle Breeze stirred fresh vegetables into a pot that had been simmering since dawn.

"Oh boy," Jesse said when she began cutting freshly washed cama root into the pot.

"She's been saving that for the day you returned," his friend the chief said.

"That's not the first time she's done that." Jesse said, and then turned a smile toward Lame Wolverine, "You've sure got a good woman there. I wish Prairie Rose was still here with us."

He said it so softly, and with such tenderness, that his friend didn't answer him right away. A few minutes passed before he turned to Jesse and spoke. "I understand how you feel, because I would also have a big hole in my heart like you do if anything happened to Gentle Breeze."

Jesse continued watching her work at the cook pot and then said in a voice barely more than a whisper, "And it would never completely heal," he turned to his friend, "as mine won't."

Jesse turned to him again after a while and asked, "Have any of those people from that little town on the other side of the hills been back over here bothering you?"

"We've kept guards out ever since that morning you came roaring down from the hills to warn us. We've seen people sneaking around out there trying to figure out what we're doing, but so far nobody has started shooting at us again." Lame Wolverine's eyes roamed out across the lake before turning back to his friend. "They seem to be watching us like we're a herd of animals and they want to know what we are going to do." A pained expression crossed his brown face, "I feel like going out there with braves and filling them full of arrows sometimes, but won't because that would just cause more bad feelings between us and the white men who want us off this land."

After he and the boys returned from Idaho with the cattle, Jesse, and at times as many as a dozen Indians, had worked on his cabin from early spring until September. It was dried in by mid summer and the exterior walls were all in place by the end of August. The room for Shadow and the mule, that Jesse named Ironhead, had been expanded to allow room for two more horses, in the event one or more of his brothers came to visit and stayed through the winter.

A friend of the diner owner, Michael O'Hannahan, offered to build the stone chimney, and diligently worked on it every day. His mother was a Flathead that married a trapper and worked the streams and lakes with him until old age took them both. "The Flatheads are good people," he said to Jesse, "but most white folks don't pay 'em no mind atol. They mostly treat 'em like they're foriners takin up space that oughta be given to white people. If you're willin t'help the Flatheads like you're doin then by golly I reckon I can sure help you build yerself a cabin."

Jesse shook the older man's hand, saying, "Jacob, I certainly do appreciate you doin this for me. My best friend built the chimney for a ranch house I had in California, but I was so busy building the place that I didn't learn much about chimneys." He grinned wide then added, "And now I'm s'busy gettin this one finished before winter that I probably won't learn much from you either."

"Jesse, you just go ahead with whacher doin and I'll build the chimney." He looked out toward the beautiful lake, and then added, "Y'might not ever hafta build yerself another cabin."

Jesse followed the man's eyes, and a moment later replied, "You're probably right, Jacob. I don't reckon there's a prettier place on earth."

By late September the cabin was finished and smoke was rising from the stone chimney.

At the beginning of spring several of Lone Wolverine's braves began trimming the limbs from fallen trees and dragging the trunks to a cleared spot near the cabin. Young boys piled the limbs on a travois and used their horses to drag them close too.

Months earlier Jesse bought a two-man crosscut saw and by working with them taught the Flathead braves how to use it.

By late fall there was enough stacked wood near the cabin to last Jesse the winter, and also a pile of logs near chief's tepee.

Jesse rode to Chief Lame Wolverine's lodge early in October and joined him at the fire. "Hola, Jesse," his friend greeted him, "join me for some sassafrass tea."

Jesse dismounted and removed the harness so Shadow could graze nearby on the winter grass poking through the light snow. "Sounds good, looks like winter found us again."

"There's no reason to hide from winter," the chief said with a wide smile, "it always finds you."

Jesse accepted the clay cup that Gentle Breeze brought him. "Thank you." He sipped the tea and then turned to the chief's wife. "Gentle Breeze, you look so much better now. You look like a healthy young woman again."

She smiled wide, but self-consciously with her eyes on the ground, "All thanks to you, White Buffalo."

He had finally accepted the honor of being called that, and smiled at her. "It was the Great Father who guided me here to help His children, The People."

After another sip of tea, Jesse turned to the chief, "Before we get heavy snow I am going back to that town on the other side of the mountain to see if I can learn what they are planning to do. Now that we have more land and a good herd of cattle I feel certain they will be planning more grief for us."

"Yes," the chief said, "I have the same feelings."

"It will be to our advantage to know what they are planning."

The chief shook his head in agreement and sipped his tea.

Two nights later Jesse was once again on the west side of that mountain. Same as before, he located the place where he'd left Shadow before the sun went down. He didn't hobble the horse, feeling certain he would remain there, but Jesse appologised for leaving the tack on, "We might need t'git outa here in a hurry, big fella." He patted Shadow's neck, "I'll treatcha to an extra big helping of oats when we get home."

Jesse checked to be sure there were no rattlers in the area, and then slipped off his boots and put on the deerskin moccasins. *I ain't walkin in there with those boots this time*, he thought, *because I know right where I'm goin now.*

He then stretched out under a huge tree and rested for two hours. After waking, he glanced up at the sliver of moon and knew that it was long enough after sunset that most of the people who were planning to go to the casino would already be there.

After filling his hat with water so Shadow could drink, Jesse slapped it against his leg and returned it to his head and headed toward town.

When he spotted the glow of a lantern, Jesse stopped next to a tree. He recalled that a lantern was left sitting on the porch of the northern-most house.

After repeatedly scanning the entire area, Jesse headed south among the big trees toward Kellerman's casino. Fifteen minutes later he stopped next to another tree. He'd moved about one hundred feet. For ten minutes he scanned three-hundred and sixty degrees. When finally satisfied that he was alone, Jesse moved forward toward the huge wooden building where he had eavesdropped previously.

He remained in the shadows of the same huge tree and scanned the area, avoiding the single window to prevent the light coming through the still filthy window from affecting his darkness-oriented eyes.

When he got close to the window he could hear the loud booming voice of Burgess Kellerman. "No, I didn't bring a herd o' cows with me cause I was too busy gettin everything set up. I got some guys bringin a small herd any day now. How many cows didja say was in the herd that white injun lover brought in for 'em?"

"Mustabeen way over a hunert, boss. That white guy and a buncha kids run 'em right down Main Street."

"I gotta find out who the hell that guy is," Kellerman's voice thundered, "and if I can't get him t'play ball with us then by God we'll bury him with a buncha them injuns."

"Boss," a weak, whiney voice came through the window to Jesse's ears, "I know a guy down in thet town near the Salt Lake what could stop by an visit with that injun lover at his new cabin and juss sorta listen and maybe find out what he's planning."

"Yeah," Kellerman slurred, and Jesse could tell that the man was getting drunk, "and them savages would send his scalped and gutted carcass back to Polson or wherever the hell you said he's from." Jesse heard bottles and glasses tinkling together, so figured Kellerman was pouring drinks. "Here, have another drink and stop trying to think. That's my job, and besides I already got a guy comin that'll get in with that guy n' learn what he n' them flatheaded injuns got planned."

"This guy kin o' yours?" a new voice asked.

Jesse strained to hear while still scanning the entire area for a possible intruder. "No, but I've known him since we was kids, back at the turn of the century. He'll be ridin in here from Texas any day now."

"Was he in your gang back in them old days?" To Jesse, the man speaking also sounded drunk. "Burgess," the man slurred, "them musta been great days. Wish I coulda rode with ya back then."

"Yeah," Jesse heard Burgess say, "we took what we wanted and if anyone squawked we just shot 'em and moved on."

A new voice asked, "This feller comin here a killer?"

"Yeah," Kellerman answered in a bold voice, "the kind that I never wondered about, because if a situation called for killin, he just went ahead n' took care of it. And he's got a scar across his stomach t'prove he ain't scared to mix it up with someone what don't see eye-to-eye with him."

"Some feller tried t'gut him, eh?"

"Didn't try, the guy did. After Tag shot that damn Mexican in the chest, the bastard lunged forward and sliced ole Tag's gut open. Tag quickly put his arm against his stomach t'keep his guts from spillin out, then shot that same Mexican between the eyes." Burgess stopped talking for a moment, so Jesse looked around quickly and was prepared to run, but he heard Burgess cough twice and then say loudly, "Damned beer went down the wrong tube." He coughed a few more times and then cleared his throat loudly before continuing. "Tag held his guts in while the bartender ran to the dentist's house to have him come n' sew ole Tag's damn gut shut." Burgess laughed so loud that he began coughing again. After a few moments he slammed his hand down on the tabletop and chuckled before saying, "Got hisself a scar that runs from side-to-side right across his belly button. I'll get him to show it to all of you when he gits here."

Jesse had heard much more than he hoped for, and even though he still didn't know exactly what Burgess Kellerman planned to do, he now knew that he and his Flathead friends were definetly part of it.

After returning to Shadow, he climbed up into the saddle to head back toward the north pass through the mountain. He was anxious to get back home and discuss what he'd learned with Lame Wolverine.

Glad I came here tonight, Jesse thought, *because forewarned is forearmed. Gotta be on the lookout for that guy from Texas and deal with him as I see fit. And then we've gotta get rid of Kellerman somehow before he builds up a powerbase of crooks and killers.*

Jesse was laying in bed thinking about the conversation he heard at the window in Kellerman's place two nights earlier. *I gotta keep a good lookout for that friend of Burgess. They were kids at the turn of this century, so he's about sixty,* Jesse thought as he stared at the moving images of moths on the ceiling caused by the kerosene lantern.

Late afternoon a week later, a man sitting tall in the saddle rode in from the north. Jesse was working behind his new house and spotted the man coming slowly around the eastern side of Flathead Lake.

Jesse carefully watched as the man appeared to be heading southeast, but then suddenly turned west toward his cabin and continued walking his horse at a slow gait.

"Howdy," the tall, thin, fair-skinned, middle-aged man said from the saddle after stopping his horse, "is that trail I been on, Jedediah Smith's last trail?" He spoke easily and smiled slightly in a very friendly manner.

"Yep," Jesse answered him casually, his small smile thin and brief, always leery of lone men on a trail.

"Good," the man said, "was hoping I had hit the right trail to take me down to Traveler's Rest."

Jesse had been through too much during his many years out in the wilderness to allow his intuitive instincts of caution to blindly accept what a stranger told him. He let the plank that he was trimming with a hatchet fall flat on the two wooden horses and then buried the blade in the top of a log so it wouldn't rust if he didn't get back to the job for a while.

He looked up at the tall stranger and said, "Climb down outa the saddle and have a seat on the porch and I'll fix us a cup of coffee."

"Thanks, a cup might perk me up, been a long trail." The man dismounted and led his horse to a hitching rail that Jesse had recently added in front of the porch. "Mighty neighborly of you, sir." He used his teeth to grip the tips of his leather gloves, and after pulling the right one off he held out his bare hand, "Augustin Pampineau, French Canadian from Quebec City, pleased to meet you, Mister McKannah."

Jesse had detected a slight accent but couldn't quite place it. He easily took the offered hand and solidly shook it, "Jesse McKannah, Irishman from California." His smile softened, "And no mister please, just Jesse."

"Okay Jesse, and everyone back home just calls me Gus." Smiling wide and friendly, he added, "There are so many people these days out pioneering this new wilderness," the stranger continued in a casual, soft mellow voice, "that they all go inside the minute they see a stranger." He grinned, "Probably to get a gun in their hands."

"It's a good way t'survive out here," Jesse spoke in a calm matter-of-fact voice, "cause y'never know when a stranger has a gang waitin behind a hill over yonder."

"Yep, that's a fact, so I sure don't blame 'em a bit for being careful, but it sure does reinforce m'faith in mankind when someone like you offers a porch chair and a cup o' coffee."

"I keep coals under the pot," Jesse said, "so it'll be strong."

"Just the way I like m'coffee." The man looped his horse's reins around the rail and walked up the steps to the shaded porch.

Jesse said from inside, "Got some sugar if y'like it."

"Nossir, juss plain black'll suit me fine."

As Jesse waited for the fresh wood to ignite under the coffee to heat it a bit more, he thought about his foreman and friend, Arliss O'Reilly. *Arliss rode in as a stranger and became the best friend I ever had until they killed him n' all my ranch hands. This guy,* he thought, *is younger'n me, and came in from the north, so it ain't likely that he's Kellerman's guy, because he said that his guy's coming up from Texas.* He watched as the wood flames heated the eye under the pot, and a few minutes later closed the damper again and poured them each a cup.

"Oh boy," the man crooned after sipping the coffee, "sure beats the camp coffee I been making."

After a sip of his, Jesse asked, "Come down from Canada, didja?"

"Yep, all the way from Quebec and lemme tell ya Jesse, that's a long ride during winter."

Jesse was relaxed now and smiled, "I know, because I was up there trapping during a few winters right along the Canadian border up above Oregon." The more he talked to the stranger the more relaxed he became. *I reckon,* he thought, *that this is just another loner traveling across this wild new country.*

"I never wandered that far west," the man said, "but I've met men from that part of the country, and they all said to come prepared if you're gonna go through in the winter."

"They told you right," Jesse said, "cause I trapped up there for a few winters." His mind drifted back to the past so he paused for a moment before continuing, "But then I was much younger and the weather didn't bother me back then."

"I reckon," the man said with an easy smile, "that I was born with blood that does not like getting cooled down like molasses, so I'm heading on down south to a waterfront town called New Orleans and gonna try m'hand at fishing for a living."

"I've heard of the place," Jesse said, "have you ever tried fishing for a living?"

"Nope, but a fella I met last year up in Montreal when I was visiting my folks in Quebec City said he's been fishing that area for a few years and is making more money than he ever earned at wages. He offered me a job on his boat, so I'm gonna give it a good try."

"M'dad," Jesse said, "left Ireland on a sailing freighter when he was still just a kid and worked on it until he was old enough to go into the mountains above San Francisco to try his hand at trapping." He emptied his tin cup before continuing, "His stories were exciting but I don't reckon I'd be worth much outa sight of land." He grinned as he picked up the stranger's empty cup and stood. "I've got a young elk that's been in the smoker for two days, so if you ain't in a hurry t'git on the trail to New Orleans you're welcome to stay overnight and we'll see how it turned out."

"Well," the man said, "I am anxious to get down there," his smile was wide and friendly, "but I ain't about t'pass up a hot meal, cause it'll be a while fore I sit down to another one."

Aleena

Aleena had been learning words in the Flathead language as she taught the children and tended to the elderly. She repeatedly heard White Buffalo mentioned when near the younger braves. It made her feel good because it was always used in conjunction with words like 'did this' or 'did that,' and White Buffalo said 'this' or 'that.' *Jesse is alive and nearby with his people,* she thought, *thank You Lord for leading me to him. You have looked after me good these past few months dear Lord, and I don't wanna seem ungrateful, but please answer one more prayer.* She remained silent for several minutes while she thought about what she should say. Finally she squeezed her eyes together tight and let her prayer flow out of her mind. *Please dear Jesus, watch over my brothers so we can all be together again. I know that all prayers must be paid for, and if You will answer this one I will make Christians of as many of these young Flathead Indians as I can.*

Aleena was walking a few feet behind the travois when she spotted an old woman lying near the edge shifting and wiggling in an attempt to get more comfortable. *She's gonna fall off,* she thought briefly, and then ran forward. Just as she arrived, the old woman's foot slipped off, and had Aleena not been there the woman would have fallen and probably busted a bone.

She helped the old woman shift farther to the inside, and then motioned with her arm for a young girl. Aleena had cleaned and bandaged an infected foot on her a few days earlier. She scooted to Aleena on her good leg and smiled. "How is foot?" Aleena asked in the girl's language, who answered that it was much better. "We will soon be home," Aleena smiled and pointed at the old woman, who was now sleeping, "no let fall off."

Aleena smiled wide when the child replied in a serious voice, "I help her like you help me." She leaned over the edge of the travois to hug the child.

When she straightened up and moved a few feet away from the travois, an older brave about her age pulled his horse up beside her and smiled, "My grandmother," he said in his tongue while nodding toward the old woman, "thank you."

Aleena looked into the kindest eyes she had seen on a man since meeting Chief Bonesetter. "This very hard for old people."

"Yes, hard for all old." He said in broken English, and then smiled warmly down at her.

"You speak my language?" Aleena felt herself blushing.

"Little bit," he grinned wide, "you brother, White Buffalo, show me how." His grin widened, "He my friend."

Aleena's brow furrowed momentarily, but then she smiled and said, "School," in his tongue. "I make school. You come?"

"You live here?" He spoke in her language.

"Yes." She smiled and motioned with her long gangly arm, "I no leave. This my home now." She could not recall seeing a grin so wide ever before when he spoke again.

"Good. I happy. Me," he pointed at his chest, "Dog Walker," his smile returned, "all dog like me so I take for walk." He then used the phrase for see you later in his tongue, and galloped off.

Aleena watched him ride away, and thought, *My, what a nice man.*

Patrick

Less than a month after Kenneth and Seamus had strapped on their custom made leather shoulder-holsters, Patrick and Joseph Alderman were watching as Mister Buchanan left his quarters and headed toward the coach they were standing beside. All had enjoyed a big breakfast prior to a trip that Patrick had prepared weeks earlier.

Patrick glanced around the campaign compound wondering where his two men were. *They said they were having breakfast with friends this morning but would be here on time to leave.*

Irish-American Gentlemen's Clubs were sprouting up in the fast growing communities along the east coast between the nation's capitol and Boston. Irish businessmen were joining with Irish politicians in an effort to counter the bad publicity that a few wild and unruly sections dominated by the Irish, had caused to be attached to all of the Irish in the northeast section of America.

Most of the members of the clubs were middle and upper middle class Irish working men. They didn't like the image that a minority of lower class Irish had cause to be associated with every Irish family from Boston to the nation's capitol.

The members liked the sound of their club's name and tried to keep the riffraff out. Patrick McKannah had visited each one personally and established a good rapport with members all along the way. Consequently the clubs were all looking forward to having Mister Buchanan and his entourages, especially the Irish lawyer from California, stop by and spend time with them.

Where in bloody 'ell could those guys be? Patrick scanned the entire compound again, and was just turning back as Mister

Buchanan approached the coach, when he heard a noise coming from the street. He was turned facing a man ten feet away that suddenly began pulling a long-barrel pistol out from beneath the belt that had been covered by his long shirt.

Patrick's pistol was in his hand when the first bullet hit the stranger. It had very obviously hit the young man in the head because he was driven straight down to the brick alleyway. Two more shots came from the roof and two other shots from the front of the compound. The stranger had not moved since the first shot hit him on top of the head, even as four more bullets hit his body.

Patrick looked up and saw Kenneth leaning out against the wall surounding the flat roof. "I'll be right down, Patrick," he yelled.

Patrick looked around and spotted Aldo in a squatting firing stance with his pistol pointing at the dead man. Patrick shook his head and winked an eye at his aide. Aldo looked around and then put the pistol back into the shoulder holster.

Seamus walked casually to the body and kicked the pistol away before checking for a pulse. "Dead as a dumbass," he said after reloading and shoving his pistol back in the shoulder holster. "Been keepin an eye of this fella all week. Som'n didn' look right the first day 'e dropped in for brew n' a bite up the street at the pub."

Kenneth walked around the corner about the same time that Mister Buchanan walked up. He glanced down, "Another nut?"

"Yeah," Kenneth said, "an Italian nut. Started saying that 'e 'adn't 'ad a bit o' luck findin a job in America and if a democrat became president 'e would probably starve t'death."

Seamus walked over and added, "Nothin that fella said made a bit o' sense. Said 'e came 'ere to git rich an couldn't even 'ave a home. Been sleepin in parks, 'e told us."

"Betcha," Kenneth said, "the guy's been a nut all of 'is short life."

"Lot of them out there," Mister Buchanan said, "but let's get going. The staff'll take care of him." He moved to the coach and stepped in, followed by Patrick and then Aldo, who had stood in the doorway watching the entire time.

Kenneth and Seamus took their positions up top beside the drivers, one on each of the two coaches.

Simon

Twenty-seven days after leaving Salt Lake City, Simon rode Dragon into Travelers Rest. During the four hundred mile trek he killed a huge wolf that had been stalking him for a week, and finally came into his camp all hunched down and ready to leap. While skinning the animal he noticed that it had a deformed lower jaw and easily saw that it was caused by a bullet. *I reckon hunger,* Simon thought, *overruled your better sense of survival, ole fella.*

Even though it was very late in the day when he finished skinning and salting the pelt, Simon moved on toward Travelers Rest. "Gotta put some distance between us n' that wolf's carcass, ole fella." He patted Dragon's neck as he spoke. "Been seeing grizzly sign along here, and I bet you've been smellin it too." He turned in the saddle to look back, "that carcass oughta keep one of 'em busy for the evening."

The day before he rode into Traveler's Rest a young grizzly stood up a short distance off the trail and growled while pawing the air. Simon knew the bear was just letting him know that this was his territory.

It had been a few years since he'd been on Jedediah's 1825 trail, but Simon knew it had been widened by pioneers and filled in where boulders had been moved to make it more passable for supply wagon traffic. *I don't wanna go all the way around this late in the day,* he thought, and then leaned forward to speak softly to Dragon. "Plus I'm 'ungry as that damn bear, and I reckon you are too."

With that said he pulled out one of his two .44 caliber Colt Dragoon revolvers and fired into the air. He'd already replaced it and had his new Jennings .54 caliber lever-action rifle out of the scabbard when the bear went back down on all four and took off running in the opposite direction. Recently purchased, the rifle held twenty-four rounds, and in the hands of a marksman like Simon the young bear wouldn't have had a chance.

While watching the shrubs and small trees shaking as the bear ran over them while frantically getting away from the noise, Simon shoved the rifle back into the scabbard, and then reloaded the pistol's empty cylinder. He gently slapped Dragon on the neck a few times, "Just like I thought, 'e was just a youngun out flexing 'is muscles."

When the horse whinnied, he added, "Yeah, I 'ope 'e keeps on goin too."

~

Like enemy ships passing close in a fogbank, Simon and Burgess Kellerman almost collided. Simon was entering Travelers Rest the next day just as Burgess and his crew was leaving. His new crew consisted of twenty-four rugged looking, cold eyed men and two lean, hungry-looking drifters that he had enlisted when they stopped at Traveler's Rest. Burgess had exaggerated the statistics of his town, Burgess Montana, but none of the men had a home or anywhere else to go, so they were very satisfied just hearing that it had several small cabins where his men that had a woman lived, and a big hotel with plenty of rooms and a kitchen with two good cattle camp cooks. Kellerman and his new *gang members* were headed toward *his town*, which was a short distance from the area where Jesse McKannah and his tribe of Flathead Indian friends had decided to settle permanently.

The two dozen men that had been waiting for Burgess in Salt Lake City were supposed to be closer to fifty. The older man with a patch where a now-dead Mexican had removed one of his eyes with a knife, also had a scar that ran from his scalp down near the patch and across his nose and cheek said, "I'm the only one that showed up in Amarillo, boss, an I had a helluva time gettin these guys to come up with me," he nodded toward the other men, "t'see what kinda cattle ranch operation you're puttin t'gether."

Burgess had worked with the one-eyed man before and knew he would do anything for money. "Patch, we've rode some hard trails t'gether, and this's gonna be our payoff." Burgess looked across the gathering of rugged trail-wise men on horseback and spoke confidently, "And all of you boys're gonna bless the day you threw in with us. From this day on, ole Patch," Burgess nodded at the huge one-eyed man, "will get his orders from me and you'll get yours from him." He nudged his horse and turned toward the north and rode out of Salt Lake City. Patch, the new men he'd acquired, and the two drifters followed. A moment later Burgess stopped his horse and motioned the other men on. "Lead the way, Patch, you been up to Travelers Rest before, aincha?"

"Coupla times." He motioned with his arm, "C'mon, boys."

The two drifters readily admitted that they were game for anything that paid well, including murder, killing Indians, and cattle rustling. Burgess never rode long with his back to anyone, so he just grinned when one turned back toward him and said, "I always figured it's easier to let a feller work hard fer a buncha stuff, and then shoot him n' take it all fer y'self, than it is to work fer it."

~

Simon nudged Dragon in the flanks with his boot heels, and headed straight toward the Trapping Supplies and Mercantile Store. When he asked the clerk about Burgess Kellerman the man told him that he was probably still in town. "He was told by my boss, Joshua Bridger, the fella that opened this here store, to stop badgering all of his customers and move on down the boardwalk aways."

Simon showed the young man his badge and then placed his leather saddlebags on the counter. "Please fill this order," he handed him a list, "and shove everything into these in case he ain't still around n' I gotta haul on outa here in a hurry."

The clerk said, "Yessir," and began reading the list, as Simon wheeled around and left the store.

For an hour Simon walked on the boardwalk or the dirt and stone streets of the small mountaintop settlement looking for Burgess Kellerman, but finally had to accept the fact that he was no longer there. It was confirmed when he stopped at the livery stable and talked to a man cutting leather into strips for new harnesses.

"He left here this mornin with a gang of the sorriest lookin buncha fellas I reckon I ever saw."

"How many were there?" Simon asked.

"Well, lemme see," the man said, putting down his cutting tool, "aside from that loudmouth Texan they was a guy with a patch and mebbe a couple dozen other fellers."

"Say where they were headed?"

"Yeah! That fathead Texas giant said he owned a town up by Flathead Lake named Burgess Montana, and it was gonna be the biggest cattle town north of some place called Sand and Tony'r som'n like thet."

Simon's first thought was to head north right away, but after thinking about it he decided to stay the night and get some rest, and then rise early and track them the following day. *He doesn't think anyone's following him,* Simon thought, *so he'll leave an easy trail to pick up.*

On May 9th the day after Simon rode out of Traveler's Rest, the two Brasco brothers from Texas rode in.

Simon was mounted on Dragon long before the sun had begun peeking over the eastern mountaintops. He decided to stay on Jedediah Smith's original 1824 trail because he was told that it ran almost right through Burgess Kellerman's town. Simon had once been on the newer trail that Jedediah had blazed in 1829 and knew that it angled off to the east before heading back toward Flathead Lake. *I reckon this guy Kellerman wants t'git to his town the quickest way.*

By the time the sun was warming the right side of his face Simon had already picked up Kellerman's trail. *This fella ain't no tenderfoot,* Simon thought, *cause he stays behind all those new guys.* "Dragon, that livery guy was right about this trail being easy to follow. Them two little fellas he said looked like drifters are ridin unshod Indian ponies and probably killed a coupla Indians t'git 'em. That Texan's a big one that's ridin a mighty big horse, same as a coupla them other guys." He leaned forward to pat the horse's neck, "Betcha Kellerman's taller'n me and carryin a full hunert more pounds o' meat on his bones." He looked down at several clear hoofprints and saw that Burgess Kellerman's horse left a print almost twice the size of most horses, and when it landed on top of all but a couple of the other horses it completely covered their print.

Each night Simon spotted their campfire ahead, and slowed Dragon to a cautious quiet walk. At a couple of hundred yards he stopped and removed the saddle and bridle. As he rubbed down Dragon the horse never made a sound. Seeing a fire ahead was all Dragon needed, to understand that a noise of any kind could bring trouble into their camp. The horse even took small amounts of grain between its lips when Simon poured it into his hat and placed it between the horse's front feet. When water replaced the grain there was no loud slurping or noise, only the quiet sound of Shadow's lips filling and the huge head rising to swallow.

Simon placed his hat over the pommel to dry and sat leaning against a giant oak to chew on some biscuits and dried beef he bought at the store in Traveler's Rest. When Kellerman's fire began dimming, Simon allowed his tired eyes to close. He knew that Dragon had silently moved closer, and would arouse him if there was movement of any kind during the night.

~

Unknown to Big John and his men, or Chief Bonesetter and his tribe, Simon McKannah was camped for the night between them, but a mile farther south.

Simon finished his coffee and covered the glowing coals of his small smokeless fire with dirt long before the sun rose above the eastern mountaintops. He was still chewing jerked beef when he climbed into the saddle and nudged Dragon with his boots.

By dawn Big John and his men were also moving north. Chief Bonesetter and his people were on the move an hour before sunrise, so by noon the valley had funneled in and brought the two groups closer together. Simon was in the same valley but still about half a mile south.

Big John, as usual, was talking in his gravely voice as they rode slowly ahead . . . and if this Kellerman fella that I met once down in Texas gits ever thang worked out, he's gonna have the biggest cattle ranch they is anywhere."

Stick spoke up. "You say he's even got a town what's named fer 'im?"

"Yeah, and there's a gamblin place what's got gals dancing on a big stage." Big John had to stop talking and take a deep breath because he got excited when he talked about going to a place like Burgess Montana. "I talked to a fella what was there, an he tole they's got themselves a big kitchen what fixes better food than y'ever et t'home."

An hour before dark, Big John was still slumped in the saddle as his horse plodded ahead. He was daydreaming about the big fancy town in Montana they were headed toward when Rupert said, "Hey boss, lookit that Injun camp up ahead."

~

Simon began seeing the tracks of the scouts that ranged out on all sides of Chief Bonesetter's large tribe and the two Flathead tribes that joined them. As darkness began blanketing the valley Simon became even more conscious of trying to spot movement.

He wasn't surprised to see several small fires ahead once it was dark. *Yep, I was right,* he thought, *those were tracks made by Flathead scouts moving along with a big tribe.*

Simon decided to make camp and do without a fire until he could move in and make contact with them the following day. *Gotta be Flatheads,* he thought, *because a large tribe of Blackfoot like this wouldn't be in this area wandering around down here.*

Simon was close enough the following morning to see in his telescope that he was right. *It's a Flathead tribe.* He the telescope together and put it away.

He nudged Dragon and began cautiously advancing toward the gathering of Indians just after sunup. The morning cooking fires had thrown off enough light earlier for Simon to observe their camp. He had spent time with Flatheads and knew how they set up a camp, so he was hopeful that when he made his presence known and asked if they knew where his brother Jesse might be, they could tell him.

Simon walked Dragon slowly toward the Flathead tribe that was moving north along a valley. When he spotted an old man and several young braves leave the group and head toward him on their horses, Simon held up his hand palm toward them and brought Dragon to a stop.

Chief Bonesetter spoke to the brave riding next to him, "I know this giant white man." When the young man turned to him, the chief said, "He's a Texas Ranger that has followed bad white men far north of where we are right now." Turning to the youth, he said, "And if I am correct about his name, he is the brother of White Buffalo."

Chief Bonesetter raised his own hand as they moved close to Simon. "Hello again, Simon McKannah, what brings you so far north?"

Simon smiled, "Greetings, Doctor Caruthers, you're a long way from home, aincha?"

"Very good memory, Simon, and yes I'm taking someone to see a relative." His mischievous smile puzzled Simon. "Come, Simon, I will introduce you to this white person, and perhaps you can help." He turned his horse toward his camp. Simon and the other men followed him.

Simon's eyebrows were pulled down as he followed the chief. *I wonder what he's thinkin? Me help someone find a relative.*

When the chief stopped they were near a group of women who were handing out apples and pieces of dried fish to the children.

The chief nimbly climbed from the bare back of his horse and motioned with his arm, "Come with me, Simon." Simon nudged Dragon, and they walked toward three women. *That one,* Simon thought, *in the sun bonnet is sure tall for a Flathead.*

Aleena turned around when she heard the chief say in English, "I have a surprise for you, Ironheaded woman."

The chief was grinning when Aleena looked at him. She was puzzled and didn't know what to say until her eyes shifted to the huge bearded man sitting on a gigantic horse. She glanced at the chief, who was grinning from ear-to-ear, but her eyes were drawn back to the big man. After a moment of staring at each other, Aleena's mouth dropped wide open, but she was still speechless until Simon laughed.

He was laughing harder as he climbed down from Dragon's saddle, "Good God, sis, we all thought sure you was dead." He stepped forward and wrapped his huge arms around her and pulled Aleena close."

"Boy oh boy, Simon," she stepped back when he released his bear hug, "I wouldn't have thought it possible for you to get any bigger but you sure have since last I saw you."

~

Cold, silent, evil eyes were watching as Chief Bonesetter and his group, which now included Simon, headed north again.

Big John lowered the telescope and rested it on the pommel. His dark eyebrows furrowed down as he continued looking at the Indians moving north along the narrowing valley half a mile or so distant.

Can't be him, he thought. Raising the scope again, he searched until Simon was once again in it. Two minutes later he lowered it again and shoved it together. *Ain't another man alive what sits a horse like thet, so it's him alright.* His eye slits narrowed until almost closed. *Gunbutt forward on the left side,* he thought, *an I bet there's one juss like it on the right. Yessiree, by God, that's the Texas Ranger what kilt ole Pucker an put this damned bullet in m'leg.* He had developed a habit of rubbing his upper left thigh where one of Simon McKannah's bullets was still lodged.

Big John wheeled his horse around and headed back to where he'd left his men waiting. "We'll move on purdy soon now," he said when he first rode in, "an find thet town named Burgess Montana." Big John didn't mention who or what he saw during his two hour absence, and none of the men were about to ask him. They noticed that he filled a tin cup with hot coffee and didn't seem to be in a hurry to get going, so they joined him at the fire and silently sipped coffee for two hours.

Wanna give them injuns n' thet damn Ranger time t'git way ahead, he thought, *cause I don't want no buncha injuns around when me n' thet Ranger settle up. The way he hugged on thet tall gal, I figger wherever them injuns decide to camp is where he'll be, so won't be no trouble atoll t'keep an eye on him.*

~

Simon McKannah had developed an uneasy feeling in his gut, something that he had learned never to ignore. So after the sun set he explained briefly to Aleena and Chief Bonesetter, and then broke away from the caravan of Flatheads. He was only a few miles from Burgess Montana as the sun slipped silently into the western peaks of the Bitterroot Range.

He nudged Dragon off the trail they had followed toward the town he had been told was nestled between two low mountains. "They's a right nice valley," the trapper relaxing in Traveler's

Rest had told him, "what runs a right smart ways tween a coupla hills, an thet's the place Mister Kellerman built hisself thet town a few years ago."

Simon didn't like anything that he had so far heard about this Burgess Kellerman fella. *Sounds t'me*, he thought as he carefully guided Dragon through the forest paralleling the trail he'd just pulled off of, *that this Kellerman guy is hell bent on controlling all of this country, even if he hasta kill Jesse and run off the Flatheads.*

Simon saw cattle tracks entering the trail from the west. *Looks like a small herd came through here a while back.*

A short time before dark Simon spotted smoke rising above the trees and moved off the trail and into the surrounding forest. He talked quietly to Dragon while guiding the horse through the trees so he would know not to make noise. "I'll find you a nice spot to graze, amigo, while I have a look around."

By the time stars had filled the sky and a full moon had risen, Simon could hear a fiddle being played, and the faint sounds of a man singing. He used the light of the moon to locate a small but cleared area with grass.

With Dragon hobbled and slowly chewing his way across the clearing, Simon began moving silently through the trees toward the music. He paused regularly as though the trees had guards watching for an enemy. An hour later he saw the first building. He was a mile or more from his horse so he didn't feel there was cause to worry that his horse would be seen or heard by anyone.

He settled into the moonlit shadows of the trees and vines a hundred feet from the trail that turned into Main Street of Burgess Montana. Within an hour complete darkness from rain clouds had spread across the woods he sat in so completely that he could not see his gloved hand when he raised it before his eyes.

Lanterns were lit in the several houses that lined the street across from Kellerman's Hotel and Casino. Remaining among the trees, he watched as men carrying lanterns left the darkness of their houses and headed toward the huge two-story building across the street at the other end of town.

Simon moved stealthily through the trees until he was behind the casino. He had considered just riding in on his horse and entering as just a traveler but decided not to risk being recognized as a Texas Ranger, since he'd tracked men into this area in past years.

He stood among the trees near the casino and watched as men filed through the front door of the building. He heard a lot of loud laughter coming from several men, and giggling from two or perhaps three different women. But since he hadn't seen a woman being accompanied by any of the men that entered the building, he figured they lived and worked there.

No rain had yet fallen, but darkness from the clouds had so thoroughly pulled a shroud over the small mountain town that Simon reminded himself not to take the darkness for granted. *That full moon can pop through any minute and light this place up.* He hadn't seen another person enter the building for an hour, so he decided that all of the townfolk must be inside. He cautiously moved closer.

There was a window low enough that Simon could listen to the people inside talking, but it was so covered with dust and soot from the wood stove that little light made it through the glass, so he felt secure standing next to it.

Constantly scanning the dark area around and behind him, Simon never-the-less concentrated on what was being said by the men inside. One booming voice stood out from all the rest, and it didn't take long for Simon to realize it was Burgess Kellerman.

When Simon distinctly heard the name McKannah he tensed momentarily and then leaned closer toward the glass. "And if that goddamned Jesse McKannah thinks he's gonna set up those stinkin Flatheads to raise cattle here on this land he's got another think comin, cause **that** ain't gonna happen." He screamed the word, that.

Simon heard laughter, and then someone yelling for the bartender to bring another bottle of whiskey, and a moment later he heard Kellerman's booming voice again. **"How many times I gotta tell ya not t'bring this damn rotgut to a table when y'see me sittin at it."** Simon heard a glass bottle smash on the wall or something else hard, and Kellerman still ranting, but his booming voice was fading so Simon knew he was up and moving around.

Simon had already heard enough at the window to know for sure that Burgess Kellerman was not only the man he'd been tracking, but he was also a dangerous and bitter enemy of his brother, Jesse. *I wonder,* he thought, *if Jesse knows that he has an enemy like this guy so close to him.*

Simon didn't want to risk dealing with Kellerman if he came outside, so he eased back from the window and looked into the darkness to get his eyes used to it. Moments later he felt rain hitting his hat as he began silently moving along the side of the building. Stopping every few feet to stand motionless against a tree trunk while scanning everything, Simon took only a minute or so to get to the rear of the huge wooden building. At the corner he paused to listen. Hearing nothing he eased around the corner, and once again stood motionless and scanned in every direction.

Half an hour later the rain was still coming down heavy, for which he was grateful. Simon was moving cautiously through the woods again toward his horse, and said a silent prayer, *thank You for the cloud cover, Lord.* After arriving at the huge sycamore tree where he had earlier stood watching the town's lanterns come on, Simon looked up at the moon, now peeking through the scattered clouds. *An hour or so after midnight,* he thought.

He got his bearings straight in his head and began moving toward Dragon. Thirty minutes later he made a soft clucking noise that the horse would recognize even through a brief deluge of rain. Simon then continued toward the area where he had hobbled the horse. The rain let up and a cloud moved past to let the moon shine brightly through, and Simon saw Dragon looking straight at him. He made that same clucking noise as he approached, and Dragon shook his huge head up and down but still remained silent while Simon approached. When he reached out and patted the horse's neck, Dragon used his nose to lift Simon's hat and knock it to the ground. It was a silent greeting thing that they had established many years earlier and Simon's grin widened as he retrieved it.

After removing the hobbles, Simon grasped the pommel and climbed up into the saddle, and then nudged the horse to move slowly back onto the trail. By the time they reached the south end of town and turned onto Main Street, Simon figured it was somewhere near 3 o'clock in the morning. There wasn't a lamp lit in the entire town as Dragon moved slowly along past the houses and the huge wooden two-story building that Burgess Kellerman referred to as his gambling casino and hotel.

The reins were looped over the pommel and Simon's two arms were casually crossed against his tight stomach with his hands resting above the two cross-draw Colt Dragoons.

He was certain that the men that he'd been listening to a few hours earlier were in bed or on a floor somewhere sleeping off the night's liquor, but unlike his brother Ian, Simon McKannah was definitely not a gambler.

He preferred a sure thing or at least as close to one as he could get. With both hands ready to pull both pistols out, he considered it a sure thing that he would give more than he got.

As he passed beyond the casino, his breathing became deeper and he was more relaxed. When they were a hundred feet beyond the last house on the other side of the street that the casino was on, Simon lifted the reins from the pommel to lean forward and pat Dragon's neck. Quietly he praised the horse's ability to move so silently. "Big fella, you're the best horse to ever carry a ranger through hostile country." He reached out and ruffled Dragon's mane, "And I sure have a feeling that this is very hostile country, especially for us McKannahs right now."

By dawn Simon was through the pass and heading toward Flathead Lake, a place he had camped a few years earlier while trailing the killer of a young pioneer family, which had included two very young children—it brought back sad memories.

Before reaching the lake he saw the small Indian village. Moments later he spotted a log cabin, which he knew would not be an Indian dwelling. He leaned forward to speak to Dragon, "Ole friend, I think you're about to meet my wild young brother, Jesse."

He saw no movement near the cabin and nudged Dragon to head in that direction. Before Simon had traveled a quarter mile, a group of twenty or more Indians came from the village sitting at the edge of the lake about a half mile away. They were not coming fast and seemed more inclined to be investigating the arrival of a white man that they had never seen in this area.

He wheeled Dragon around to face them and brought him to a stop.

The Indian, who seemed to be the chief that Simon later learned was Lone Wolverine, smiled and then said to the Indians gathered around him in their language, "I believe this man is White Buffalo's brother but they have not seen each other for a long time."

When the braves and their chief stopped, Simon surprised all of them by speaking to Lame Wolverine in the Flathead dialect of the Salish language, "I have not seen my brother in many years, but if this house is where he now lives," he nodded at the cabin, "Then I am happy to see that he has chosen The People to build his life among."

"I am called Lame Wolverine, and I am the chief of this tribe." He spoke in his language. "Yes, that is the cabin your brother built, but he has not been seen today, so he must have gone to the white man's village to buy supplies."

The Wolf

The wolf had watched the stranger ride in the day before. Instincts cause him to freeze and remain motionless until the man was engaged in conversation with Jesse.

When the human that had befriended him and the strange human moved to the porch out of his sight, the wolf moved swiftly into the forest and began circling to the rear of the cabin.

The wolf had no conscious reason to be moving into position to observe the area where the two humans sat talking. Every fiber of the wolf's mind and body was vibrating and behind his eyes a red alert signal continuously flashed.

One hundred yards in the distance, the wolf cautiously looked in every direction to be certain that he was not being observed, and then began carefully moving from side-to-side.

While burrowing down into the thickly piled leaves, the wolf stopped regularly to scan the area all around to be sure he had not been seen.

He was still lying there when the sun began dropping into the distant mountain tops on the western horizon. The wolf's eyes were adjusted to the darkness so well that his pupils were dilated wide open.

An hour after dark he heard movement at the cabin by the stranger and the human that he instinctively knew had saved his life by providing him with food during the time that his leg was healing.

The wolf intuitively knew that humans must be avoided, but while tracking a wounded elk, the wolf had become careless. As he limped into the thick forest, a man yelled, "Hey Jody, I juss shot a wolf tryin t'sneak up on that elk you shot."

The wolf had unsuccessfully stalked several deer, a few rabbits, and even a groundhog, and was suffering badly from starvation when Jesse spotted him.

Now healed and healthy, the wolf somehow sensed that he owed his survival to the white man who built the huge wooden cave and was honored by the dark people who lived in the pointed animal skin caves.

The darkness had been complete and impenetrable to human eyes for only an hour when the wolf heard a noise. He neither moved nor blinked as his eyes scanned the porch. Both chairs were in the same position as when the two humans had entered the wooden cave earlier.

The clean blue aura of the human that had saved the wolf's life remained around the chair he had sat in, but the aura of the other human was an evil shimmering red aura that pulsed like a beating heart. The wolf's yellow eyes remained locked on the red aura—unemotional and motionless. His mind however was busy sorting through emotions that the wolf had never before encountered.

Moments later the wolf's mind cleared and he slowly rose to all four feet—*the human that saved my life is in danger*. With his eyes still watching the red shimmering aura the wolf moved silently toward the cabin.

Instinct let the wolf know that he must not spook the horse tied in front of the wooden man-cave. Without moving his head he determined that the wind was blowing from the northwest, so he altered his approach to downwind. Once he was behind the wooden cave the wolf moved past the area where the man he now thought of as the good human and the other one that he now considered the evil human, had talked as one remained standing, and the other sat on a horse.

The wolf was a hundred feet southeast of the porch lying on his stomach beside a very large tree when the light inside was extinguished. A moment later the evil human came out alone. The man's entire body was a mass of shimmering red aura as he moved to the stable where the wolf knew the good human kept his horse.

Jesse had tirelessly worked to teach Shadow that the wolf was not his enemy. He had also explained the situation to his friend, Lame Wolverine, and all of the Flathead Indians understood it, because their relationship with the wilderness and all things in it was different than most white men. "You have now made a very good friend," Lame Wolverine said to Jesse, "who will be your companion until his time is over."

The wolf lay motionless amongst leaves beneath the tree as the evil human led the good human's horse to the place in front of the porch where his own horse was tied.

The red aura then disappeared into the wooden cave. A short time later he came out with a large bundle on his shoulder. After dumping the bundle across the saddle, he tied it securely and climbed into the saddle on his own horse.

The wolf had no basic understanding of human activity. He simply knew that the good human and his brown friends treated him with respect, and did not fear him as an evil being, but he did not understand why. The wolf simply accepted it as the way life went at times. He recalled playing with a dog that followed an old human, but later a pack of dogs were used by a man who tried very hard to kill him. The wolf learned a good lesson from that, but also now understood that there were humans that he could exist among.

The wolf followed the evil human at a distance that would allow him to flee into the forest if other evil humans glowing red were waiting in the canyon they were going through.

Broderick

The three men stopped at midnight, and after getting a small smokeless fire going to heat the jerked meat in their water tin, each tended to his horse. All were so tired that they lay down with their tin cup of broth and jerky and chewed while moving around on their groundcloth to get the lumps out. Broderick was the last to set his empty tin cup down and pull the horse blanket up over him. He positioned his holster against the saddle so it would be an easy reach, and after glancing at their horses he drifted off into a shallow sleep.

Three days before they rode into Fort Hall, Liam was riding a short distance ahead. Aidan and Broderick were moving along behind Liam and talking about seeing Jesse again as they all rode carefully along this area of the rugged trail that was considerably narrower than any they had been on.

Just as Broderick looked up at Liam, who was about fifty feet ahead, the big palomino horse Liam was on reared up on its hind legs, whinnying loud and pawing the air with its front hoofs.

Broderick and Aidan had a difficult time restraining both of their horses that were not yet comfortable and adjusted to their new riders.

When Liam's horse was back down on all four legs and being backed up toward Broderick and Aidan, Liam began cursing in a loud and agitated voice, "Damned badger musta staked 'is claim on this 'ole bloody mountain."

Broderick yelled, "Damned thing's big as a small bear."

"I reckon I'd rather 'ave a small bear after me than a cranky bugger like 'im." While Aidan was speaking he was backing his mount away from the badger that had followed Liam as he backed his horse away.

Satisfied that it had frightened the intruders away from its meal, the huge badger growled and hissed at the three men on horseback a few times and then turned and scurried back around the bend in the trail where Lian had encountered it.

"Biggest damn badger I ever saw," Aidan exclaimed while shaking his head, "betcha that stout bugger'd pull up a thirty kilo chunk o' lead."

"Whacha reckon we oughta do now, Brod?" He turned in the saddle and looked at his boss.

Before Broderick could reply, Aidan said, "Shoot that cranky sonuvbitch so we can 'ead on to that fort n' git some decent food in our bellies b'fore we git juss like 'im."

Broderick looked hard at the trail beyond the bend that the enraged badger had just wobbled around, and then surveyed the boulders and forest on both sides of where they sat. Before speaking he lifted his chin and looked at the sky. Finally he said, "We really don't 'ave a clue what's up ahead, good, bad, or otherwise, an I ain't gonna 'and down a death sentence to a magnificent animal like that courageous fella just so we can 'ead on to a fort that may very well give us the same reception 'e did." He motioned with his chin toward the area the badger disappeared to.

Aidan twisted his lips and screwed his face up while lifting his leather hat to rub his sweating forehead with his shirt sleeve. Positioning his hat again he spoke with obvious embarrassment, "Sorry, fellas, juss loss me 'ead fer a moment. Could not shoot 'im even if y'tole me to, Brod."

"I know that." Broderick turned again and looked back along their trail.

"Whadaya reckon we oughta do now?" Liam's speech was garbled as he positioned the new wad of tobacco into his cheek.

"Well," Broderick answered, "It's not yet noon, so let's go back along the trail a ways an 'ave a cup o' coffee n' dip some o' those sourdough biscuits. By the time we've 'ad ourselves some rest an a bite o' grub, ole nasty there," he motioned toward the area now dominated by the badger, "will probably 'ave dragged 'is kill into the forest."

An hour and three very hard biscuits soaked in coffee later, the three men cautiously approached the bend around the boulder again.

"Lookit that." Liam, still in the lead, pointed at a small deer leg severed at the first joint.

"No wonder 'e was so cranky," Aidan said, "musta just took down a fawn 'alf again as big's 'im, an 'ere we come ridin right through 'is bloody dining room."

"Tough little bugger." Broderick lifted in the stirrups to look into the forest, hoping for a glimpse of the badger dragging the kill to his den. Sitting back down, he said, "I reckon if we was to weigh everything, including us on 'orses, an the two mules n' all that's strapped on 'em, we'd be more'n fifty times the weight 'o that badger, and there 'e was in the center o' the trail, all by 'is lonesome standin guard on wh' 'e knew was 'is."

Aidan lifted in his stirrups hoping to see the badger, "Tough as they come, I reckon."

Liam turned in his saddle and grinned, "An you wanted to shoot the scrappy lil bugger."

Aidan sat back down and mumbled but made no reply.

Two days later they rode into Fort Hall. Broderick had taken time at each stop to add to a letter he would leave for his brother, Ian. In it he listed all he'd heard about Burgess Kellerman and where the town he established was located. He also included what little he heard from trappers about a tribe of Flathead Indians living near a big lake up near the Canadian border. "Ian, I believe we are gonna find Jesse living right there with those Indians. I don't know any of the details, but they call a white man that lives with them, White Buffalo, and I won't be surprised to learn that it's Jesse."

Ian

Ian and his two men arrived at Traveler's Rest on the 12th day of May—now only a day behind Broderick, but about three behind Simon.

Two days earlier, the Brasco brothers rode in at noon, several hours after Burgess Kellerman, and his recently acquired men to strengthen the numbers of his gang, rode out toward his town he was now calling the Northern Territory's new cattle empire, Burgess Montana.

While Lon and Solomon MacKandle secured their horses and the two mules to the hitching rail in front of Emil Gustafson's Mercantile Store, Ian McKannah went looking for a telegraph office, *if*, he thought, *there is one on top o' this bloody mountain.*

"Nope," the old man behind the pastry and candy counter said, "but there's talk of a tellygraf comin in purdy soon, so's the cavalry and the sojers can keep track o' what them damned Blackfoot injuns're up to."

Ian stood there thinking for a moment before asking, "Is there a place where travelers can leave a letter or message for someone comin along behind them?"

"Yep!" The old man pointed in the direction that Ian had just left the MacKandle brothers. "Emil has a sorta post office at his store. You can buy a little stick-t'gether bag from him an leave a message in it."

Ian tied his horse and walked into the store. Lon looked up and said, "C'mere Ian, n' listen t'what this fella 'as t'say." He had a wide grin on his face, which made Ian think things were going their way.

"Ian McKannah," he said with his hand out.

The short chubby man standing behind the counter in a white apron took it with a wet hand so limp that Ian shuddered inside. "I spoke to both of your brothers, I do believe." His red flushed face broke open into a speckled grin as sweat ran down across a ragged field of pimples and pockmarks. "I have two packets here for you." He grinned again, "I actually created these myself." He handed Ian two of his open-ended home made envelopes that were glued together with what appeared to be schoolhouse type, flour and water paste.

Ian thanked him and squeezed one to spread it. He could see writing inside and when he allowed it to close, he saw his name under TO and above that was FROM with Broderick under it.

The sweating man reached beneath the counter saying, "Here is a letter opener you ca...

Before he finished the word, Ian engaged the trigger holding the razor-sharp, double-edge dagger in the leather sheath on his left arm. The dagger magically appeared and he was slicing the envelope open when the gasping fat man spoke in a shaky voice.

"Oh my," the man mumbled and stepped back so fast that he hit the wall so hard that two wicker baskets full of knitted doilies fell from the top shelf.

"You okay?" Solomon had to work hard to keep the grin that wanted to jump out stay inside.

Lon just glanced at the man and shook his head.

"I'll be right back." The sweating man almost ran into the rear of the store.

As Ian read the message from Simon to Broderick, who then added a note to Ian, Lon looked at his brother, "Wh' d'ye reckon 'is problem is?"

"Can y'not smell it?" Solomon grinned.

Ian abruptly looked up from the letter, "What the bloody 'ell is that smell?" He looked at one then the other.

Solomon nodded toward the rear of the store, "I reckon that Arkansas toothpick," he nodded at the dagger still in Ian's hand, "scared the shit outa the poor lil fat fella."

"I'm 'eadin outside t'read the other one." Ian opened the door and stepped out, followed by both MacKandles.

They had plenty of supplies strapped on the mules, so all three agreed to get back on the trail. "We're not far from where Jesse is living with the Flathead Indians, according to what Broderick has learned, and I don't like what I've heard about that Texan, what's 'is name," Ian lifted the letter again, "Kellerman. Burgess Kellerman."

"Boss," Lon said, "four men 'ave told us 'e acts like a con man and looks like a killer, so I say let's close the gap."

"Yep," Solomon added, "smells like that fat clerk back there."

Ian and the MacKandle brothers followed directions that would eventually lead to the lake where the Flathead Indians lived on a government reservation. The directions were given to Ian by a trapper working out of Traveler's Rest, another of many who didn't like Burgess Kellerman.

Unknown to Ian or Broderick, Simon had already made contact with their sister, Aleena, and Chief Bonesetter. Simon's instincts had caused him to break away from the Indians and head for Burgess Montana.

Neither Simon nor Broderick knew that Big John, an old enemy of Simon, had spotted him and was also heading toward Burgess Montana.

None of them knew that the Brasco brothers from Texas were in the area on a long-awaited mission—to kill the man who killed their father three years earlier—Burgess Kellerman.

Jesse

Shadow plodded along at the end of a lariat tied to the saddle of the horse ahead. Shadow sensed that the human sitting in that horse's saddle was the man who put the bundle across the saddle on his back and secured it there with rope several hours earlier.

The horse knew it was Jesse inside the canvas bundle, but it had no idea why he was lying across the saddle instead of sitting in it as he had always done.

Daylight finally began to penetrate the dense forest, which the man and the horse ahead and Shadow had slowly walked through all night. A while later Shadow's senses began sending signals to its brain that let the him understand that he and Jesse had been there together before.

Less than an hour after passing the spot where Jesse had left Shadow when he first reconnoitered the town of Burgess, and then again later when they came there on another dark night, the man on the horse ahead moved out of the trees and led them to a small cabin on the north edge of town.

Many hours earlier Jesse's brain had begun the slow process of recovering from the concussion he received from the blow on the back of his head. As consciousness became permanent rather than allowing the head-wound to heal by shutting down the brain intermittently for shorter and shorter periods during the night, Jesse was able to begin sorting through the events that put him in the predicament he was in.

I brought inside that hindquarter of smoked deer and sliced off enough meat for dinner and breakfast....told Gus that I would tie the remaining hindquarter in a flour sack so he could take it with him in the morning after breakfast...told him that I was glad he stopped because it's always nice to meet another pioneer moving through this wonderful new country...after we ate the smoked venison, wild sweet potatos, and fresh baked sourdough bread, we moved to the porch and sat quietly enjoying the star-filled evening sky...by midnight we had exausted the few topics we could mutually talk about, and both of us were tired ...said it was time for me to hit the sack...told him to sit out on the porch as long as he wanted, and I'd see him in the morning...Gus said he was also tired and was gonna turn in too... said that bed in the room that I'd set up for my brothers was callin him...followed me through the door...I recall sayin okay Gus, I'll see you in...that's the last thing I remember sayin...felt som'n hit the side of my head...next thing I can remember is wakin up laying across this horse's saddle, which I reckon is Shadow, tied inside a huge blanket or something that's lashed to the saddle...Gus knocked me out...he must be the guy that was hired by Burgess...can't be...he's not old enough...Burgess said they was kids and growed up together...damn! Let m'guard down...musta rode out after dark...nobody even knows I'm not in the cabin...been climbing up for a while now...must be goin through the canyon...probably headin toward Burgess' town.

Similar thoughts continued running through Jesse's mind as he lay inside the thick bundle across Shadow's saddle. *Getting a bit dizzy again...hard breathin through this damn gag that he put in my mouth...gotta try to relax n' concentrate on breathin through my nose if I'm gonna get outa this mess.*

Jesse remained silent when the horse stopped. His headache was gone and he had overcome the brief panic caused by not being able to easily breathe through the bandana tied across his mouth. Jesse's keen hearing, inherited from a mother who, from a sound sleep could hear one of her children several rooms away sneeze in the middle of the night, determined that the man had dismounted. Jesse lay limp across the saddle when he heard Gus coming toward him to begin removing the ropes.

Jesse stayed limp and silent as the man easily transferred him from the saddle to his shoulder. *Gus,* he thought, *must be a logger or som'n similar, because he's stronger'n he looks.* Jesse began trying to free his hands earlier once his head stopped aching, but after an exhausting hour realized that it was a futile effort. *This guy knows rope...got m'hands tied behind my back so good he'll hafta cut the rope...maybe he's a fisherman instead of a logger.*

He remained limp and silent, hoping the man might put him in a room or a cave while he found Kellerman to make a deal. *We just went up some steps onto a wood porch...he's using a key to open a door...we're inside a house...oooomph, he just dropped me onto a bed or som'n soft.*

Jesse listened as the man walked away, then moments later he thought, *he's walking around inside this house, or whatever it is.*

"Damn, Tag," Jesse held his breath when the man spoke, "you never was much for cleaning up, but this cabin o' yours is a damn pigsty." *Tag must be somebody he knows who lives here.* "Well, Tag ole pal," Jesse strained to hear what he was saying, "all yer worries're over now," Jesse could hear him better now, "cept the flames, heh, heh, heh, betcher havin a hot ole time down there now." When he laughed again, Jesse thought, *Gus sounds like a completely different person than when we was talkin...mebbe he's one o' those dem psycho killer guys I heard Simon talkin about when we was kids...I bet he killed that guy Tug, or Tag, or whatever his name was, so he could live here in his house.*

The man returned to Jesse and began removing the rope that was tied around the canvas ground cover that he wrapped Jesse inside back at the cabin on Flathead Lake. Jesse remained silent as he was turned onto his stomach once the cover was opened and removed. His feet, which were still in his leather boots and tied tightly together, were pulled up by Gus and secured to his bound hands.

He felt the man's fingers on his throat, and momentarily had to fight off panic. Jesse realized that the man was worried that he had died while lying across the saddle, and smiled inside. *I'm doin a good job of acting.*

The man held his two fingers to Jesse's carotid artery to feel for a pulse. He finally removed them and spoke softly to himself, "Reckon you ain't as tough as that Kellerman guy told Tag you was, but I'm sure glad you're alive, cause I damned sure couldn't get a deal for a corpse." He chuckled softly and reminded Jesse of an evil troll he read about as a young boy, *he doesn't look like the monster that lived under the bridge in that book, but he sure sounds like him.* Gus opened the door and left the building. Jesse heard the door being locked, but remained motionless on the bed until he rode away on his horse.

So that guy Tag must be who was s'pose to grab me for Kellerman. Jesse lay on his side wishing Gus had removed the gag, but after a moment thought, *at least I can see where I'm at now...mebbe I can figure a way outa this mess.* He began moving as much as he could to see what the rest of the house loked like.

Aleena

Aleena was walking behind a travois that was carrying mostly old men and women that walked as long as they could, and then took the place of others that had been resting.

Chief Bonesetter smiled as he rode along behind on his big palomino and watched as Aleena helped the old people on and off the travois. *If all people, white and Indian, only had this woman's compassion for others, this would be a much nicer world to live in.* He nudged his horse closer to her and spoke. "As soon as we get to the top of this hill, Aleena, you will see the village where your brother lives with The People."

"Doctor Caruthers," she replied, looking up at him with a wide smile, "I am now thinking of The People as my people."

"That is a wonderful attitude, Aleena McKannah, and **our people**," he grinned down at her after emphasizing the two words, "will be very pleased to hear that, because they consider you a member of our tribal family now."

"I'm so happy about that, because if my brother Jesse has a room for me in whatever he's living in, then I ain't ever leaving here."

"One of their chief's scouts told me that he lives in a large log house that the tribe where we are heading helped him build, so I'm sure he'll have room for you."

"Oh my God," she said as they approached the top of the hill, "I'm so excited I feel like a teenager again." The chief smiled when she skipped ahead nimbly to help an old woman scoot a bit farther ahead on the travois so she could lay down.

The young boy that was sitting on the horse that pulled the travois pointed and said excitedly, "Look at that beautiful lake where The People are camped."

When the chief translated what the boy said, Aleena looked

past the horse and saw what the boy was still pointing at. "This is far beyond any beautiful scene that my mind has created during this trek."

"It has been many years," the chief said, "since I have been here, and I too had forgotten how wonderful this place is."

Aleena held to the travois as the tribe began moving down from the hilltop toward the lake, but her eyes were very busy taking in everything before her. Finally she pointed, "That new log cabin must be the one The People helped Jesse build."

"Yes," Chief Bonesetter said, "it is just as the scout described it to me. Get on the travois, Aleena, and move to the front." He then shouted instructions to the boy on the horse to stop for a moment and let the sister of White Buffalo get on the chief's horse. Aleena moved cautiously past the old people until she was at the front. The chief brought the huge palomino close and Aleena grabbed the old man's hand and climbed on behind him.

The boy nudged the horse and the travois began moving toward the camp beside the lake, as the chief and Aleena walked the palomino toward the new cabin.

Before they were halfway there, a small group of Flatheads were riding toward them. The chief and Aleena got there ahead of the others, so he maneuvered the horse close to the porch and Aleena easily slid off.

"I am Lame Wolverine, chief of the tribe living here on this reservation." He smiled warmly, "And I know who both of you are, even though I have never met you. Welcome to the home of your brother, who you call Jesse, and my people know as White Buffalo." He smiled at Aleena, and then turned, "And you are the great Doctor Caruthers, and also Chief Bonesetter, the legendary man who became a trained doctor to help The People enjoy a better life for more years than I have had life." He raised his arm and put a fist on the end, "Welcome both of you to your new home." The dozen Flathead braves with him raised their fists and screamed a welcome to the two people.

Lame Wolverine's demeanor changed and he nudged his horse closer. "I must now tell you what has happened in the last two days."

Aleena could tell, even though she did not understand their language, that something was not right, so she stopped smiling and listened intently as the two chief's spoke in their language.

"Simon McKannah came here after leaving your group to see what was going on in the town on the other side of those mountains." He nodded with his chin toward the west. "When I told him that the people from that town had tried to attack us in our sleep, but were unsuccessful, because at that moment White Buffalo came riding down the same hill that you just did and was screaming and shooting his gun. Simon is a hunter of men and can see things that other men, even our warriors, often miss. Simon said it was a bad pain in his head and an evil aura surrounding his brother's cabin, where we are now, that caused him to look inside this cabin." Lame Wolverine shook his head, "Simon walked inside and then all around the cabin, and when he returned all he said was something is wrong, bad wrong, and I'm going back to that town." Lame Wolverine looked toward the mountain, and he just shook his head back and forth. Finally turning back to them, he said, "That was earlier this morning. He told me not to follow because it might hurt his chances of saving his brother. He said it would be better to stay here to meet you when you arrive. Simon said that a huge tribe like we will now have is the best way to keep bad white people like those from trying to start trouble. I am very upset because Jesse is the best friend that I have ever had, but I know that Simon is right.

Chief Bonesetter listened without saying a word. When Lame Wolverine stopped talking, the chief told him that he would translate all he had said to Aleena.

When he finished translating, Chief Bonesetter leaned back into his saddle to contemplate all he had heard. Aleena looked in the direction she had been told that Simon rode into. Turning sad eyes toward Lame Wolverine she spoke softly but in a confident voice, "My brother Simon is the best man-hunter alive according to letters that I received from my brothers." She paused again to look at the mountains west of where she stood. "If anyone," she said in a stronger, more confident voice, "can bring Jesse back to us it will be Simon."

"Chief Lame Wolverine," Chief Bonesetter said while turning toward him, "if you will ride with me we will guide my people and the tribes that joined us, to where they can assemble their camps temporarily until we have this current situation under control."

One hour later, the two chiefs sat at the cooking fire to watch

Gentle Breeze prepare their lunch. After a sip of hot coffee Chief Bonesetter smiled, "This tastes so good." After another sip he grinned, "You can easily see that I have adopted some of the white man's habits during my years in his presence."

"I too love the drink made from the bitter beans." The much younger chief sitting beside Chief Bonesetter placed his empty cup on the split log and turned toward the old chief. "We have had only one encounter with the white men from a town on the other side of those mountains," he motioned toward the western Bitterroot Range, "but White Buffalo is certain that more will come."

"From what Simon McKannah has told me, I believe they are planning to develop this entire area into a big cattle ranch." After finishing his coffee he added, "And to accomplish that they must have this flat land and the lake." The old chief looked at the man sitting beside him and spoke softly, knowing that Gentle Breeze was nearby cooking. "And the first task they face is us. They will have to get rid of us one way or another."

Lame Wolverine was still contemplating what the old chief had just said when Gentle Breeze began silently placing bowls of hot food on the split log in front of the one they sat on.

As the men ate, and long after, they talked about Jesse's plan to teach the children and young men who were not yet old enough to become warriors, how to be cowboys and gardeners.

Before going to his own tepee for the night, which the women had already put up, the older chief who had joined his tribe with the group heading to Flathead Lake, stood and said, "I know that it will be very difficult to make the young people see that it is necessary, but the man your people call White Buffalo is right." The old chief pursed his lips and shook his head, "But if we are to survive as a tribe and move into the future, we must do as he suggests." He stretched a moment then turned and grinned at the other men, "I think I might have enjoyed being a cowboy when I was young, but planting corn, and potatoes, and......he shook his head vigorously and grinned wider, "I do not think I would have enjoyed that." He waved his hand and walked toward his people's camp.

Wolf

The wolf lay flat against the ground as the human with the evil red aura surrounding him rode silently west through the canyon. He continuously checked the light breeze to be certain that he remained downwind from the human with the evil aura. His yellow eyes were constantly drawn to the bundle lying across the saddle of the horse that the good human usually sat on. Even though there was no sign at all of the soft sky-blue aura that surrounded those few good humans that were able to live in perfect harmony with the natural world around them, the wolf knew that the good human was in the bundle.

When the evil human turned south and began walking on the dirt road leading to Burgess Montana, the wolf stayed up on the side of the mountain, moving stealthily through the thick forest. Fifty yards away and staying downwind, the wolf could easily see the shimmering red aura surrounding the evil human.

When a few dim lights could be seen, the wolf remembered coming through this area when his leg was injured. He was with the good human that had killed a goat and some rabbits for him when he was moving with a large herd of animals.

Those yellow predator eyes were riveted to the evil red aura. It stopped, and then moved a short distance and disappeared. He moved silently toward the last place he saw the red aura. Several moments later the wolf was lying beside a huge boulder in a stand of golden-leafed aspens directly across from the cabin that the man had carried Jesse into. The wolf silently burrowed into the thick layers of leaves so he would remain unseen if another evil human approached. He laid his head down on the muscular outstretched front legs and let his eyes move back and forth from one end of the cabin to the other.

When he heard the door being opened, every nerve-center in the wolf's muscular body was sending signals to the brain. The body didn't move when the eyes locked onto the red aura. The evil human was so casual that the wolf felt no danger as the man rode past on his horse. The wolf was still downwind, and had masked much of his smell by burrowing into the leaves. His yellow eyes were now following the red aura as it moved toward the faint lights that he had seen come on a short time earlier.

Patrick

Patrick had been working tirelessly to organize everything since he and his two men had arrived at James Bucanan's Presidential Campaign Headquarters. He was extremely pleased to find that Joseph Alderman was not only a loyal democrat but a hard working aide that wanted to see his friend, James Buchanan, elected president. "Patrick," he said one afternoon as they walked across the courtyard to the dining room, "we both worked so hard," he looked up at Patrick, "James and I that is, on those three earlier attempts to place him in the White House as our president. But events," he said somewhat whimsically, "beyond our control caused many people," he turned to Patrick again, "even democrats who had always been loyal supporters of Mister Buchanan, to begin turning on him."

The two men walked on in silence for a moment, but as they approached the private dining room where all key players in the campaign effort met each week on Friday to discuss strategy and options, Joseph stopped abruptly and turned to Patrick, "Mister Buchanan placed his lifetime dream in your hands, Patrick, and I honestly believe your tactics are working."

"I hope so, Joseph, because I met Mister Buchanan while I was still in lawschool at Harvard, and admired his knowledge of our government and the laws that he helped write and put into effect to run this government. In reaching out to my people," he looked down at Joseph, "the Irish, that is, I'm hoping they see that he will be a president who will help them fulfill their own dreams."

At dinner that Friday evening Patrick mentioned the plight of a tribe of Flathead Indians that his brother had explained in several of his letters. Mister Buchanan listened, but made no comment until dinner was over and everyone began leaving. When Patrick started to rise from his chair, his friend pressed down on his hand and whispered, "I want to have a word with you after everyone is gone."

When they were alone, with the exception of Aldo Calaveras and two old waiters who were full time employees of Mister Buchanan, he turned to look directly at Patrick when he spoke. "Patrick, I believe I have a very good chance of being elected president this time, and if I am it will be in great part due to your willingness to come so far to be here with me to oversee everything. I have long sympathized with the Indians, so tell me what your younger brother is doing to help them and I will do all I can to assist him."

It was almost an hour later when Patrick stretched out on his bed, fully clothed and completely exhausted. With the light out and his fingers locked behind his head, he thought about Jesse, Simon, Ian, and Broderick. *You're probably all together now. Wish I was with you fellas. I'll be heading home fore too long, so I'll stop by. Jesse, I think you're gonna have a powerful man on your side now.* His tired mind at ease, Patrick drifted off into a deep sleep.

Simon

The sun was going down behind the mountains when Simon got to the pass and headed west through it. While there was still a bright sun overhead, his powerful tracker's eyes concentrated on a trail that was still very fresh. Twice he climbed from the saddle to closer inspect the tracks he was following. The second time that he remounted Dragon, he thought, *whoever y'are you're leavin some easy tracks t'follow. That second horse is tied to the first one 'cause the gap stays the same and it's always right behind; never off t'one side'r the other.*

Just before the last faint rays of sunshine faded away, Simon spotted a small bush that was recently crushed by a horse's hoof. *I'm purdy sure he's gotcha tied in the saddle, Jesse, so juss hang on n' I'll find you, and then together again we'll take care o' this sonuvbitch.* A hard unpleasant smile crossed Simon's face, *we might juss take care of all these sons o' bitches before Brod n' Ian get here.*

Since it got dark, Simon moved ahead very slowly and with extreme caution, knowing there might be men stationed along the trail to intercept all strangers coming in from any direction. *If I let this buncha worthless bastards grab me we're both gonners.* Simon could tell by Dragon's gait that the horse intuitively understood the need for careful movement and silent as possible.

He stopped Dragon and dismounted when he saw the glow from a candle in one of the cabins ahead. As he led the horse into the forest, Simon's mind was working. *Ain't but about an hour till sunup...gotta git Dragon situated...there'll be guys up n' gittin som'n t'eat before daylight...gotta git in close n' learn what they're plannin.*

After getting Dragon situated, Simon cautiously approached the dirty window again on the side of Burgess Kellerman's huge building. He recognized the loud voice he'd heard before. **"Yes, dammit, I said four eggs**." Simon heard the chair being shoved back as the man screamed, **"Do I look like a two egg man**?"

Yep, that's Kellerman. Simon scanned the area while trying to hear what was being said.

"Gus, or whatever the hell your name is, I been thinkin on whacha told me yesterday. Tag asked ya t'come here with him an help snatch that squawman, but b'fore y'all gotcher gear t'gether he up n' died on ya, eh?" He stopped talking and Simon waited.

"That's right, Mister Kellerman, I reckon his wore out old heart just exploded, it happened so fast."

After a short pause, Kellerman said, "Okay, Gus, but if it turns out you're a damn lawman, or I find out you killed ole Tag, I'll be smiling when m'boys hoist you up by the neck."

"Fine with me, Mister Kellerman, 'cause I sure ain't no damn lawman, an Tag's family there in Amarillo all came out t'bury him. They all know the doctor that told us what happened. Said Tag's heart musta been bad, and an artery busted." There was a moment of silence before Kellerman spoke.

"You want the hunert in gold that I promised Tag if he'd grab that squawman and then you wanna stay here n' help us clean out them stinkin injuns. That right?"

"Yessir, and I'd like to stick around and ride cowboy for you, cause ole Tag said you're a man that gits things done."

Simon was about to move and be out of the area when the sun came up, but stopped when he heard Kellerman laugh.

"Okay, itsa deal Gus. Goddammit, ole son I like your style. It kinda reminds me of how I was, way back when I was your age. Where y'got that squawman stashed?"

"In Tag's cabin at the north edge o' town. Got him hogtied up real good."

Kellerman laughed harder than he did the first time, and then said kind of breathless, "Oughta put a bullet b'tween your eyes fer makin me deal for the sonuvabitch when he was right under m'nose all along, you smart-alecky goddamm whipper-snapper." He continued his boisterous laughing until he said, "Here's breakfast, let's eat n' go have a look at the injun lover."

Broderick

The two brothers, Aidan and Liam, followed Broderick into Traveler's Rest late in the afternoon on May 11th, the same day that the Brasco brothers rode out at dawn.

Before arriving, they had agreed that Broderick would find the post office to see if Simon had left him a letter, and the two men would purchase food that could be eaten in the saddle. It turned out that all three men met again minutes later at the same place.

In less than an hour and a half they were heading north out of Traveler's Rest on Jedediah Smith's 1829 summer trail. While still in sight of the cabins, shacks, stores and buildings, Aidan spoke around a mouthful of fried chicken. "Simon was told by a trapper that a big tribe of Flatheads are moving north in a valley just this side o' that lake, eh?"

Broderick held up his hand and continued chewing. After he swallowed, he turned in the saddle, "Yep, said they was movin north toward Flathead Lake where he heard Jesse's livin."

Liam then asked, "How far y'reckon it is t'thet lake, Brod?"

"Best I can figure from the map Simon put on the back of this letter, we're about fifty miles from the lake right now."

"When we git to that valley where the trapper tole Simon he saw the Flatheads, we oughta be able to make good time." Aidan turned to look at his brother riding beside him, and then looked at Broderick who had turned in the saddle again.

"I'm countin on it," Broderick said.

Unknown to anyone other than themselves, the two Brasco boys were only a few hours ahead, and following the map to Burgess' town that a trapper who was cheated by Burgess Kellerman had gladly made for them.

~ The long list of people that the boisterous Texan had cheated
and stolen from in the past was now working against him ~

Ian

When the three men were back on the trail, and heading north toward the lake, Lon asked, "'ow long y'ad that wicked lookin dagger on yer arm, boss?"

"So long," Ian said with a grin, "the damn sheath 'as grown to me bloody arm."

Solomon chuckled, "An as y'kin see, brother Lon, 'e juss loves scarin the livin shit out of a puffy lil fairy like that fella back at the store."

The sun was still just a short distance above the tips of the eastern mountains as the three men pressed their mounts to close the gap between them and Simon and Broderick.

Ten miles ahead, Big John and his *gang* were moving steadily in the direction he was told earlier that Burgess Montana lay nestled in the hills just east of the Bitterroot Mountains.

Two miles behind Big John, two determined young men moved cautiously north. Neither knew what lay ahead, but judging by the few things they were told along the way up from Texas, the man they had sworn to kill, and vindicate the death of their father, would not be easy to take down.

Ian, Lon, and Solomon all now knew that they were entering into what might become extremely hostile territory. The casual banter that helped pass the time was ceased. All three were men who missed very little of what happened in their vicinity. As though choreographed by one of Ian's stage directors, one-by-one they turned in their saddles and surveyed the terrain in every direction. Guns were double-checked, and sheath knives taken out and honed. Three pairs of eyes penetrated the forest in all directions as far as humanly possible. A long journey was ending and each felt certain that blood would run.

They were going to do all they could to see to it that it wasn't theirs.

Jesse

The cabin that Jesse was tossed into had a terrible odor. He hadn't paid attention to it when he was first dumped on the bed like a sack of dirty laundry, surviving the ordeal he was in being foremost in his mind.

Now that he was out of the groundcloth that the stranger had wrapped him in, the odor, even hogtied on a filthy bed with the gag still in his mouth, was overwhelming. He closed his eyes and concentrated on the memory of the fresh scents of the trees and bushes surrounding his cabin back by the lake.

Lifting his head he could see a little of the room he was in. It had no door, just a square-cornered passageway. It led from the room he was in to what appeared to be the only other room. He saw a wood-burning stove against the far wall, which was only about fifteen feet away. Beside it was a small counter to prepare food on, with a few chunks of firewood stacked beneath it. A small wooden table had two chairs shoved in under it, and all were obviously home-made and very crude.

The door we came through, Jesse thought, *must be right around the corner on the side my head is pointing at.* He scooted across the bed, as best he could, in his hogtie rig. Once he was positioned in the middle, Jesse took a moment to catch his breath. *This dern gag,* he thought, as he struggled to breathe, *sure makes it hard t'git some air in m'lungs.*

With his breathing once again under control he very carefully rolled over on his side with his face toward the distant wall in the other room. *Good,* he thought, *don't wanna fall off to the floor, cause if that bastard returns n' figures out that I'm tryin t'git loose he might tie me up tighter'n I am now.*

He was lying there trying to think of some way to free himself when he heard a voice outside. *That's Kellerman,* he thought. The next voice he heard didn't surprise him. *That's Gus, or whoever the hell 'e is.*

The door opened, confirming in Jesse's mind where it was located, and a tall huge man with a head the size of a five-pie pumpkin, and carrying an enormous belly, stepped into the cabin and turned to look straight at him. Even before the man spoke, Jesse knew it was Burgess Kellerman.

Wolf

The wolf remained motionless beneath the leaves. Only his yellow eyes moved. Even in the light of day the red aura covered the evil human he had followed to this place, and now there was another one—an enormous evil human surrounded by a bright red aura pulsing like a giant heart.

He watched the two men enter the place where the good human was carried in by the evil human. The wolf remained as silent and motionless as the boulders around him. His yellow eyes were locked on the door the two evil humans had entered. He felt neither hate nor anger. His emotions understood that he owed a debt—the good human had fed him when he couldn't feed himself—the evil humans were holding the good human captive just as an evil trapper had held him while he was still a pup—a brown man killed the trapper and freed him—he must help this good human.

Burgess Kellerman

"**W**ell, well, well, whada we have here, Gus?" Jesse could smell the whiskey as he stared up at him. "Kinda looks like one o' those damn squawmen what can't handle white wimmin." His guffaw sent a wave of whiskey laden air toward Jesse, but he didn't even blink as he continued staring at the huge man weaving back and forth in front of him.

He must be seven feet tall, Jesse thought, *and I ain't never seen a head big's that on any man. He's gotta weigh over four hundred pounds.*

"Good job, Gus."

Jesse watched as the giant slapped Gus on the back, almost knocking him to the floor.

"C'mon Gus, I wanna have Patch get fifty, or however many men I've got right now, together an go run those stinkin damn Flatheads clean outa here, now that we got the troublemaker." Burgess twisted his huge mouth into a smirk and leaned toward Jesse, "An I already tole Patch to bring a coupla young squaws so they can see what I do to their goddamm White Buffalo, so all them other injuns'll know better than to mess with me."

"What the hell's that White Buffalo thing all about?"

"That's what they call this squawman." Burgess laughed, "I been hearin about it long fore them Flatheads got here, but never paid no mind to them injun superstitions." He raised his flabby but huge arm and pointed at Jesse, "Then he come ridin in that morning we was gonna wipe the bastards out, an I been hearin about White Buffalo ever since." Jesse watched as he fished the small silver flask from his pocket and took a drink. After shoving it back into his pants, Burgess grinned and looked so evil that a slight shiver ran through Jesse. "When them squaws see what I do to their almighty White Buffalo they ain't never gonna give no white man any more trouble."

"Whadaya got planned," Gus asked.

"Was gonna hang the injun-lovin bastard, but changed my mind n' decided to burn the sonuvbitch at the stake. Been gittin it ready ever since I tole ole Tag t'come up here n' tie in with me. Looks like you ain't gonna have any problems takin his place, Gus. Let's go flush them lazy turds o' mine away from the bar so Patch'll have a sober bunch t'ride with him." He grinned and snorted through his huge nose, "As sober as any of that bunch ever is."

Wolf

Yellow eyes watched as the two evil men left the cabin. The wolf had never seen such a bright red aura of evil surrounding a human. It ignited urgency in the wolf's brain, but also made it aware that stealth and cunning were more important than ever—*I must help free the good human.*

After a very thorough search of the terrain surrounding the cabin, and the area the wolf had been lying in fifty yards east on the side of a hill, it moved swiftly toward the cabin.

While constantly scanning the area, the wolf began looking for a weak spot in the cabin's exterior where he could enter. When he arrived at the area on the opposite end from where Jesse lay bound and gagged, the wolf saw something that was not part of the cabin's pattern.

By sniffing with his extraordinarily sensitive nose he learned that the small two foot square door was a means of entry. It was a door that swung inward on leather hinges at the top and was used to get a supply of cooking wood near the stove without carrying it through the cabin. Once the stovewood box was filled, the door was secured by shoving a wooden peg into a hole carved in the floor.

Jesse

While the wolf was testing the small door with its paws, Jesse was turning himself around in the bed so his knees would be against the wall with his legs and feet shoved against his back. He was exhausted by the time he had both knees against the wall, but Jesse knew he didn't have much time. *They'll be back soon—gotta get that knife outa my boot—what the heck was the name o' that black bootmaker that usta be a lawyer up in Canada—he made the sheath so soft and sewed it in so perfect that I never have felt the knife when I walk—can't believe I forgot his name.*

Once he got his knees up on the wall as far as he could, Jesse flushed everything else out of his mind and concentrated on shoving his feet closer to his hands.

Twenty minuted later his wrists were bleeding and he was gasping for air. He got his fingertips almost to the tops of his boots but no matter how much he strained, he could not get them closer. *If I can just get a little slack in the rope he tied my hands and feet together with I think I can reach the knife—it's only about an inch from the top o' the boot—Ruben, that was his name.*

Just as Jesse had his breathing under control again, he heard a noise outside. *Oh my God, they're back already.*

Wolf

The wolf looked all around to be certain that there were no humans, and then lunged through the air and hit the small door with his head. He felt the door move. Again he looked around, and then the second time he backed away farther to give himself a little more room to run.

The old leather hinges gave little resistance the first lunge and almost none on the second. The weathered old door peg and hinges snapped off and the wolf was inside.

Jesse's eyes were bulging out as he watched the wolf, now healthy and huge, wriggle through a small door that Jesse hadn't noticed. Without hesitation the wolf approached the bed. With no hesitation at all he was up on his hind feet and in one brief chewing, severed the rope holding Jesse's feet to his hands.

Jesse swiftly slipped the razor sharp double-edged knife that his brother Ian had given him years earlier, out of the sheath. He severed the rope binding his feet and hands first, and then swung his feet over and onto the floor. As he struggled to sever the bandana holding the gag in his mouth, he looked at the wolf and smiled. It was sitting a few feet away watching intently as though it might be something that he would have to do some day.

The wolf was actually watching the soft blue aura rebuilding around the good human.

Once his hands were free Jesse stood and reached out to pet the wolf on the head, "Good boy amigo. Lame Wolverine was sure right when he said I would have a very good friend for life. C'mon big guy let's get outa here, we're both dead meat if they catch us."

Simon

Remaining high up on the side of the hill that was thick with aspens, Simon moved along silently as he kept an eye on Burgess and the man who had apparently waylaid his brother, Jesse.

He watched as the smaller of the two men used a key to unlock the door. He scanned the entire area around him to be certain that one of Kellerman's gang wasn't tracking him. When he was satisfied that nobody was watching, Simon placed one of his boots against a small aspen and lay back. The hill was steep, so even lying on his back he could still see the cabin's door.

He pulled his left pistol out with his right hand and checked it to be sure it was fully loaded and ready to fire. After doing the same with the other pistol he replaced it to the leather holster and pulled out his Bowie knife. Satisfied that the edge was sharp as a straight-razor, he replaced it and then removed the perfectly balanced tomahawk that he'd carried for over thirty years. At fifty feet he could bury it in a target pumpkin on a fence post every time—at half that distance he could also bury the blade of his Bowie in the center of another pumpkin.

Simon McKannah was a devout believer in the theory that to be efficient with any tool you must practice. As a Texas Ranger his weapons were his tools, so when he was alone he practiced with all of them regularly.

Few people had ever seen him do it, but with four pumpkins on four fence posts, Simon could simultaneously draw both of his butt-forward pistols from their leather holsters and hit two of the pumpkins dead center, and after reholstering them, place the razor sharp blade of his tomahawk in one of the remaining two pumpkins and then bury the Bowie knife in the other.

"Practice makes perfect," was his advice to all of the young Rangers entering the elite Texas brigade of lawmen.

While Kellerman and the stranger were inside the cabin, where as far as Simon could determine his brother was being held captive, he slowly descended down to a distance where his pistols would be more efficient. He wanted to remain unseen if they emerged without Jesse. *If they bring Jesse out with 'em,* Simon thought, *they're both as good as dead.*

A short time after the two men entered, Simon heard the door open. He kept both boots against the tree he was behind, and with a small branch from a bush he had busted off earlier, he brought one eye out to peer through the leaves on the branch. *Alone,* he thought, *Jesse's still in there.* He used the branch to conceal himself and watched as the two men walked back the way they had come. He waited until he could no longer see them, and then Simon began very cautiously moving down through the aspens. Knowing that if he was spotted by anyone before he rescued his brother, he might be sentencing them both to death, so he proceeded slowly.

At each new tree he placed a boot against it, and remaining behind the leaf-filled branch off the bush, Simon surveyed the entire area before moving on down the hill. While scanning the area, Simon spotted movement off to the side in his peripheral vision. When he saw movement again, Simon was surprised that it was a wolf. Finally realizing that the wolf was stopping every few feet and cautiously looking around before moving ahead, he thought, *that wolf is trying hard not to be seen.*

Puzzled, Simon sat still and watched. He could easily see the entrance door and all of one wall from where he sat. He watched the wolf disappear on the opposite side of the cabin, so after scanning the area thoroughly, he moved on down the hill.

Simon stopped when he heard a loud thump reverberate from the far end of the cabin. Before sliding on down to the next tree he heard another thump and wood breaking. He didn't know what to make of it and thought, *that wolf might've fallen into a trap of some kind covered with thin wood.* One more very careful scan and then Simon moved on down, but paused before crossing the dirt road. He had almost made it to the front porch—when the door opened and the wolf walked out.

Kellerman

Okay, Patch," Kellerman said, "you n' the boys know what t'do when y'git t'thet injun camp." He let his eyes pass across the gang of forty-seven thieves, outlaws, bandits and killers waiting on horseback for Patch to give the order.

"Sure do, Boss." A warped mind caused a twisted sneer to cross his one-eyed face, "Kill as many as we can but bring a coupla young squaws back t'watch thet White Buffalo cook." Several that had heard of Burgess Kellerman's plan for Jesse, laughed and jeered until the one-eyed man raised his arm and yelled, "Ready to ride?"

More jeering erupted and the gang headed north out of town.

Burgess took another pull from the silver flask then offered it to Gus. "No thanks, boss, too early for me." Burgess grunted, and after shoving it back into his pants pocket turned to the other man standing nearby. "C'mon Larson, let's go inside." The man followed his boss and Gus into the casino while trying to clear his whisky-soaked mind enough to remember what he was supposed to do. "Git them two fellas in the kitchen t'come out here while I fill this flask."

The tall muscular red-headed man had been told by Burgess that he was going to be the one to pull Jesse up and hold the rope until he stopped kicking his legs. It was all he thought about since Burgess had told him. *I been lookin fo'rd to thet hangin cause I ain't never hanged nobody.* His weak mind was also whiskey-soaked, so he simply stood there thinking about being cheated out of something that he had been looking forward to, and watched as Burgess pulled the silver flask out and went behind the bar to locate the type of whisky to fill it with. When Burgess realized that the man was still standing there he screamed at him, **"Go git 'em now, you goddamn simple-minded moron**."

Moments later the three men emerged from the kitchen and approached Burgess. "Whacha need, boss?" the tall skinny man who did the cooking asked as he wiped his hands on the filthy apron.

"Got some fancy cookin for ya t'do, chef." Burgess laughed hard. "Gonna have us a big party later tonight when Patch and his boys git back. While it's still light outside, Larson n' you two git s'more dry wood piled up around that pole I had you n' Toad there," he nodded at the short man beside him with warts all over his face and neck, "bury in the ground a few days ago."

"Will do boss, c'mon Toad." The two men headed toward the door behind Larson. The one called Chef by everyone asked, "Have either of you ever seen a Texas Stake party?"

"Nope," Larson said, "but I love any kind of party, especially when there's steaks." Toad just shook his head and held tight to Chef's apron.

Larson's thoughts would make him glow red if the wolf saw him. *Maybe Burgess'll let me shoot that injun lover in the knees or arms before he burns up.*

The Brasco brothers

The two young men, still in their teens but fully grown, had moved close enough to the casino and hotel, described to them by a trapper in Traveler's Rest, to see the assembled men ride out of town. They also got a good look at the man they met on their father's ranch in Texas almost four years earlier.

"That's him," whispered Sam, the older by a year.

"Yep," seventeen year old Justin whispered, "ain't another man on this earth with a head big's that."

Each held a double-barreled 12 gauge shotgun loaded with buckshot, and had a leather bag attached to his gunbelt with a dozen more that a gunsmith friend of their father's had made and waxed for them—knowing full well what they planned to use them for. He had also provided each boy with a five shot revolver that had just come on the market a short time prior to their departure. The long time friend of their father spent a week with them as they learned to shoot the pistols and hit what they aimed at. The gunbelt and holsters he gave them had a pre-made .44 cartridge shoved into each loop. The morning they rode out, all he said was, "Godspeed."

Each boy nodded while touching his wide-brim hat, and then rode slowly north.

Now, these many months later, they were constantly looking in all directions, as they moved cautiously ahead after the men on the porch went inside the casino.

"You skeered, Sam?"

"Yeah," he whispered back, "but not as skeered's that guy's gonna be when he sees us."

Broderick

Aidan was first to see the two horses. His brother, Liam was riding beside Broderick when they came to the clearing where the two horses were hobbled on an open area with good rich grass all around.

Aidan turned in the saddle, "Brod, these're probably the two 'orses we were told those two 'eavily armed young fellas askin about Burgess Kellerman were ridin."

Broderick looked both horses over very carefully and agreed. "That one's a palomino with three white boots and the other's a Comanche paint. Looks like they caught up with that Kellerman guy they were askin about."

Liam came in with, "This Kellerman doesn't sound like a guy that would lose any sleep after shootin a coupla boys."

"Check your guns fellas," Broderick said as he pulled his out of the leather holster on his belt. He looked up after opening the cylinder to be certain it was full. "We might be riding right into a hornet's nest."

288 The McKannahs ~together again~

Ian

Solomon had insisted that he ride ahead fifty yards and take the point position once they came to the well-worn trail coming from the west. Looking in both directions he said, "This trail was cleared of trees a good while back." He turned in the saddle and looked at Ian. "We're gettin close to that town, and from the looks o' the trail we've been followin, that Texan's got a buncha fellas ridin with 'im now. I'm gonna move ahead n' ride point, Ian, cause I can spot things that might be a problem long before either o' you two." He looked at his brother, "Keep a sharp eye out, Lon."

Lon nodded, and Solomon nudged his horse to gallop ahead. Ian watched a moment before speaking. "Solomon feels right at home out here in the wilderness, doesn't he?"

"Always 'as," Lon answered as he nudged his horse ahead. "I remember as kids when a bunch of us got t'gether to play 'ide n' go seek, Sol could track us down no matter where we went." He chuckled softly while turning in the saddle to look down their back trail, "I once climbed all the way to the top of a big sycamore tree out be'ind the barn t'keep Sol from findin me." He chuckled again, "But after 'e found everyone else, ole Sol juss kept on lookin for sign and sure enough, juss b'fore dark 'e figured out where I was. I had to hang on up in that tree till daddy came 'ome a couple hours after dark, cause I was too skeered t'climb down."

"Too scared of Sol?"

"Nah, Sol n' I never did fight much. I was up there s'long that I couldn't remember 'ow I got up so high."

"How old were ya?"

"Five, I think, mebbe six."

Ian said, "Sounds like som'n a McKannah boy mighta done."

Big John

Just after Patch and his men rode out to attack the Flathead Indian camp at the edge of the lake, Big John and his two men rode into Burgess Montana. The town was not at all what he expected. The dumpy shacks and cabins scattered about were a very big disappointment. The huge, dilapidated old wooden building they stopped in front of dissolved all of the images that had been floating around in Big John's weak mind.

The big man leaned forward and rested both arms on the pommel of his saddle and looked up at the three boards that had recently been nailed on the building just above the porch roof. He read the words on each board slowly, "Kellerman's Hotel Casino." A deep rumbling laughter coming from Big John caused the other two men with him to also laugh.

Burgess had nodded and said okay a few minutes earlier when Gus informed him that he was going to walk up to the cabin where Jesse was being held captive and ride his horse back and tow Jesse's behind.

Burgess was now walking toward the front of his casino to see what the noise he just heard was. When he saw the huge man sitting on a horse with two men on horseback beside him, anger began rising inside. One thing that Burgess had never tolerated was to have a man as big and powerful as he was working with or for him. He remained in the shadows beyond the screen door as the huge man read the new signs he had a man in Polson make for him a few weeks earlier.

Big John took a big deep breath, but still chuckled a little as he said, "This has gotta be a joke. Hotel casino my ass! I bet the guy built this damn barn to put a few old worn out whores in it what couldn't git no work in a regular town." He was about to laugh again when Burgess opened the screen door and walked out on the porch with the long-barrel pistol in his hand. Big John had never been intimidated by anyone in his life, pistol in hand or not. He sat up straight in the saddle and asked, "Who in the hell are you?" He had gained so much weight that Big John didn't recognize him.

"Burgess Kellerman," he said loudly through a frown, "and this's my goddamm town, so git movin on down the trail."

"We might just do that," Big John said, "but we're gonna stay long enough t'git a bite to eat an drink some whiskey."

"**No y'ain't**," Burgess screamed as he raised the gun and shot Big John in the heart, and then before either of the men beside him could get their pistols out, Burgess calmly stepped forward to the edge of his porch and shot both men in the chest. "You're all gonna stay right here permanently." He stood looking down at Big John's body for a few moments to be sure his deadly aim had not deteriorated in the few months he hadn't used his pistol. He then stepped a few feet more to look down at both of the other men. Satisfied that they were also dead, he shoved the pistol back into the leather holster and staggered back inside.

Simon

Jesse turned when his brother said, "Here, she's fully loaded." He watched as Simon unwrapped a pistol that he'd taken from one of his saddlebags. He extended it butt first, and after Jesse took it, Simon put the cloth bag that the pistol was in back into his saddlebag. "I end up with a lot o' those from men who won't need 'em any longer, but most are junk so I toss 'em. But that one," he nodded toward the small revolver that Jesse was inspecting, "is a good one."

"Thanks, Simon." He shoved it behind the wide leather belt holding his pants up, "Mine's back in my cabin by the lake," he paused a moment and added, "I hope it is anyway, along with my Bowie and tomahawk."

Simon looked down at the wolf that was standing beside his youngest brother. He smiled as only he could under stressful circumstances and motioned with his bearded chin toward the wolf, "That's probably a story worth listening to."

Jesse grinned, "It is." He looked down at the wolf adding, "I hope it ends the way I want it to."

"Brother," Simon said seriously, "I've been writin the end o' my own stories for a long time now. Let's git up in those aspens and work our way t'ord the palace or whatever that place is n' see what's happening."

Flathead Indians

Chief Lame Wolverine and Chief Bonesetter had invited the other two chiefs to sit with them and drink coffee made from the beans that Jesse brought with him. As they sipped the coffee, a rare treat for them all, the young chief of the first tribe to join the caravan spoke. "My people are now setting up their lodges and are very happy to be part of this large group. My head scout, Night Hawk, and fifty warriors have joined your warriors," he nodded respectfully at Lame Wolverine, "and all have joined with a hundred of Chief Badger's warriors." He nodded at the stout old chief that was sipping his favorite drink, who simply nodded and continued to sip the hot coffee.

"What you both have told us about the white men on the other side of the hills makes us think we must remain constantly alert until we learn what they plan to do." They all turned when three scouts were seen riding toward them. All remained on their horses as the one in the center spoke.

"A large group of white men on horses is coming through the canyon toward us."

"How long until they are through the canyon?" Chief Badger stood as he spoke.

"Two more cups of hot sassafras tea," the scout replied. He had not yet tasted coffee.

Twenty minutes, Chief bonesetter thought.

Chief Badger, the old Indian, spoke. "Tell all of the warriors to follow the plan that we made. Let the white men through the canyon but do not allow them to return. We will settle this now. Go, I will alert our people, and those with guns will remain here to protect the women and children."

Chief Nighthawk stood, "I will do the same with my people."

Chief Lame Wolverine and Chief Bonesetter mounted their horses and did the same.

Patch

Even with only one eye, Patch could spot things in the wild that many so-called wilderness men missed. He had spotted the Indian on a hilltop off to the south as he and his men rode through the canyon. His survival instincts kicked in and he instantly began considering all of the alternative moves now open to him. Fifteen minutes later, as they approached the end of the canyon, they would soon be riding across the flat plain leading to the lake and the Flathead camp. Patch could see the Indians on ponies off to both sides.

He pulled his horse over to the side and motioned vigorously with his arm for the riders to hurry along. After the last few men rode past, Patch walked his horse slowly, as he watched the first men exit the canyon.

When he saw the Indians move in behind the last riders, Patch immediately understood what they were doing. He put the spurs to the horse's flanks and leaned forward on its neck and up the hill through the trees they went. *Looks t'me like they's more injuns there than Burgess was tolt.*

The Brascos

Sam, the older brother, turned and held a finger up to his lips, and motioned toward the front. They had silently worked their way down the hill behind the casino when Sam heard Burgess yell. They moved swiftly toward the front of the huge wooden building. Each had the pistol that their father's friend had given them shoved into a leather holster, and each carried a double-barreled shotgun with buckshot in each chamber and both hammers pulled back. With the barrels pointed up they moved ahead. Both boys heard someone yell **Burgess Kellerman** loudly, and then a moment later three gunshots. The two boys stopped just short of the corner and lay flat against the building. The porch was only four feet away when they heard the exact same voice that said Burgess Kellerman earlier, say loudly just after the shooting, **"You're all gonna stay right here permanently**."

Sam thought, *that's Kellerman.* He quickly stepped out and raised the barrel of the shotgun, and before Burgess had time to realize that he was in a very bad situation, the first barrel filled his chest with lead and the second nearly took off his left arm.

His enormous body slammed down on the wooden porch so hard that two clay pots with aloe vera plants in them fell over. He was still moving and trying to say something when Justin stepped forward to shove his shotgun's barrel close to Burgess' face and say, "This is for you, pa."

After the second trigger was pulled, there was very little left of the enormous head.

Both Brasco boys were breathing hard as they broke open their shotguns and removed the spent shells. After refilling both barrels they put their backs to the wall again and used their bandanas to wipe Burgess Kellerman's blood off their faces while carefully surveying everything around them.

Sam exhaled slowly before speaking in a very soft voice, like a whisper. "Took us a while, Justin, but we finally took care of that bastard that took our pa from us."

Justin didn't speak, but looked at his brother and slowly shook his head up and down.

Wolf

Both boys heard the man screaming and turned to see Gus riding toward them. He had already dropped Shadow's rope when he first heard the gunshots, and spurred the horse into a full gallop.

Sam and Justin both froze for a moment when they saw the man riding fast toward them. What they saw next remained in their memory until they were old men and had told the story to everyone who wanted to hear it.

A San Antonio Texas newspaper eventually heard about it and sent a reporter to their uncle's home in Austin, where they were living for a while after returning from Montana.

Sam was always the narrator of the two, so he told the story. After the newspaper verified it by sending a reporter to the Texas Rangers home office, who talked directly to Ranger Simon McKannah, they published the following story.

Justice—Texas style

Two young Texans finally learned the name of the man that murdered their father, Texas cattle rancher, John Brasco, over three years earlier. After following the trail of Burgess Kellerman, a known counterfeiter, cattle and horse rustler, murderer and an escaped convict, the young Brasco boys found him near the Canadian border in a small town named Burgess Montana that he created to shelter killers and rustlers that would help him build a large cattle ranch.

After confronting Kellerman outside of his hotel and casino on Main Street, he went for the gun that he had just killed three men with and were still lying in the street. He learned the hard way that a pistol is no match for two double-barreled shotguns in the hands of two vengeful Texans, even if they're just boys.

All four hundred pounds of Kellerman fell to the porch of his casino. After reloading their shotguns the boys were startled to hear a man screaming as he spurred his horse toward them. At that same moment they spotted movement in the trees. The largest wolf the boys had ever seen was running toward the tall man sitting in the saddle on the galloping horse. It lunged at the man and clamped powerful jaws on his throat, sending both man and beast to the ground.

The boys waited until the wolf departed to walk to where the man lay. His throat had been torn open and his glassy eyes stared sightless at the sky.

He was later identified as Augustin Pampineau, a French Canadian from Quebec City. He was wanted for murder in Texas and Louisiana, and bank robbery in Montreal. He had also kidnapped Jesse McKannah, brother of the legendary Texas Ranger, Simon McKannah. Augustin and Kellerman had planned to kill Jesse so they could run off the Flathead Indians that Jesse had befriended.

When Simon McKannah was asked about the wolf, he simply said that wolves can often tell the difference between good and bad humans.

Aleena

When Aleena saw the white men galloping out of the canyon she wondered briefly if Jesse might be riding with them. When the Flathead braves began firing back and the white men started falling from their horses, she knew it was another attack by the men that she had been told lived in a town on the other side of the hills, and hated Indian people.

The scene was unfolding over a mile away, but she could see that the white men were badly outnumbered. Some tried to get to the canyon and return to the town, but Aleena could see that other Flatheads had positioned themselves at the entrance to prevent the men from regrouping with others to attack from a new direction.

Men were falling from their horses at the entrance to the canyon. Others tried riding up the hills on both sides, but were cut down. Aleena saw several white men riding north away from the Flathead camp, and was pleased to see that the Indians did not follow. She spotted a small group of four or five riding hard in the direction of the flat plains that she had recently walked through behind the travois, and again was pleased to see that no Indians tried to prevent them from escaping.

Aleena could see that the battle was over because the Flathead Indians were casually gathering the riderless horses—a valuable commodity to all of the Indians she had even known.

Broderick

Liam turned toward Broderick when three gunshots rang out not far away. "Bloody close," Aidan said quietly.

"Jesus," Broderick said as a scowl crossed his face, "I hate the thought of two young boys trying to even a score against a killer like this Kellerman guy seems t'be"

Just as Liam was about to speak, two loud shotgun bursts were quickly followed by two more.

Broderick's lips were twisted and one eyebrow was raised as he turned first to Liam and then toward Aidan. "Maybe," he said slowly, "Kellerman underestimated those two boys from Texas."

"Let's 'ope so," Aidan said softly, almost under his breath.

"Only one way t'find out," Liam said as he nudged the horse gently with his spurs.

"Let's stay together on this wide road," Broderick said, "but spread out. I'll take the center." He pulled out his long-barrel pistol to be certain it was fully loaded. After shoving it back down in the leather holster on his belt, he pulled the smaller gun from the shoulder holster and checked it too.

As he did this, Liam and Aidan checked their sidearms then opened the double-barreled shotgun that each carried in a leather scabbard attached to their saddle. Each saw a shell in each barrel and closed the weapon.

With the shotguns resting on their thigh, barrels pointing up, fingers near cocked hammers they spread out and headed slowly toward the gunshots.

Ian

Solomon held his arm up when he heard the three gunshots in the distance. After scanning the trail they were on, and the dense forest on both sides, he motioned for the other two men to move ahead.

When both had moved up beside him, two shotgun blasts were quickly followed by two more. They stayed where they were to see if a small war had begun, but when there was no more gunfire for a few minutes, Ian suggested they move cautiously ahead.

"If yer right," Lon said turning to Ian, "about those 'orses we just passed, we might find a coupla dead boys up a'ead."

"Jesus, I hope not." Ian just shook his head.

"Remember," Solomon added, "what that livery stable fella said when we stopped at Traveler's Rest. They looked, 'e said, like two tough young men on a mission, so maybeeeeeeeeeeeee," his voice trailed off into silence.

"Maybe," Lon answered, "we'll find 'em both safe n' lookin down at a fat cadaver."

"That'd suit me just fine," Ian said as they headed toward Burgess Montana.

Simon

Jesse stopped when he heard the three shots and turned to look at his brother. "Simon," he said quietly, "it sounded like those shots came from the casino."

Before Simon replied, they both heard the four shotgun blasts reverberate through the forest. He knelt down next to Jesse and spoke softly, "Two young boys from down my way have been on Kellerman's trail for a few months. Best I could learn along the way was that he killed their pa about three years ago. I been on his trail too, cause I reckon he's the one that killed an old pal o' mine, a Ranger that saved my life."

"Damned fool kids," Jesse shook his head, "oughtn't t'go for a ruthless sonuvabitch like Kellerman." He took a deep breath, and then added, "If he shot 'em, I'll skin that bastard alive."

Before Jesse could move, Simon knudged his arm softly and nodded down the hill. Jesse scanned the area until he finally spotted the wolf. He was sitting beside a giant cottonwood tree looking straight up the hill at Jesse.

"I've only run into a few wolves in all these years," Simon said, "but seldom had a problem with 'em. Always thought they had a sorta wisdom about everything in their world, and could tell what was good and what was bad."

"Let's go down n' see what those gunshots were about."

"Okay Jesse, lead the way, I'm a stranger up here."

Kellerman's Casino

Jesse, Simon, Broderick, Liam, Aidan, Ian, Lon, Solomon, and the Brasco brothers, Sam & Justin, all sat around two tables that were pulled together inside the casino.

Simon went into the kitchen and pounded some coffee beans and boiled them in a pot. Sam followed him in and carried four tin cups to the table for him and his brother Justin, Jesse, and Simon. The rest were enjoying a glass of Kellerman's Canadian whiskey.

Broderick took a long slow sip, and when he set the empty shot glass down said, "Why is it that those buggers up there can make whiskey that's so much better'n ours?"

"I've 'eard of a few fellas makin a whiskey in Kentucky called bourbon," Solomon said, "and a coupla guys that tole me they tried it said it was the best whiskey they ever tasted."

Ian shook his head in agreement, "I used mostly Canadian in The Shamrock, but I'd get rum from the Caribbean Sea at times and on a few occasions I bought some barrels of that bourbon the folks in Kentucky make." He nodded at Solomon, "He's right, it tastes good, but ain't as smooth as Canadian."

"There's a fella in Tennessee," Aidan said as he set his empty shot glass down, "named Daniels, that folks say makes the best tastin whiskey they ever 'ad."

Simon stood and carried his coffee to look outside through the screen door. "I wonder where those fellas I tracked ridin with Kellerman went?" After a sip of coffee he continued, "There was twenty or more riders with him and musta been more here waitin on him." He took another sip of coffee then added, "Wonder where'n the hell they all went, and I also heard some wimmin talkin in here while I was listenin at the window." He paused a moment before adding, "And there musta been some wimmin livin in some o' them crappy little cabins." A moment later his head jerked and his hand went to one of his pistols, but he didn't pull it out, "Well, I guess me talkin about 'em flushed a couple out, cause here they come." He seemed relaxed again so nobody stood, but they were all watching Simon.

"**What're you three fellas lookin for**?" Simon's deep voice boomed so loud that it startled the small man and he jumped behind the tall one wearing an apron and a chef's filthy white hat.

One said, "I'm Larson, a sorta handyman roun here, and we was wondering what the shootin was all about."

"Y'all got guns?" Simon said.

"Nope, not me," Larson said loudly while Chef shook his head side-to-side. Toad leaned out from behind Chef and nodded no.

"C'mon," Simon said as he walked to the screen door.

All three men moved ahead and stepped onto the porch when Simon opened the screen door. He pointed toward where Big John, Stick, and Rupert lay. Their eyes were glued to the three dead men. Chef finally looked up at Simon, who had stepped aside and stood at the edge of the porch. "Me n' Toad," he nodded at the short man that had stepped out from behind him but still held on to his friend's shirt, "work in the kitchen for Mister Kellerman. Everybody aroun here calls me Chef, Larson's a handyman like he said, and this here's Toad." He nodded at the small young man clutching his shirt, "He's not right in the head but he kin wash pots n' dishes, and carry plates o' food to the men."

Simon nodded at the porch area behind him, "Looks like you're all out of a job then."

Chef stepped ahead and Toad followed. He looked across the deck, and when he spotted the bloody remains of a head on the huge body, his neck seemed to telescope out. "Oh my God, I ain't never seen anybody blowed up like that. Oh sweet Jesus, his head is nearly all blowed off."

Chef looked at Larson, and then down at Toad and so did Simon when the small man said loudly, "**Good riddance**."

Simon turned toward Larson, "You got a horse?"

"Nope, not any more. Got hit by a rattler a while back n' had t'shoot him when the leg wouldn't heal."

"Pick one o' these then," Simon nodded at the horses that Big John and his men rode in on, "and you three fellas drag these four bodies and that one over there," he motioned with his arm at the one the wolf took care of, "out back somewhere n' bury 'em all in one hole. When y'git done, all three of ya gitcher stuff n' git on these horses," he motioned at the three still standing near the bodies, "an keep on headin t'where ya were goin when ya stopped here, cause we're gonna burn this buncha shacks n' shithouses down, including this barn," he nodded at the casino, "so s'more rotten apples don't set up here n' spoil this whole area." He stared at Larson, and then at Chef. Toad was hiding behind Chef, but he leaned out and nodded rapidly when he heard Simon say loudly, "**Got it**?"

Both other men said emphatically, "Yessir."

"Before y'all leave, tell me som'n. There were some wimmin in here," he nodded at the door, "an I reckon there were more livin with men in them cabins." Simon stared at each man, "You know where they are?"

"Nope." Larson looked at Simon a moment, but when the big man just stared at him, he shifted his eyes down toward his feet. "But if thet yaller surrey with the red canvas top ain't inside thet little shed over there," he pointed at a small building across the road and a hundred feet or so south, "then I reckon all six of 'em jumped in it n' headed t'ard Missoula when the shootin started, cause thet's where they come from." Toad leaned out again and nodded.

Simon went to the door after seeing the men tie Big John's cadaver to the horse and drag it behind the building. He went in and explained to the others what he planned to do.

"Good," Jesse said, "there's probably a lot more like Burgess out there waitin to fill up a place like this again."

"I was gonna suggest it, Simon." Broderick said.

"The only downside of that idea, boys," Ian said grinning, "is there's gonna be a million termites lookin for a place t'eat."

"Yeah," Jesse said with a chuckle, "that cabin I was staying in briefly has more holes in it than that good chesse they make in a place called Switzerland."

It was long after after midnight when all thirteen cabins and several outhouses were burning, and they set fire to the hotel. Rain clouds had been building again, so Simon smiled when he felt the first drops fall, because he knew that all of the old buildings would still burn to the ground. He was riding beside Jesse, who had turned in the saddle to look back at the flames.

"I never thought I'd be happy to see a building burning, but that blaze sure looks good t'me."

"Yeah," Simon responded, "y'ain't gotta worry about anyone like Kellerman settlin in there n' givin y'all a hard time. Them Flatheads're good people and will do well if this government'll just do right by 'em."

"I'm gonna do all I can," Jesse said, "to see to it they honor the terms of that treaty the bigshots in the east used in order to cheat 'em out of their land."

"If they appoint a good man as Indian Agent, like they been saying they would everywhere, then these Flatheads'll have as nice a place to live as any I've seen."

"That's why I bought the land here n' built the cabin, Simon, cause I ain't ever seen a better place t'live."

They rode along in silence with the rest following them for a long while before Simon spoke again. "I'm gonna retire outa this manhunter game fore too long, Jesse. Gettin too damn old to be livin on the back of a horse, so I just might be droppin in on you again purdy dern soon t'see if there's a piece o' land I could buy t'build m'self a cabin on."

"Simon," Jesse said turning to his huge brother, "I ain't told anyone but the Flatheads, and they don't talk to white men, but I bought two hundred and thirty thousand acres including half the lake, so when y'git ready to settle down, how does a few thousand acres backed up to a beautiful lake for one dollar sound?"

Simon turned toward Jesse, who could see his white teeth in the moonlight showing through his full black beard because he was grinning wide before he spoke. "Damn, little brother, you're one o' those high pressure land salesmen now, huh?"

"Yep, I been lyin around here these past coupla days thinkin on how I could prosper with all the land I have."

The men following them smiled when they heard the two men ahead laughing.

Aleena

It was just getting light enough outside to see the men and tepees when they rode out of the canyon and headed toward the Flathead camp. It was almost three times as large as it was the last time that Jesse saw it. His eyebrows furrowed down as a soft, "Wow," made Simon turn in the saddle and look at Jesse.

"What's that wow about, Jesse?"

"That camp," he turned toward his brother, "is three or four times the size it was the last time I saw it."

"Been so busy," Simon said, "that I juss forgot to tell ya that Chief Bonesetter," he turned to Jesse and grinned, "an Indian I met a long time ago when I was stabbed and he fixed me up, because," his grin widened, "he's also a trained medical doctor." Simon laughed too when he heard Jesse laugh as he shook his head. "As I was sayin," he stopped laughing but couldn't hide the grin, "he was bringing his tribe up here lookin for you, and along the way some other tribes joined him, so there would be strength in case the Blackfoot jumped 'em."

"Lookin for me," Jesse said, "why were they lookin for me?"

"Cause Chief Bonesetter's son and some braves that were out huntin, came across Aleena after some crazy old guy, in a wagon home like that tinker that usta come to daddy's ranch traveled in, beat her and tried t'kill her."

He watched as Jesse's eyes widened and his mouth dropped open. "Aleena," Jesse finally was able to say in a whisper, "she's alive, our sister Aleena is alive?" He was now almost yelling.

"She's alive n' looks healthy as ever."

"Oh my God." Was all Jesse could say.

"She's been with Chief Bonesetter's tribe for quite awhile and told me she ain't leavin here if you have room for her. Them Indian kids in every tribe really love her, so she's gonna be their school teacher."

They were about half way to the Indian camp when Simon pointed, "Look, Jess, that's her runnin this way. She's seen you, and you know Alleena, she can't wait for us t'git there. Man, she ain't lost any of her speed." Simon watched as Jesse nudged his horse into a gallop. A few minutes later Simon smiled as he saw Jesse climb from the saddle and put his arms around Aleena. *She loved us all,* he thought, *because she's a loving woman, but nobody ever shined in her eyes like Jesse.*

Simon watched as Jesse climbed back into his saddle, and then helped Aleena mount Shadow behind him. He leaned forward and patted Dragon's neck, "We'll just take our own sweet time, big fella, and get there when we get there." He had to smile when Shadow fanned his lips and shook his huge head.

By the time Simon got to Jesse's cabin and removed the tack from Dragon, so the horse could wander around and locate the best grass, Jesse had warmed the old coffee he'd made the night he was waylaid. He and Aleena were in rockers on the porch talking. Simon smiled as he climbed the steps up to the porch. "Sis," he said, pointing at a group of men riding toward them, "y'recognize that blonde runt ridin with that feller with the Rusty red goat's beard?" He smiled and waited as she strained to see who he was pointing at.

"Oh my God," she said and began a slight bouncing up and down on her toes as she watched the group of riders approach. "Ohhhhh," she moaned, "I wondered there for a while if I would ever see you guys again."

"Well sis," Jesse said, "we're together again now."

"All but Patrick." She smiled and turned back to watch.

Flathead Camp

Many changes have taken place since the town of Burgess was leveled by flames. The Flathead hunters now had another area in which they could search for game where there was no threat.

During the period when they worried about the white men attacking their camp again and barely days prior to the arrival of Chief Bonesetter and the two tribes that joined him, another big threat presented itself. While scouts were ranging far to the north to determine if the Blackfoot tribes were preparing to attack the Flathead tribe on the Lake Flathead Reservation, signs of enemy scouts were seen.

One week prior to the arrival of Chief Bonesetter's new tribe, the Flathead scouts spotted a dozen or more Blackfoot scouts in a thick forest five miles north of the lake.

"My Chief," the scout sat on his horse while Lame Wolverine came through the flap of his tepee, "I and my braves have seen Blackfoot scouts among the whitewood trees north of here."

The chief stood looking into the fire thinking about this new threat. Finally he spoke. "If they are that brazen and come this close to our camp, then I believe they intend to attack us in force soon." After a long pause he said, "I will talk about this with White Buffalo tomorrow, but for now bring all of your scouts back into camp and prepare for a battle."

The following day, Chief Lame Wolverine listened as another of his scouts told him that a large caravan of Flatheads was heading toward Lake Flathead. "There are many, my chief." He waved his arm and said, "Three times as many as we are now."

The chief stood motionless looking into the embers. When he looked into the scouts eyes he saw no fear; only concern for his people. "The Great Spirit has seen the need of The People, and is sending more warriors so that we will be strong again."

The Blackfoot scouts were hidden in the thick forest and watched as Chief Bonesetter led his huge group of Flathead Indians into Chief Lame Wolverine's tribal reservation. A short time later they were still trying to gather enough information to present the situation to their own Blackfoot chief back across the border in Canada, when white men rode through the canyon. They were in trees watching in awe as the Flatheads slaughtered most of the white men.

The Blackfoot scouts remained in the trees until after dark and then retreated cautiously to their waiting mounts and rode north.

The Blackfoot chief listened impassively to all of the details then spoke. "The Great Spirit has let us see the new power that the Flatheads have. We will wait and watch. One day they will be weak and we will be stronger. That is when we will strike."

Reunion

Aleena moved into the spare bedroom in Jesse's cabin and her three brothers, plus their men, along with the two Brasco boys moved into a spare tepee. It was a project undertaken by Lame Wolverine's wife, Gentle Breeze, plus several women both young and old, and a crew of boys and young braves. The huge lodge was assembled near Jesse's cabin.

Young Flathead braves used their ponies to pull a travois that was loaded with the spare tepee wall-skins, and another heaped high with sleeping-skins to coat the inside floor with.

As Gentle Breeze and her friends were sorting the rolls of stitched together skins that would become the walls, several young braves rode in on ponies towing freshly cut lodgepole pines that would create the frame structure to attach the wall skins to.

Jesse and Aleena watched as the men cut the long narrow pines to the same length. As children they had both seen small tepees being made, but never one this large. Jesse admired the way these men worked smoothly together as though they had done it many times, but in fact, Lame Wolverine had told him that it would be the first tepee the young Flatheads would make unassisted by an experienced member of the tribe.

An old man who had constructed many tepees sat nearby leaning against a huge tree. He would only interfere when a very serious error was about to be made, otherwise he would remain silent, and then report to the Tribal Chief later. His evaluation of their finished product would have long term effects on their status in the tribe.

Once the site had been made as level as possible, four poles were laid side-by-side. Two of them were then moved 180° so the narrow tips of two were overlapping the narrow tips of the other two. They were then loosely tied together and a long rawhide rope brought out. A nimble young Flathead took the end, and climbed high into a giant sycamore tree to lower the end down to another young Flathead. The rope was then secured to the four poles and the balance of the rope laid out straight so that the poles could be controlled as they were pulled up.

The larger butt ends were then moved in as two others hoisted the lashed-together smaller ends up until each butt was placed next to a pre-determined shallow hole. Jesse noticed that the old man leaning against the tree shook his head slightly up and down, indicating that he was pleased with the position chosen by the builders.

Jesse watched with admiration as the young men began the task of getting these four main poles, which were over thirty feet long, pulled up and the butts positioned.

The boy in the tree stayed there to be certain that the rope went smoothly over the tree limb as the men on the ground beneath him pulled the poles up.

Two stout young men held the other end of the rope as the four poles, now resembling a big A without the crossbar, were being pulled. It was their job to see to it that the poles were stopped once they were standing straight up.

At the larger, butt end of the poles, two men held them in the shallow holes as the small ends were swiftly pulled up into a verticle position. Jesse and Aleena marveled at the swift and efficient way this task was accomplished.

With very little verbal communication the poles were straight up and being held in that position by the men on each end of the rope. Without a word, two men moved one pole around and into position to create part of the temporary pyramid, and a third who had followed with a grub hoe dug a shallow hole for the large butt end to drop into.

"My goodness," Aleena said as two other men repeated that same task with the fourth pole, and suddeny there were the four corner-poles of a pyramid, all lashed together at the top with rawhide. As a long pole was shoved up, and the big butt placed in a shallow hole, two young men brought another pole, and the process was repeated until a large circle was completed with the space between the large butts was uniformly three feet.

Two agile young men placed a small coil of rawhide around their necks and with ease, scampered up to the top and began to tie together the smaller ends of the lodgepole pines.

One hour later, Aleena, who had been watching the boys jump around up at the top, turned to Jesse. "I can hardly believe what I just saw."

"Yeah," Jesse answered, "first time I've seen one this big put up from beginning to end." He stood leaning against one of his porch's roof poles, "They pulled all those lodgepole pines up an got 'em tied together faster'n I woulda ever thought possible, especially since this's the first time these guys have ever done a job like this."

"Really," she exclaimed while shaking her head, "first time?"

"Yep! That's what Lame Wolverine told me yesterday when he said it was decided that a big tepee should be built for all the guys to stay in until they're ready to head back home."

Five hours later the tepee was covered and the soft skins were put inside to cover the floor. Jesse and Aleena had stayed on the porch and watched the entire time.

Young men cut laterals from saplings that were brought and piled nearby. The laterals were lashed in place on the long poles by boys that could climb up them like monkeys. As soon as they had a section completed, young men unrolled the wall hides and pulled them to the top, while old women secured them at the lower levels. Next, the young women scurried up securing them as they went toward the top.

Simon, Broderick, Ian, and all of their men, plus the two Brasco brothers returned from Burgess. They went back to see if all of the buildings had burned completely. Seeing the huge tepee sitting near Jesse's cabin they could hardly believe their eyes. When his brother, Broderick, asked Jesse about it, Simon just smiled. He had spent time with various Indians and knew how easily they could construct all sorts of lodging.

Broderick was still in the saddle when he spoke to Jesse. "I can hardly believe that tepee was built while we were over in Burgess, or what's left of that place."

"Wasn't much to it, brother Brod." Jesse nodded toward his sister who was sitting beside him on the porch. "Aleena said if I would go out n' cut a few trees down she'd stitch together a few o' them skins I had in the horse shed, and we'd make you fellers a nice lodge to stay in while you're here visiting." He kept a straight face as he turned toward Aleena, "Ain't that right, sis?"

Unwilling to lie, even as a joke, she just kept rocking, but a big smile crossed her face.

"Remember the goose," Broderick said as he looked at Jesse, "that pa once penned up n' force-fed, so we'd have som'n special when the Monsignor from Yerba Buena came to visited us that Christmas?"

"Yep!" Jesse kept a straight face and looked right at him.

"Well, little brother," Broderick said softly, as he shook his head slowly up and down, "that's what you remind me of right now."

"Well dern, sis, whadaya make o' that?" He turned to look at Aleena.

Smiling wide she said, "I think he's saying you're full of it."

Everyone began laughing as they climbed down and began securing their horses to the long hitching post in front of Jesse's cabin.

They all went through the weather flap to look at the inside of the tepee. Aleena and Jesse could hear them commenting on the structure. Sam Brasco was the first to come out. "Boy," he said, "I never saw one that big. These Flatheads really know how to build 'em fast." He stopped to look around, "There wasn't a thing here on this spot when we left this morning."

"Built good too." Simon walked over, "I've been inside plenty of different lodges, and I reckon these Flathead Indians build the best. When I first met Doctor Caruthers," he looked at Sam, and Justin who had just walked up, "he was livin with a Flathead tribe back west o' here, near the Colombia River, and they all lived in permanent lodges built of cedar planks n' beams, except when they were forced to follow them big buffalo herds." He motioned toward the tepee with his bearded chin, "Then they built more portable lodges like these, but," he motioned again at those in the camps below them, "smaller like those."

Simon sat on the porch and leaned back against one of the roof supports, "Jesse, y'really got me t'thinkin. I just might turn in my badge fore too long n' take you up on that offer." He removed his huge hat and looked all around, "I don't reckon it gits any purdier'n this, no matter where ya go." He ran his eyes across the front of the cabin before continuing. "Nice job y'did on this cabin, Jess, but I ain't spent much time inside a regular house, so if I come up here I'll build m'self one o' them t'live in." He motioned with a huge thumb toward the big tepee.

"Soon's y'get here," Jesse said, "an pick out yer spot, I'll get out the axes n' files an we'll go find a mess o' lodgepole pines n' git started."

"Oh my goodness," Aleena said after hearing that, "I can just picture us all here together again and living out our days in this little paradise with these wonderful people."

"Well sis," Broderick said as he approached from the tepee, "I agree it's a paradise," he grinned, "buuuuuuuuuuut," he drew out the word, "I wouldn't build any plans around me n' Ian or Patrick moving here, cause we're all pretty darn citified," but I can sure see all of us comin here two'r three times every year to kinda lay back n' take it easy for a while."

Jesse nodded at the big tepee and said, "The chief told me today that it's gonna stay there, so when any of you fellas wanna stop by for a visit you'll have a place t'stay for as long as y'like."

Simon turned to his brother from the city, "Broderick, when you fellas git back here for a visit I'll probably have one o' them," he nodded at the tepee, "right here on the lake som'rs for you guys to stay in, and it'll be bigger'n that one, cause I ain't gonna leave ole Dragon out in the cold during winter."

"By then," Broderick said, "I hope the government's got men working on the trails so we can use our coach to get here."

"Probably will," Jesse offered, "according to what my land agent said. A big outfit's gettin a contract to carry the mail, so they're putting a buncha new stage coaches in service for that, and also so folks can travel to places a lot easier, even up into mountains like these."

"Dern," Broderick said, and then grinned, "dunno if I'd want to miss all of the scenery a fella gets t'see from the saddle."

Justin Brasco came out of the tepee followed by Ian's two men, and a moment later Broderick's two followed them to the porch. After introductions, Aleena told them that the chief of the tribe that found her and nursed her back to health, wanted them all to come to his lodge an hour before dark and eat with them.

Liam Beckett wobbled his bushy eyebrows, "Mmmm, boy, a home cooked meal." His stomach actually growled, so he gently rubbed it saying, "Easy big fella, we'll be sending som'n down there to ya purdy soon." Everyone laughed, including his brother Aidan.

"That chief," Aidan said with a wide smile, "mighta made a bad mistake inviting that fella to eat." He motioned with a slight nod toward his brother.

"Wait'll you see the size of the iron cauldrons we hauled here for the women of his tribe to cook in when they invite people to eat with them. The women have probably cut up a few fresh deer by now and are adding all kinds of yummy things."

Several of the men looked at the western horizon. Justin was the first to speak. "That's only an hour or so from now."

"Didn't realize how hungry I was," Ian commented, "until you said som'n about food, sis." He shook his head, "Man, I'm starving now."

"Chief Bonesetter's scouts all have wives that can cook great food with whatever's available, but when they have fresh meat like deer, or bear, or elk, mmmmm, boy." Aleena wobbled her eyebrows too, "And Nosey Doe, one of the scout's wives, makes the best dumplings I've ever eaten." She squinched up her face a moment then added, "Hope she's makin 'em today."

An hour later, Simon rode Dragon up beside the porch and yelled for Aleena, "C'mon sis, let's ride over n' see what's in that food kettle."

She was on the porch in a flash and was still wearing her Levi Straus pants, but had put on a freshly ironed red and black checkerboard wool shirt. The big change that Simon noticed was her hair. It had obviously been thoroughly brushed and was tied back with a yellow ribbon.

Before Aleena stepped over onto Dragon's back, Simon said, "You're a mighty handsome woman, sis."

With a huge radiant smile, she answered, "Why thank you, big brother. That's som'n every woman likes t'hear now n' then."

Once she was settled in behind his saddle, Simon turned to her and smiled. "What's his name, sis?"

Without missing a breath, she said, "Dog Walker."

Simon turned around to smile at her, and while shaking his head up and down slowly, Dragon turned his huge head all the way around and gave her a long whinny as he shook his head up and down too.

316   The McKannahs ~together again~

~ better late than never ~

Everett Bullock, the Indian Agent from Fort Connah rode into
the Flathead Reservation on the third day of January 1857. He
was accompanying seven wagonloads of long-promised but not
delivered food and supplies stamped PROPERTY of US ARMY.

The wagon train had departed Independence, Misouri almost
a month earlier with a U.S. Calvary escort of twenty armed
soldiers, plus two armed regular calvarymen as drivers on each
wagon. Captain Foon Mills O'Leary carried a dispatch signed by
James Buchanan, who would be sworn in on March 4th of this
same year as the 15th president of the United States of America.

It stated that in the event of an emergency of any kind, the
captain and his men should be given assistance to fulfill orders
given by the Secretary of the Army, which he received directly
from the President. The captain was to deliver the seven wagons
to the Flathead Indian Reservation in Northwestern Montana,
including armed escort if deemed necessary. All assistance
given by civilians will be paid upon receipt of a bill signed by the
aforementioned captain.

It was signed by James Buchanan and the Secretary of the
Army.

Jesse was chopping and splitting firewood when Aleena yelled to
let him know that a wagon train was coming. Jesse buried the
axe into the end of a log, and walked up the steps to the porch
and accepted a hot cup of coffee from his sister.

Everett broke away from the wagons and headed toward the
cabin. He had always stopped there first when he visited the
Indians, but never had a grin on his face like the one he wore
this day.

"Mornin ma'am," he touched the rim of his hat and smiled at Aleena, "hello Jesse." He motioned toward the wagons with a nod, "I 'ope yer oldest brother will not 'afta face a firing squad for puttin the barrel of 'is pistol against the 'ead o' the new president an insistin 'e send these poor people some o' the supplies they was promised a coupla years ago."

Jesse grinned, "Just one Irishman negotiatin with another of 'is own kind."

"By Jesus lad, 'e must be one o' th'best at it there is."

"I've 'eard," Jesse said with a grin, "that judges 'ho don't even know 'im well, still cringe when told 'e will be the lawyer for the defence."

"I believe y'lad, an that's why I 'ave 'is address in me desk."

"C'mon up n' getcherself a cup o' coffee Everett, an I'll ride down with ya."

They were sitting on the porch the night after Jesse returned, when he began explaining to Aleena about the food and other things that were in the wagons. "And," he said, "The captain told all four chiefs that another wagon train as big will be arriving in two months, and then every three months after that until there are enough food supplies in reserve to last through the harshest of winters. After that there'll be one coming every four months year round."

Tears began running freely down Aleena's cheeks, "These are such good people, Jesse, and I just hate the way so many white people that I meet when we go to Polson act like they're so much better just because they were born white."

"I do too, sis, and I truly think a lotta that's because those white folks know that these Indians're smarter, stronger, and can live through hard times that would kill off most whites."

"I think that's why so many people are afraid of wolves, Jess, they never took time to learn about them or get t'know them." Aleena's eyebrows knitted down as she looked around the terrain extending out from the cabin. "Where's Woolie?"

Jesse grinned and nodded at a shaded corner of the porch, which extended half way across the front of the area that Jesse added for his horse and mule, so they could get inside out of the weather when it was too cold.

She looked at the box that he had recently built and put at the end of the porch against the wall of what she refered to as, the animal room. "Wollie's in there?"

"That's where he went when I got back from watchin that stuff git unloaded."

"He was down there among all them dern soldiers?" Aleena cocked her head when she said it.

"He was," Jesse grinned, "because he's a curious fella, but none of 'em knew it, at least none of the sojers."

"Ha," she laughed, "didn't think he woulda lost his good sense that quick." She stood and walked to the box and folded back one of the two heavy blankets that were overlapped in the middle so he could go thru the same way she entered the tepee. "Musta went on in to check on Shadow and ole Ironhead."

"Yeah," Jesse said, "cause he's comfortable goin in there, now that I cut a hole in the other wall and put blankets over it too so he can come n' go thru there."

After a long silence, Aleena said, "I think Simon's right about wolves being able to tell good humans from bad ones."

"Wouldn't doubt it, sis, because I can see wisdom in those yellow eyes when him n' me look right at each other."

Epilogue

Patrick and his three men rode into the Flathead Reservation one week after the first seven wagonloads of supplies arrived. He was first to ride to the top of the hill overlooking the lake, and sat there admiring the view as the others reined their horses in beside him.

Aldo had ridden horses as a child, and again when he was on the McKannah ranch working for Jesse's father, Sean, and later on for Jesse. He was a bit sore, as were all the others for the same reason, too long out of the saddle.

"It's even more beautiful than your sister described in her letters."

"You're right Aldo," Patrick said as the other two joined them, "it's a surreal scene off a canvas of one of the great ones."

"Yes," Aldo said almost in a whisper, "an early da Vinci."

"Or one by a very talented young man named Monet. One of the professors at Harvard brought some of this young man's work back from Paris and he displayed them at his home. Broderick and I were invited to a party and Doctor Sheffield took everyone on a tour of his gallery. This boy Monet is still in his teens but is destined, I believe, to be one of the great artists of our time."

"I'll look for his work," Aldo replied, "the next time I visit the gallery in San Francisco."

"Wheweee," Kenneth blew out as he admired the scene.

Seamus did the same and said, "I thought we'd already seen the best this country 'ad t'offer, but this beats all I ever saw." His head swiveled as his eyes took in everything. "Phew, it's no wonder your sister says she's never leaving 'ere, an yer brother Simon's gonna give up buryin garbage an settle down 'ere."

After they settled into the big tepee all three of his men rode to the lake while Patrick sat on the porch with Jesse and Aleena.

"Sis, that letter from Broderick telling me about you being here was the best news I ever received." He looked at her and smiled, then said, "He also mentioned that you have met a man here in the camp that you like." He nodded his head saying softly, "I was so happy to hear that sis," he paused a long moment before adding, "I sometimes wish I could find a woman that I could spend the rest of my life with," another pause, and then a wide grin, "but I reckon I'm so set in my ways, and now that I'm a member of the over the half-century mark, it's very unlikely that I'll be meeting Miss Right."

"I felt the same way, Patrick, but when I looked into Dog Walker's friendly brown eyes, something inside me that had been dormant for many years came alive." She smiled, "And I'm in my half-century year too, so who knows what might happen."

He cocked his head a bit and raised his eyebrows, "Only thing I know about the future is that it's a very uncertain place." He turned to Jesse, "I'm riding up to meet Everett Bullock tomorrow Jess, would you mind riding along?"

"Not at all, Pat, I've come to like that old scott."

"I read the dispatches that he regularly sent to the capitol, Jess, and I could see right away that he sympathizes with the Indians, so I did some digging." He took a sip of his coffee while it was still hot before continuing. "He ran his own trading post near the border up north of here for many years. He married a Chippewa in Quebec when he was younger, and had just arrived from Ireland. Everett took her trapping with him, and when they found a place they liked, he built that trading post. It sits on a river," he looked at Jesse, "I don't recall the name of it, but it was a good size river and they did real well for over forty years. Raised four boys and a girl and probably planned to stay right there, but a small war began between him and a guy that was born in Quebec. The Canadian opened a trading post about a mile away on the same river, planning no doubt to run Everett out of business. Everett gave everyone a fair deal on whatever they brought to him or bought from him, so he had lots of good loyal customers. The Canadian hadn't counted on that, so he wasn't doing much business, and decided to burn Everett out.

Word got back to him in time to be ready, so when that guy came with his gang, Everett and his boys were waiting for 'em." Patrick sipped the last of his coffee and shook his head no when Aleena asked if he wanted more. She was glad, because she always enjoyed the stories her brothers told.

"Anyway, this guy was a little cagier than Everett realized, because once the shooting started, another group of the guy's pals showed up. While Everett and the four boys were shooting at the Canadian and his gang, the other bunch lit fire to the trading post and then apparently retreated into the forest.

Everett saw two of his boys shot dead and the other two burned up trying to get the fire under control. He was also shot three times but managed to get in one of his canoes and escape. He learned later that he and his boys had already killed the Canadian and two of his sons. He learned all of this from a newspaper after he got down to Missoula and had the bullets removed." He shook his head a moment before continuing. "He thought sure he'd have someone go up n' bring his wife down here, because he'd taken her to a small cabin on the river that he'd built a long time earlier. But she returned to help, and when she saw her boys fighting that fire she climbed through a window to help and burned with 'em. That newspaper article about killed him, cause he wasn't heard from for five years, so he musta stayed drunk. He'd made good friends though, and one of 'em got him this job as Indian Agent."

Jesse shook his head, "I figgered he was about sixty or mebbe sixty-five, but he's gotta be way older'n that."

"Best I could figure, Jess, he's pushin the hell outa eighty."

"Tough ole bugger, eh?"

"Yeah," Patrick agreed, "but, Jess, those dispatches were very interesting. Everett is an educated guy and probably did it all on his own by reading the right books. He's also extremely dedicated to the Indian people, because he pointed out the many treaties that were broken, and never by the Indians. He also pointed out that the bad feelings between the Blackfoot Indians and the Flathead Indians could be resolved if both governments would simply honor the treaties they made with these people."

Patrick's courtroom tactics took over and he began pacing on the porch. A sly smile briefly crossed Jesse's face, so Aleena put her hand up over her mouth and coughed to keep from giggling. "Much of the cause regarding the poor service the Indians have received is due to a policy that has allowed men to remain in the position as Indian Agent when they have no interest in helping anyone but themselves. I put together a list of qualifications that must be met before anyone is registered as a Government Indian Agent, and President Buchanan is going to see to it that it becomes policy, and the ones who have been ignoring their duties," he waved his arm through the air covering the entire reservation, "like not listening to men like Everett telling them that people are starving because of inaction in the nation's capitol, will be promptly removed and replaced."

Patrick and Jesse's visit with Everett reinforced his gut instinct that there are still a few men like him that sees the Indians as the original Americans. As Everett Bullock stood in the doorway and watched the two men ride away he felt better about the future of the Flatheads than he had since accepting the job.

A telegram was carried by a friend of Jesse's to Michael in Polson and handed to him in his restaurant. The first person that came in to eat that he knew he could trust got a free lunch every day for a week to carry it down to Jesse.

After reading it, Jesse turned to Aleena, "I sure do wish Patrick could have stayed a while longer because this is from Simon and he's coming here to live."

Aleena's wedding to Dog Walker was delayed until her brother arrived. When Simon saw her come out in her new outfit made by her husband's mother from beaded and embroidered doeskin Simon told her that she was the prettiest bride he'd ever seen. She gave him the biggest hug he'd ever had.

After Simon completed his huge tepee with plenty of help from the village, he and Jesse and many of the Indians who had learned how to build a cabin with wood by working with Jesse on his, began a large log schoolroom so Aleena could move her outdoor school inside. One of her students had to sit in the rear because he was too tall for the children to see over. Dog Walker wanted to learn his wife's language and also know how to read books.

Surprising to everyone but Jesse and Aleena, the giant brother of White Buffalo became the best thing to ever come into the Indian children's lives. Simon enjoyed reading stories to them and making toys they could play with. He was always willing to stop whatever he was doing if asked by only one child to read a story. When a child was sick, or had a toothache, or was just bored, he would sit beside their bed and entertain them for hours to keep their mind off of their problem.

Chief Bonesetter brought much better health and even a little dentistry to the village. His brother, the tribe's Medicine Man, finally let his brother treat his liver, which no longer tolerated his hot pepper habit. After a full month of real white man's medicine, and abstinence from hot peppers, he admitted that he felt better than he had in many years. But if a serious problem presented itself, he still treated a few of his old patients with rattlesnake skin, opossum tongue, ground bear bone, and many of his other tried and true, secret cures.

Two events occurred that could not possibly have been foreseen by anyone—except perhaps Chief Bonesetter's brother, the tribal Medicine Man. He had painstakingly created three small dolls that were lifelike in every detail. One was a large girl doll and the other two were boy dolls that were also larger than any of the many others that he had previously carved. They hung unnoticed beneath the opening at the top of his small tepee, and each time he chanted and sprinkled his mysterious dust on the fire, they all danced in circles.

The first event was when Singing Swan, a thirty year old widow from Chief Badger's tribe, fell in love with and married Simon, and then later announced that she was going to have a baby daughter.

The second event happened a short while later, and surprised not only Aleena, but everyone in the village—except the tribal Medicine Man. Aleena was grinning with happiness when she informed her husband, Dog Walker, first and then everyone else, that at age 52 she was pregnant. Her midwife soon told Aleena that she would have twin boys, and she'd never been wrong in the 40 years that she had helped bring new blood into the tribe.

~ O ~

One year later, Patrick, Aldo, Kenneth, Seamus, Broderick, Aidan, Liam, Ian, Lon, and Solomon rode into the village to visit with everyone, but specifically to see a huge adorable infant named Issabella and twin boys named Sean and Oliver.

THE END

About books by this author

• **Dark Caribbean**… is a true story. Two friends, both offshore lobstermen, battle thieves and pirates on the Florida coast, the Caribbean, and the Bahamas for years. They eventually begin smuggling drugs, in hope of recovering some of the fortune that had, over the years, been stolen. Airplanes, airboats, 150 mph pickemup trucks, vodka, gunfire, riding gators, wild men, vodka, wilder women—it's all in this one…and it's all true.

• **The McKannahs**…is a western adventure novel that begins in 17th century Ireland and moves to early 18th century America. 5 McKannah sons and 1 daughter spread out across this wild new country to build their life.

• **The McKannahs ~together again~** … the four McKannah brothers come to Montana and stand with Jesse as he confronts men intent on wiping out his Flathead Indian friends. Their sister, Aleena…well, she……….

• **Carib Indian**…this is the only novel written specifically about these courageous freedom fighters. Holding wooden spears in their hand-carved canoes, they took on mighty ships full of modern soldiers that had entered the Caribbean Sea in search of slaves.

• **The Face Painter**…is a book of stories for young readers 8 to 88.

• **The Black Widowmaker**…was a beautiful black woman who made widows of many women, but after reading her story, you might find yourself sympathizing with her.

• **Satan's Dark Angels**…is a collection of frightening stories, and now accompanies The Black Widowmaker…making 2 novellas in 1 book.

- **America**…is a book of western and other short stories that are anything but traditional.
- **A Sacred Vow**…A Memoir…The author swore to his beloved wife, Dottie, that he would never let her languish in pain and discomfort in a nursing home, when all quality life was gone.
- **It's A Dog's Life**…the author's 15 year old, blind, Jack Russell(ish) terrier always wanted to write his autobiography. With help from Rick he finally finished it. All proceeds will go to homeless animal caregivers.
- **80 Stories**…is great for folks who don't like to face one long story in a novel. You'll find almost every genre in this one. Sad, funny, unbelievable, maddening, frightening, whacky, true, thought-provoking, award winning and some you will read over-and-over. (There are now 81 stories. Caribbean Revenge is a true story. A bonus for the people who bought the book because their friends recommended it)
- **Ghosts of Chokoloskee**…Many ghosts have been sighted in and around the 100 year old Smallwood Trading Post/Museum on Chokoloskee…once a small fishing village just beyond Everglades City, Florida…the place where locals gunned down Edgar Watson, the infamous killer that carried a pound of lead to his grave.
- **Uninvited**…A frightening look at the pythons that have now taken over the Florida Everglades, which will soon be void of all wildlife.
- **CALUSA ~warriors from a distant past~**
Follow these incredible people as they cross the landbridge to North American people on down the west coast to Baja California, and then across the Sea of Cortez to Mexico, and on down to Central America. From there they follow a river to the Caribbean Sea and the many emerald-like islands and the crystal clear water surrounding them. Following the tales of the traders, they land in Cuba to rest and restock in preparation for the journey north to flat lands that are always warm. Once established in Florida, they become Calusa Indians, and hold Southwest Florida for 2,000 years.

• **Ladybug and the Dragon**...is the true story of Tampa native, Katia Solomon. At 2 she was diagnosed with leukemia. Rather than write a story about her, as he was asked to do by a magazine editor, Rick decided to write a small book instead. He ordered 5,000 copies and sent the Solomon family all of the money to assist them during that difficult time. Katia turned 15 in 2015 and remains in remission, but now their small house in Tampa has been re-possessed—the one her mama was raised in, and Katia loves. . . . . *Never rains, that it pours.*

Go to his email and order a $10 signed copy...every cent is sent to Katia.

magersrick@yahoo.com

Many times, a small generosity from a stranger will brighten the day for someone like Katia.

A writer without a loyal following

is just another unknown writer.

Many thanks to my many readers.

Rick